THE PHOENIX
OF PRAGUE

By the same author

The Triumph of Bacchus
The Talinin Madonna
The Estuary Pilgrim

THE PHOENIX
OF PRAGUE

Douglas Skeggs

St. Martin's Press ⚞ New York

Library of Congress Cataloging-in-Publication Data

Skeggs, Douglas.
   The Phoenix of Prague / Douglas Skeggs.
      p.   cm.
   ISBN 0-312-15189-6
   I. Title.
PR6069.K34P46   1997
823'.914—dc21   96-46339
                                    CIP

First published in Great Britain by Little, Brown and Company

First U.S. Edition: February 1996

10 9 8 7 6 5 4 3 2 1

For Imogen

AUTHOR'S NOTE

This novel is set in Prague in 1991, a year after the communist regime collapsed: a grim, impersonal city where footsteps echoed in cobbled streets and every foreigner was treated with suspicion.

The characters and some of the places in the book are fictitious, but the story reflects the reality of what is happening in the city today.

CHAPTER ONE

Prague, 1991

The department tends to work on a need-to-know basis, and in this case it didn't reckon I needed to know much. All they'd given me was a photo of a painting, a name and an address.

The name was Pavel Pesanek, the address was for an ancient tenement block in the Mala Strana, a picturesque enough place if you've a taste for flaking plaster and dodgy plumbing. The garbage bins were kept in the hallway to prevent them from being nicked and the disinfectant didn't quite manage to cover the smell.

Pesanek's flat was on the top floor. I tried the lift but a note that must have been there as long as the lift itself said it was out of order. So I trudged up the four flights of coiled steps, past linoleum-covered corridors and blank doors. Somewhere a Hoover was droning; above it a woman's angry voice added the occasional descant.

When I came to Pesanek's door I paused for a moment out of respect for my pulse rate before giving the bell a prod. There was no answer. I gave it another, longer this time and harder, holding the brass nipple in with my thumb. The thing was working, I could hear it buzzing away inside like an angry wasp but no one seemed to be listening.

It might have been clever to have come back later but I'd come a long way to see him and I wasn't giving in that easily. I rapped on the door and it moved.

Not much. Just a fraction of an inch. A sliver of light appeared down the doorframe.

I stood quite still.

Putting my finger to the door I gave a push and it swung open the rest of the way.

Pesanek's flat was never going to excite an estate agent. It was a single room tucked up under the eaves of the roof, one wall sloping inwards. Bookshelves lined the inner wall and a few pieces of modern furniture stood around the floor, aimless and out of place like the first arrivals at a cocktail party. Pesanek himself was sitting on the steps leading up to the gallery.

He didn't look pleased to see me. His head was pressed against the banisters, his face set into an expression of mild annoyance.

I didn't apologise. There was no point; I could see now why the door had opened so easily. The catch had been torn off and lay a couple of feet away, small splinters of wood spearing out from the empty sockets where it had been. It wouldn't have made much noise as it broke; about the same as kicking a hole in a cardboard box.

Pesanek was still staring down at me.

Gently, as though not to disturb him, I shut the door and went over to where he sat. His eyes remained fixed on the closed door as though he was waiting for someone else to come in behind me.

He was a stringy little fellow in his early fifties, his head balding, the flesh slack around the jaw-line: professorial, avuncular, the kind who wears slippers indoors, the kind who keeps the top of the milk for the neighbour's cat. One knee was drawn up under his chin, an inch of ankle showing above his sock. His hands were white and bony. Sitting there on the staircase, with his peeved expression and threadbare clothes, he could have been listening to one of those complicated pieces of modern music that takes a lot of concentration to be appreciated.

I lifted his head away from the banister but there was no visible damage to his neck or face. I checked his hands and fingernails but there was nothing there either. His flesh was cold and waxy. When I pressed down on the skin of his wrist the dimple came out slowly like a punctured football.

It was then that I noticed the blood on his cardigan. There wasn't much, just a thin black stain in the fold of the knitted wool above his heart. I guess whoever had killed him had done so with a fine blade. It leaves practically no trace. The wound seals up before the bleeding can begin.

A sound caught my attention. It was a faint hiss, coming from somewhere high in the room. Stepping over Pesanek's body I went up to the gallery. It was a makeshift addition to the room, fitted out as a simple kitchen with a table and a couple of chairs. The sound was coming from a saucepan on the cooker. It contained some reddish substance which might have passed for soup in its youth but now looked more like a failed submission for a chemistry exam.

By rights I should have left it as it was. Never touch anything unless it's really necessary, that's the golden rule. But smoke and flames and neighbours rushing around shouting 'fire!' was the last thing I needed. So I turned off the heat and the skin on the soup sagged inwards, making angry little crackling noises as it went.

Taking out my handkerchief I cleaned the fingerprints off the knob and then going back to the door I did the same to the handle. I wasn't wearing gloves, you see. I hadn't thought they'd be needed. Back in the office they'd told me that this was going to be a routine piece of work: a few questions and a written report when I returned. Nothing fancy; no reason to cover my tracks. I wasn't expected to be in Prague for more than a day.

So much for the office. Now I was going to have to make the best of a bad job; find out what I could and then get the hell out of the place.

It took me less than twenty minutes to go over the flat. There was nothing of any interest; just letters and bills and all the other irrelevancies of domestic life. Nothing to suggest a sudden rush of wealth, certainly nothing to suggest that around thirty million American dollars had passed through Pesanek's bank account in the last year.

When I was through I went back to the entrance and opened the door. On the floor below two women were talking, their voices tinny in the confined space. I waited until they were gone before going out. As I closed the door I glanced back at Pavel Pesanek.

He still didn't look pleased to see me.

The Mala Strana district of Prague stretches down from the castle to the Vltava river. It's a tangle of small streets and alleys with buildings that lean in on each other for support.

It was early March and drizzling with rain. The cobbles glistened like a Byzantine mosaic. Above the rooftops, the soft green snout of St Nicholas dome was pressed into the belly of the low cloud.

A hundred yards down the hill I found a bar. There were only three men inside but they managed to make the place seem full. None of them looked round as I came in. I ordered a glass of beer. It was sweet and dark as treacle, a taste that brought swift, sharp memories. In Paris it's the smell of baking bread that makes you realise you're back; in Vienna it's the sickly taste of whipped cream. In Prague it's the beer.

'Have you got a phone?' I asked the barman.

He nodded to the passageway behind. It was one of the old-fashioned affairs set on the wall in a plywood booth next to the gents'. I pushed in a few coins, dialled 158 and asked to be put through to the police.

'What do you want?' asked the officer.

'There's a dead man in my apartment block. On the top floor.'

There was a pause while the idea sunk in. Then the suspicion

that's latent in every Czech policeman's mind hit the surface.
'How do you know?'

'I saw him there. The door's open and I saw him lying there
on the stairs.'

'Who are you?' he asked.

'I'm just telling you what I saw. It's nothing to do with me,
I'm just passing it on, okay?'

'What's the address?'

I gave it to him and the seconds passed away as he searched
for paper and pencil. God knows what he'd do in a real
emergency.

'This is straight up, is it?' he asked after I'd repeated it to
him. 'You're not pulling my leg or nothing?'

'On my mother's grave.'

This wasn't good enough. Maybe he guessed that my mother
was alive and well and giving piano lessons in Cheltenham at
the last count. 'I need your name. We can't look into it unless
you tell me who you are.'

'Just check it out for yourselves,' I told him. 'He's up there
on the top floor, dead as a bedpost.'

I hung up and the coins clanked down into the machine.
There was graffiti scrawled on the wall. Subconsciously I
read it; there'd been a time when it was the only way of
knowing what people in this upside-down, rat-infested city
were thinking.

'Get through?' the barman asked as I returned. He was
polishing a glass slowly and deliberately. Above the till a
loudspeaker was giving its version of 'Blowin' in the wind'.

I nodded and drank some more of the beer. It's said that
you should be able to stand up a matchstick in the head on
Czech beer. This stuff looked as though it would be lucky if
it could take one lying down. The barman wanted to make
conversation.

'You from these parts, then?'

'Just passing through,' I told him. 'On business.'

He repeated the word to himself. Then setting the glass

down on its head he placed both hands on the bar and said, 'You can sell anything in Prague these days. Did you know that? Any bloody thing you like.'

'Is that right?'

'You know what you should be doing?' He had the thin, pinched features of those who want what's beyond their reach. 'If you want to make some money – real money – you know what line you should be in?'

I told him I had no idea. I was sitting on the bar-stool, half-turned so that I could watch the street through the rain-smeared window.

'Videos,' he confided.

'No kidding.'

'That's what I'd be in if I had the cash: videos.'

From the bored expressions on the faces of the others at the bar I guessed I wasn't the first to be offered this business expertise. I nodded towards the speaker. 'You'd need something a little more up to date than your music.'

'You don't sell them,' he explained. 'You just rent them out, all dubbed up nice in Czech. Make a fortune.'

'I'll bear it in mind,' I promised. From down the hill I heard the thin wail of a police siren approaching. It flashed past, its tyres thrumming on the wet cobbles. The barman didn't give it a second glance.

'What line you in then?'

'Cosmetics.'

This was beyond his range of expertise. 'There's no money in that, is there?'

'Enough to open a video shop,' I told him. Getting up from the stool I moved over to one of the tin tables in the window. From there I could see up the street to where the police car was parked. The ambulance arrived ten minutes later. There was a small crowd of onlookers around the passageway now. A man came into the bar and passed on the news that a stiff had been found in the apartment. It took the barman's mind off videos for a while. He went and stood outside. Raindrops fell from the faded awning onto his head but he didn't seem to notice.

I left it an hour before going back to the apartment building. The ambulance with its covered stretcher had gone. The police car had gone also but another had arrived in its place.

Tied across the passageway was a piece of plastic tape. A policeman leaned against the wall. There was a gun at his waist and gum in his mouth.

'You can't go in there,' he said as he chewed.

'I live here.'

He gave a disinterested nod. 'Okay. Make it snappy.'

I ducked under the tape and he went back to pounding his gum. On the second floor was a delegation of women. They were standing in their doorways talking in low, urgent voices, united in the face of tragedy.

'You can't go up,' one of them informed me as I went towards the next flight of stairs. 'The pigs are turning the place over. No one's allowed up there until they're finished.'

'What's happened then?'

'Old fellow,' she said. 'Snuffed it.'

'What's that to the police?'

Her eyes narrowed. She was wearing a thick green jumper that managed to make a shapeless figure one degree more shapeless, her arms folded above her bosom. 'Why do you want to know?'

I flicked an identity card from my wallet. It was the security pass for the office back in London as it happened, but it was plastic-covered and official-looking with my photo on the front.

'CTV news.' I gave her the name of one of the TV stations that broadcast from the concrete tower on the east side of Prague.

The woman leaned forwards without unfolding her arms and quizzed the card. The others watched on, letting her take the decisions. 'It's in foreign,' she said.

'That's where I do most of my work.'

Her eyes came up slowly and searched me over with lazy interest. 'He was done,' she said after a moment.

'Done?'

'Someone stuck a knife in him.' Her voice held a shade more enthusiasm. Then, looking over my shoulder she asked, 'Where're the cameras then?'

'They're coming,' I promised her. 'How do you know this?'

'One of the pigs told us.'

'Burglars,' another woman said. 'They're everywhere. Makes you scared to be alive, doesn't it? It could have been any of us.' There was a murmur of agreement all around. An hour from now they'd have worked themselves into hysterics.

'Who was he then?' I asked.

'Old-man Pesanek,' the first woman said. She can't have been much younger than Pesanek herself but I could understand that she should think of him as an old man. He had probably been an old man when he was a child.

'Why do you think burglars should have picked on him?' I asked.

She rolled her tongue around in her mouth, tasting the answer before coming out with it. 'Because he was worth more than anyone else here. Got his own business. Turned in a tidy stash, I reckon.'

'What did he do?'

'Carpentry,' she said. It sounded vague so she clarified. 'He made bits of furniture and stuff. Real nice if you like that sort of thing.'

That explained the slick-looking table and chairs I'd seen in the flat.

'Where did he work?'

Again the woman turned cool on me. She leaned back against the doorpost. 'Why do you need to know all this?'

'Background information,' I told her. 'It helps to paint a

picture for the viewer.' Prague was changing fast. Three years ago she'd never have cross-examined anyone who smelled of officialdom. She'd have answered the questions and kept her opinions to herself.

She shrugged. 'He had a workshop somewhere over in the Smichov area, I think. It can't be far. He always used to walk there.'

I asked her how she could know this and she said, 'When it was raining he used to come in wet. I told him he should buy a car. "You should get yourself a car, Mr Pesanek," I said, "or you'll catch your death." He said he didn't need one when he could walk to work. That's how I know.' She looked round at the other women in triumph.

'You don't know the address?'

'Not the exact name of the street. But it was Smichov way.' There was the sound of footsteps and two policemen appeared from the floor above. The women ducked back into their doorways like nervous rabbits. The policemen scowled at them as they passed.

I went back outside into the covered passageway. There were rows of dustbins, a pile of building bricks and that air of dilapidation that you find in the Mala Strana. At the upper end of the passage the police were standing around their car. The plastic tape was still in place. The lace curtains of a window above twitched back and an old man's eyes looked down at me. That's the way it is in Prague: everyone watches everyone else. Sneak on them too if they get the chance. But no one was watching Pavel Pesanek when he was killed, or if they were they weren't letting on. That's the real tragedy of it.

I walked away in the opposite direction. After ten yards a voice behind me said, 'Mister?'

I turned. It was a small boy who'd called.

'You want to know where the old man worked?' he asked.

'Do you know?'

'Could do.' He can't have been more than eight years old

with the words 'Laser Atomic' splashed across his T-shirt and that crafty smile on his face that kids get when they've learned to live by their wits. 'Depends what it's worth to you.'

I told him, 'Fifty crowns if you can give me the exact address.'

'And what if I don't?'

'You get a clip round the ear for wasting my time.' I had gone back to where he stood waiting with his feet spread wide, his hands in pockets. Taking a note from my wallet I held it up as evidence. The boy considered the deal.

'Smichov,' he said eventually. He gave me the name of a street and took the note at the same time. As I moved to go he asked, 'And what if I'm telling you a fib?'

'Then I'll be back asking your mother why you aren't in school at this time in the afternoon.'

'It's the honest truth, mister.' His voice took on a note of urgency. 'I took a package over there for him a few weeks back. It's by a shop with vegetables. You can't miss it.'

Andrew Slater was waiting for me in the tram-stop in St Nicholas Square. The market was closing up for the day, damp pigeons hopping around the trestle tables on the off-chance there was something in it for them.

I sat down at the other end of the bench from him. Between us was a man reading a newspaper and a woman burdened with shopping bags and a fretful child. We waited until a tram came by and removed them. Then Slater said, 'Jesus, you took your time.'

'There were complications.'

'I've been sitting here over two hours,' Slater complained. He had red hair, rather sparse for his twenty-five years so that it only just managed to cover his large head. Beneath it, round spectacles gave him a limited view of the world.

'You got to see him, did you?' he asked.

I told him I had.

'What did he have to say for himself?'

'Nothing. Someone got there before me.'

The tram had wobbled away across the square and dived under a narrow arch in the Letenska, fitting through it as neatly as a thread going through the eye of a needle. Slater watched it disappear before saying, 'Oh shit.'

It was roughly my thought.

'How long ago?' he asked.

'Half an hour before I arrived. Maybe less. There was some soup on the cooker, it was only just beginning to burn. It was a professional job. Someone pushed in the lock and stabbed him with a stiletto before he had time to get down the stairs.'

'Did they know you were coming, do you think?'

'Possibly.'

Slater stood up and flapped his arms around himself. 'I'll have to talk to London.'

I'd never met him before that day but I knew the type well enough. He was one of that public-school, Oxbridge breed that the Foreign Office puts its faith in, all snap decisions and positive thinking. He'd got a rowing blue and a first in Greats and about as much knowledge of the eastern bloc as you can get from the inside of a rowing eight. It's always said that the talent scouts of MI6 approach the Slaters of this world in the public conveniences of Trinity and Magdalene colleges. Personally I think it's just the excuse they give for hanging around these places.

He'd picked me up from the airport, scuttling around with my luggage in a friendly sort of way and making it abundantly clear on the way back that people like me weren't needed in Prague any more. And he may have a point. I haven't been in Prague since the revolution – the Velvet Revolution as sentimentalists like to call it. A lot had changed since then.

'Where do we go from here?' Slater asked.

'You go back to the embassy and stay there. If you want to make yourself useful, find out what you can about Pesanek: personal things, small details.'

'And you?' He sounded sulky.

'I'm going to have a couple of drinks, maybe take in a show later.'

'You're staying on, are you?'

'For a bit.' Another tram was approaching. I stood up to go.

'But you're due back in London this evening,' Slater said.

I stepped out into the drizzle, felt it prickle against my face.

'Bugger London.'

CHAPTER TWO

I would have liked to have gone round to Pesanek's workshop then and there, but it was getting dark and it's never wise to search a place in the dark. Ask any cat-burglar. You need light to see what you're doing and even the smallest pen-torch is visible from outside.

Instead I checked into a hotel and went in search of a restaurant off the Bethlehem Square. I've known the place for years; it has bare floors and uncovered tables. The chef leaves the kitchen door open so he can talk with the customers; slivovitz comes in clouded glasses and the cooking is as good as you'll find anywhere in Prague.

The restaurant was exactly where it had always been. The kitchen door was closed and the menu had nothing much beyond steak and chips. The bill at the end came to four times what it used to be; there was a service charge and the waiter expected a tip on top of it. I guess it's the price you pay for democracy.

So it wasn't until the next morning that I took the metro down to Smichov. It's one of the industrial districts of Prague with juke-boxes that blare from café doors and laundry hanging from wrought-iron balconies. Praguers will tell you the place is full of gypsies but they say that about anywhere they don't like.

Pesanek's workshop was up a cul-de-sac. It must have been one of the only deserted streets in the area and that wasn't good for business in the grocery shop next door. The cardboard boxes of cabbages and potatoes that stood out on the pavement looked as though they'd passed their anniversary.

I pressed the doorbell on Pesanek's workshop but there was no answer. It was the right place: his name was there above the button, an engraved business card that had been cut down to fit the brass slot. I tried again and when there was still no reply I forced the lock. It had been put on the door to keep out burglars. It kept me out for less than thirty seconds which means it would have kept out any burglar worth his salt for half that time.

It was dark inside with that musty smell that comes with old plaster and bare wooden floors. A flight of steps led up to the workshop, a huge space in the eaves of the roof. In the way of most craftsmen, it was kept meticulously tidy. Seasoned timber was stacked in the rafters, tools hanging from pegs beneath. Hefty pieces of machinery stood along the walls, dark and ghostly in the sallow light of the overhead windows. As I'd expected, there was a small office at the far end of the room, a partitioned-off area beside one of the lathes. In it was a filing cabinet, a distant ancestor of the ergonomically designed affairs you find in London offices, but functional.

For half an hour, hampered slightly by the gloves I was wearing, I went through the plump green files. I didn't find what I wanted but they taught me quite a bit about Pesanek's business. There were photos, drawings and receipts for pieces of custom-built furniture. Some of them had made their way abroad: a four-poster bed to a pop star in Beverly Hills, a conference table to Brussels. By Prague standards the prices he asked were astronomic but then they probably took an age to make. Each one was a labour of love.

I've never had that sixth sense you hear about, the ability to feel the presence of someone in a room, to know when you are being watched in a crowd and so, as I reached down to open the third drawer, the butt of the pistol hit me without warning.

Fortunately, my head was slightly turned at the time so it caught me on the side of the neck rather than the spinal column. Otherwise I would have gone out like a light. Instead I was treated to an explosion of garish colours, a sudden sunset, that erupted before my eyes and pitching forwards I collided with the filing cabinet. As I slumped to the ground there was a roaring in my ears not unlike the opening bars of Mahler's third symphony.

I twisted round as I fell and kicked out with one foot with the vague hope of tripping my attacker but he was too quick, or rather I was too groggy to catch him. Jumping back out of range he stood with his feet apart, waiting for my next move. I hadn't got one in mind. Giving a shake of my head I looked up at him.

Two thoughts registered at once. The first was that the gun that he had used as a club was now pointing at me. The other was that it wasn't a man but a girl.

'Get up!' she shouted.

It was easier said than done. The roaring of the music was still in my ears but it was now coming in slow, sickening waves that made the room rock from side to side. I pulled myself up, back against the cabinet, and then gave up the effort and sat down.

The girl stood where she was, poised and alert. The majority of women have no idea how to handle a pistol. They hold it close to their faces and squint along the barrel. If they did pull the trigger the best they could hope for would be a bullet through the roof and a broken nose from the recoil. But this one had it out at arm's length, both hands on the butt, her body braced against the kick.

'Get up.'

She spoke in a quieter tone but I did as I was told. The weapon she was holding was one of the old Zastava Model 70s that used to be issued to the Yugoslav army when there was such a place, an ancient piece with brownish patches of steel showing through the blueing, but I wasn't deceiving myself. It would work all right. Bury one in the ground for a year and it will still knock a hole through a man the size of a drain-pipe.

'Put your hands up,' she ordered.

I placed them on the back of my throbbing head which was roughly where I wanted to put them anyway. She studied me with cold eyes over the sights of the gun.

'What are you doing here?'

'I was looking for Pavel Pesanek.' I tried to sound surprised and a little offended but she pounced on the remark.

'Don't lie to me! Pavel's dead; you know he is. I saw you round at his home yesterday.'

'I was looking for him there.'

'You killed him!'

'No,' I replied with a calm that I was far from feeling. 'He was dead when I arrived. I called the police.'

'You killed him!' She hissed the words back at me.

'Why should I do that?'

'I don't know. You went to his house and afterwards he was dead. He wouldn't harm anyone; he wouldn't harm a fly. You had no reason to do it; no reason at all.'

She was pale with anger. Beneath the white T-shirt I could see her chest heaving but the gun didn't waver. Taking my hands off my neck I held them up in a gesture of surrender and, in the fewest words I could come up with, I told her how I had found Pesanek in his flat: the broken lock, the slumped figure on the steps. She listened without comment.

'You're lying,' she said as soon as I'd finished.

'I have no reason to lie. I came in from London yesterday to talk to him. That's all.'

'What about?'

'About the paintings he's sold.'

'Paintings?' For the first time she had the grace to sound puzzled. 'He doesn't have any paintings.'

'Then you know less about this affair than me. Look – ' I tried a smile, which given the gun aimed at my chest and the virtuoso drum performance in my head, was some feat of acting – 'we have two possibilities here. Either you put down that piece of dated ordinance and listen to what I have to say or we stand here like a couple of lemons until one or both of us dies of starvation.'

I had moved away from the filing cabinet and back towards the main workshop as I spoke. She didn't like it.

'Stay where you are!'

I put my hands back in the air. They were touching the wall now. Beside the right one was a heavy duty electric switch.

'I'm not going anywhere,' I told her and as I made the promise I pressed the button.

The lathe beside the girl started up with a bellow of energy from its engine.

Jump? She must have lifted two feet in the air, mouth opening, eyes startled. The gun was suddenly pointing in the air.

If you look in the unarmed combat manuals there are probably some classy ways of taking advantage of these situations but I contented myself with stepping forwards and barging her over with my hip before she could recover her balance.

She went down on the floor in an untidy heap of legs and arms. Standing over her I wrenched the gun out of her grasp. It came free easily enough but she wasn't giving in so easily. Coiling herself around my arm with the speed of a striking cat, she sank her teeth into my wrist.

'Jesus Christ!' A bright circle of blood sprang up from my wrist. 'What the hell did you do that for?'

She had pulled herself into a sitting position now and was glaring at me in triumph. I switched off the lathe and there was silence in the gloomy room.

'Who are you?' she asked.

'That doesn't matter.'

'It does to me.'

'Let's get one thing straight.' I pointed the butt of the pistol at her. 'I'm the one holding the gun now so I get to ask the questions, okay?'

'If you like.' She gave a shrug and with a quick athletic movement of her body she got to her feet. 'It's not loaded anyway.'

I pulled out the magazine. She was right.

'Pavel used it as a paper-weight.' There was more contempt than anger in her voice now.

I put the gun down on the window-sill. 'Are you a friend of his?'

'Yes,' she said shortly and then nodded over to the work-benches. 'And I work with him.'

'Heavy work for a woman.'

'I don't make anything,' she replied. 'I design it.'

The expression on my face must have been incredulous because she frowned and with a touch of pride she added, 'I'm very artistic.'

'But not artistic enough to know about his paintings.'

'No.' She missed the sarcasm in my voice. 'Pavel had no interest in paintings. He was only interested in his work.'

I could have left it there. Looking back on it, it might have been better for all concerned if I had done that. But this was the contact, the link with Pesanek's past, that I had been looking for.

From my wallet I took out a photo and showed it to her. 'Have you ever seen this before?'

'No.' She hardly glanced at it.

'Do you know what it is?'

'Yes, of course. It's a Rembrandt.' She deigned to give it a second look. 'A portrait of his son Titus by the look of it.'

It never fails to amaze me how girls with wide cheekbones and straight noses seem to know these things. A knowledge of art must come with the bone structure. I'd had to have it spelt out to me by the Dutch painting specialist at the National Gallery.

'That's right,' I agreed. 'It's the Rembrandt that Pavel Pesanek put up for sale in Sotheby's last week – that's an auction room in London.'

'I know what Sotheby's is.'

'It fetched just over thirty million dollars.'

'I don't believe you,' she said curtly.

'I can show you the receipt.'

'I mean I don't believe it was Pavel. He would have told me about it. There was nothing he didn't tell me.'

'It was him,' I assured her. 'His name and address were on the receipt and he'd signed it. I can show it to you if you like.'

She was leaning against one of the work-benches, her hips in their stone-washed jeans thrust forwards. She fiddled with one of the metal clamps as though that might help her to understand what I was talking about. Then in a voice that had shrunk to half its original size she asked, 'Is this why he died?'

'I expect so. He didn't own this. He was just a front for someone else. I need to know who that is.'

'And you thought he would tell you?'

'He might have. I went round to his apartment yesterday to find out. Unfortunately someone got there before me.'

'They knew you were coming.'

'Possibly.'

'So you did kill him,' she said bitterly.

'Not directly.'

With sudden emotion she buried her face in her hands, her short blonde hair closing around her grief like stage curtains. 'Oh God! I can't believe this. I've never heard anything about any paintings. He never even mentioned them . . .'

I moved away from the lathe. 'What were his politics?'

'Politics?' she asked, looking up at me above her splayed fingers as though I'd said a rude word. 'I don't think he had any. He wasn't that sort of man. He kept himself to himself—' A sound outside in the street made her pause. She glanced back at the staircase.

'We must talk about this somewhere else,' she said quickly. 'The others will be turning up in a minute.'

'Others?'

'The other people who work here.' She brushed her hand around at the benches. 'Come, I know a place near here.'

She took me round to a café in the next street. Her name, she told me as we sat down at a plastic table in the corner, was Jarka Surova.

'What's yours?'

'Jan,' I told her. 'Jan Capek.'

Solemnly she offered me her hand across the table which, in the light of our first encounter, struck me as faintly absurd. As I took it she noticed the blood on my wrist.

'Did I hurt you?'

'Nothing that a week in intensive care won't cure.'

'I'm sorry,' she said. From the tone of her voice she didn't sound as though she were sorry. It was just a formality.

Calling the waitress she ordered coffee with slivovitz. After it had arrived she took a sip and looked at me steadily over the rim of the glass with cool grey eyes. She was rather beautiful. Beneath the helmet of shiny blonde hair she had a broad, firmly sculpted face with a Slav gravity to it and a wide, generous mouth. She reminded me of the women in those heroic communist posters that used to be all the rage around here: tall, straight-backed Amazons with frowning brows and magnificent breasts. Instinctively, I glanced down to see what hers were like. She caught the movement and staunched it with a question.

'Why did you ask about Pavel's politics?'

Taking the photo of the Rembrandt from my wallet I propped it against the bottle of ketchup that stands as mute testimony to the new world order in every café in Prague. I'd seen the original painting back in London. It was about the size of a hardback novel, a sketchy portrait of a boy wearing a floppy red hat.

'Your friend Pesanek has sold four or five paintings in the last few months,' I told her. 'Each time he said he was acting as an agent for the Czech government, selling them on their behalf.'

'Isn't that possible?'

'Perfectly possible. He sent all the right papers with all the right stamps on the bottom so no one blew the whistle on him.' I tapped the photo. 'Until this one.'

'What's different about it?'

'The difference is that this one definitely doesn't belong to the Czechs and never did. The others could have, you can't tell, but not this one.'

'What makes you so sure?'

'Because for the last twenty years it's been hanging in the Presidential Palace in Bucharest.'

It took a moment for the significance of this address to register in Jarka's mind.

'You mean . . . ?'

'I mean it belonged to President Ceauşescu.'

'Oh my God.'

I took a sip of coffee. 'As you say,' I agreed drily, 'Oh my God.'

'I didn't know he owned any paintings.'

'What do you think he had on the walls? Postcards from his grateful subjects?'

Her eyes flashed at me. 'I mean, I didn't know he had anything as valuable as this.'

'And a great deal more. At the end of the war a lot of art treasures were caught on the wrong side of the fence. They were there for the taking. Ceauşescu helped himself, built himself quite a little collection, I'm told.'

'How do you know this?'

'There are people back in London who make a hobby of knowing these things.'

'No, I mean how do you know that this painting was hanging in the palace?'

'It was seen there a few years back by a British workman.'

'Workman?' The eyebrows went up. 'And he was an expert at recognising Rembrandts, was he?'

'I doubt it. He was over there to do a job in the palace. When he was finished he took a photo of his handiwork. Not the kind of behaviour that was encouraged by the management but useful just the same.'

'And this painting shows up in the photograph.'

'Clear as day.'

She picked up the photo and studied it seriously. Then her face brightened. 'Maybe Pavel was selling it for the Romanian government. That's possible, isn't it? He could have just made a mistake about the name.'

She was looking for a solution, an easy way out of the problem. I hated to be the one to tread on it.

'That painting doesn't belong to the Romanian government or any other government. It was removed along with all the rest of his private collection at the time of his execution.'

'You mean it was stolen?'

'Spirited away would be a more accurate description. What I want to know is how it wound up in the hands of your friend Pesanek.'

The question just hung there. She didn't seem to notice it. There was a moment of silence in the café. Then her head jerked up and the grey eyes were on me again.

'You think I have the answer?'

'You're the one who knew him.'

'Not this side of him I didn't,' she said quickly. 'I don't know anything about paintings or how he got them.' A slight flush had come into her face as though I was accusing her of complicity.

'Did Pesanek have connections in Romania that you know of?'

'No—'

'Money problems?'

She shook her head violently from side to side so that her hair lashed across her face. 'No, there was nothing like that.

We've been doing well of late. New orders had come in; things were looking up. He had no need to be doing these beastly things.'

'Was there anything strange of late? Did he have any new friends, anyone different he was seeing?'

'No,' she said.

'There must have been something.'

'No!' She was answering petulantly now, resisting my suggestions without considering them.

'Are you sure?' I pressed her. 'Think about it.'

She looked up at me, her eyes suddenly accusing. 'Who are you?'

'I told you.'

'No, I mean who do you work for?'

I had gone too far down the line to lie. Besides, I've learned it's better to tell the truth in these situations. It avoids a lot of difficult questions later.

'I'm a civil servant,' I told her. 'With the British government.'

With a little inward breath, like a child who's just realised something, she said, 'Oh my God, you're a spy.'

It must be the most abused word in current use and not even true. 'No,' I said. 'I'm just someone who asks questions.'

'Is there a difference?'

'All the difference in the world.'

She looked away to the bar where a waiter was coaxing coffee from a consumptive espresso machine.

'I don't like your sort of questions, Jan Capek,' she said after a moment. Her eyes flicked back to me and then down at the table. 'None of this would have happened if you'd kept them to yourself.'

'You can believe that if it makes you feel any happier.'

'Why's all this so important now, anyway? Pavel's dead; it's finished.'

'Pesanek was just a front, Jarka. He was passing the money on. I need to know where it's going.'

She gave a little shrug, as though this couldn't be of the slightest interest to anyone. 'I imagine it's gone to someone who's made himself very rich.'

'But who?'

'Does it matter?'

'Have you any idea what thirty million dollars could do in this city?' I asked her nastily. 'Have you any idea of the chaos it could cause in the wrong hands? Not everyone thinks the collapse of communism is the best idea since sliced bread. There are quite a few who aren't too happy about it. They were doing very nicely for themselves and may be hoping to do so again if they get the chance.'

Jarka listened in silence. I don't think she had the slightest idea of what I was talking about. I stood up, tucking the picture of the painting back in my wallet.

'I need to know where these pictures are coming from. I think you can help me.'

I dropped some money on the table. Jarka stayed where she was, her feet pushed out underneath the table.

'I don't want to help you,' she said sulkily. 'I want you to go away and leave me alone.'

'I'm going.' I wrote a telephone number on a piece of paper and put it down in front of her. 'Think it over. If there's anything you remember, anything at all, give me a call.'

I'd made a right mess of that, I told myself as I walked back over the Charles Bridge. It was no good bullying her. She was frightened and upset and that had made her defensive. It would have been wiser to have coaxed her into co-operation. Too late now. The chances of extracting anything useful from her now were about a thousand to one.

The hotel where I stayed when I was in town was up in the Josefov, the old Jewish quarter of Prague. It's a solemn building, with an elaborate Viennese Secession façade, that was put up at the turn of the century and has been coming down again ever since. For the last thirty years it had been under state control, now it was back in private hands but the mattresses still felt as though they were stuffed with coal.

As I crossed the courtyard I could hear Zora's raised voice. I stepped into the darkly lit foyer and stopped dead in my tracks.

Coming towards me were two policemen.

CHAPTER THREE

You can recognise a country by its police force. Put two English policemen in a hotel foyer and they will be sulky and embarrassed like a couple of shy girls at a ball. The French will be self-important, the Italians operatic but this was Prague and these two came towards me with their heads down and shoulders hunched as though they were members of an occupying army whose sole purpose in life was to barge pedestrians into the gutter.

If they'd bothered to look at me as they passed they might have wondered why I'd hesitated at the sight of them. But then again they might not: everyone hesitates at the sight of the Czech police.

I went over to the reception desk where Zora Novotna leaned on beefy elbows.

'Having a spot of bother there, Zora?'

'Pigs.' She said the word slowly and succinctly as though it had been in her mouth a long time and was making a nasty taste. Waddling over to the rack she unlatched my room key and slapped it down on the counter. 'It's Michal.' She sank back on to her elbows as she offered the explanation. 'He's had his car stolen.'

I waited for her to start on about the rise of crime in the city in the last few years but she wasn't in the mood for it.

'In broad daylight,' she added and her little black eyes regarded me without blinking. 'He had it taken in broad daylight. What sort of a man allows that to happen? Now he's the only taxi driver in Prague without a taxi.'

I wouldn't have liked to have been in her husband's

shoes when he broke the news to her. It's no fun to be on the wrong side of Zora Novotna: hotel proprietress, town gossip and Olympic gold medallist for foul language. I tried a conciliatory tone.

'It'll probably show up in a day or so.'

'The police think he's hidden it to claim on the insurance.' She glowered at the door they'd left through. 'Communist pigs.'

'They're not communists any more, Zora.'

She gave a grunt, a small internal upheaval that scarcely shook her mountain of flesh. 'I know they're not communists,' she said. 'You know they're not communists but has anyone tried telling those bastards that they're not?'

I went up to my room. It was on the first floor with en suite wardrobe and easy access to the bathroom at the far end of the corridor.

As I came in the telephone was ringing.

It was Slater. He didn't sound too happy. By the time I met him that evening he was hopping wild.

'You were going to stay in contact,' he said.

'I left the number with the Embassy.'

'They had no knowledge of where you were. I had to get in touch with your secretary back in London – and she was only guessing. It's too bad.'

I leaned on the railing. We were in the Letna Park, a huge characterless space on the hill above Prague. It was here that they used to roll the columns of tanks and missile launchers on those grey May Day Parades. Then the park had a huge statue of Stalin but the Russians decided he wasn't the hero they'd always imagined him to be and they blew the thing up. Now there's a fifty foot metronome in its place. It was swinging from side to side like a windscreen wiper.

'Did you learn anything about Pesanek?' I asked.

'What's there to learn? He didn't do anything apart from make his furniture. Once a week he played a game of chess over at some club and occasionally he went to the opera. Apart from that, nothing. He was like a hermit.'

We walked down the long ribbon of steps that reached down to the river. Heavy clouds were building behind the Petrin Hill and the fretful wind that precedes rain was blowing.

'Any women in his life?'

'A sister over in Pilzn and that's it. Nothing on the side if that's what you mean.' Officially Slater was a Private Secretary at the Embassy. There was a time when they tried to pass intelligence officers off as passport officials but they stuck out like a sore thumb. Added to that, they found themselves processing so many visas that they hardly had time for anything else. So now they give them these nebulous titles.

'How about his politics?' I asked.

'He was a communist.'

'Everyone was.'

'No.' The fresh air had brought two spots of red to Slater's cheeks. 'Pesanek was a real believer, a fully paid-up party member. He used to go round the factories spreading the word.'

'When was this?'

'Way back. Just after the war.'

'He can't have been more than a teenager.'

'They're always the eager ones,' Slater said. A barge had come round the curve of the river and was working its way downstream. The single screw left a long white scar in the water.

'There must be something,' I said. 'Pesanek was being blackmailed.'

'How do you reckon that?'

'I saw his bank account. Money came in after each painting was sold. A few days later exactly the same amount went out again. There was no percentage in it for him; no payment. Nothing.'

Slater hunched his shoulders and nodded. The first spits of rain hit us.

'They must have had something on him,' I said.

'God knows what. I've heard of nuns with more vices. He thought that having a drink in the afternoon was a sin.'

We walked down the rest of the steps. When we reached the river I asked, 'Did you get on to London?'

'I did.'

'What did they have to say?'

'They want to know what you are doing here.'

I had no answer for that. I didn't really know what I was doing in Prague any more than he did. There was no plan in my mind. I was just picking up the scattered pieces of the past and trying to put them together again. It was like mending a broken daisy chain. Not that London would understand. As far as I know, their only knowledge of fieldwork comes from the cricket pitch.

'Tell them I'm taking the waters at Marienbad,' I said.

Slater wasn't amused. His steel-rimmed spectacles twinkled at me. 'They have a right to know,' he said primly. 'As a matter of fact, I have a right to know.'

'What are you going to do with the information? Put it into code and file it away in a safe place?'

'Pass it on to the police.'

'Are you out of your mind?'

The little runt smiled: the tight, tolerant smile of those who know better. 'The cold war's over, Capek,' he said. 'We work with the full co-operation of the police nowadays.'

'You don't want to trust them.'

'Prague's changed.'

'Not that much it hasn't,' I told him as I left. 'And for your information the cold war's not over, Slater. It's just had a change of rules. I don't know what they are; you don't know what they are. And so until we do I'll handle things the way I know best.'

*   *   *

No doubt Slater saw me as a dinosaur who's passed his extinction date and he may be right. I've made enough mistakes in my career and I've generally had to pay for them. But the one thing they've taught me is to keep my mouth shut. That way there are fewer surprises.

Turning up my collar against the rain, I walked into town, past the Municipal House, the big, art nouveau building that holds the Smetana Hall. The place has recently been reguilded and repainted so that it now stands in the street like a huge cream-puff.

A horn hooted as I passed the taxi rank but I didn't pay it much attention. A moment later a yellow Mercedes cruised alongside. Its hub caps were missing, as was the ignition on one of its cylinders. Leaning from the window, cigarette in mouth, was Michal.

'Want a lift, captain?'

'Michal. What are you doing here?'

'Nothing.' Michal gave a smile. He's got a beautiful smile, all teeth and no cares; you can get a suntan just standing in front of Michal's smile.

'I thought this thing had been nicked,' I said as I climbed in beside him.

Michal gave a nod, as though this was a common mistake.

'I found it,' he said, enunciating the central word carefully in case I hadn't heard it before.

Swinging the car out into the Na Prinkope he crashed through a couple of gears in quick succession and trod on the accelerator. The car lurched at a pedestrian who was making the mistake of trying to cross the street.

'What do they know, eh captain?' he inquired as the wretched man leapt to one side. 'They think we're still driving those old rattlers.'

In physical terms, Michal couldn't be much more different to his wife.

Where Zora was plump, Michal was thin; where she was

sleek, he was wiry, with the cracked, rumpled hide that comes to old leather. It was as though one had been preserved in olive oil, the other left out to dry in the sun.

'Where was it then?' I still hadn't fathomed the secret of his stolen car.

'Up by the Holsovice Park where I left it.'

'You left it there?'

'Of course, captain.' He glanced at me, apparently surprised that I couldn't see the wisdom of this. 'Otherwise I'd have caught it in the neck from Zora.'

'You did anyway.'

He shrugged, both hands coming off the wheel. 'That'll blow away. When she sees the car she'll be so pleased she'll forget she was angry.'

'Why did you have to lose it in the first place?'

Michal thought over the options on an answer for this. Then he tapped the side of his nose to indicate that we were now entering the inner sanctum of his confidence and said, 'You're a man of the world, aren't you, captain?'

'I guess so.' I was certainly more of one than Michal whose entire knowledge of the outer world was confined to a six-month stint on the German border during his National Service.

'Me and a few others play a few rounds of poker from time to time,' he explained. 'Zora thinks I'm on night shift. So if I win a bit she doesn't notice the difference, but if I lose I have to make it up some way.'

'Like pretending your car's been nicked and turned up again with the cash box raided.'

'She checks how much I make every day, writes it down in a book.' Michal was offended. 'What sort of wife does that?'

I could have said: a shrewd one who knows what a shiftless layabout she had married in a fit of optimism twenty years before. But I couldn't bring myself to it. Michal had his heart in the right place, and he was giving me a free trip into town.

We stopped at the lights. Beside us passive faces stared out of the grimy windows of a trolley bus. Michal lowered his voice a notch. 'You won't tell her, will you?'

'I doubt whether she'll ask me.'

'You know how these things are, captain.'

Ever since I've known him he's called me captain. I don't know why. I've never told him of my years in the Royal Marines or of my rank when I left.

'Could you use a beer?' Michal asked.

'If it were for medicinal purposes.'

We went to some dive in the Nove Mesto where the ceilings were low and the carpets sticky and drank a couple of pints of U Fleku beer which affects your head in much the same way as the kick of a donkey's hoof. Then we ordered dinner and talked of old times.

'Prague's changed,' Michal said. 'The whole spirit is different. Everyone's on the take.'

'They were always on the take.'

He nodded thoughtfully. 'But in the old days there was nothing worth taking. That was the good thing.'

It was well after eleven by the time we left. Michal disappeared into the night saying he must drum up some business or he'd have to get his car stolen again and I walked back to the hotel. The rain had stopped. Stars frosted a clear sky. As I came into the courtyard a shadow detached itself from the wall.

I stopped dead in my tracks.

'There you are,' she said, coming forwards into the light that shone from a window.

'Jarka. What are you doing here?'

'I need to talk to you. Can we go somewhere?'

'You don't mind me coming round?' she asked as we came into the Old Town Square. 'I telephoned but you weren't in, so I thought I'd come round and wait.'

'Why didn't you go inside?'

'I tried but there's a vile old woman in reception. She didn't want me there. I think she had me down as a call girl.'

The huge square was almost empty, the buildings glowing against the night sky. A couple scurried past us, arm in arm, their breath puffing out ahead. Jarka bounded up the steps at the base of the Hus monument and sat down on a bench.

'I was thinking about what you said this morning,' she said as I joined her.

'I'm glad.'

In the light of the street lamps her face was pale and intense. She looked at me for a moment and then twisting round, one knee clasped in her arms, she stared away into the distance.

'You asked me about Pavel; whether there was anything on his mind before he died. I wasn't thinking clearly – the way you'd turned up like that, the things you told me. It was such a shock. I didn't know what I was saying.' She was speaking quickly, muddling her words as she tried to explain what was troubling her.

'There was something?'

'Yes.' She said the word cautiously. 'It's true: there had been something bothering Pavel of late. At first I thought it was the workshop. We'd taken on so much new business, he wasn't sure whether we could keep up with the demand. We were going to need new tools, maybe more space; it was all going to cost a fortune. But it wasn't that; it was something else, something more personal.'

'Did he say what?'

She paused, gazing back into the past, then shook her head. 'Not directly, but there were times when he was very distracted. He'd lose his temper for no reason, just fly off the handle. It wasn't like him. I tried to talk to him but he told me it was nothing.'

'How long had this been going on?'

'Two months, maybe a bit longer. There was one day I remember particularly.' From the bag over her shoulder she pulled out a little book and began shuffling through the pages, holding it out in front of her to catch the light. From the direction of the Týn church came the thin sound of an accordion.

'He went out just after lunch,' she said. 'When he came back he was in a terrible state. He went into his office and just sat there for over an hour. I checked when it was in this. Here . . .' She passed the opened book across to me, pointing to an entry.

It was a diary, a week laid out on each page. The day she was indicating was a Thursday in late January. There was only one appointment. It read: '2.30pm. See Z'.

'Where did you find this?'

'It was in his desk.' She was leaning towards me, her head cocked to one side as she studied the page, so that I could smell the perfume in her hair. 'You wouldn't have found it,' she said. 'There was a special place where he kept it, a sort of secret drawer. I picked it up this afternoon.'

'Do you know who this "Z" is?'

'It's here.' Eagerly she took back the diary and flicked back a few pages until she found another entry. It said: 'See Z – 118a Cerninska'.

'You think the two are connected – his mood and the visit to this place?'

She nodded, her grey eyes wide and concerned. 'I'm sure of it.'

'It may be the address of his bank manager.'

'No,' she said. 'He would have told me if it was anything like that.'

'Or a mistress. He wouldn't have told you about that.'

She was suddenly cross. 'You're not taking me seriously. I should have realised you wouldn't.' She tried to snatch the diary back from me but I stopped her.

'I am. I just want to check. It's no good jumping to conclusions.' I handed the little book back to her as a peace offering.

She studied me warily in the darkness. She really was very

beautiful. After our first meeting I hadn't been sure, but looking at her now there was no doubt. It was a wild and rather fierce beauty.

'What are you going to do about it?' she enquired.

It was the question everyone seemed to be asking me these days. I gave a shrug. 'I'll go round there tomorrow.'

'I'll come with you,' she said quickly.

'No.'

'I must. He was my friend. I have a right to know—' At that moment the accordion stopped playing. It had been midway through a tune when it was cut short, the note dying away like a sigh.

Jarka swivelled round.

'Oh God!' She had jumped to her feet, her hands buried in her short blonde hair.

Across the square, in the cloisters of the building that straddles the church, two figures were standing over the huddled form of the accordionist. Slowly and relentlessly they were kicking him, taking it in turn, each blow aimed methodically. They made very little sound as they went about their business, but the grunts they exerted with the effort were amplified by the vaulting so they carried to where we stood.

'Bastards,' she hissed under her breath.

I must have made some movement because she caught me by the sleeve.

'No, stay here! Don't get involved with them – they're dangerous.'

'Who are they?'

'The SL,' she said. 'Nazis.'

As abruptly as they'd started, the two men stopped their work. I watched them run off up the Celetna, their distended shadows leaping across the walls ahead of them. They were short, brutal-looking men in dark clothing, and they ran with their heads down, bodies pitched forwards, their boots clattering on the cobbles.

A small crowd had materialised around the prone figure of

the accordionist. He was in a bad way, lying on his back with his head resting against the wall. Even from where we were I could see the blood splashed across the stonework. Above him, one of the men had scrawled a symbol: a crude circle cut through with a right angle. I'd seen it before, on street walls and hoardings.

Jarka was still clutching my sleeve as she stared at the scene in the cloister.

'Why did they pick on him?' I asked.

'I don't know. Maybe because he's a gypsy, maybe because he was begging for money. Does it matter?'

'No – probably not.'

'The city's crawling with the bastards.'

In the distance came the wail of a police siren. Letting go of my sleeve, Jarka turned on her heel. 'Come on,' she said sharply, 'let's get out of here. It makes me sick to watch.'

CHAPTER FOUR

The address that Jarka had found in Pesanek's diary was for a stonemason's yard in one of those crooked streets above the Loreto church. The entrance passage was wide enough to take a van but only just, judging from the paint scrapings along the brickwork. The place had no name that I could see but carved on to the wall above the entrance were two grasshoppers.

For some reason I'd decided the address was going to be for a private house and had come armed with various reasons for being allowed inside. As it was I needn't have bothered; I just walked through into the inner yard.

Slabs of stone were piled up like giant children's building bricks, some of it old and frayed around the edges where it had been chewed by acid rain, some freshly cut and white as unsalted butter. Propped against one wall were some carved figures that must have come off a dilapidated church and in the far corner stood a vast statue wrapped up in cellophane.

From the single-storey lean-to beyond came the whine of a circular saw, and loitering in the open doorway were two men in blue denim overalls.

'Can I help you?' one of them asked. He took the cigarette from his lips only after he had put the question.

'I'm looking for someone who works here,' I told him. 'I don't remember his name exactly, I think it begins with a Z.'

The cigarette went back into the man's mouth. He drew on it, then gave a little jerk of the head. 'Zemek?'

'Could be.'

'He's the foreman here.'

'That sounds right.'

Rolling his body around the doorpost, the workman raised his voice above the din of the saw. 'Milos! Someone here to see you.'

He was in his forties, this Zemek, a short man with a balding head and massive chest from which his powerful arms stuck out on either side as though he were carrying a couple of invisible buckets. He reminded me of the pugilists you see in those old prints except the stone dust that clung to his clothing and hair had turned his skin milk-white giving him a cold, deathly appearance.

'You looking for me?' His voice was surprisingly mild coming from such a formidable physique.

'Milos Zemek?'

'That's me.'

'I was given this address,' I said with a suggestion of apology, turning away from the other two men who still stood in the doorway watching with bored interest. 'I hadn't realised it was a stonemason's yard.'

Zemek's expression didn't alter but he gave a little shrug, as if to say this wasn't his problem.

'Cemetery work is it?' I asked.

'Restoration,' he replied in the same quiet, flat voice. 'Churches, historic buildings.'

'That should keep you busy.'

He gave a suggestion of a smile, his hand reaching out to feel the block of stone beside him, his thick fingers automatically testing the finish.

'What can I do for you?' he asked.

'I was looking for a friend of mine. He said he was down here.'

'Friend?'

'Pesanek – Pavel Pesanek. He's a cabinetmaker; has a workshop not far from here.'

I watched to see whether the name registered but there was nothing. Zemek ran his hand along the top of the stone and shook his head.

'Doesn't mean anything to me.'

'You were doing some work for him, I believe.'

'Can't think what.'

I wasn't doing too well. Looking around the overcrowded yard, I improvised. 'A marble top for a table, I think he said it was – something like that.'

'We don't do much marble.' Zemek wiped his hands across his broad chest, his eyes watching me. They were pale blue but in the floury whiteness of his face they glowed like two gentians.

'That's strange,' I said. 'He left a note saying he was here. Maybe he's coming later.'

'Maybe.' Zemek was unflustered. 'I don't know no Pesanek.'

'I'll tell you what.' I dug my wallet from my jacket and took out one of the business cards I keep there. Resting it against a block of masonry I scribbled a note on the back. 'I'll leave this with you.'

Zemek accepted the card, turning it over in his hand. The message I'd written was in English so it was unlikely he could understand what I had said.

'If he turns up maybe you could give it to him.'

Michal's taxi was parked at the end of the street. The door was hanging open and he was sitting across the front seats reading a newspaper. I'd given him a flat rate for the morning so the metre wasn't running. In the back seat was Slater.

'Any luck?' he asked, leaning forward as I got in the front beside Michal.

'The foreman's name begins with Z but he's never heard of Pesanek. Didn't bat an eyelid when I brought up the name. So we'll have to wait and see.'

Slater grunted his disappointment and sat back into the flabby upholstery of the Mercedes. I'd told him about the diary but not that Jarka had given it to me. As far as he was concerned I had just found it for myself.

'Like some coffee?' Michal asked. He crumpled the newspaper together and stuffed it down at his feet.

'That's not a bad idea.'

'It's Zora's,' he told me, which was no surprise as the only time Michal ventured into Zora's kitchen was to pinch drinking money out of her handbag.

'What's he saying?' Slater demanded, pulling his head forward between us, his spectacles twinkling with displeasure. I'd already discovered that his Czech was minimal. It's generally expected of intelligence officers that they have a grasp of the local language but they tend to make an exception with the Central European countries. It's just too difficult to pick up in a crash-course of evening classes. Not that I should complain: it's how I keep my job.

'He was asking whether you wanted any coffee.'

'No,' he said shortly, sitting back again. 'I don't.'

It was just as well, I'm not sure whether Michal's invitation had stretched to him in the first place.

With a sly smile, Michal pulled out a bottle of slivovitz and put a slug into the two cups. Solemnly we touched them together and drank our mutual health. Outside it had started to rain again. I stared through the wet windscreen to where I could just make out the entrance to the yard before the street dipped away out of sight.

'What's the weather forecast?' I asked in Czech.

'More rain,' Michal said. 'It always rains at this time of the year in Prague.'

'Same in London. Only difference is it doesn't remember to let up in summer.'

Michal drank his coffee reflectively. 'London.' He repeated the name with reverence. 'I've always wanted to go to London.'

'Nothing stopping you these days.'

'Are there black'uns in London?'

'Some.'

He drew in on his teeth, a tiny whistling sound. 'I've always wanted a big black'un. They don't have them here, you know, captain. Vietnamese, there's some of them, but they're not the same; not the same as a big black'un.'

'What's he talking about?' Slater asked.

'He's complaining about the weather.'

Slater was making some comment to the effect that it would be better if taxi drivers picked up a smattering of the Queen's English, when a figure appeared out of the stonemason's yard. He was dressed in an overcoat, an umbrella over his head but I recognised the powerful frame just the same.

'That's him.'

Zemek was in a hurry. Head down, eyes fixed on the pavement in front, he walked up into Pohorelec Square. Close to the statue of Tycho de Brahe and Kepler, he caught the 22 tram.

We followed, fiddling our way through the traffic, keeping a distance behind as the tram went clanging down the hill into the Mala Strana. Despite Michal's predictions the sky had cleared and a hard white sunshine had broken through the low cloud, flashing on car windows and puddles.

'He's going over the river,' Michal predicted as we crossed the upper end of the Mosteka and headed on down the Karmelitska. At the far end of the Legii bridge, where the trams funnel up into Narodni Street, Zemek jumped off, walked a few yards up the pavement and dived in through the glass doors of the Slavia bar.

'Get in there and see who he's meeting,' I told Slater as Michal dropped us on the other side of the road.

Slater was gone ten minutes. When he emerged he sauntered over to where I was waiting in the heavy gothic arches of the National Theatre.

'He's at a table on the far side,' he told me. 'Talking with some fair-haired fellow. They've got the note you gave them.'

I couldn't see them through the large windows. The Slavia bar is one of those big, noisy cafés which seats over a hundred people but it has only one entrance so we couldn't miss them when they left.

'How did you know they'd meet in person?' Slater asked me, as he leaned against the stone pillar. 'He could have just rung to say you'd been round.'

'Stonemasons can't read English on the whole. If anyone wanted to know what I'd written on that card they were going to have to look at it themselves.'

'You didn't put your name on it, did you?'

'I didn't have to. It's printed on the other side.'

Slater looked at me as though I had gone round the bend.

'It's no good pussy-footing around,' I told him. 'If we're going to get anywhere we've got to let them know we're here.'

'Are you two waiting for someone?'

The voice came from a tired-looking prostitute with per-oxide hair and smudged mascara, who was leaning against the back wall of the theatre smoking a cigarette.

'Sorry, love,' I said. 'There's nothing I'd like better to but we're staking out the Slavia bar.'

'Who's a funny man then?' The reply came back slowly and sourly with twin jets of smoke exhausted down the nostrils.

'Saucy cow,' Slater said.

'That one isn't a cow,' I told him as the slim-hipped figure teetered away. 'It's a bull.'

'Oh, Christ . . .' Slater's adam's apple rose as though he was about to add some telling remark but he kept it to himself. I don't think Prague was turning out to be quite as he expected.

It was five minutes later that Zemek came out of the bar. Crossing the street he waited at the tram stop.

'Let him go,' I said. 'He'll only be going back where he came from.' It was the other one I wanted. We didn't have to wait for long.

'That's him,' Slater murmured.

Coming down the steps of the Slavia was a neat, slightly

effeminate-looking man in a green Loden overcoat. On his head was one of those natty Tyrolean hats with a jaunty little feather that raises the faint suggestion that the owner spends his weekends boar-hunting. Glancing in either direction he set off into town.

We followed him through the mid-morning crowd to an office block off the Na Prinkope, one of those heavy piles of masonry they stuck up in the last century to show that they knew what business was about. After he had gone inside, I passed the doorway. There must have been twenty firms registered in the premises.

'Wait over there,' I told Slater, pointing to a café that was minding its own business diagonally across the street. 'If he comes out again stick with him.'

'How can I stay in touch?'

'Take the phone number. If you're not there when I come back, I'll hang around until you call. And don't get too excited,' I added as I left him, 'I may be some time.'

As it was, I was back in less than an hour, bringing 'Father' Oldrich with me. I'd picked him up on the Charles Bridge. It's the old medieval river crossing that had once linked the two shores of Prague. Now the traffic has been banned and it's more like a street market.

I leaned against one of the statues and watched the crowds pushing their way between the stalls of bohemian crystal-ware, puppets, painted eggs, Soviet army hats and glass jars of caviare. From what I hear, you have to watch the caviare. I've never opened a jar but I'm told it's likely to be full of lead-shot and oil.

A few artists were at work, painting those cheerful little views of the castle which, despite the weather, always come out with green trees and bright blue skies. The thin sound of a recorder came across the air and an old man had got himself lost and was asking for directions. He had a big map of the city that was flapping in the faces of the passers-by who paused to help him.

After a while he gave up his quest and trotted off down the flight of steps that lead into the Na Kampe. I took the identical ones on the other side, cutting under the arch of the bridge and ducking into a doorway in the little alleyway that leads down towards the river bank.

As the old man came past I took him by his tie and pulled him in off the pavement.

'How's tricks, Oldrich?'

He gave a little choking gasp as his head jerked back and he caught sight of me. 'Mr Capek—'

'Still pulling the old map routine?'

'Really, Mr Capek . . . that's no way to talk to a man, no way at all.'

I let him go and he tottered back a couple of paces. He was bald as an egg and pink in the face.

'Had a good morning, then?'

'I don't know what you mean.' Fussily he patted his tie back into place, readjusting the little gold pin that held it in place. He was deeply offended by the implication of my remark.

I reached into his overcoat. He didn't resist but turned his eyes upwards in supplication.

'No respect,' he murmured. 'There's just no respect left any more, Mr Capek.'

It wasn't a bad haul he'd made on the bridge: five or six wallets, a gold bracelet and a couple of passports. I put them in my pocket.

'I thought you were going straight, you naughty old goat.'

'Straight. Ah yes, straight. The chance would be a fine thing, Mr Capek, a fine thing indeed. What with the inflation and the rising prices, it's not easy, you know. And at my age . . .'

'At your age you should know better,' I told him.

Oldrich – 'Father' Oldrich as they call him – is the best in the business. I've seen him remove a man's watch with one tap on his wrist, take the gold fillings from his teeth given a couple more seconds, and there isn't a lock that holds any mystery for him.

'True,' he agreed, his eyes never leaving my pocket. 'Very true. So easy to be wise after the event.'

'I want you to do something for me.'

'Oh yes?' His lips pouted with the word. I guess those little cherubs you see in baroque paintings will all get to look like Oldrich when they reach pensionable age. 'And what would be in it for me?'

I patted my pocket. 'You get to keep this stuff, Oldrich.'

'Ah, dear me—'

'And I'll forget to turn you over to the police.'

'Really, Mr Capek.' He smiled, the virginal smile of a schoolgirl caught necking behind the bike shed. 'As if you would do such a thing . . .'

Slater was still in the café when we turned up, an empty cup of coffee in front of him. He looked up at me, then at Oldrich who was gazing round at the other clients with the fond expectation of the aficionado.

'Who's he?' Slater asked.

'Oldrich – an old friend of mine.'

Grasping the situation, Oldrich gave a bow and held out his hand across the table. As Slater was about to take it, Oldrich made a deft little movement of the palm and there in his hand was a fan of visiting cards. Slater looked at him in astonishment. With another flick of the wrist, the cards vanished and the plastic rose which had been on the table a moment before appeared in their place.

'Jesus Christ,' Slater said.

Oldrich handed him the rose. 'They just don't know,' he murmured to me. 'The younger generation, they just don't know.' And drawing out the chair he sat down opposite

Slater, a composed smile on his face, and relapsed into silence.

'Any sign of our friend?' I nodded across the road.

Slater was still watching Oldrich as though he was a genie who had sprung out of the ketchup bottle.

'No,' he said. 'He hasn't come out; not that I've seen.'

And so we sat and waited. To keep the waitress happy, I ordered more coffee and a beer for myself, while Oldrich accepted a glass of crème de menthe which he drank in tiny sips, dabbing his lips on a white handkerchief. Around a quarter to one, just as the café was beginning to fill with the lunchtime trade, I gave him a nudge.

'That's the one.'

Across the street, Zemek's friend had appeared out of the office. He was still wearing his hat and green coat but now he carried a rolled umbrella over his arm.

'Ah yes.' Oldrich nodded in satisfaction. 'Very nice, Mr Capek, very nice indeed. If you'll excuse me . . .'

He got up from the table and removed himself. I'd already told him what I wanted before we arrived.

'Where's he going?' Slater asked.

'He's just going to check him over. It may take a little time. I suggest we have some lunch while we can.'

I ordered more beer and goulash for two. It arrived steaming hot with plum dumplings. As we ate I asked Slater whether he knew anything about an organisation which called itself the SL.

'Oh yes.' He was concentrating on his plate. 'We've run up quite a dossier on them in the last few months. Why do you ask?'

'No reason – I saw them give some wretched gypsy a kicking last night.'

Slater turned down the corners of his mouth. 'Nasty bunch. Started up in some of the factories around Brno and Pilzn a few months back. Since then it's been spreading.'

'Fascists?'

'With all the trimmings: black shirts, paramilitary outfits. They've even designed themselves up a slick little banner which they parade around. They might be funny if they weren't so scary.'

'What does the SL stand for?'

Slater had dissected one of the dumplings and was inspecting its steaming innards. He shook salt over it but when it didn't flinch he said, 'It's short for "The Sons of Libuse", whatever that means.'

It meant a lot to me. Libuse was a semi-mythical figure in ancient times, a somewhat unbalanced princess who had married a ploughboy and proceeded to give birth to the Czech nation; no small achievement when you think about it.

'What's their line then?' I asked.

'Anti-Semitic, anti-Catholic, anti-communist. You name it, they'll put the boot into it. They're out to cleanse the country – that's their word, not mine – which means they've given themselves the right to kick the hell out of anyone they don't like. Arson's their latest trick. They burnt down a factory a few weeks back because the manager didn't allow a rally to take place: big bang, lots of smoke and no questions asked afterwards.'

'How are they funded?'

'Protection rackets, kick-backs from the drug trade. They're well organised. It's not going to be easy to put them out of business.'

It wasn't a pretty picture. I might have pressed him for more had Oldrich not shimmered into the café at that moment. Giving one of his bows he handed me a wallet, a black crocodile affair with gold corners. Slater had been chewing but, at the sight of this, he swallowed hard, his throat distending around a mouthful of dumpling. As soon as it was clear he said, 'What's that?'

'His wallet.'

'You mean he stole it?'

'We were thinking of asking him to leave it to us in his will but that might have delayed matters.'

Slater was visibly horrified, he looked round at Oldrich who had slipped into the chair beside him.

'Christ, he's a pickpocket.' It was probably the thought of how he was going to phrase his report that was worrying him.

'The best in the business.'

Grasping the drift of the conversation, Oldrich patted Slater on the hand in a fatherly way.

'The boy seems upset,' he said to me.

'He's had a closeted upbringing.' Digging Oldrich's loot from my pocket I passed it over to him and he spirited it away in his overcoat with the speed of a vicar pilfering from the collection bag.

'A pleasure doing business with you,' he said, getting to his feet. 'A real pleasure.'

'I'll see you around . . . oh, and Oldrich.'

He turned as he was leaving, a look of angelic innocence on those lips. I gave a snap of my fingers.

'Give it back.'

'Mr Capek?'

'Give it back,' I said.

With a sigh, Oldrich handed Slater his watch. I held my gaze on him without speaking. He met it for a moment and then with an air of supreme sacrifice, handed over a silk handkerchief and a pen. 'Just a whim, Mr Capek. Just a whim. No offence meant.'

From the black wallet I took the wad of notes and handed them to Oldrich. 'Here, you'd better keep these.'

'Most generous.'

Seeing Slater's shocked expression, I added, 'It's got to look as though a thief took it.'

'A thief did take it,' Slater pointed out, strapping on his watch and tucking the pen in his upper pocket. Whatever else he'd got from his Oxbridge education, it wasn't a sense of humour.

'Charming friends you have,' he said when Oldrich was gone.

I was going through the contents of the wallet. From the credit cards, driving licence and season ticket for the railway I learned that this friend of Zemek's was called Ivan Teige. He was the editor of a newspaper and lived in a town on the outskirts of Prague. It was as much as I needed to know for the time being.

'How did you meet him then?' Slater asked.

'Who, Oldrich? I was in jail with him.'

There was silence from the other side of the table. I lifted my eyes to him.

'Didn't you know you were working for a jail-bird?'

'Well yes . . . of course.' Slater was embarrassed; he would have read my file but didn't like admitting it.

'Don't worry,' I said kindly. 'You'll get used to it.'

They say that we only remember the sunlit days of our childhood. Unfortunately it's not the same for the adult years. I could recall every detail of the months I passed in that prison: the dull clank of the locks turning, the smell of disinfectant in the passages, the sound of raised voices muffled by the walls and steel doors so that they appeared to come from miles away. Above all I remember the silences, the long, unbroken silences that come when men are packed close together: thinking, scheming, dreaming in the darkness.

It had happened during one of the border-crossings into Austria, the last I ever made before the revolution. I had some scientist with me, a microbiologist that they wanted in the west, or didn't want remaining in the east, which ever way you want to look at it.

We were holed up in a god-forsaken guest-house near the frontier. It was getting dark, I was lying on the bed reading a newspaper when a car pulled up in front of the house. The scientist – Cervinka, I think his name was – jumped up from the chair and went across to the window. Whether he realised what was about to happen, I don't know, but he suddenly waved his arms in the air. I shouted at him to get down but my voice was drowned in the burst of gunfire, the window pane blowing inwards, his body leaping backwards as though he had been hit by an express train.

I'll never forget the sight. With his arms spread and the headlights behind him, the shards of splintered glass fragmenting into a strange, glittering halo, he looked like one of those visions that severely repressed saints used to come up with. Then he hit the wall and the brains that someone had thought might be useful to the free world were smeared across the wallpaper.

The court case was brief. The newspapers didn't get hold of the story and no one from the office turned up to testify. That was to be expected. The British government had never heard of anyone called Jan Capek.

On the positive side, I was sent down as a criminal rather than a political prisoner and so I was sent to a normal jail in Slovakia rather than one of the mental hospitals I might have warranted otherwise. But that was just for their own convenience. I was under no illusion: they'd locked me in and thrown away the key.

It was the revolution that changed that. The new president, who'd spent a few years cooling his heels in a communist nick himself, declared an amnesty and on a freezing December morning, with a clear blue sky and pigeons grumbling around the fountains in Trafalgar Square, I found myself back in London.

Somewhat to my surprise, the department took me back. I might be wearing a dunce's hat the height of Nelson's Column, but this was 1989 and the whole of Central Europe was in chaos. Anyone with contacts and experience was suddenly valuable. They had set up a new office to assess the situation and there was a desk in it for me.

You might say I should have told them what they could do with the job, but I was a 35-year-old Czech with no other practical skill to his name. It wasn't going to be easy to find anything better. But my pay was docked and for the last two years they'd kept me on menial tasks.

That was until now.

'Here he comes,' Slater said.

I pulled myself out of my reverie and glanced out of the café window.

Ivan Teige was hurrying back to the office with the flustered air of a man who has found he can't pay for his lunch.

After he had gone inside I let him sweat on his misfortune for as long as it took me to have a cup of coffee and settle the bill. Then I went up to see him.

His office was on the fourth floor. A grim-faced woman with the sex appeal of a steamroller asked me whether I had an appointment.

'Not as such, but I have something he might be pleased to see.'

She let me through into an open office cluttered with filing cabinets, typewriters and telephones. A couple of employees sat amidst the loaded ashtrays.

'How can I help you?' Teige's voice was brusque. He was sitting behind a desk in his little glass cubby-hole beyond.

I flapped the wallet down in front of him. 'You left this behind.'

Teige picked it up, slowly and carefully as though it could be a mirage that would disintegrate in his fingers.

My first impression of him had only been half right: he was effeminate, almost girlish, but he was older than I'd thought at first, maybe the wrong side of fifty. His fair hair, which was brushed straight back over his head, was making that imperceptible shift into grey, and his skin had a translucence to it as though it had gone thin over the years. It made you feel you were looking straight at his skull.

'Where did you find it?' he asked.

'In a gutter off Wenceslas Square.'

Teige had lost his earlier reticence and was now busily thumbing his way through the contents of the wallet.

'There's no money left,' I told him. 'If that's what you're looking for.'

'Bastards.'

'I had to take a look to find your address.'

'There was five hundred crowns in there,' he said angrily, tucking the wallet into his upper pocket. He paused, his hand held there over his heart, and said, 'It was that boy. I remember now, there was a boy who barged me in the street. He must have had it then.'

'There's a lot of it around.' I let him have his deduction if it made him feel better and strolled over to the glass frame that separated him from the lesser beings in the office.

'Auditors, are you?'

'No, we run a magazine,' Teige replied shortly, getting to his feet. Now that the wallet was back, he wanted me off the premises but I wasn't going that easily.

'Which one is that, then?'

'*Vysehrad.* You've probably heard of it.'

'Can't say that I have.'

He gave me a tight little smile which I took to be sympathy for someone who's been living on another planet for the last ten years and said, 'It has quite a circulation.'

'I'll look out for it.'

'Yes,' he said. 'Do that.'

I went over to the door and Teige followed, more affable now that I was going. 'And thank you for coming round, I'm most grateful, Mr – I'm sorry, I didn't catch your name.'

'Capek. Jan Capek.'

I had to smile as I walked out through reception. If you'd put electrodes on Teige's testicles and coupled him up to the national grid you couldn't have got a more startled expression on to his face.

CHAPTER FIVE

Sometime around three, after I'd packed Slater back to the embassy, I went round to see Jarka. She lived in the narrow street that runs up from the Town Square to the Estates Theatre. A dark, vaulted passage led through to a courtyard of faded canary yellow with a spider's web of telephone wires above. In an old bathtub were the first green shoots of daffodils. There were more on the first floor balcony outside her apartment. I knocked but there was no reply.

'Are you Jan Capek?' A door at the end of the landing had opened and a young man's head appeared in the crack.

'That's right.'

He looked me over, deciding whether I suited the name. 'She's over in the Petrin Hill; she said to tell you.'

'You don't know where, I suppose?' The door had opened a fraction wider now and I could see he had a soft, fleshy body, the kind that looks as though it's made of blancmange. It was wrapped – and not that well wrapped either – in a silk dressing-gown.

'Wish I could tell you,' he said with a sigh. 'I'm just the messenger boy. I don't get told anything.' His eyes were wandering over me with the professional interest of a tailor. 'You a friend of hers then?'

'Kind of—'

'She said she wanted to stretch her legs.' He touched the side of his mouth as though he had lipstick that had smudged. 'Can't see it myself,' he added. 'All this fresh air; it's hardly natural. But then she's like that, isn't she? So full of energy.'

'I'd better go and look.'

'I envy her; I really do. Yes, you run along.'

On the way over to the Petrin Hill, I stopped and bought a copy of *Vysehrad* from a newsagent in the Karlova.

It made grim reading. Back in his office, Teige had called it a magazine but it was nothing so glamorous. It was a list of those with influential positions in the government, industry and business who had once been members of the Communist Party. There must have been hundreds of them denounced in that one edition alone. For some it simply stated their name and present post, for others there was a more detailed biography, complete with dates and facts and photos. It was all there. As I flicked through the cheaply printed pages, the accusations of fraud and embezzlement shouted out at me, the message clear as the 'Wanted' posters they used to pin up in the saloons of the Wild West.

I found Jarka without much difficulty. She was sitting cross-legged on the edge of a path high up on the hillside. There was a pad of paper spread across her knees and a box of watercolour paints on the grass beside her. Seeing me coming she waved her brush above her head.

'You got my message then?' she asked as I climbed up to her.

'I did.'

She smiled as though I'd passed some hidden test and bowing her head over the painting she added a couple of extra touches. The cold had brought the colour to her cheeks.

'What do you think?' she asked after a moment.

I cocked my head to get a look. It was a curious painting, the spires and roof-tops of the city worked in weird colours: soft reds and blues. It made the place look as though it was glowing like a coal fire.

I said, 'It looks good to me.'

Holding the pad out at arm's length, she examined it critically, her head tilted to one side.

'Yes,' she said gravely, 'it is.'

'Do you sell them?'

'Sometimes. There's a gallery in town that takes a few when it suits them. But they don't pay much.'

'Why do you use those strange colours for the buildings?'

'They aren't the colours of the buildings,' she replied. 'They are the colours of the people who live in them.' She glanced up from her work to see if I was going to make some comment. When I didn't she said, 'People have an aura to them, a sort of energy. The closer they get to each other the stronger it becomes – you must have noticed that.'

'No, I can't say I have.'

'Then you've been living in the west far too long, Jan Capek.' Her voice had the brisk tone that women assume when they've spotted a weakness in a man.

Putting the painting aside she cleaned each brush in turn, rattling it in a glass of clear water before fitting it into a compartment in the paint-box. It was all very orderly and neat, a ritual to mark the end of the creative process.

When it was done she clasped her knees in her arms and looked up at me expectantly like a child waiting to be read a story. 'So, did you go round to that address I gave you?'

'I did.'

'What did you find?'

There was no reason why she shouldn't know so I gave her an amended version of the events of the day. She listened attentively, her grey eyes never leaving my face. It was only when I came to the bit about *Vysehrad* that she showed any reaction, her eyebrows arching in surprise.

'*Vysehrad*?'

'You know it?'

'Yes, of course. Everyone knows it. It's that rag that tries to expose communists.'

'You don't approve?'

'No,' she said after a pause in which she weighed the argument in her mind. 'I don't think I do. In fact I think the government should ban it. What happened in the past is over. It's best left alone now.'

She was wearing a brown jumper, belted at the waist, with a wide roll-neck that fell open so that as she stared down at the city I could see the full curve of her throat and the cleft between the collar-bones.

I said, 'Your friend Pesanek was a communist.'

She turned and looked at me in silence for a moment, trying to gauge what I was getting at. Then quite gently she said, 'Everyone was a communist before the revolution, Jan. It's not important.'

'No, Pesanek was the real thing. A true believer. That's what this crew who run *Vysehrad* had on him.'

Jarka twisted one finger of her left hand with the other hand, as though toying with an invisible ring.

'You mean he was forced to sell these paintings because he had once been a communist?' She sounded incredulous.

'I imagine it was more simple than that. Either he did as he was told or they'd put a match to his workshop.'

'Would they do that?'

'If they can kick in a man's head in the town square they can set fire to a few pieces of furniture.'

'You mean it was the SL?' She lowered her voice at the mention of the name.

'Arson's their favourite pastime.'

'They didn't leave that sign of theirs.'

'They'll leave it when they want people to know who's done it, not when they don't.'

She looked down at the invisible ring that she was twisting in her fingers. 'Poor man,' she said softly. 'It doesn't seem fair. A lot of people were communists in the beginning, weren't they?'

'They were.'

'They did it for the best reasons.'

'It was going to save the world.

She gave a little shiver and getting to her feet she brushed down the sheepskin bomber-jacket she had been sitting on and put it on. Collecting her painting equipment together she packed it into a canvas bag and swung it over her shoulder.

The light was going fast as we walked down the hillside together. On the distant horizon the clouds had been slashed open and a thick syrup of light was spilling over the city.

'How long is it since you were married?' I asked.

She stopped dead in her tracks.

'What makes you think I was married?'

'From the way you keep fiddling with a ring that isn't there any more.'

She looked down at the hand that had given her away. Then, with a little shake to rid it of the habit, she said, 'Do I? How very stupid of me.'

She was smiling now but for an instant back there another expression had registered on her face. It had passed so quickly I didn't have time to read it. It could have been surprise or shock. It could even have been fear.

'I couldn't help noticing.'

'Oh, it's no secret,' she said as she moved on. 'Just something I like to forget.'

We came to an intersection in the path. The bell of the Carmelite church was chiming the half-hour. Jarka muttered a curse to herself and checked her watch.

'Is that the time?' she said. 'I must get going.'

'Which way are you heading?'

She jerked her head towards the castle hill but made no move in that direction. Instead she studied me appraisingly, the grey eyes slightly hooded. 'You like to know about people, don't you?'

'It's a habit, I guess.'

'Not a very nice habit.' The reply came back sharp enough but there was no real animosity in her voice.

I watched her walk away in the twilight, her stride long and purposeful, the short hair bouncing above her collar. She must have felt my eyes on her for after she'd gone twenty yards she swung round and called back to me.

'What do you do in the evenings, Jan Capek?'

'Not much—'

'If you came round later I could make you supper.'

'What time?'

'Eight.'

I was late. Not a few minutes late but seriously late. I was late enough to expect a slap in the face for turning up at all. But when she saw the state I was in she forgave me.

After I'd left her in the Petrin Hill I'd gone over to the café in the Hotel Pariz and had a couple of drinks with Radek Holy. He must rate as my oldest friend. I don't mean my closest, we haven't seen enough of each other over the years for that, but he's the friend I've had longest. As children we lived in the same apartment block which, in a satellite city of the Soviet Union such as Prague, meant we played in the same streets, went to the same school and nicked fruit from the same stalls. And that gives you a lot of memories in common.

Radek sat at a table by the window and flicked through the pages of *Vysehrad*.

'Nasty little rag,' he said.

'Been around long, has it?'

'A while. This one started up about a year back.' Radek stirred his coffee and took a sip, pulling a face at the taste. There are fourteen different types of coffee in the Hotel Pariz and none of them win prizes.

'There've been others have there?' I asked.

'Several. They come and go. Different name and different format but the message is always the same.'

'Are any of their claims true?'

'Who cares?' Radek flashed one of his quick smiles. He had sharp white teeth and bright eyes. It gave him the appearance of a small predatory creature. 'People read it, Jan. That's all that matters. They want to believe it's true so they do. Everyone here's looking for a scapegoat for the past. The communists are the best they can come up with at present. They're a dirty word.'

I thought of the contempt in Zora's voice when she talked of the policemen, of the empty stone plinths where smiling statues of Lenin had stood until a couple of years ago, of the scrawled graffiti on the walls.

'A woman has bunions,' Radek said, 'she blames the commies. A man can't make it in the sack, he blames the commies.'

'Who's behind it?'

Radek shrugged. 'It's the way of things.'

'I mean, who's behind this magazine?'

'Anyone's guess.'

'What's yours?'

He tasted his coffee as though that was on what I was requiring an urgent opinion.

'Kupka.'

The name didn't mean anything to me. 'Should I know him?'

Radek put the cup back on its saucer and pushed them away from him. 'No, not necessarily.'

'Who is he?'

'Jaroslav Kupka.' He tested the name in his mouth. 'He's an empire builder, Jan. Rolled into town just after the revolution with a lot of ideas about rebuilding the country, setting up a new Nation State – you know the sort of stuff. He's set up an organisation called the National Reform Party. It's got quite a following.'

'Will anything come of it?'

'It could do. Of course he'd need luck on his side.'

'And money.'

'He's got plenty of that,' Radek said. 'Throws it around as though it grows on trees.'

*   *   *

'I thought they had you grounded behind a desk these days,' Radek said as we came out into the street.

'I got time off for good behaviour.'

'I'm glad.' He hailed a taxi with a raised hand. As it drew into the kerb he opened the rear door then paused. 'Will you take a word of advice?'

'I might.'

'Handle Kupka with great care. He's a dangerous animal.' He threw himself into the rear seat, folding the tails of his coat around his knees and looked up at me. 'You're putting on weight, Jan.'

'It's this office life.'

'Sex,' he said thoughtfully. 'You should have more sex. It's the only exercise an executive can rely on.'

It was after seven when I got back to my hotel. Slater had rung a couple of times, leaving urgent messages to say he wanted me to return the call. I didn't. Instead I went upstairs and took a shower. As I was emerging, the telephone rang. Still dripping, I sat down on the edge of the bed and picked up the receiver. It wasn't Slater. The voice on the other end spoke in Czech with that soft, rather oily tone of those that have something to sell.

'You don't know me,' it began. 'I work at the Two Grasshoppers.'

It took me a moment to remember the carving above the entrance to the stonemason's yard.

'What can I do for you?'

'It's what I can do for you,' the reply came.

'And what's that?' These conversations are like a game of grandmother's footsteps, each side trying to get to the subject without the other one noticing.

'You were asking about the death of Pavel Pesanek. I think I can help you.'

'So help me.'

'No, it's not me personally.' A slight whine came into the voice. 'Someone else . . . He might be useful to you.'

'I'd like to talk to him.'

A moment's pause. 'Do you know the gardens on the Kampa Island?'

'Yes—'

'I'll meet you there in half an hour.'

The Kampa is not really an island, just a narrow strip of land that is separated from the Mala Strana by a canal. The gardens stretch along the river bank. There are practically no flowers, just some benches and bony swings for the children but the swans like it. Their droppings cover the grass like a convention of giant worms.

I stood in the sickly glow of a street lamp and waited. The lights of the city jittered on the water. At regular intervals trams thundered over the Legii Bridge which towered above.

Just after eight a couple appeared, walking arm in arm along the river bank but they didn't even notice me as they passed. It was getting cold. I'd put on a thick fisherman's jersey under my coat but it had forgotten why it had been brought along and let the night air straight in. I stamped my feet and moved closer to the bank. As I was looking at the water lapping against the shore a voice said, 'Mr Capek?'

I turned around.

It was one of the two characters who had been loitering around the doorway of the stonemason's yard, a thin man with an anorak and a beret shadowing his face.

'Are you alone?' he asked.

'Yes.'

With a brief glance around, he said, 'Come with me, please.'

I followed him across the gardens and up the steps of the bridge. He walked with his shoulders hunched, his hands in his pockets, keeping a few paces in front to bar any further conversation. Ahead of us, at the end of the long dark perspective of the bridge, the city was lit up like a stage set. It reminded me of the painting Jarka had made that afternoon and I glanced down at my watch. Damn it, it was already eight-forty. I'd wanted to ring her before leaving, to warn her that I might be late, but I didn't have the number.

Half-way across the bridge, my guide glanced over his shoulder to see that I was still with him and ducked down a flight of steps. They led down to Strelecky Island, a boat-shaped patch of land in the current of the river. In summer people go there to picnic and fish from the banks but now it was deserted. Even the stray dogs who sniff around the litter baskets had better things to be doing that night.

Threading our way between the trees, we went across to the water's edge and here the man stopped. Without speaking he nodded his head to where a single figure was seated on a park bench further up the shore.

With that he removed himself, silently disappearing into the darkness of the trees.

It was a trap, of course. I'd known that from the moment the telephone rang in my room. I walked towards the figure on the bench. He was wrapped up warm in a scarf and overcoat, a narrow brimmed hat perched on his head. He didn't make a move as I approached but sat staring out over the river.

It was a good vantage point he'd given himself. Across the narrow strip of water he was looking straight at the gardens where I'd been waiting. It had given him ample time to assess whether I was alone.

It was only as I reached the bench that he responded, suddenly standing up and turning towards me. There was no expression on his face. His eyes touched mine then moved to a point just over my right shoulder.

I turned around.

There were three of them converging in on me. It's always best to have three. Just to be certain. With two there's a slim possibility of losing the advantage. But not with three.

They were dressed in black and emerged from the darkness quickly and silently on rubber-soled shoes. If I was hoping for a honeymoon period of discussion and mutual recrimination I was in for a disappointment. They came straight in, fanning out to attack from two sides at once.

The one on my left swung a punch but he must have been reading a book on how to get it wrong because he wasted time drawing back his fist. I dodged to one side and clasping my hands together I drove my elbow into his ribs as he passed.

He gave a grunt and staggered but he was built like a concrete pillbox and I was under no illusions that I'd inflicted much lasting damage.

Before I had time to collect my wits, the other two were on me, coming in from behind. A punch like the kick of a horse hit me on the back of the neck and I went sprawling across the arm of the bench, landing on the hard earth beyond. I rolled over with the force and came up on to my knees. With the bench between us, I had time to grab one of the rocks that lay around. It was about the size of a cricket ball and snug in my hand. As they came at me again I jabbed it into the stomach of the nearest.

Even the weight of a coin in your hand dramatically increases the impact of a punch. A rock puts it into a different league. I felt my fist burying into his gut, the muscles giving way like the broken springs of a bed. He made a noise which would have done credit to a schoolboy who has spied a large cream bun in a shop window, and crumpled over my fist.

If I had been in a boxing ring I'd be jumping around with my arms above my head by now. But this wasn't a fair fight. The Marquis of Queensberry had been given the night off and was back home tucked up in bed. As the winded man fell aside, his legs rucked up beneath him, the other two got in close, pinning me to the ground.

After that it was a massacre.

With one holding me down, the other kicked me in the head. I saw stars in front of my eyes. A couple more kicks and I was in the London Planetarium. Hauling me to my feet, arms clamped from behind, they began to punch me with the slow deliberation of those who know there's going to be no retaliation. Even the one who'd taken the rock in his guts recovered well enough to join in. And he was in a spiteful mood.

After one hard blow to the head I went unconscious. I don't mean I passed out, just that I appeared to. In the circumstances it was the only option I had left.

They let go and I slumped to the ground. A foot prodded under my shoulder and gave a heave. I rolled over on my back, mouth gaping open. Taking me by the arms they dragged me to the edge of the water. I could hear them talking now: short sentences punctuated by heavy breathing. Rough hands went through my coat pockets, searching for identification but I could have told them there was nothing there. A brief pause and I felt my jumper pulled aside and a heavy weight was pushed up onto my chest. Then the coat was buttoned up to the neck.

Until then I didn't know what they intended. If they'd wanted to kill me they could have shot me where I stood without bothering with the GBH. But I realised now they didn't want to leave that kind of evidence behind them.

Drowning was cleaner.

Even as it came to me, I felt myself picked up and pitched into the river. I heard the splash, felt the sudden paralysing grip of the cold.

Then darkness closed over my head.

CHAPTER SIX

'Oh my God!'

Jarka opened the door the moment I knocked. She was probably reckoning on slamming it shut as soon as she'd told me what she thought of men who turned up two hours late for dinner. But as she caught sight of my wet clothing, the blood on my face and shirt, her face fell.

'What's happened?' she asked.

'I had an accident.'

She was still standing there, one hand on the door handle, the other out to her side, the fingers splayed wide in surprise.

'Do you mind if I come in?' I asked.

'Yes . . . yes, of course.'

She stepped back to let me pass. As she closed the door again I saw her glance quickly up and down the passage and then push the bolt.

'I would have gone back to my hotel but it doesn't look good for a well-connected businessman like me to turn up looking like this.'

'No,' she said. 'No, it was right you came here.'

I was dripping on the carpet. Propelling me through into the tiny kitchen she damped a tea towel in the sink and pressed it against my forehead.

'Hold it there,' she ordered and standing back she reviewed the situation. 'God, you look a mess. Who did this to you?'

'A bunch of goons. I didn't catch their names.'

She was looking at me in dismay as though I were a large shaggy dog who had just padded across her newly cleaned floor with dirty paws. 'You must get out of those wet things,' she said decisively.

'I clean forgot to bring a change.'

'That doesn't matter. I'll borrow some from next door. Go into the bathroom and have a wash.' She indicated where it was with a straight arm, jiggling the hand so her bracelets clattered on her wrist. 'I'll see what I can get.'

'Not the dressing-gown,' I called after her.

She put her head back round the kitchen door, not understanding what I was talking about.

'The dressing-gown?'

'If it's the guy who lives at the end of the passage, I don't want his dressing-gown.'

After she'd gone, I looked at myself in the bathroom mirror. It wasn't a pretty sight. My face has already had thirty-seven years of natural wear and tear, now it had mud streaked across it and a swelling around the right eye and cheek where it had been kicked. The skin was broken and blood was caked back as far as my ear. When the bruising came up it was going to look as though I'd been through an accident in a paint factory.

I had been intending to use the basin but it looked so clean and white with its little feminine clutter of bottles arranged on the shelf above that I didn't have the heart. Instead I stripped off completely and stood in the shower.

When I returned to the living-room ten minutes later, a towel round my waist, Jarka was waiting for me.

'That's better,' she said without conviction. 'There are some clothes through there in the bedroom. They should fit.'

Why she should think that, I don't know. Her neighbour was three inches shorter than me with a waist that went outwards rather than inwards. The sweat-shirt was all right, the trousers showed the full length of my socks and there was room in the cardigan to throw a small cocktail party. Fortunately it came with a natty little knitted belt that took up some of the slack.

'What do you think?' I asked Jarka for her honest opinion as I returned to the living-room.

'It's not really you, is it?'

'No?'

Jarka gave one of those little smiles that is supposed to show that there's nothing to smile about and went away to get a plaster. I sat down on the sofa and let her plant it on my forehead. With the warmth of the apartment, a weariness was coming over me. 'You don't have a drink, by any chance?'

'I've got a bottle of wine open, as it happens.'

'Ah, yes. I'm sorry—'

'But you had a more pressing engagement, yes, I know.' Her voice was brusque as she finished the sentence for me and went to get the wine.

'I would have brought some flowers,' I called after her. 'But the cemeteries were all closed for the night.'

It was an old joke and got the silence it deserved. I looked round the room. It was neat and colourful with thick rugs on the floor and big, loose-limbed pot plants. Pinned on the wall were some of her watercolours. I recognised the blues and pinks of all those auras getting together.

Jarka returned with a bottle and took a glass from the table. With a twinge of guilt I noticed it was all neatly laid ready for dinner. She poured a generous measure of wine and handed it me. It was one of those soft reds from Moravia and tasted fantastic.

Fixing some for herself, she cradled the glass in her hands and looked at me thoughtfully. She was still in her jeans but now she had on a white silk shirt with baggy sleeves and a thick gold necklace around her neck.

'Are you hungry?' she asked.

I was. It wasn't until she said so that I realised it. 'Don't tell me,' I said. 'You happen to have a nice little casserole for two all ready in the oven.'

'No.' Her smile told me I should think myself so lucky. 'I was going to make omelettes. I still can if you like.'

When those three goons chucked me in the river they made the mistake of assuming I was unconscious. And that's what gave me the chance to escape.

I have to say that it didn't seem like much of a chance at the time.

As the water closed over me, the rock they'd put on my chest jerked me downwards. Strangely, although I knew I was sinking, I had no real sensation of movement. I was just aware of revolving aimlessly in darkness like an astronaut cut adrift in space.

Then I hit the river bed and the mud pressed into my face. There was a foul taste in my mouth and nostrils. I could feel the current tugging at my clothing, dragging me along the bottom.

All the while I was tearing at the buttons on my coat. Dry, it was light enough but down there it had me in a bear-hug. I had the upper two buttons free and was wrenching at the next when the current spun me over. I felt a sudden pain in the leg. I gave a gasp and water came into my mouth. Frantically I lashed out with my legs, trying to regain control. My lungs were beginning to hammer, my throat was constricted. I choked out water and my breath went with it, silver bubbles ripping past my eyes as quick as a shoal of fish. In desperation, my back arching with the effort, I tore at the coat and felt some more of the buttons give.

After that, the rest came more easily. I must have been almost upright as the coat opened because the rock spilled out of its own accord.

I was free.

But for a terrible moment there was no reaction. Instead of floating upwards I stayed where I was, suspended in the water. But it must have been an illusion for suddenly I broke the surface and lay there, arms and legs spread wide, gasping in the night air.

God, it tasted good. You have no idea what a sensual

pleasure it is to breathe fresh air until the supply has been cut off for a while.

Somewhat to my surprise there was no sound from the river bank, no shout of recognition. Turning my head I looked around myself. I could see the far shore, prickled with lights and, further round, the dark smudge of Strelecky Island. It was some fifty yards away now. I must have been under water for longer than I thought.

At that moment there was a sudden jolt as I hit the weir. It was a six foot drop in the level of the river, a stone fortress wall over which the water fell in a white torrent. For a few moments, the river roaring around my ears, I hung on to the lip. It seemed like a good idea at first. But I was nearly suffocating from the force and let go, slithering down into the blackness below.

Up above there had been no sound and now I realised why. All the sound was down here. It was like thunder: the noise that a spider must hear as it is washed down the plug-hole. The good news was that with this din no one was going to see or hear me now. Keeping close to the weir I began swimming for the shore. The weight of my wet clothes was slowing me down. I pulled off my coat and after that I made some progress.

There are trees along the river bank by the Charles Bridge. Catching hold of a root that dangled into the water, I pulled myself up and lay face down on the ground, letting my heart get used to the idea that it didn't have to pound so hard. A few people walked past but they gave me no more attention than they would to any other drunk.

It was the cold that roused me. As my clothes began to dry they set solid as though they had frozen. I struggled to my feet. My leg was hurting so it wasn't easy to walk but with a few pauses for rest and reflection I made it over here to Jarka's house.

*   *   *

'Do you have a car?' I asked her when we had finished eating.

'Yes.' She said the word lightly as though it could have no possible bearing on the situation.

'Do you mind if I borrow it for a while?'

She looked up. 'You're not going out, are you?'

'I have to.'

Getting to her feet she collected the plates and carried them through into the kitchen, clattering them down loudly on the draining board. 'You're in no condition to go anywhere,' she said, as she returned with a tray in her hand.

'This is important.'

She began to clear the table, her whole concentration on the job.

'Then I'll drive you,' she said. Her eyes met mine across the table, daring me to argue.

I did.

'That's not a good idea,' I said.

She disappeared again and I heard the taps in the sink running. I went to the kitchen door.

'I'll only be gone a couple of hours.'

She had her back to me, her hands buried in the soap suds. Taking out one of the glasses, she rinsed it in cold water and put it on the draining board.

'What's the rush?' she asked. 'What's so important that you have to go now?'

'There's someone I must talk to.'

'Can't it wait?'

'No.'

She turned round to face me, wet hands on hips. 'You wanted this to happen, didn't you?'

'Why should you think that?'

'You wanted them to go at you, didn't you? You provoked them. You made them do it.'

'I needed to see who they were, Jarka.'

'And that's the way you go about it, is it?' She was really

angry now. 'Letting them kick you in the head. Letting them drown you in the river. That's what you call "getting to see them", is it?'

'It's just a job—'

'Oh yes? And I suppose you're too stupid to get a proper job, are you? I suppose you can't do anything that doesn't involve being kicked and punched? They must love you back in London, Jan – the poor little Czech boy who can't do anything better. You've got a problem over in Prague. Don't worry. Send Jan Capek. See if he gets his head kicked in.'

'It's not like that.'

'No? Have you looked at yourself in the mirror?'

She was closer to the truth of it than she realised but this was no time to be discussing the ups and downs of my career.

'I need the car, Jarka.'

'I'll drive you; I told you.'

'I don't want that.'

Stripping off the pink rubber gloves she was wearing, she went across to a drawer and took out a bunch of keys.

'Either I come along,' she said, her temper suddenly transformed into a smile of triumph as she went over to the window, 'or I'll throw them outside.'

'Don't be silly.'

'It's your decision, Jan.'

We checked the directions in a road map and Jarka drove. I'd expected her to own one of those eastern bloc cars with an engine that sounds like a hair-drier. But it was a second-hand VW Golf with a clock that had recorded forty thousand miles before it'd broken.

'Ever heard of someone called Radek Holy?' I asked her.

'No,' she said. 'Should I?'

'Not particularly. But I thought he had the monopoly on selling these bangers.'

Jarka swung out into the fast lane. 'Never heard of him,'

she said, hitting the horn as she passed some unfortunate. 'And for your information it's not a banger.'

We'd left Prague on the Strakonika, following the line of the river southwards. Jarka drove with the same flair and confidence as she showed in everything else she did. And she talked incessantly, asking me about the rendezvous I'd made with the man from the stonemason's yard, how they had contacted me, whether I could recognise them again.

Shortly after we had passed the racetrack she turned off to the right, taking a smaller road that wove into the hills.

We found the town easily enough. It was one of those two-horse affairs of small private houses with high-hipped roofs that like to think they are in the Austrian Tyrol. Or maybe it's the owners who like to think they're there.

Jarka stopped and went into a bar to get directions. The address we wanted was on the outskirts of the town, a rather more modern-looking building with metal framed windows and a black door. It was set back from the road behind a neat garden. There was a miniature wrought-iron gate that had to be opened first. It's odd how house-proud people always put a lot of obstacles in the way of their guests.

We parked half a mile further on down the road and I got out.

'You stay here,' I told Jarka.

She looked rebellious and for a moment I thought she was going to start with the arguing routine. But she relented with a nod.

'How long will you be?'

'I can't tell.'

The house was in darkness. There was a garage off to one side but no sign of a car. I went round to the patio at the back. White chairs were arranged around a table. A barbecue stood on three legs in the corner. Beyond it, one of those gardens that looks as though it gets used only on Sundays.

The windows were all locked but security isn't what it

might be in the eastern bloc. With the blade of my penknife I flicked open one of the catches and climbed inside.

It was the living-room. I could make out easy chairs and a bookcase, all in the same gaunt style of the house. Taking off my shoes, I made my way through to the hallway. A flight of stairs led up to the first-floor landing. Keeping to the side of the steps to stop them from creaking, I went up and checked the rooms.

There was only one person in the house and that was a woman. She was sleeping in the bedroom at the end of the passage, almost invisible under a pile of bedclothes. Her hair was tucked into a bedcap and she didn't stir as I pushed open the door. On the floor beside her was a heap of magazines.

Returning to the living-room I searched the desk. In the top right drawer I found a Beretta. I tucked it into my pocket, and sitting down in a comfortable chair I prepared to wait.

I must have dozed off because the sound of a key in the front door jerked me awake. I glanced at my watch. It was just before midnight.

Ivan Teige came in and closed the door behind him quietly. Without putting on a light, he took off his coat and hat and hung them in the cupboard under the stairs. As he was about to go up I reached out and switched on the lamp beside me.

For a moment Teige stood stock-still, one foot on the stairs. Then he came forwards and stared at me. I doubt whether he believed in ghosts – he didn't look the type – so it must have been that much harder for him to believe it was me sitting there in his living-room.

'What do you want?' he asked.

'To talk to you.'

'Talk?' He repeated the word as though it had no meaning. There had never been much blood in his face but now the final corpuscles had drained away and he was white as a sheet.

Until then his eyes had stayed fixed on me, but now they flicked over to the desk. I shook my head and lifted the gun from my lap.

'The trouble with being orderly is that it makes you predictable,' I told him.

'The wallet.' He spoke mechanically, as though forcing himself to respond. 'You found my address in my wallet.'

I let him work it out for himself. There were more pressing matters to discuss.

'It was very stupid of you to try having me drowned,' I reproved him. 'I can't be any help to you if I'm dead.'

'Help? What help can you be to me?'

A light came on at the head of the stairs and a woman's voice said, 'Ivan? Is that you, Ivan?'

Without taking his eyes off me, Teige half turned. 'It's me, dear. Go back to bed. I'll handle this.'

She appeared on the staircase, wrapped in a dressing-gown, her face blank with shock. For a moment she gaped at us, her eyes drinking in the scene.

'Go back to bed,' he repeated.

Silently, she crept upstairs.

Teige turned back to me. He was calmer now, sensing some sort of deal. 'Help,' he said warily. 'You said you can help me.'

'That's right.'

'How?'

I smiled. My face wasn't in the mood for a smile but it came up with a substitute. I said, 'I can sell your paintings.'

'Paintings?'

'Don't play games with me, Teige. You have the Ceauşescu collection. I can sell it for you.'

CHAPTER SEVEN

When I got back to the car I thought Jarka had gone. But she was asleep in the back seat, only one knee showing in the rear window. She leapt up when I tapped on the pane and wriggling between the seats she let me in.

'Did you get to talk to him?' she asked, as she swung the car around in the road.

'We compared notes.'

'And—'

'I've had a change of career. I'm now an art dealer.'

'You're what?'

'I'm going to get the job of selling the Ceauşescu collection.'

The car jerked to a halt, its nose in the verge. Jarka stared at me in the darkness. 'What on earth do you mean?'

'They need someone to sell them now that Pesanek's gone. I put myself forward for the job.'

'And he went for it?'

'Not at first. But he's coming round to the idea. Are we going to sit here in the ditch all night, or can we get going?'

With a grinding of the gears, Jarka reversed up the car and headed back the way we'd come. As we buzzed along, the shadows of the cherry trees flicking over the windscreen, I gave her the gist of my conversation with Teige.

'He didn't like it when I first put it to him. In fact he was distinctly unfriendly. But I suppose you can't blame him. He had a couple of problems to contend with. The first was he didn't want to admit to me he knew anything about any paintings. And the second is I don't think he likes me.'

'You can see why.'

'But I managed to talk him round.'

'I can't believe I'm hearing this.' Jarka had her eyes fixed on the road ahead.

'I pointed out that there's no way he's going to be able to sell any of his pictures on the open market any more. The London auction rooms have just rumbled one. They're not going to touch another in a hurry. What he needs is a good dealer.'

'But you're not a good dealer,' she said with devastating female logic. 'You're not a dealer at all.'

'He doesn't know that.'

'He'll soon find out.'

It was perishing cold in the car. I fiddled with the controls of the heater but it didn't appear to work.

'So what happens now?' Jarka asked when I'd given up the attempt.

'He's going to think it over. Which means he's going to have a talk with his boss.'

'His boss?'

'Teige's not running the show. He's just the oily rag. Any decision is going to come from someone a great deal more important.'

'Do you know who?'

'Not for sure.'

We'd reached the outskirts of Prague. The car halted at an intersection. I watched the colours of the traffic lights wash across Jarka's face. As they reached green her eyes flickered towards me. 'So are you going to tell?'

'Tell what?'

'Who is it that Teige works for?'

'Ever heard of someone called Kupka?' I passed on the name that Radek Holy had given me.

'Kupka?' She shot it back at me in amazement. 'Jaroslav Kupka?'

'You know him?'

'Of him, yes, of course. I thought everyone did.'

'Not me.'

'You've been living in another world.' She was speaking quickly, almost breathlessly. She pulled the car off the road and stared at me in the dark. 'Jaroslav Kupka. Oh Christ, Jan. You can't start throwing accusations at Jaroslav Kupka. He's a powerful man.'

'I didn't think he'd be a mouse.'

'He'll eat you alive.'

'I'm not going to accuse him of anything. I've just offered to flog his paintings.'

'You may be wrong,' Jarka said. She sounded suddenly hopeful. 'It may be someone else.'

'Possibly. We'll find out.' I didn't particularly like her estimation of my chances.

'But you don't know the first thing about paintings, Jan.'

'Who needs to know about them? As far as he's concerned I'm a businessman with a sharp eye for a deal.'

'No,' she said firmly. 'You'd be bound to know something about pictures. No businessman would handle something he knew nothing about.'

I told her I'd have to risk that but she shook her head.

'You must know something about them.' She was adamant about it. 'I'll have to teach you.'

And that's exactly what she did. For the next two days we walked around the National Gallery of Prague looking at pale Italian Madonnas, fat cherubs, grim-faced Dutch burghers and cubist still-lives that might have been made from smashed glass.

She went about her task with some enthusiasm, breaking the pictures down into their constituent parts, explaining incomprehensible words like composition and iconography, pointing out details of technique, and drumming dates into me until my head spun.

I can't say I was a star pupil. What I did discover in this

time was that it takes more than a few days' cramming to become an art expert. But Jarka was relentless.

'First try to see which country a picture comes from,' she said. 'Then which century it was painted in. After that you can take a guess at who did it. You may not get it right but at least you won't make a complete ass of yourself.'

That was her opinion. Privately I was beginning to think there was every chance I could make an ass of myself. Not that I liked to say so, she was so determined to help. But somewhat to my surprise I did begin to pick up the rudiments of the subject so that by the third day of our crash course I'd reached the point where I could recognise the major movements and create the impression that I was, if not informed, at least an inspired amateur.

'You should take this up professionally,' I told her.

'Do you think so?'

'If you can teach me you can teach anyone.' We were having lunch in her flat. Jarka was sitting across the table peeling an apple, carefully cutting the skin so that it fell away without breaking.

'Maybe.' She watched the movement of her fingers through her lashes. 'I'm going to need something now that Pavel's gone.'

It was the first time she'd referred to her job since our first meeting. I'd almost forgotten it.

'Is it a problem?' I asked.

She put down the apple and searched around the flat with her intense eyes. 'Unless I can start earning something soon I won't be able to keep this place for a start.'

'What about your ex-husband? Doesn't he give you anything?'

She shook her head violently, the crop of gold hair whipping across her eyes. 'No. Nothing like that.'

'Do you know where he is?'

'Yes,' she said. Folding her hands she looked down at her plate as though she were saying grace. 'I know where he is but I wouldn't ever go to him for money. He's never been very' – she searched for the right word – 'kind to me.'

In the last few days, between the dates of the Italian Renaissance and the principles of foreshortened perspective, I'd picked up quite a bit about her brief and troubled marriage. Her husband was some sort of diplomat. They'd met in Prague but lived in various cities around Europe. When the break-up came they were in Paris. He'd left; Jarka had stayed.

'He hated Paris,' she'd told me.

'Too much rich food?'

'No, it was all this.' She waved a hand at the piece of sculpture we were standing in front of at the time. 'He couldn't stick knowing less about something than me. It really hurt him.'

'Hardly the ideal recipe for togetherness.'

'There was never any question of togetherness,' she said quietly. 'He wanted to rule me. Everything I said or did had to be approved by him. I wasn't his wife, just one of his subjects.'

'Why did you marry him?' It was a dangerous question and might have snapped her closed like a clam but she looked over the sculpture – Rodin I think it was – with great concentration as if the secret to the question was hidden in one of its bronze crevices.

'I don't know,' she said after a while. 'He just bowled me over. I was very young, only eighteen, and he was so forceful. I've never known anyone as forceful as him. Whatever he wanted he got.'

'And he wanted you.'

'Yes,' she said. 'For a time.'

I knew the type. I should do, there are enough of them around the foreign service. Hard men whose ambition is buried beneath the sleek skin of sophistication that their education and training have moulded on to them. They hurt the people they love in much the same way that a small child breaks its favourite toy.

When lunch was finished, Jarka fetched a bottle of brandy and a couple of glasses. Putting them on the coffee table she took down a stack of art books.

'We haven't done much on the nineteenth century yet.'

She settled herself cross-legged on the floor and began searching through the illustrations. I poured a measure of brandy into the glasses and pushed one across the table to her.

'What's this?' she asked, twisting a book around.

'It's French.'

'That's right. What style would you call it?'

I studied the picture. It was dark and cold and looked as though it was painted by someone who had never heard a joke in his life.

'Neo-classical?'

'No,' she said. 'French Realism; it's by Courbet.'

She bent her head over the book again, her hair spilling across her face. I studied the curve of her neck and the soft down of hairs that lined it. Sensing the contact, she looked up at me.

'How about this one?' Her eyes were large and serious.

'Delacroix.'

She turned her attention back to the book, leaning forwards so that the ridge of her spine was printed clearly across her tightly stretched shirt. I put my hand on the material, running it up into the cleft of her shoulder-blades.

'He was the leader of the Romantics,' I added and leaning closer, I kissed her on the neck.

'You shouldn't do that,' she whispered.

'I know.' My nose was nuzzling the lobe of her ear, pressing her away from the book. With a little murmur of complaint, she rolled on to her back and lay beneath me, her arms and legs curled up tight, like an overturned woodlouse.

'I can't help it,' I told her. 'I always get a crush on my teachers.'

'We're meant to be in the museum, Jan.' There was a look of panic in her eyes.

Gently I stroked the hollow of her belly. Then, parting the brass stud at the top of her jeans with my thumb and forefinger, I slipped my hand inside, the zip opening with the movement. Jarka put back her head and gave a moan as though it caused her pain.

'No, Jan—'

'The museum will wait.'

'This isn't a good idea,' she wailed, but even as she formed the words I felt the resistance give in her body. Her hands came up into my hair and she drew me down, her lips meeting mine half-way. They were soft and eager, the tongue darting out in greeting.

Struggling up on to her knees, Jarka crossed her hands over her chest and stripped off her shirt in one movement, tugging it over her head so that her breasts in their lacy white bra stood out firm and proud as a ship's figurehead.

She fell back again, brushing the table with her arm as she pulled me down with her. A book was knocked off the table and dropped open on the carpet by her bare shoulder. I kissed her on the pale, silken flesh between her breasts, then raising my head I glanced across at the opened page.

'And that one's by Manet.'

'Is it?' Her eyes were closed.

'*The Bar at the Folies Bergères*.' I read the title off the page as I pressed her jeans away from her hips.

'That's very clever,' she murmured. Pulling up her knees she kicked her legs free and locked them around my waist.

'Do I get a prize?' I asked.

'I think you've got it already.'

Around five that evening she dressed to go out.

'You can stay here, if you like,' she said. 'I'll be back in an hour or so.'

I watched her brushing her hair in the mirror. She had put

on a pale lemon-yellow dress with a white polo-neck jumper beneath. I didn't know why she didn't wear a dress more often: she had marvellous legs.

I rolled off the bed. 'No, I'll come with you.'

With a last glance in the mirror, as though reassuring herself that no sign of our love-making showed, she turned to me with the quick smile of a woman who is finally satisfied with her appearance.

'Ready?'

'Where are you off to then?' I asked as we walked up the street. It was getting dark, the shop windows splashing light across the cobbles. Jarka put her keys into her handbag.

'I've got to see someone,' she said vaguely. 'Which way are you going?'

'Back to the Josefov—'

'I'm going this way. I'll see you later maybe.'

She walked away, tall and slender, her yellow dress a note of sunlight in the shadow of the St Gall church.

I don't know why I followed her. It might have been that I had nothing better to do, or it might have been the time. Five o'clock. Jarka always seemed to have somewhere to be going at five o'clock.

Crossing the Melanchikova, she dived into the crowded market-place, threading her way between the stacks of cardboard boxes, the packed trolleys and shuffling women. At one stall she paused. I saw the purse come out of her handbag, money exchanged and a little brown paper parcel go back in return. Then she moved on.

I waited a few minutes before passing the stall. It was selling biscuits, those flat gingerbread affairs that are cut into shapes of hearts and teddy bears and decorated with thin strings of icing.

'That girl in the yellow dress,' I said. 'What did she buy?'

The woman looked me over, trying to decide whether there was something weird in the question. She gave a shrug.

'One of those.' She pointed to a stack of round biscuits.
They had shaky handwriting on them.

'Which one?'

'Does it matter?'

'I want to know what it said on it.'

She gave me a hard stare. Then leaning over she inspected
the display. I suppose she could only work it out by checking
the omission.

'It had "Tomasovi" on it.'

'Tomasovi? You're sure?'

'That's what it said.'

It confirmed what I'd already guessed, or half guessed.
Not that I particularly wanted it confirmed. But it added an
important piece into the jigsaw that was Jarka Surova.

On the way back to my hotel I stopped and bought a new
overcoat, a light grey herring-bone like the one I'd lost. The
material was coarser, the cut baggier than those you would
buy in London but I preferred to wear Czech clothes when
I was in Prague, it made me feel at home. As I came out of
the shop a man cannoned into me.

'Sorry, mate,' he mumbled.

I stepped aside but he was still there.

'Got the time?'

'Just before six—'

He had his hands in his pockets, barring the way. His voice
was reasonable.

'Would you get into the car, please, Mr Capek.'

He nodded towards a long black machine that was parked
a few yards further back. Another figure leaned against
the side.

'No trouble, please.'

I didn't give him any. You always know when there's
no point.

We drove over the river. No one spoke. When you come down
to it there wasn't much to say.

The man who had been waiting by the car was driving. He wore a blue anorak and his haircut was so short he wasn't going to need to have another for over a year. He was chewing gum. The squelching sound it made in his teeth was the only sound in the car.

The other sat beside me in the back. He kept his hands in his coat pocket so I had to assume he held a gun in there. I wasn't going to check. It makes for very dull conversation.

At the Mala Strana metro station, the car swung off to the left, curving around the high wall of the Wallenstein Palace, coming to a halt beside the small door that is hardly noticeable in the expanse of soot-blackened brick.

The driver jumped out and opened the rear door.

After the tight knot of streets where trams, cars and pedestrians all fight for space, the sudden openness of the gardens comes as something of a surprise. There are fountains and hedges and avenues of bronze statues that invite you to wander around in an aimless sort of way.

But my companion wasn't in an aimless mood. As we stepped in through the doorway, he gave a nod, directing me down a wide pathway that led off to the right. The place was officially closed and the crunch of our feet on the gravel was a lonely sound.

We came to a large circular pond. In the middle was a statue of Hercules – seventeenth-century Italian if Jarka's teaching was anything to go by – and off to one side an enormous greenhouse. In the ghostly light of the castle that loomed above I could see that it was a dilapidated shadow of its former self, panes of glass missing, the roof sagging in the way that greenhouse roofs do after fifty years of communist neglect.

My companion pushed open the door, ushering me in with another of his nods.

It was dark in there. Unloved plants stood racked up in tiers on either side like scruffy spectators at Wimbledon. The air was musky with their decay. Seated further up the nave of this decrepit establishment was a single figure. His legs were crossed and he was smoking a cigarette.

'Mr Capek?'

I said, 'You've made an embarrassing mistake if I'm anyone else.'

The cigarette went to the shadowed face. I saw the tip glow red and then it came away again, turning upwards as the palm fell back in a graceful and slightly feminine gesture.

'Quite,' he said. 'I take your point. It was a shade piratical; rather vulgar. I do apologise, Mr Capek. But you're a difficult man to contact.'

'Why should you be wanting to contact me?'

The cigarette went back into his lips. Smoke drifted upwards, suddenly writhing in a shaft of light.

'To ask what it is you are doing in Prague.'

'Minding my own business.'

'Your business, Mr Capek, is exactly what concerns us.'

'Who are you?' I asked. 'Police?'

'Heaven forbid—'

'StB?'

At the mention of the Czech secret police, he smiled. I couldn't actually see him smile but I could tell he was smiling from the tone of his voice. 'StB?' A suggestion of reproach was added to the smile. 'There's no such organisation in the new republic. You know that as well as I do.'

'Just the same pack of heavies working under a different name.'

'Possibly. Let's just say I perform much the same role as you do yourself.' He stood up, a movement that appeared to require no physical effort, and offered me his hand. 'But I'm forgetting myself. My name's Vlasek, Major Ludvik Vlasek. My friends just call me Vlasek.'

'I expect you get called Major most of the time.'

'Quite.' This appeared to be a favourite word of his. He used it to end one line of conversation and open another. 'Earlier this week you were dispatched from London to

interview a certain Pavel Pesanek. Unfortunately he proved
to be unavailable.'

'You mean he'd been murdered.'

Vlasek made a small circular movement with his cigarette to
indicate that this meant much the same thing in his dictionary.
'If you prefer,' he agreed, moving away towards the door.
'That is a matter for the police to handle. What I must
ask myself, Mr Capek, is why you have remained here in
Prague.'

'Just social reasons: looking up a few friends.'

He nodded as though this was understandable. 'Yesterday
you visited the offices of a magazine called *Vysehrad*.'

'I thought there might be a lead. But it was nothing.'

'Is that so?

We came outside and for the first time I had a good view
of Vlasek – Major Ludvik Vlasek – of what, until the Velvet
Revolution, had been one of the most efficient secret police
organisations in the eastern bloc.

He was slim with that unruffled elegance that is the luxury
of those who have minions to do their dirty work. His hair
was brushed close to his head; the cigarette, that appeared
to be an extension of his right hand, lodged in a short
amber holder. It would only have taken a monocle and a
silver topped walking-stick to have completed the impression
that he had been wafted here from an earlier and more
graceful age.

'What made you think there was a connection between
Pesanek and that magazine?' He was looking at me keenly
as though he too needed this moment to assess who he was
dealing with.

'I found a few copies of it in his studio.'

'There were none when the police searched the place.'

'I took them with me.' It wasn't true but it was a simple
enough explanation to be plausible and Vlasek went for it. He
let the subject drop and turned away. Taking a deep breath,
he filled his lungs with the night air.

'I've always liked these gardens,' he said. 'So peaceful.'

'For those who can afford to be here by themselves.'

'Absolutely.' To give Vlasek his due, he didn't deny the privilege but flashed a quick smile to acknowledge the irony of it. 'I wish everyone could be so fortunate. But that's not really practical.'

'Probably not,' I agreed. 'You must be one of the first people to be here alone since Wallenstein.'

'Do you think so?' He seemed interested by the idea. 'I rather hope so. I've always felt an affinity with the man. He was a great general in his own way and a man of destiny.'

He said this last word carefully as though it was so out of fashion that he might have trouble in pronouncing it.

'Do you believe in destiny, Capek?'

'I can't say I've thought about it much.'

'Nor me,' he agreed quickly. 'And yet of late I find small events in my life falling into sequence, forming a pattern you might say. I can't help but wonder whether there is not some logic governing it.' He glanced round at me to see whether I found him too fanciful and hurried on to explain what he meant. 'About ten years back I was assigned to the task of uncovering a suspected agent operating in Prague. He was a Czech by birth although he'd lived in England for much of his life. He claimed to be a businessman selling cosmetics. It was most convincing. He never made the mistake of being either too obtrusive or too secretive. But I studied him: every move that he made, every café he drank in, every person he spoke to.'

'And now you find yourself talking to him in person.' I cut short the rest of the story for him.

Vlasek paused at the intrusion.

'Quite,' he said. If you'd put the word on the washing line it couldn't have come out drier.

'It could be destiny,' I told him. 'Or it could be that you just couldn't resist meeting him in the Wallenstein Gardens to tell him how clever you were all those years ago.'

The cigarette went to his lips.

'What I'm here to tell you – ' there was a touch of steel in the voice now – 'is that I know you, Capek. I know how you think and how you operate. And I'm telling you that you aren't hanging about in Prague to look up any old friends. There is nothing social about your stay. There isn't a sentimental bone on your body. You're here because you know something about Pesanek's death that you are keeping to yourself.'

'If you say so.'

His eyes were on me, sharp and unblinking as a ferret's. 'I want you to tell me what it is.'

'Why should I?'

'Because it would be worth your while.'

'And if I refuse?'

'If you refuse.' He smiled and made a small gesture with his hand as though we were entering a realm of speculation that was inconceivable in the circumstances. 'I would have no alternative but to eject you from the country.'

'That would be embarrassing for your government.'

'And yours.'

'I can stay here if I want. This is a free country nowadays.'

'It is,' he agreed. 'But, as you know as well as I do, a free country doesn't mean everyone has the freedom to do exactly as they like, does it?'

As soon as I got back to the hotel I put a call through to Slater. He sounded less enthusiastic to talk than usual.

'Vlasek.' I put the name to him. 'Mean anything to you?'

'Yes, of course.' Slater was rapidly trying to get the gist of a conversation he hadn't heard. 'He's spoken to you, has he?'

'He gave me a conducted tour of the Wallenstein Gardens complete with background biography of his days in the StB and a free introductory offer of threats at the end.'

'What did he say?'

'He offered to have me kicked out of Prague if I didn't tell him what I was doing.'

'You can't blame him, Capek.'

'Probably not but I just couldn't see anyone else around to take the blame instead.'

'We're supposed to be co-operating with the Czechs on this.'

'You're supposed to be co-operating, Slater. No one's told me I have to.'

'Vlasek's a good man.'

'Good man?' Slater must had been brought up on the *Boy's Own* book of self-deception. 'And while you've been so busy co-operating with him did you find the time to ask who he was?'

'Yes, of course. He's the—'

'He's the bastard who had me put away, Slater.'

There was a moment's silence. Then he said, 'I didn't know that.'

'Well, when they publish the thirty-six-volume, leather-bound edition of things you don't know, Slater, you must remember to add this new item in the back page.'

I put down the phone. It was only then that I noticed the envelope. It was propped against my pillow.

There was no stamp, just my name neatly written in the centre. Inside was a ticket for 'Bedrich Smetana' and the time: 20.15 hrs. It didn't have a date so I could only assume it was for today.

I went back downstairs.

'Did anyone come here asking for me?' I asked Zora.

She hadn't moved since I came in; the hands were still planted on the counter. She shook her head impassively.

'Someone left a note in my room.'

'I didn't see anyone.'

Smetana was one of Czechoslovakia's leading composers but the ticket didn't say whether it was for a performance of his music or for a concert in the hall named after him. I checked the programmes for the day in the newspaper but it didn't help.

'Oh, it's not that,' Michal said when I showed it to him. 'It's the name of a boat.'

'A boat?'

'Sure, the 'Bedrich Smetana'. You see it on the river in the summer. It takes tourists on trips around the city.'

She was moored below the Palacky Bridge, a squat vessel with a black hull and white superstructure topped by a tall yellow funnel. From the look of her, she had started life as a tug and been conscripted, grudgingly, into the sightseeing business in retirement. Her deck winches and towing tackle had been stripped away for extra space and a white awning fitted overhead. It all looked jaunty enough but, up close, she was showing signs of her age. There was a beard of rust hanging from each scupper and the boat davits were gummed up with paint.

I showed my ticket and went up on to the foredeck. It was raining again and the place was practically deserted. A couple were necking in the shadow of the wheel-house and an overweight man sat in the bows morosely eating his dinner. Down below, in the lower regions of the ship's hull, lights were burning and loudspeakers were playing music that I couldn't identify: it could have been a piece by Smetana but if it was it had lost something in translation.

I leaned against the railing and stared out over the river. The rain was turning the surface matt-black and dulling the details of the distant shoreline so that the floodlit buildings glowed like the dying embers of a bonfire.

'You English?' a voice behind me asked.

I turned around. It was the overweight man with the dinner on his lap.

'More or less.'

'Me too.' I couldn't place his accent but that wasn't surprising as his mouth was crammed with bread and sausage.

'We're late,' he complained. 'Eight-fifteen it says on the ticket and that was ten minutes ago.'

'It's often the way here.'

'Bloody chaotic, that's what it is: the whole country. I asked the captain why we don't get going. He said they were waiting for someone important. Go without him, I said, teach him to be on time in future. But they don't have the balls, do they? Here, would you like something to eat?'

I didn't want anything to eat; I didn't want to be making small-talk with this mountain of flesh. I shook my head and turned back to the river but he wasn't giving in.

'I was going to have dinner in the restaurant down below but I couldn't face another dumpling. Dumplings and cabbage, that's all you ever get here; it's not surprising they can't run anything on time.'

Getting to his feet he came across to the railing. It was a strangely graceful performance. His feet were so tiny beneath his monstrously fat body that just balancing was an achievement; walking required the skill of a ballet dancer.

We were moving now. The lines had been cast away, the ship swinging round across the river, the steel deck shuddering as the engines picked up speed. The fat man pressed his belly against the railing and stared at the curl of the wake.

'Go on a boat trip. That's what they said. See the city by water. There's nothing like it. Bollocks.' He gave a belch that started in his gut and reached his cheeks by stages, blowing them out without making a sound. He was wearing a see-through plastic mackintosh that gleamed like steel in the rain that was plastering his hair to his forehead.

'Looks as though they've given up on that important person,' I observed.

'Serve him right.'

Getting into the stream of the river we cut under the Palacky Bridge. Then the ship swung round, the propeller churning, and headed into the shore again. As we drew close I saw a long black car parked on the wharf. Two men in black suits were standing beside it, their feet set apart, hands folded across their privates as they watched the boat dock.

'This isn't scheduled,' the fat man said peevishly. 'We're not meant to be stopping here.'

A line was thrown out, the hull bumped against the wicker fenders and the gang plank was run ashore. The fat man drew himself up, almost wearily, and tipped the remains of his dinner over the side.

'But now we're here,' he said, reverting to perfect Czech, 'we might as well go ashore, don't you agree, Mr Capek?'

I guess the look on my face must have been comical because he chuckled, a deep throaty sound that made his shoulders quiver. With a quick movement he took out a flask, flicked back the lid and took a swig at it. He offered it to me but I shook my head.

'You must forgive my little deception, Mr Capek,' he said, tucking the flask away. 'If I have a weakness it's for play-acting.'

'Your English is very good,' I said.

'It is, isn't it?' He was pleased with the compliment. Taking hold of the upper button of his mackintosh he gave it a tug. When it didn't give, he dug the fingers of both hands into the feeble plastic, and dragged it apart, throwing the tattered remains overboard. It was a simple enough act but for some reason it seemed almost obscene.

He smiled, as though reading my thoughts, the flesh puckering around his bright eyes.

'Let me introduce myself,' he said. 'My name is Kupka – Jaroslav Kupka.'

CHAPTER EIGHT

'Ah,' he purred in satisfaction, 'I see you already know of me.'

'I've heard your name mentioned.'

'Good, that's good.' Pushing himself away from the railing he waddled across the deck. 'It's just vanity, of course,' he added over his shoulder, 'but I do like to be recognised. I pay a public relations firm a fortune to arrange it but it still gives me a little thrill when it happens. Slightly childish, I suppose.'

I didn't like to tell him that his name had only been tossed into the conversation by Radek Holy, and then it wasn't in entirely complimentary terms.

Kupka had turned, his hands in his pockets, and now stood waiting for me. 'Well, are you coming then?'

'I've got a ticket for a trip round the city,' I told him. 'Why should I want to get off here?'

'A trip round the city? Oh, I think we can offer you better entertainment for the evening than that, Jan Capek.' He trundled down the gangway, his hands out on either side like the wings of a penguin. As he stepped ashore, he nodded his thanks to the captain of the ship. 'Frightful fellow,' he confided. 'Drinks too much and beats his wife, but who am I to cast aspersions?'

There was a strange intimacy to the way he talked. It was as though he had known me for years and this meeting on the boat had been nothing more than a happy coincidence.

The car was waiting. Kupka threw himself into the back seat, winching himself over so that I could join him. Without further instruction, we drove into the town. As we crossed the Jirasuv Bridge I glanced down at the river. The *Bedrich Smetana* had cast off again and was heading upstream, a dark beetle of activity on the shining water.

Kupka was in high spirits, humming to himself in anticipation. The back seat of the car was designed to take at least three. There was just the two of us and we were a tight fit.

'You're going to enjoy this, Jan Capek,' he said. 'You wait and see.' Taking out his flask he had another pull at it, letting his breath out through his teeth in appreciation. 'Capek: now that's a good Czech name. Any relation to Karel Capek?'

'No,' I said. It was a question I'd been asked often enough: Karel Capek was an author of the 1930s. 'But I am related to Petr Capek.'

'Petr Capek. And who's he?'

'My father.'

Kupka drank some more. 'Oh yes, very good.' His laugh bubbled up through the slivovitz so that some of it trickled down his chin. 'I like that, your father. Yes, that's very good. I like a man with spirit.'

I was about to point out that he was the one with the spirit in him when the car swung in off the road.

'Ah,' he said, 'I think we've arrived.'

We were in a large courtyard, lit only by a single lamp high on the wall. As we climbed out of the car Ivan Teige materialised from the shadows. He was dressed entirely in black so that his pale hair and bloodless face shone above his collar like a minor moon.

Kupka stretched out his arms.

'We're late,' he informed Teige. It wasn't an apology, just a statement of fact. 'Boats, you know. Unreliable machines at the best of times. And they make you sick. Can't see the romance of them myself.'

Teige gave a little bow to show he understood perfectly.

'This is Jan Capek,' Kupka added. 'He'll be coming along

for the ride – but of course you know him already, don't you?'

'We have met.' Teige turned towards me for a moment. His eyes were icy, in fact he was an icy little fellow in general. If you put your hand on his forehead it would probably stick there.

'Are we all set?' Kupka asked.

'Everything is ready.'

Across the yard was parked a crane, one of those heavy-duty lifting rigs they use on high-rise buildings. Its extendable arm was lowered and lying beside it on the flat top was a huge, shapeless object wrapped in cellophane. I didn't know what it was but I recognised it just the same. The last time I'd seen it, it had been propped up in the corner of the Two Grasshoppers masonry yard.

'Stay here,' Kupka ordered and, hands thrust deep in pockets, he crossed the yard to talk to the crew. They stood in a knot: wary, unhurried-looking men, dressed also in black.

Beside me Teige said, 'This wasn't my idea, Capek.'

'Come again?'

'Having you along this evening. It wasn't my idea.' He was standing close, his voice soft.

I gave him one of my cheerier smiles. 'No, somehow I didn't think it would be. Ideas aren't your strong point are they, Ivan?'

The eyes blinked. He didn't like me using his Christian name. 'Have you any idea who you are dealing with?'

'A construction crew on double overtime by the look of it.'

'Keep your eyes open, Mr Capek. Watch, listen and learn. You'll find this evening an education.'

One of the crew had jumped up into the cab of the crane. With a roar the engine fired into life, the flap on the vertical exhaust fluttering on the stream.

Above the noise, Kupka shouted, 'Don't just stand there, Capek. Get on board.'

I did what I was told. There were five or six men on the crane already, perched between the giant wheels. I clambered up the side and sat beside one of the mud flaps. A few minutes later Kupka joined me, struggling up with assistance from below. By the time he arrived in place his face was streaming with sweat.

'Beats boat trips on the river, eh Capek?' he shouted in my ear as soon as he'd regained his breath. He gave a signal and the crane nosed its way out through the entrance and headed along the river bank.

'Where are we going?' I asked him.

'You'll see – you'll see.'

That has to be the strangest journey I've ever made. We were only doing forty but even at that speed the crane was bucking and jolting like a wild animal, the massive wheels throwing up a spray of water that drenched everyone on board. I moved closer to the mud flap and hung on for dear life. If there was a suspension system on that machine it had taken the day off. And the steering was like a tank's, a matter of locking the wheels on one side to force it round, which didn't make for a smooth ride. But the driver had it down to a fine art and hammered his way through the traffic, swerving in and out of the lanes, sounding his klaxon at anyone stupid enough not to get out of the way.

Crossing the river we thundered up the Ujezd into Mala Strana Square. Above us the castle was lit up like a child's birthday cake. Kupka had clambered to his feet and now stood clutching the crane arm. He was like the commander of a ship up there, the rain splattering his face, his enormous body swaying dangerously to the uncertain rhythm. From time to time he would shout something down at us but it was lost in the wind and racket of the engines.

A cavalcade was developing in our wake. When we'd set off there had been only one car following but as we progressed up towards the Cechuv Bridge a couple of vans fell in behind, then a larger lorry, its cargo covered by a tarpaulin. By the time we had re-crossed the river and were heading up Parizka Street, past the red tiled roofs of the Old Jewish Synagogue, we were like a small advancing army.

At first I'd thought Kupka was staging this exhibition purely for my benefit but I was beginning to realise that I was just a spectator – a privileged spectator with a grandstand view but still a spectator.

The centre of the old town of Prague is banned to traffic. But it didn't deter Kupka. The crane took the ramp at speed with a jolt that nearly cost me the fillings in my teeth, and charged on up into the Old Town Square. Here, right in the middle of those venerable medieval buildings, it came to a halt and stood smoking in the cold air. The vehicles behind fanned out and parked at prearranged points.

There was a hush in the square, broken only by the ticking of the crane's engine. Kupka looked around, checking that everything was in place. Then jumping down to the ground with remarkable agility he said, 'Come on, Capek. It's time we faded into the background.'

We stood beneath the tower of the Town Hall. Kupka leaned against the wall, flask in hand. I could smell the alcohol on him now. It was like a perfume. If someone nearby had lit a cigarette they might have witnessed one of the rare cases of spontaneous combustion.

A small crowd had gathered around the crane, sensing some sort of event but as yet unaware of what it might be. There was a burst of life from the engine and the crane arm lifted, slowly raising the wrapped package, tipping it over on its end and setting it down on the ground. The men who'd been riding beside it began stripping away the covering.

Beneath it was a stone statue. It must have been fifteen foot tall, a grey granite figure, wobbling uncertainly on its base. At that moment a spotlight on one of the vans across the square came on. The hard white beam wandered across the side of the crane and then steadied on the statue.

The crowd recognised it and gave a gasp.

'Know him?' Kupka asked me.

The carving was of a slight-looking individual with birdlike features, one hand outstretched in that patronising fashion made popular by the statues of Lenin.

'Zetlivsky, isn't it?'

'That's right,' Kupka agreed. He seemed disappointed that I should recognise it so easily. 'Vaclav Zetlivsky, Minister for the Interior for the Communist Dictatorship of Czechoslovakia. We found it standing in a town square out east. They were going to junk it in the canal. We thought he deserved a more fitting end.'

The crowd had multiplied as he spoke, drawn to the spotlight like moths to a flame. There must have been five hundred in there now. Kupka took a swig at his flask.

'Justice,' he said, reverting to English. 'It has to be done and it has to be seen to be done. Isn't that what they say?'

'That's what they say.'

Music had started to blare out from the van beside the spotlight. It was a cheerful Bohemian dance. The crowd began to clap in time. It was turning into a party. Kupka gave another of his chuckles; it was rich and deep, the sound of the entrepreneur who is giving his audience what they want and can see a healthy profit in it for himself.

'Zetlivsky,' he said gazing at the statue. 'Now there was a bastard. He was in office for only five years and in that time thirty thousand Czechs vanished from their homes. Artists, writers, intellectuals; none of them ever seen again.' The crane was gunning its engine once more, the roar of the exhaust rising above the music. Slowly the arm began to rise, and the figure lifted, swinging pathetically at the end of the line like a hanged man. 'Yes,' Kupka murmured, more to himself than me. 'We thought he should have a proper send off.'

I must admit he knew how to draw a crowd. It was all in the

timing. As the crane arm extended, each section telescoping out in turn, bearing the statue up into the night sky, another spotlight came on from the other side of the square. They held the condemned figure in the cross beam.

When it reached its full height, the music stopped, the engine was cut off and there was silence in the square. The crowd pressed back, realising what was coming.

For a full minute the statue hung up there, slowly revolving. Every face was turned upwards: a sea of expectant white expressions. There must have been some sort of remote control mechanism because I heard a detonation, a sharp crack like a rifle shot, and the cable parted.

It lashed upwards.

But for a moment the statue didn't seem to move. It just hung in mid air. Then it was coming down. Suddenly accelerating – height converting into energy – a terrifying, uncontrolled force plunging into the crowded square. There were screams of fright. People scattered.

The statue hit the ground about ten feet in front of the crane with a crash that echoed around the buildings. Its impact could be felt as well as heard. Some of the crowd had fallen down in shock.

Strangely, the statue didn't appear to break. It stood undamaged on the ground where it had landed. It seemed inconceivable. But it was only an effect of the dust that had momentarily preserved the image of the shattered figure.

As it drifted away I could see the remains of the stone figure scattered far across the cobbles. The torso had fallen on its back, arms and legs gone. The head lay on its side not twenty feet from where we stood. The nose was broken, the lower eye buried in debris. The other stared up at us, slightly startled but still benign.

Kupka raised his flask to it.

'So long, Vaclav.'

His voice was no more than a whisper but in the stunned silence of the square it carried. Someone gave a little cheer. It was picked up by others, spreading, doubling and redoubling in strength. A sudden exhilaration was gripping the crowd. It was almost hysterical. There was laughter and wild clapping. The music had started again and people began to wave their arms and dance.

Kupka studied the scene for a while, his expression momentarily vacant, like a general reviewing the aftermath of a victorious battle. Then turning to me he said, 'Beats a boat trip up the river any day, eh Jan?'

'What we need is a drink,' he said.

'That flask of yours run out?'

'No, not this stuff,' he said. 'What we need now is a real drink; something to celebrate with.'

We went round to the Golden Tiger. It's a beer cellar off the square where intellectuals go to get away from their brains. Kupka laid in a couple of litres of beer and settled himself at a table. He seemed to be well known in the place and fielded the nods and greetings that came his way with good-natured swats of his hand.

'Did you see it then, Jan?' he asked. Putting the glass to his mouth, he drew off a few inches of beer and let out his breath. 'Did you see it hit the ground? What a bang. You won't hear a better bang than that until Judgement Day.'

'It was quite a sound.'

'And it burst, didn't it? Burst like an egg. They told me it wouldn't break from that height. Just hit the ground and fall on its face.' He gave a laugh at the absurdity of the suggestion. 'What do they know? If that wasn't breaking I don't know what is. What a sight, eh Jan?'

He was talking to himself rather than me, rolling the memory around in his head. I don't know what it was that had made me think he was fat. Sitting there in his black overcoat with its astrakhan collar, he was massive, solid, like a great bear. And like a bear, it was impossible to be sure whether he was docile or dangerous.

'They'll be talking about this for years,' he purred.

'Maybe.' I couldn't get out of my head the idea that we were on a stage here in the centre of the bar. All around us people were listening, watching us.

'Oh yes,' Kupka said. 'This was history in the making.'

'There's a lot of things have happened in that square over the centuries. No one's talking about them now.'

Kupka studied me. His eyes were just slits in his face, the brilliant blue pupils almost invisible. 'Do I take it you weren't impressed by our little display?'

I shrugged. 'The crowd seemed to be impressed.'

'And you?'

'Does it matter what I thought?'

'It matters to me,' he said softly.

'If you must know, I found it all rather theatrical.'

'Theatrical.' Kupka repeated the word slowly, evaluating it in his mouth. 'Yes,' he said. The eyebrows over those Tartar eyes lifted. He placed the beer glass on its mat with studied care. 'That's exactly what it was – theatrical. Sometimes it's necessary to be theatrical, Jan. Sometimes it's the only way to make people wake up, to make people see what's happening beneath their noses.'

His voice didn't increase in volume but a new energy had come into it. 'For forty years we put up with the communists. We let them take our farms, our homes, our jobs; we let them sap the life from our country. Then along comes the revolution.' He raised one arm, opening his fingers at the top as though tossing a feather into the air. 'We sack the communists. A bloodless coup. No fighting, no executions. A velvet revolution – hooray. The whole world applauds; they tell us we're a civilised nation. But what has changed?'

He paused, offering me the chance of putting in an answer. When I didn't he gave a smile. 'What has changed?' He repeated the question more softly, as though it were faintly obscene. 'Do you realise only nine members of the communist regime were forced to resign after the revolution? Nine – the rest kept their jobs, kept their pay, kept their privileges. It's the same everywhere else. The army is still run by the same officers as before, the civil service by the same bureaucrats, the factories by the same foremen, the hospitals by the same administrators. We sacked communism but in our enthusiasm we forgot to sack the communists.'

Like all good politicians, he had a way of phrasing complex issues simply and neatly. What he said could be remembered and quoted later. Kupka seemed to read my mind because, taking a swig at his glass, he wiped his mouth with the back of his hand and grinned.

'You agree, don't you?'

'I can see your point.'

He wagged a thick forefinger at me. 'No, Jan. Don't give me that reasonable-man rubbish. You agree with me; you know I'm right. I can see it in your face.'

'I can't see that making a lot of mess and noise in the town square achieves anything.'

'It helps to remind people.'

'Of the past?'

'It helps remind them that the real work is still to come.'

'You mean you want to start another revolution?'

He nursed the beer glass to his chest. His eyes were sullen and for a moment I thought I'd pressed him too hard. But then he gave a little grunt and said, 'It's not what I want, Jan Capek. It's what the people want that's important.'

'How do you know they want it?'

'You saw them in the square just now. They were dancing.'

'That was a side-show,' I said. 'Everyone likes a side-show. They don't care what it's for.'

'You're a hard man to please, Jan.' Kupka stared at me for a moment, then gave a wave of his paw, brushing aside this conversation as though it were a fly that was irritating him. 'But this is boring. We didn't come here to talk politics.'

He glanced around. Through the cigarette smoke and

jostling figures I noticed that Ivan Teige had slipped into the room. He was leaning against the bar.

'From what I hear,' Kupka continued, turning back to me, 'you've put yourself to a great deal of trouble and effort to meet me. I'm intrigued to know what it is you wish to discuss so urgently.'

'The Ceauşescu paintings.'

Kupka smiled, the innocent smile of a lollipop man as he watches his tiny wards cross the street.

'The Ceauşescu paintings?'

'You have them.'

'What ever makes you think that?'

'You wouldn't be here now if you didn't.'

'Is that so?' he nodded thoughtfully. 'Well, that may be true. Very well, let's talk about them.' The combined effect of beer and whisky began to tell. He gave a belch. Putting his hand to his mouth, he held out the other in a gesture of restraint. 'But wait. First things first. If we're going to talk business you'll have to excuse me a moment. I need a pee.'

He clambered to his feet, patting me on the shoulder as he passed. 'Get in another round; I won't be a moment.'

After he had gone, I drained my glass and pushed my feet under the table. The tension, the adrenalin that had been running through my veins since I'd first met Kupka on the boat, began to drain away. Now that we had come to the business in hand, I felt easier. Calling the waiter I put in an order for more drinks.

Teige hadn't moved from the bar. He was looking away towards the doorway. The waiter returned. He flicked a cloth over the table, dealt out a mat and placed a single glass of beer in the centre. I was about to point out to him that I'd ordered two when a hush settled over the room.

Two policemen had come in.

Brushing aside the heavy curtain they stood in the doorway. Thick necks, pistols at their hips, bellies tight in their tunics.

I glanced round but Kupka was gone. There was only one

glass on the table. It was a trap. I realised it – and I had realised it a second too late. There was no escape.

The two policemen were coming towards me.

'Is your name Capek?' The senior of the two put the question.

Out of the side of my eye I caught a glimpse of Ivan Teige. He was watching the scene with an expression of strained, almost painful concentration on his pale face. That's why he had come into the bar. This was his moment of revenge, his moment of triumph. There was nothing on earth that would make him miss it.

I looked up at the officer. There was no point in denying who I was. I'd been framed as neatly as any painting.

'It is.'

'I'm arresting you,' he said, 'for the murder of Pavel Pesanek.'

CHAPTER NINE

They took me to a police station somewhere in the south-eastern sector of the city. There were no preliminaries: no signing of papers, no formal statement of rights. They removed my overcoat and jacket, emptied my pockets and threw me in a cell.

For half an hour I sat on the iron bed with its hard mattress and single blanket folded at the end. Then they took away the bed and I sat on the concrete floor.

It was cold in there, the damp, aching cold that penetrates your clothing and creeps into your bones for comfort. There was only one window in the place. It was high and small and covered with a rusty grill. The walls were scratched with graffiti. They'd taken away my belt and the laces from my shoes in case I hung myself. By rights the only person who needed to hang himself was the interior designer of that rat hole.

I should have guessed that something like this was going to happen. Kupka was never going to deal with a complete stranger, someone who'd come at him with no credentials, no references. It was optimistic to think he might. What annoyed me was how easily he'd played with me. It was painfully obvious now that he'd never intended to discuss his paintings; he'd just wanted to teach me a lesson. And once he reckoned I'd learned it he'd had me chucked in here.

There was one spark of hope, however. He must still want something. He'd never have gone through all this performance unless there was some way I could be of use to him.

For over an hour I sat staring up at the ceiling, turning these thoughts over in my mind until they were worn as smooth as pebbles on a beach. Then the door burst open and two policemen came in.

They were both rookies with thin, expressionless faces. Their hair was cut to bristle, their necks long and scrawny above their collars.

Locking my arms behind my back they dragged me from the cell. My feet were dangling between them like a puppet with broken strings. Out in the passage was a third policeman. He held one of those obscene little sub-machine-guns that squirt bullets so rapidly that it's not necessary to take proper aim.

Up one flight of stairs. Through two sets of fire doors, the policemen kicking them open with their boots, and into a small office.

It was glowing with warmth.

There were two of them in there. The sergeant who'd arrested me sat cross-legged in an armchair by a coal-fired stove. His khaki tunic was open, his vest-covered belly bulging. The other sat behind a desk. It was stacked with paperwork and rubber stamps; there was a kettle on the stove and the scent of beeswax in the air. Between them they created that cosy atmosphere of provincial officialdom.

The sergeant nodded towards an empty chair.

The two rookies sat me down and strapped my wrists to the arm rests with leather belts. Then they removed themselves.

As the door closed, the sergeant swivelled his chair towards me. He leaned back and it creaked comfortably. I'd learned earlier that his name was Kurz.

'I thought we should have a talk,' he said, clasping his hands over his gut.

'Fine – for a start you can tell me where they've taken my bed.'

Kurz ignored the request. He picked up a business card. It was the one that I'd given to Zemek at the Two Grasshoppers masonry yard. Kurz studied it closely.

'It says here that you're in cosmetics.'

'I am. You can check with London if you like – that's if your English is up to scratch.'

'How long have you been in this business?'

I shrugged. 'Twelve years, maybe more.'

'And why did you go to see Pesanek?' Kurz asked. He had a thick neck and the small, malevolent eyes of a pig. 'Pesanek was a furniture maker; he had no reason to be involved with a peddler of cosmetics.'

'He was a friend of mine.'

Kurz stood up. He hitched his trousers over his belly and, with a leisurely back-swing, hit me in the face. The other policeman sat and watched.

'There now, I punished you, laddie,' Kurz said. 'Do you want to know why I punished you?'

I didn't need to ask; I think I could work it out for myself.

'You lied to me,' he went on evenly. 'And every time you lie to me I'm going to punish you. It'll come a little harder each time, a little more painful. In the end you'll be begging to tell me the truth. Do you understand me, laddie?'

I said, 'I was in business with Pesanek.'

'In what way?'

'Furniture. I was going to sell his furniture in England—'

He hit me again. This time the hand was closed into a fist. It jerked my head to the side and I felt the skin tighten from the impact.

'There's money in furniture,' I said. 'Good money.'

This time the punch landed on the other side of my face.

'What do you expect me to tell you?' I shouted.

'The truth, laddie. The truth.'

'I didn't kill him—'

'We know that.' His voice still had the reasonable tone of a schoolmaster but he was beginning to breathe more heavily. It could have been the effort, or it could have been that he found some pleasure in the activity. 'What we want to know is why you went to see him in the first place.'

'I've told you.'

Kurz straightened and turned away. He ran one finger round the upper rim of his vest. 'You'll give me an answer, laddie. Don't think you won't. Before the end of this night you'll be singing like a dicky bird.'

He rapped on the door and the two rookies appeared. They pulled me out of the office and down the stairs to the cell. Here they held me up against the wall, arms spread, face hard against the rough plaster with its shaky graffiti.

From down the passage came the drumming of a tap on aluminium and then Kurz came into the room. He had one sleeve rolled to the elbow, a bucket of water in his hand. Without further discussion he came up close and poured it over me.

'See if that helps your memory, laddie,' he said.

The two rookies let go of my arms. Kurz kicked my legs away and I rolled on to the floor.

As soon as they'd gone I sat up and tugged the shirt over my head. The icy cold of the water was already gripping me, squeezing the breath from my lungs. I stood up and flapped my arms but it had practically no effect. Dropping down again I began to do push-ups; not something I usually indulge in, but this was different. Cold saps the strength, weakens the will to resist.

After fifteen minutes of exercises I was clammy with sweat but the cold was still with me. It ate into my flesh. I sat against the wall, knees rucked up to my chin. My teeth were chattering, long shuddering spasms shaking my body.

With an effort, I lay down and started the exercises again, putting myself through the same routine, driving the thought of the cold from my mind, concentrating on the work.

I don't know how long it was – it felt like a lifetime although it was probably no more than an hour – before I heard footsteps outside. I slumped against the wall.

The two rookies came in without speaking, took me by the arms and dragged me back into the warm office.

'Chilly down there, is it, laddie?' Kurz eyed my bare chest as I was strapped back in the chair. 'I thought it might be.'

He sat comfortably, legs spread wide. Opening the doors of the stove, he riddled the glowing coals with a poker. I couldn't feel anything as yet but my whole body craved the warmth, cried out for it in gratitude.

'Why did you go to see Pesanek?' Kurz asked.

'He was a friend—'

He reached forward and hit me.

'I was doing business with him.'

He hit me again and now he kept on hitting me, slowly and systematically, aiming each blow accurately, punctuating its delivery with a grunt of exertion. All the time he kept up a patter of talk. 'Don't lie to me, laddie . . . Spit it out then . . . Do yourself a favour . . .'

The other policeman sat and watched with the flat, dispassionate stare of a man watching goldfish swimming round a bowl. Eventually I'd had enough. I rolled back my head.

'Paintings,' I said hoarsely. 'It was the paintings.'

'Paintings?' Kurz straightened. He was sweating hard, his face pink and shiny like a boiled sweet that's been sucked in the mouth. 'What paintings, laddie?'

'He had some paintings to sell . . . valuable paintings . . . I wanted to do a deal.'

Kurz sat down and drew up his chair.

'What sort of a deal?' His tone was encouraging.

'I could have got more . . . a better price for them.' The numbing of the cold was lifting now and every part of my body was screaming with pain.

'How could you do that, laddie? How could you get more?'

'I have contacts.'

'What sort of contacts?' His voice was in my ear, close as a priest in the confessional.

'I know people who are prepared to pay above the odds.'

Kurz's sweating face was floating before my eyes. I could smell his breath. 'Can you, laddie? Who are you, then?'

'A dealer,' I whispered. 'I'm a dealer.'

'And who do you work for?'

'Myself . . . I work for myself.'

'Don't lie to me. Don't lie now, laddie. Tell me who you work for.'

I was becoming confused. 'No one.' I lifted my head to look at him. 'I work for myself. It's God's truth, I swear it.'

'Don't bring God into this,' he warned. 'We don't want him in here. Not now, not just as we were doing so well.'

'I'm a dealer . . . in London.' There was a screech of desperation in my voice. 'I can get a good price for paintings.'

'You tell me who you work for and we'll let you go; we'll forget that you tried to lie.'

'It's the truth.'

Kurz pushed back his chair, its castors rattling across the wooden floor. Reaching down he drew the poker from the stove. Its tip was red and smoking, a blunt sword in his hand.

With a crab-like scuttling of his legs he brought it back.

'Now laddie, let's stop playing silly buggers shall we?' He held up the tip of the poker. I could smell the acrid, unclean stench of the hot iron, see the flecks of black ash that dappled its head.

'I just wanted to make a deal,' I shouted. 'That's all. I wanted to find out who owned those paintings, make a bit on the side for myself.'

The poker didn't waver. 'That's just the half of it, laddie.'

'No. That's all – that's all there is.'

'Who sent you here?'

'I came by myself—'

With the deliberation of a craftsman, Kurz lowered the poker to my bare chest, holding it half an inch from the flesh.

'I'm going to have to punish you now, laddie,' he whispered.

I could feel the heat of the thing parching the skin, already sense the pain as it touched. Kurz's tiny eyes were on the poker. The lizard of his tongue had slipped out. It was pressing on his lower lip.

'I'll tell you,' I screamed. 'I'll tell you what you want to know.'

'Too late for that, laddie.'

'I work for the British government—'

The head of the poker quivered. Kurz looked up, wary, uncertain. 'Go on.'

'Take that thing away!' I cried. 'I'll tell you what you want to know. Just take that damned thing away.'

For a second the poker hung there. Then, like a swordsman, Kurz swung it out to one side.

'That's better, laddie,' he said softly. 'That's better. No need to make it hard on yourself.'

My head had slumped. I was drained of all strength, drained of all emotion. 'I was sent here to find the Ceauşescu paintings,' I mumbled. 'I was to find out who owned them . . . where they were coming from.' The words were hostages stumbling out to freedom. 'Then when I found Pesanek dead I saw my chance. I thought I could replace him, make some money for myself – real money.'

'You expect me to believe this?'

'It's the truth. What I said just now. I'm a dealer back in London – on the side, that is. I have contacts.'

'Your bosses won't like it.'

'They don't know. I haven't told them anything. They think I'm washed up, wasting my time. They don't know what I'm doing.'

'No, laddie. I'm not having this; you're one of them.'

'One of who?'

'You work for the British. You're one of their men. You'd never rat on them.'

'The British?' I spat the word back at him with all the energy I had left. 'I don't owe the British anything. For ten years I did their dirty work. Ten years I ran their errands; did as I was told. And how did they repay it? They let me rot in jail. Disowned me. I'm not one of them, you see; I don't belong. They used me when it suited them and when it didn't they forgot I ever existed. I was expendable.'

Kurz's tiny eyes were watching me, drinking in the words.

'I don't work for the British any more,' I said sagging back in the chair. 'I don't work for anyone.'

At dawn they let me go. There wasn't an explanation. They gave me back my clothes and a brown envelope containing the small change from my pockets and then bundled me out into the street.

It was a diamond-hard morning, the sun shining from a pale blue sky. I took the metro in the centre of Prague and walked up into the Old Town Square. My face was bruised, every limb stiff. If I live to be ninety I'll never feel as old as I did that morning.

Work had already started to clear away the remains of the statue. A lifting rig was parked by the headless torso while men in blue overalls tried to work out how to get a chain around it. A small group of spectators had gathered on their way to work. They stood silently watching like disconsolate sparrows.

'Jan!'

I turned around.

It was Jarka. She had wriggled her way out of the crowd and was running towards me. Her expression was wide-eyed, but with the morning sun in her hair and the cold bringing the colour to her cheeks, she was looking wonderful: young and healthy and warm as new-baked bread.

'Jan, where have you been for goodness sakes?'

'It's a long story.'

'I was looking for you last night. I thought you were going

to come round.' She stopped and stared at me. 'Christ, what have you done to your face?'

'I met a police sergeant who's perfected a primitive form of plastic surgery.'

'Where was this?'

'In jail,' I said. 'I'll tell you all about it later, but first, do you have anything back at home to eat?'

'Yes, I think so.' She was suddenly concerned. 'Didn't they give you anything?'

'I can't even remember what it's like to eat.'

'You poor thing, you must be starving.'

As we moved away the crane started up, its thin blue exhaust trailing up into the air. Jarka turned to watch as the legs of the statue were hauled up off the ground.

'Were you here last night?' I asked.

'No, I only heard about it on the radio this morning.' She sounded preoccupied. 'I came out to see,' she added shortly.

'Did they say who was throwing the party?'

She shook her head. 'Something about right wing extremists – no names.'

'It was Kupka.'

'Are you sure?' She was suddenly listening.

'It was Kupka – all eighteen stone of him. I was standing beside him.'

'Did you speak to him?'

'I spoke to him, drank with him. Hell, I could have eaten his supper at one point.' I was still feeling a little sore at the way I'd been treated. 'It was a set up. He called me over to some rust-bucket on the river and asked me along to watch the festivities. I thought he was just trying to impress me, show me what a big noise he is around town. But then, as soon as the show was over, he had me chucked into jail.'

'But he can't arrest you.'

'He knows a man who can.'

'The police sergeant.' Jarka's mind was running to keep up.

'We were sitting in some dive off the square when in come a couple of goons and arrested me.'

'For what?'

'The murder of Pesanek.'

'But you didn't do that.' She was becoming angry.

'You know that and Kupka knows it. But no one in there did.'

When we reached her flat, Jarka hung up her jacket and went through to the kitchen. I sat at the little table and watched as she put a pan on the stove and began rummaging through the fridge in a businesslike fashion. She was wearing blue jeans and a thick woolly jumper, belted at the waist to emphasise the curve of her hips.

'What makes you think it was Kupka who had you put in jail?' she asked over her shoulder.

'The timing; it was too good to be true. One minute we were drinking together; then Kupka suddenly ups and removes himself and this bastard Sergeant Kurz comes in through the door bang on cue. It had to have been staged.'

'He could have followed you from the square.'

'The police weren't there. I noticed it at the time. They'd taken the night off.'

Jarka cut a thick slice of bread and put it in the pan. The warm scent of hot oil filled the air. 'But why should Kupka want to put you in jail?'

'To check my credentials.'

Jarka glanced around, hair spilling over one eye. 'How do you mean?'

'Kupka wants to know what I'm doing. This was his way of finding out. Clever idea if you think about it: you've got a few questions to ask, don't ask them yourself, get a psychopathic police sergeant to beat the answers out for you.'

'But you didn't tell them anything, presumably,' she said quickly.

'Oh yes I did. I told them everything.' I didn't want her getting the impression I was any sort of hero. 'They knew, you see. They knew exactly who I was. I don't know where they get their information but it's good. I tried giving this ape Sergeant Kurz the line about being an art dealer back in London but he wasn't having it, smacked me in the face every time I brought up the subject. So in the end I gave in and spilled the beans.'

Jarka put a plate down in front of me. It was heaped with sliced bread, eggs and mushrooms. She watched as I began to eat.

'You told him that you work for the British government?'

'I didn't have much option. He knew it already. What he didn't know is that I'm not doing this for the British. I told him that I've come to Prague to set up a deal for myself. Clever, don't you think?'

Jarka smiled, suddenly intrigued. 'Yes,' she said. 'That was clever.'

'Kurz wanted an answer to take back to his lord and master. I gave him the answer I wanted him to have.'

'But will he believe you?'

'Who, Kupka?' I chewed for a moment. 'I think so. He knows that after two years in the clink I've got no reason to love the British. I told Kurz I had a whole lot of contacts in the art world and I wanted to use them, make a bit of real money for myself. He just might go for it.'

Jarka sat down opposite me. She rested her elbows on the table, hands folded beneath her chin, and regarded me thoughtfully.

'Are you, Jan?' she asked quietly.

'Am I what?'

'Are you working for yourself?'

I ran a piece of fried bread round the plate on my fork. 'What do you think?'

'I don't know,' she said seriously. 'I can't ever tell when you're telling the truth.'

'Let's hope Kupka has the same problem,' I said. Jarka was watching me intently. This was evidently important to her. 'No,' I said, to put her mind at rest. 'If I had all those fascinating contacts in the art world I might be tempted. Unfortunately I haven't.'

Jarka thought about this. Then she gave a slow, seraphic smile. 'No, you don't, do you? What you know about art could be written on the back of a stamp.' She glanced down at my empty plate. 'Was that good?'

'Brilliant.'

'I could make you some more, if you like.'

I shook my head. 'I must be on my way.'

'Where are you going?'

'To bed, for a start.'

'You can sleep here,' she said.

'What would the neighbours say?'

'Who cares?' she said, getting to her feet. 'It's nothing to what they get up to. Wait a moment, I'll just go and make the bed.'

'I can sleep on the sofa.'

'Nonsense,' she said as she went through to the bedroom. 'It'll give you a terrible stiff neck.'

I didn't bother to undress, just kicked off my shoes, rolled myself under the cover and slept like a log. When I came round it was dark. I lay quite still, cruising on the edge of sleep. After a few minutes the door opened and Jarka came into the room. She sat down on the end of the bed.

'What time is it?' I asked from the pillow.

'About two-thirty.'

I turned my head and looked at the window, realising the darkness was caused by the curtains.

'I drew them after you'd gone to sleep,' she said. 'I didn't want you to wake before you were ready.'

I ran my hands over my face. There was a dull ache from the bruise on my right cheek, but other than that I was feeling as well as can be expected.

Jarka drew her feet up on the bed, clasping her knees in

her arms, and studied me thoughtfully. I had a feeling that she'd been thinking things over while I'd been asleep.

'I should get going,' I said, raising myself on one elbow. But she wasn't going to be deflected so easily.

'Why do you do it, Jan?' she asked lightly.

'Sleep?'

'This job.'

'It pays more than you can get cleaning the public conveniences on Waterloo station, and there's the luncheon vouchers.'

'What are they?'

'The last word in western decadence.'

'Seriously.' There was a note of impatience in her voice. 'It's all so cold, so brutal. When I first met you I thought that you were someone who knew no better; I thought you were just part of it. But it's not like that, is it?'

I didn't like to point out that when we first met it was she who had hit me with the butt of a pistol.

'I can't see why you want to be doing this.'

I could have given her a dozen good reasons, but this wasn't the time or the place for any of them. 'It was a way of getting back here.'

'To Prague?'

'Yes, to Prague. It's my home. I haven't lived here for a long time, but it's still my home. Working for the Foreign Service was the only way I knew of being here.'

Jarka was silent.

'You think that sounds silly?'

'No,' she said. 'I don't.'

'Prague was a long way away when I was growing up. It was behind the Iron Curtain and that put it in another world. I wanted to find a way of getting back, that's all. It's not much of a reason.'

'No, it is,' she said with sudden energy. 'I understand. It was the same for me. You have to be where you belong; it's the most important part of living. When I first went to Paris I thought I'd stay there for ever. It was so bright and exciting. But in the end I found I couldn't. I just didn't belong there. It's hard to explain to people who haven't felt that way.' Getting up off the bed she went across to the window and stared out at the view. 'Besides,' she said, 'Prague's the most beautiful city in the world. I like being here.' Through the crack in the curtains a shaft of light touched her, carving out the profile of her face, flaming on her hair. 'At least,' she added, 'I did until recently.'

'You mean until they started smashing statues in the square.'

She nodded thoughtfully, her whole attention fixed on the view. 'Why did he do it?'

'For effect.'

'The communists weren't all bad, were they?' She put the question as though she was trying to convince herself. 'I know they were corrupt and dangerous and never let anything get into the newspapers that they didn't want, but they can't all have been like that. Some of them must have just been doing their job, trying to make a living, to get by as best they could.'

It wasn't the first time she'd put in a plea for the communists.

'Are you thinking about Pavel Pesanek?'

'Yes, him,' she said. 'And others.'

I couldn't help wondering quite who it was she had in mind. I should have asked; I should have pressed her to explain what brought on these sudden introspective moods, but then there are a million things I should have done and haven't.

Getting up, I washed and shaved as best I could with the tiny razor Jarka used for her legs, and went back to the hotel. The reception desk was deserted; Zora was backstage shouting at someone in the kitchens. I drank a couple of cups of coffee in the little café next door and read the newspapers. Just after four I went out into the street.

Michal was leaning against his taxi, the wizened remains

of a cigarette hooked to his lower lip as he studied the legs of the girls who passed on the pavement.

'Ah, captain,' he said, coming to attention. 'What do you think?' Pinned to his lapel was a large silver medal with a red ribbon attached.

'Very fetching.'

'I thought you'd like to see it.'

'What did you do?' I asked him. 'Win it at a fair?'

'No.' The idea was outrageous. 'I was given it by a Russian general. Get in the back, captain. No one will see you in the back.'

We drove over to the Stare Mesto. The evening light was settling, the rush-hour traffic, such as it is in Prague, beginning to jostle around us. As we searched through the streets, Michal told me about his medal.

'General Ivan Rustokski.' He rolled the name out on his tongue. 'I was his private chauffeur for over a week while he was here. At the end he gave it to me.'

'Why did he pick you?' I could have put it more tactfully but my attention was on the cars parked along the kerb.

'I know the town like the back of my hand; I know the history and all those things. And he liked me to get girls for him.'

'No problem for you.'

'No, it wasn't; no problem at all. Actually,' he said in the interests of honesty, 'it wasn't as easy as we'd expected. The general didn't like to pay for anything in hard currency. And there's only a limited number of times the girls will accept medals.'

'I can see their point.'

'The Russians weren't as rich as they used to be. It was a bit like your aristocrats in England.'

'The only difference being that our aristocrats weren't trying to dominate the world. At least, not recently. There it is.' I pointed to where Jarka's dark blue VW was parked.

Michal backed up, tucking the car into the kerb. Sensing we

were in for a wait, he lit his cigarette and stretching his arm along the seat he reminisced about other passengers entrusted to his care. After ten minutes of this Jarka appeared, hands deep in the pockets of her jacket.

'That's her,' I said.

Michal gave a whistle. 'Holy Mother and all the Saints.'

Unlocking the car, Jarka threw herself into the driver's seat, started the engine and drew out into the road almost before she'd shut the door.

'Now there's one,' Michal said in admiration.

'There's one what?'

'One that the general would have wanted to give a medal.'

CHAPTER TEN

Rats come in for a lot of bad press. They've lent their name to anyone who is low and sneaky; anyone who can't be trusted; anyone who turns on those who show them affection. Whether it's fair to rats I don't know, but if it is then, as we followed Jarka's car through the evening traffic, I was one of them.

At the same time I didn't have much alternative but to be doing what I was. In my line of business there's no point in following up what you already understand; it's what you don't understand that matters; it's all the irrelevant little details, the inconsequential facts that don't amount to much that need checking out.

Crossing the river, we wound up the hillside above Prague. It was a clear, cold evening, the spires of the ancient city rising from a sea of lilac mist. Orange lights glittered in the dark. For all his other failings, Michal was a good driver and he kept in touch with the blue VW, only getting close when there were intersections or twists in the road, falling back when it was clear.

At the top of the hill Jarka swung off to the left and drove down the long avenue of trees behind the castle. After half a mile the indicator light flickered and she turned off again, weaving her way through some smaller streets until she reached the Strahov monastery. She parked alongside the wall. I watched her climb out, slinging her bag over her shoulder, and run up the steps.

'Wait here,' I told Michal as she disappeared inside.

The Strahov monastery is like those Russian dolls they still sell in the markets. Buried inside the pastry work of Baroque architecture, with its twin onion-towers, is an earlier gothic structure, and for all I know another one inside that. The monks were kicked out in the Stalinist years and the place fell into disrepair. Now scaffolding is creeping up the walls like ivy, but much of the place is still derelict.

By the time I reached the gates, Jarka was half-way across the courtyard, a dark figure in the shadow of the trees. She was walking quickly with her head down. A single light was burning in one of the buildings. It lit up her hair as she passed. She didn't stop but headed straight for the archway in the far wall of the monastery.

The moment she had vanished I stepped in through the gates. The ground was soft and made practically no sound beneath my feet as I hurried after her.

The archway led out to a rough terrace high above the city. Lights glittered in the darkness, gold on black, mystical colours, a breathtaking sight if you paused to look. But I needed my breath right then so I hardly gave it a glance.

As I came out of the monastery I thought I'd lost her. The track that led downhill was deserted. But then I spotted her. Quite close, in the garden of one of the houses below. I realised now why she had come by this devious route. It was to avoid being seen from the street.

Brushing under the branches of an apple tree, she knocked at the back door. It was opened almost immediately by an elderly woman. A sudden splash of light, the glimpse of a passageway beyond. And then Jarka had slipped inside and the door was shut.

I went up closer and examined the place. It was four storeys tall, although I daresay this was increased by the slope of the hill; from the other side it would be three. The only other light that I could see was in a window on the first floor. From where I stood I couldn't see much, just the ceiling and part of the upper wall.

I looked around. Back on the other side of the path was a

shrine, one of those curious little buildings, half chapel and half bus-stop, that marks the place where some forgotten saint ended his time on earth.

I scrambled up on the roof, hardly respectful behaviour, but I'd left respectability behind the moment I started to follow her. Standing up I had a view of the inside of the room. It was from quite a distance but it gave me everything I needed to know.

The old woman was standing at a stove tending a kettle. In front of her was a table, laid out for a meal. Jarka was seated on one side, hands clasped, elbows spread wide. I couldn't see her expression but from the way she was tossing her head as she spoke she seemed animated, cheerful. Opposite her was a small boy. I'm not good at judging the age of children, but I'd say he was around five years old: slim, blond haired, like her.

I think I knew then. Not the exact details, they would come only later, but as I stood there on the roof of that shrine I think I understood the whole tangled, sordid business.

What I didn't have was any premonition of what the consequences of it would be. Had I done so, I might have left her there with her child that she kept hidden in this house high above Prague.

I let Michal go and walked back down into the city, my face buried in the folds of my scarf. In Mala Strana Square I stopped for a drink. Sometimes it's easier to think in the loneliness of a crowded bar.

At eight I knocked on her door. She greeted me, smiling in welcome, her arms held out away from her clothes.

'I can't get any closer,' she said, inclining forward to kiss me. 'I've got flour all over my hands.' I could smell the scent on her hair, feel the warmth of the kitchen on her cheeks. 'Do you like *Hovezi gulas?*' she asked as she went back to the stove. 'I've got a marvellous recipe for it somewhere but I can't find it, so I'm doing it from memory. It may be a disaster so you mustn't make any of your remarks.'

She wasn't making it easier for me. I opened the bottle of wine I'd bought at the shop on the corner. Pouring two glasses I drank some before it had time to breathe, wishing it was something stronger.

'What have you been doing this afternoon?' I asked. I think I was still hoping that she'd tell me where she'd been, offer some simple explanation that I had overlooked.

'Nothing much,' she called through the doorway. 'A bit of shopping.'

Maybe I should have just left it there, changed the subject and let her keep her secret to herself. But I'd come too far.

'Why do you keep him hidden?'

Jarka stopped what she was doing and came to the door. She regarded me with that grave beauty of hers.

'What do you mean?'

'Your son,' I said. 'Why do you keep him hidden in that house?'

She stood and stared at me, lips parted, cheeks drained of colour. Then in a tight voice she asked, 'How did you find out?'

'I followed you.'

'How dare you,' she whispered.

'I knew you were going somewhere in the evenings. I needed to know where.'

For a moment I thought she was going to fly at me. Her hands came up, fingers spread. She took a step towards me, then stopped. 'Oh God, you stupid interfering fool!'

'You could have told me.'

'Why should I? It's got nothing to do with you.' Her voice was rising, more in panic than in anger. 'None of this has anything to do with you. Damn you . . . damn you!'

'I'm sorry. I had to do it.'

'You had to do it?' She spat the words back at me. 'Is that all you can ever say? Why can't you leave anything alone?

Why do you have to come here asking questions, prying into things that don't concern you?'

'No one else saw you.'

'Oh yes?' She rounded on me like a tigress. 'How do you know?'

'I checked—'

'You don't know what you're talking about! You've no idea.' She tossed her head in disgust. 'Why don't you just go back to London and leave us alone! We were doing fine until you came along with your questions.'

'What are you hiding him from?'

'It doesn't matter! Can't you get that into your thick skull? It's got nothing to do with you.'

'There must be something.'

She paused and dropped her gaze and for a moment I thought she was going to answer. But when she lifted her chin her eyes were cold.

'Get out,' she said quietly.

'It would be best to talk about it.'

'Just get out!'

The streets were almost deserted, a chill wind biting up from the river. I wandered up into the town square. A few of the *pivnices* were open, the thin sound of a jazz band leaking out of one. I thought of going inside, having something to eat. But the idea of sitting alone at a table didn't appeal. It would give me time to brood and I didn't want to brood. Come to think of it, I didn't want to eat either.

I headed back towards the Josefov. As I was passing that scraggy bust of Kafka, a figure stepped out into my path.

'Good evening—'

'Major Vlasek. What brings you out at a time like this? I thought you'd be back home putting your dossiers to bed for the night.'

'Quite.' Vlasek smiled briefly, his teeth clamped over the amber cigarette holder. It gave him the look of an aristocratic pirate. He was dressed in a long black overcoat with a velvet collar, a white silk handkerchief spilling from his breast pocket. 'I was rather hoping to bump into you,' he said.

'Looking for a night out on the town, are you?'

'No,' he said slowly, as though this was an interesting possibility that hadn't occurred to him. 'There's something I want you to see, if you have the time.'

I didn't want to go anywhere with Vlasek but it was distraction and that's what I needed right then.

'I think you'll find it interesting,' he added.

'I can hardly wait.'

We drove down towards the Nove Mesto in the back of the car that was parked further up the road. It was warm and comfortable with a rich aroma of leather. Even at sixty it moved with that silky smoothness which only the very rich can expect from a car.

Vlasek studied the lights licking past the window for a while before saying, 'I think I might have given you the wrong impression when we met the other day.'

'In what way?'

'It's so easy to get off to a bad start, isn't it? To let the conversation drift away from the point.' He didn't strike me as a man who ever let a conversation drift in any direction other than the one he wanted. 'What I didn't perhaps convey,' he went on, 'is that you can be of immense help to us.'

'Really?' I wasn't in the mood for enthusiasm. 'That's never been top of my list of priorities.'

'No.' He touched the cigarette to his lips, drawing in a feather of smoke. There was no smell of cigarettes in the car. It must have been air-conditioned. 'No,' he agreed. 'I can see your point. You have no reason to trust the police. But I hope you'll reconsider in this case. You see, in many ways you and I are alike. We both find ourselves working in a changed world. The old objectives have gone, the new ones are unclear. And curiously we find ourselves on the same side.'

'Do we?'

'Oh yes.' He turned those pale, educated eyes on to me. 'Make no mistake about that.'

'And how do you imagine I can be of help to you?'

He drew in more smoke. Nothing was ever rushed. 'You were with Jaroslav Kupka last night during that vulgar little display in the square.'

'What makes you think that?'

'We have pictures,' he said sadly. 'I can show them to you if you like.'

'The police weren't there.'

'No, they weren't, were they.' He smiled faintly, as though this touched on some private joke that I couldn't be expected to understand. 'Conspicuous by their absence; isn't that the expression they use? But we were there.'

Who he meant by 'we' was never fully clarified in Vlasek's conversation.

I said, 'I just happened to be standing beside him.'

'Come, come; you're too modest.'

The car had drawn to a halt. Vlasek jumped out and knocked on the door of a low brick building. It was opened by an orderly in a white tunic. Without waiting for instructions he led us along the passage, down a short flight of steps into a bare room with a white tiled floor. There were no windows; the air held the reek of formaldehyde. Three of the walls were plain white, the other was a bank of steel cabinets.

It was a mortuary, sterilised of germs, colour and character.

'Take a look at this,' Vlasek said.

The orderly opened one of the cabinets. The body that slid into view was covered in a thin sheet. It carried the imprint of arms and thighs, the obscene mound of genitals. Reaching over him, Vlasek took the two upper corners of the sheet and folded it back, arranging it around his shoulders as neatly as a maid turning down a hotel bed.

'Recognise him?'

The face he'd uncovered had shrunk in death. The eyes were

closed, mouth open. A stubble of beard had grown along the jaw. It was the same grey as the bristle of hair on his head.

'Sergeant Kurz.'

'Exactly so.' Vlasek spoke as though I'd passed the first stage of an IQ test. 'I believe you had some trouble with him?'

'You could say that. How did he die?'

'He was shot; driving back from work this morning.' Vlasek turned the sheet back further, the second fold identical to the first, revealing the man's chest. Two small holes had been punched into the white lard of Kurz's flesh, one close to the heart, the other further across, beneath his armpit. The skin had puffed up slightly, discolouring around the rim. Together they looked like the burrows of two tiny rodents. The view on the other side would be a great deal less attractive.

'A sniper at the turn in the road,' Vlasek said. 'Two shots through the windscreen; both on target. Laser-guided sights, I should imagine. A professional piece of work.'

'Congratulations.'

Vlasek glanced round. 'Oh, don't get me wrong. This one isn't down to me.'

'No?'

'Absolutely not.' He gave the ghost of a smile at the thought of it. 'If I went after every bent policeman in Prague, I'd never have time for anything else. No, this is Kupka's work.'

'How can you be sure?'

'A little bird told me.' It was his way of saying that his sources didn't concern me. 'The city's full of them,' he added. 'It's practically an aviary. Kupka used this man for a job and then he had him executed. I imagine he knew too much.'

Vlasek paused to see whether I'd care to enlarge on this. When I didn't he said, 'I thought you'd like to see the kind of man you're dealing with.'

Kurz lay between us, head back, hands smartly at his side; standing to attention as he went to meet his maker. It was only hours since he'd been sprawled in that easy chair of his, full of the lazy, insolent authority that he'd thought of as life.

'How does Kupka recruit men like this?' I asked.

'He pays them for a start; pays them very well from what I hear. But he doesn't have to bribe them. A man like Kurz used to be an influential figure in the old days, someone to fear. He'd have been taking bribes, taking his pick of black-market goods, breaking the heads of anyone who stood in his way. A right little tyrant. Then when the revolution came along he lost the whole lot.'

'And now Kupka's offering to give it all back to him.'

'It's a powerful incentive. There are a lot of Sergeant Kurzes around this city. Men who've lost their status, lost their authority, and will give anything to get it back again.'

'It doesn't worry them that they're working for a completely different party?'

Vlasek smiled. 'Who cares about politics?'

We went back upstairs and out into the cold night air. The black car stood waiting by the kerb. Its engine was already running, a column of exhaust rising from the rear end.

Vlasek had a word with the driver and then came back to me. 'Shall we walk? I find a breath of fresh air is no bad thing after that place.'

He moved off down the pavement, his hands sliced into his pockets, thumbs hooked over the rim. As we came up into Charles Square, the car silently shadowing us in the road, he said, 'I've tried getting someone into Kupka's organisation but so far I've failed.'

'By the sound of it, he's had more success infiltrating the police than you've had infiltrating him.' I couldn't resist giving the knife a twist.

'Quite,' Vlasek agreed drily. 'But it's not just the police. He's worked his way into the civil service, the legal profession, even the military.'

'How about your outfit?'

'Them too,' he said thoughtfully. Vlasek was considering how far to take me into his confidence. 'That's what interests me about you.'

'I thought it might.'

'For over a year now I've been trying to get someone into Kupka's outfit. I mean right into it; the holy of holies. But nothing. Then you arrive in Prague and in a matter of days you are standing there beside him, for all the world like his right-hand man.'

'How do you know I'm not?'

'Because I know you. You're a loner; you're bloody-minded towards anyone who tries to help you. But I know where your loyalties lie. That's why you are the one man in Prague who can be trusted.'

'A strange state of affairs when the only person you can trust is an old enemy.'

'As I said, our fortunes are mixed.'

'It seems they always were.'

'Quite.' Vlasek flashed his piratical smile again. 'As I understand it,' he continued, 'you are convinced that Kupka has amassed a large collection of valuable art treasures.'

'He has the pictures looted from Ceauşescu's place. He's already sold some of them.'

'Has he more?'

'Oh yes. A great deal more.'

Vlasek was studying me with the keenest interest. 'Can you get to see them?'

'Possibly.'

'You must,' he said. 'If he has these paintings they must be discovered and exposed. The public must hear of them; the western press must hear of them. Then they can be handed back to the Romanian authorities to whom they belong.'

'It may not be that easy.'

'No,' he conceded. 'But it's essential that you do it. Without the financial resources of those paintings his organisation will be crippled.'

'He may find other ways of raising money.'

'He can and no doubt he will. But it would take time and we could use that time, Jan.'

It was the first time he'd used my Christian name. Strangely, it brought home to me, more than anything else that had passed between us that night, the alliance into which we found ourselves drawn.

I said, 'You're assuming that I get to see him again.'

'Oh, you will.'

'I wish I shared your confidence.'

From his upper pocket Vlasek drew out an envelope. 'This was delivered to your hotel this evening,' he said. 'Since you weren't available at the time I took the liberty of opening it myself.' He spoke with the infinite sadness of a man who has broken the common law of decency. 'Kupka wants to see you tomorrow.'

'Did he say where?'

'St Peter-in-the-wall.'

CHAPTER ELEVEN

I can't say I'd ever heard of the place but that doesn't mean anything. There are hundreds of churches in Prague, some of them old, some of them beautiful and some of them just functional spaces where you can shoot off a couple of prayers. You'd have to be very excited by churches to have seen them all. But Michal knew it.

'St Peter-in-the-wall,' he said, drawing in his cheeks knowledgeably. 'It's off Narodni Street. You wouldn't have noticed it there, captain. It's in a terrible state.'

I walked over there on the following afternoon. It was a clear, cold day, the streets and domes of the city lost in a sugary light. But I wasn't too interested in the view. I was thinking of Jarka, as I'd been thinking of her all day. Already some of the exact words she'd thrown at me were fading and all that remained, sharp and painful, was the look in her eyes, the sense of disbelief and outrage in her voice.

It was just after four when I reached St Peter-in-the-wall. As the name suggests, it was once part of the fortification walls of the city, but they've all gone, leaving the church stranded, squat and medieval, between higher buildings. Its windows were boarded up, tiles missing from the roof. One end was buttressed with scaffolding.

The studded door was locked. I knocked but the wood must have been three inches thick and absorbed the sound. A temporary bell had been rigged up to one side. I gave it a push.

After a few minutes a bolt was drawn and the door opened wide enough to show that the way was barred by a man in overalls.

'Yes?' He had the air of a bouncer.

'I've come to see Jaroslav Kupka.'

'Name?'

'Jan Capek.'

He stood back far enough to let me in.

The floor was gritty, the air dank with builder's dust. Powerful working lamps cast a hard white light on bare brick walls and wooden scaffolding. Over to one side a concrete mixer was thudding away to itself.

I walked into the nave of the church and looked around. There must have been twenty men at work in there but none of them gave me so much as a glance.

'Can you picture it, Jan?' The voice came from above.

I glanced upwards.

Suspended from the inside of the dome was one of those workman's hoists. In it stood Kupka. With the fierce glare of the lights behind him his massive physique was just a black silhouette. As I looked up at him he spread his hands, presenting the inside of the desecrated church to me.

The workman beside him manipulated the ropes and the hoist began to lower, the pulleys creaking. Kupka's arms remained spread outwards, a smile of welcome on his face.

Did he just happen to be up there, I wondered as I watched him come down to earth, or did he stage these effects?

'Can you imagine what it will look like when it's finished?' Kupka asked as he stepped over the side of the hoist. 'Thirty years ago this was one of the most beautiful interiors in Prague. White and gold; a vision of paradise.' He gazed around himself as he spoke, seeing it as it was. 'You'd never guess it from the outside, would you?' he said in wonder. 'From the outside it looks so unpromising, so pedestrian. The best you could hope for is some worm-eaten pews and the smell of damp rot. And then this. Come, let me show you what we're doing.'

The workman who had been operating the hoist climbed out to let us in. It was Zemek, I noticed, the mason from the

Two Grasshoppers. He stood to one side, watching us with those gentian blue eyes of his.

'There's only room for two, I'm afraid,' Kupka explained. Turning his back to me, he cranked down on the rope and we began to rise into the air. 'It seems a little precarious at first but don't worry, if it can take me I reckon it can take anyone.'

From below the dome hadn't appeared particularly high but as we swung upwards, the ground seemed to fall away at an unnatural speed, the figures below shrinking to the size of insects.

Kupka tied off the rope and we hung in space, swaying gently like the basket of a hot-air balloon. The light from the work-lamps was blinding up there. Kupka studied the crumbling masonry above our heads. 'The whole structure has been weakened. We're having to insert steel joists into the fabric. I've been assured they won't show once it's done.' He glanced down at me and said, 'I hear you've made an interesting business proposal, Mr Capek.'

The sudden shift in conversation took me by surprise.

I said, 'That's right.'

'I thought you might. Some of the others were all for dismissing you. But from the start I had a feeling you might have something for us.'

'It's a pity you didn't trust your instincts earlier.'

'Ah yes.' He took my meaning. 'Sergeant Kurz. A good man in many ways. Unfortunately he can be a little abrupt. I do apologise. But we needed to know who we were dealing with.'

'I trust you won't be calling on his services again.'

'No,' Kupka said slowly. 'I'm sure that won't be necessary.' He held up one hand, shielding his eyes from the light as he studied me. 'You say you can find buyers in the art world.'

'I can.'

'Prepared to pay top prices?'

'That depends on the pictures.'

He leaned back against the wooden wall of the hoist and the whole thing sagged alarmingly. 'Who are they then?'

'Private clients.'

'And they are discreet, are they?'

'Provided they get what they want they'll be as silent as the grave.'

'They'll need to be, Jan,' he said softly. 'They'll need to be.' He turned and stared around the domed ceiling above us, slowly drawing in his breath as though he was trying to inflate himself. Then he took a swig at the flask, a quick salute from its stainless steel base, and said, 'As you know, I have some pictures I wish to sell. Maybe you could take a look at them. Give me an idea of what they might fetch.'

'When?'

'Whenever suits you.'

'Tomorrow?'

'If you like,' he said. 'Shall we say midday?'

'Where are they?'

'In the party headquarters. Do you know it?'

'I can find it.'

He gave me the name of a street I'd never heard of. 'I'll see you there tomorrow.'

'Why do you want to sell these things in such a hurry?' I asked as the hoist began to lower.

'Is that any concern of yours?'

'Just curiosity.'

'You've got a nerve,' Kupka said. 'I'll grant you that; you've got a nerve.' Turning his back he concentrated on the rope he was playing through his hands. I took it as a sign that he wasn't going to give me an answer but as we reached the ground he said, 'Does the Easter Coup mean anything to you?'

'I've heard of it.'

'I'm surprised.'

I didn't like to point out that in my line of business you

know about every subversive act that has taken place, however small. You know when it happened, why it happened, and you know the names of those involved. They're the tools of the trade.

'But "coup" is the wrong word, isn't it?' I pointed out to him. '"Failed coup" would be a more accurate description.'

'Maybe.' Kupka stepped out of the hoist, rocking his bulk from side to side like a galleon wallowing in a high swell. The workmen had all packed up and left while we were up in the roof. The church was empty and silent.

'But you're right,' he conceded. 'It failed. It was bound to fail. I don't think anyone realised that at the time. Still, it was a bold attempt. For twenty-four hours they held the city. They took over the radio and television stations. There was support all over the country. Had luck been on their side they might have succeeded. But history was against them. It came too early. I don't think we understood that at the time. Ten, even five years later and it might have been a different story.'

'You were part of it?'

'Oh yes,' he said. 'I was part of it; I was there from the start.' His voice had sunk as he spoke. Taking that flask of his from his upper pocket he took another swig.

I said, 'I don't remember which year it was.'

'Nineteen-fifty-eight,' he replied. 'I was just eighteen.' He gave a little backward toss of his head as though he couldn't believe there'd ever been a time when he was so young. 'They sent in the tanks. I was in Narodni Street when they came. We'd formed a barricade: overturned carts and lorries, pieces of furniture from the houses around. But what use are a few broken bedsteads against tanks? Half of us were killed then and there in the street; the rest scattered. Some came in here.'

He stared around the church, his mind back far away, reliving the past. 'There must have been fifty of us. All jammed together in here; all shouting ourselves hoarse, everyone giving orders, nobody listening to a word. It was madness of course; we'd cornered ourselves; there was no possible way of escape. We piled everything we could find against the doors but there wasn't much we could do about the windows. They threw in incendiary bombs. The place caught fire. That was the end of it.'

It came out short and disjointed. A few terse words to describe an atrocity that would nowadays scream its way across the headlines of every newspaper in the world.

'How did you escape?' I asked.

'I found the crypt.' Kupka made a downwards movement of his palms as though patting some invisible dog. 'There's a crypt under here. Its entrance isn't easy to find but I knew a bit about these old churches. I knew there must be one somewhere. So I searched for it. There wasn't much time, the place was filled with smoke but I worked out where it was; got down there and hid until the fire had died down.'

'Why didn't you take the others with you?'

There was a moment's silence and then he said, 'I couldn't.' The question had hit a nerve. He lifted his head, contemplating the awesome responsibility he carried for his decision. 'I just couldn't do it. One body missing from that charnel house was neither here nor there. Had all of them been gone they would have come looking for us. It would have defeated the purpose. I had to go down there alone or not at all.'

'Quite a decision.'

'You think it would have been better if I'd stayed up here, do you?' His voice was soft now. 'You think I should have stayed up here and died with the others? That's what the English would do, isn't it? All for one and one for all. The whole cricket team out together.' He'd switched to English, pronouncing the words in a curious sing-song voice that he took to be a well-bred accent. 'At least this way someone survived,' he said, reverting to Czech. 'At least this way there was someone left to tell the tale.'

'They searched the place did they?'

'Oh, they didn't just search it, they tidied it up, removed

every trace of what had happened. They were like that, the communists. No one was ever allowed to know what they did; no one was allowed to see how they treated those who defied them. They carted out the bodies, chucked them in a hole somewhere and washed their hands of the whole thing. I heard them do it; it was going on just above my head. I could hear them clearing away the evidence. Then when they had gone I emerged.'

'Like a phoenix.'

'Yes.' Kupka nodded thoughtfully. 'Like a phoenix – a rather grubby phoenix.' He turned and looked at me, returning to the present like a swimmer coming up for air. 'Does that answer your question?'

'Are you telling me you are selling a major collection of pictures just to rebuild a church?'

'Not just a church,' he said. 'The whole country. It's the whole country that must be rebuilt. It's been weakened by generations of corruption. Crime is running out of control. Mafia organisations are tearing the place apart. You must have seen it yourself, Jan. Prague's becoming a breeding ground of vice. It must be stopped; it must be stamped out.'

'You reckon you can give the country back its soul by kicking in the heads of a few gypsies?'

'Gypsies? What's this to do with gypsies?'

'The SL.'

'Oh, them—'

'Aren't they part of your bright new future?'

'The SL are nothing to do with me,' he said. 'They're just a bunch of thugs – peasants. I'll deal with them when the time comes.'

'Do you think so?'

Kupka turned, his shoes scratching on the gritty floor, and stared at me. His little eyes were suspicious. 'You're sounding more and more like an intelligence officer by the minute, Jan.'

'I've been one for the last fifteen years.' I'd gone too

far, pushed him too hard, and I gave the answer quickly.

Kupka contemplated it for a moment. Then he nodded and took another mouthful of whisky. 'Sell the pictures, Jan,' he said thickly. 'Sell the pictures and leave the thinking to me.' He glanced down at his watch. 'But I can't stand here talking all evening. I must go. I'll see you tomorrow.'

It must have been around five-thirty when I came out of that sad little church. The sky was still pale but darkness was piling up in the road and a nasty breeze had got up to remind everyone that it was still March.

As I walked up the street I came across Michal. He was leaning against his car, watching the world go by with the supreme indifference of those that can dedicate their entire thought and ambition into the smoking of a home-made cigarette.

He took the butt out as I reached him and said, 'Evening, captain.'

'You waiting for me?'

'Thought you might like a lift back home.' He nodded down the street. 'Cadillac.'

'What of it?'

'Your friend – Kupka – drives a Cadillac. Except he doesn't. Some silly bugger in a black suit does the driving. He just sits in the back seat about a hundred yards behind him and gets driven around the place.'

I got into the taxi. Michal put the cigarette in the ashtray. He didn't stub it out, just shut the lid and let it die of suffocation.

'What's it cost then, a Cadillac?'

'If you need to ask you can't afford one.'

He nodded thoughtfully. 'That much?'

We drove down Narodni Street, past the new theatre that looks as though it's still wrapped in protective bubble-plastic.

'Why did he want you to see that church then?' Michal asked.

'He's doing it up.'

'That must cost a bit. What's he want to do that for?'

'He was there when it burned down.'

'Kupka was?' Michal swung out on to the embankment, flashing his lights at the car in front. 'That would interest the police. They always wanted to know how it started.'

'There's no doubt, is there?'

'Could have been lightning.'

'During the coup?'

Michal glanced round at me. 'Which coup?'

'The Easter Coup.'

'It didn't burn down then, captain.'

'According to Kupka it did and he was there. I reckon he should know.'

'Jesus, captain. He told you that? He must have been winding you up. St Peter-in-the-wall didn't burn in any coup. It went up just after the war. Electrical fault they reckoned.'

'Are you sure?'

'Cross my heart. We used to play in the remains of it when I was a nipper. And that's back way before the Easter Coup. What are you looking at me like that for?'

'Just checking the view from the top end of the garden path.'

Michal dropped me at the hotel. I suggested we should have a drink but he was in a hurry to be off. He didn't say where he was going but from his faintly roguish manner and his tendency to treat pedestrians on the zebra crossings as a potential blood sport, I'd already guessed he was off to his weekly poker game.

'Hope your cash box doesn't get raided,' I said as I left him. It was just a joke but Michal took it seriously.

'It's time my luck changed, captain.'

Zora was sitting behind the reception desk, gloomy as a

tax demand. I asked her for my key and she aimed a plump finger at me. 'There's someone been looking for you,' she said. 'Someone important. He said to tell you that he'll be in the Black Crab for a bit. Might still be there.'

There aren't many who rate as important in Zora's book. I went over to see who had been awarded the title.

As I might have guessed it was Vlasek. He was sitting at a table by the window, an empty cup of coffee in front of him, his hands clasped above as though he was praying it would go away.

'Did you see them?' he asked as I sat down.

I shook my head. 'Tomorrow.'

'Really?' I don't think he'd been expecting anything so positive. 'You don't know where they are, do you?'

'I've got to go round to some place off Blahnikova Street.'

'That'll be the party headquarters.'

'He wants me there around midday,' I told him. 'It might be worth putting some surveillance on the place in the meantime.'

'We have already,' Vlasek said sadly. 'As a matter of fact we've been watching that ant heap for the past two years.'

'Old habits, eh?'

Vlasek nodded thoughtfully. He wasn't agreeing with me, just considering the situation. 'The place is like a rabbit warren. It doesn't look much from the outside but it's got cellars going down fifty feet into the ground. We had a couple of men in there a few months back.'

'Faulty telephone line?' I was sympathetic.

'Suspected gas leak as a matter of fact.' He gave the ghost of a smile then getting to his feet he buttoned his coat, checking that all the details of cuffs and collar were as they should be. 'Give me a ring tomorrow morning,' he said as he left. 'First thing.'

After he'd gone I ordered a glass of beer and unhooking a newspaper from the wall I checked my horoscope. It told me I was not making enough of my potential and should think carefully about my future career. It's horoscopes like that which remind you that you don't believe in them. As I turned to the crossword puzzle a shadow fell across the page. Someone was standing at my shoulder. I glanced up.

It was Jarka.

CHAPTER TWELVE

'Hallo, Jan.'

I put down the paper and stared at her in surprise. She gave a wry little smile.

'Do you mind if I sit down?'

Without waiting for an answer she pulled out the chair that Vlasek had just left and dumped herself into it, elbows spread on the table top. Her face was pale, the cheekbones pronounced. Her eyes were dark rimmed as though she'd been rubbing them with sooty fingers.

'Do you want a drink?' I asked.

She gave a quick shake of her head. 'I'm not staying.'

'How did you find me here?'

'That old woman in the hotel; she knew where you were.' Jarka glanced to one side, as though someone had called her name, and looked around the nondescript café. Beneath her sheepskin bomber-jacket, she was wearing a silk shirt with a high collar that sheathed her throat. I don't know whether she'd covered herself in this way intentionally but curiously enough it gave her an air of smouldering sexiness, like a governess letting rip on her day off.

'I wanted to find you,' she said shortly. 'To explain things a bit better.'

'You don't have to—'

'I didn't mean to shout at you. I was scared stiff when you said you'd followed me. I thought you might have wrecked everything. I didn't really know what I was saying.'

'It was my fault.'

She shook her head. 'It's not that—'

'I wasn't at my most subtle.'

'I thought he was safe up there. That's what frightened me. I realised that if you could find him so easily my husband could too.'

'Is that who you're hiding him from?'

She nodded. 'He's in Prague. He wants to take Tomas away with him.'

'Can he do that?'

'I don't know. Probably not. But that wouldn't worry him. He can be quite . . . ruthless. Particularly when he can't get what he wants.'

'Why not go to the police?'

'I couldn't.'

I told her that I could if it was easier but she dismissed the idea with another shake of her head.

I said, 'I've got a few connections.'

'No, don't.' There was an edge in her voice. 'Don't tell the police about this; don't tell anyone.'

'Why not?'

'You mustn't.'

'They could help.'

'It's not as easy as that,' she said. Taking a toothpick from the centre of the table she twisted it around in her fingers. I could feel the tension in her body; it was a tangible presence, a third person at the table. 'I'm not sure he'd be allowed to stay in the country. If the police heard about him I think he might be . . . deported.'

'Why on earth should he be?'

'He was born in France.'

'So?'

'He's not in the country officially. He's not registered here, I mean.' She paused, coming to a decision. 'Neither am I.'

Until then she'd been fiddling with that damned toothpick of hers, but as she said this the grey eyes flashed up to me for an instant, wary, challenging. 'I didn't go through the customs check, you see. I just walked over the border. Everyone was doing it. It was the revolution. I drove into Hungary, left the car and walked. Tomas was only two years old; I carried him in a basket.' She shrugged. 'It was as simple as that.'

'But why didn't you go through customs? You're Czech; you must have a passport.'

She held the toothpick poised between her fingertips and carefully broke it in two. Then she arranged the two pieces together and broke them again.

'Because I'm not allowed into the country,' she said.

'Why? Have you committed some kind of crime?'

'Not me.' Her head was down, the gleaming wing of hair shielding her face. 'My father. And it wasn't a crime, unless it's a crime to be part of the government.' Brushing the pile of wood aside she looked up at me, the grey eyes suddenly defiant. 'In the last government, I mean; the one everyone hates.'

'High up in the government?'

'Minister of the Interior.'

'Zetlivski?' I said the name softly, a little theatrical maybe, but the realisation of who she was came like a punch in the stomach. 'You're the daughter of Zetlivski?'

She gave a sad smile as though she'd known I'd react in this way. 'Yes, Jan. I'm the daughter of Zetlivski. The man who was banished from the country, the man whose statue they smashed in the square the other day.'

I said, 'I'm sorry.'

It sounded inadequate, weak and rather remote, but what can you say to a girl who has been exiled from the country from which she was brought up, particularly to a girl who has refused to be treated in this way and has crept back over the border?

Mind you, it made sense. The moment she came out with her father's name I heard the pieces clicking together in my mind. Those moody silences that came at any reference to the communists, her inarticulate attempts to justify the past, the curious way in which she kept her child tucked away in that house.

'So no police,' she said. 'I don't think they'd have much time for someone who isn't meant to be here.'

'You may be right.'

'I am right,' she said flatly.

'Do you think your husband will tell them?'

'He might do.' She pushed her fingers up into her hair so that it stood out in golden spikes. 'He might do it out of spite. He hates what I am; hates knowing who it was he was married to.'

It sounded a bit thick. 'He must have known who he was taking on; when you first met, I mean.'

She rolled her head in a dreamy sort of way, as though this were both the tragedy and the beauty of it all. 'I didn't tell him. When I went to Paris I changed my name. Terrible, isn't it? Even then I didn't want people to know who I was. He was furious when he found out.'

'And divorced you?'

'No,' she said. 'He likes to think that's why. It gives him a nice cosy reason that he can tell his friends but it's not true. We got divorced because there was no love to hold us together.'

'And you came back here.'

'Yes,' she said. 'I came back here and I changed my name again. I always seem to be changing my name. But it didn't do any good. He still found me.' She frowned. 'How did he do that? I never told him where I was going; I never told anyone. How did he find out?'

'Probably chance.' I knew all about coincidence; the more unlikely it sounds, the more likely it is to happen. 'Someone spotted you in the street, someone heard you were around. Prague's a small place.'

'I suppose so.' She stared across the café as she contemplated this quirk of fate. 'Anyway,' she said. 'That's why Tomas is living up there with Elena. I needed to put him somewhere safe, somewhere where he couldn't be found. I thought I'd found the right place until you came along.'

'You still have,' I said. 'He'll be as safe there as he'll ever be.'

'Maybe.'

I was feeling sorry for her, believe me. Not a brief, passing sorrow either, but deep down where it means something. She must be scared out of her wits, running and hiding and then running again, never knowing who to trust, never knowing where to go next. I'd been in much the same situation myself, back in the old days – when her father had been master of Prague. Ironic when you think about it.

'I wanted you to understand,' she said. 'That's why I came to find you. I wanted you to understand why I yelled at you the other night. It wasn't . . . anything personal.'

'I'm glad you came.'

Jarka stood up, pushing back the chair. She swung her bag over her shoulder, half turning away from me. She fumbled with the catch, head down. Then she let out her breath in resignation.

'Do you want to see him?'

'Who? Tomas?'

'Do you want to see him?'

'Won't he be in bed?'

'Yes or no, damn you!'

'Yes,' I said carefully. 'I think I would.'

And so we went back up the hill to that house below the Strahov monastery, Jarka relieved now and talkative, me feeling distinctly nervous. I wasn't at all sure how to handle the scene that awaited us. I'm not good at talking to children, as most men who haven't had children of their own are.

But I needn't have worried; Tomas was too excited by the mystery of this unscheduled visit from his mother to worry about making small talk with me.

I was right about one thing, however: he had been in bed when we arrived and came into the kitchen in his pyjamas, his hair clean and shining and brushed for the occasion.

'Jan's a friend of mine,' Jarka explained, her eyes flashing up to me as she said it. 'He's come to see you.'

Tomas shook my hand and said he was pleased to see me, which wasn't strictly true but he was unmistakably pleased to see Jarka and sat at the table and chattered away to her while she watched him with the hungry eyes that only mothers who are separated from their children can have.

As I'd thought when I first saw him, the boy was a dead ringer for Jarka. He had the same penetrating grey eyes, the same carved features that gave them the look of those sculpted gold Pharaohs you see on Egyptian coffin lids. Even his crop of blond hair seemed to be modelled on hers.

It was strange sitting there in that kitchen which I had only seen from outside, like watching a play from behind the scenery. The place was smaller than it had appeared from the garden, and drearier too. The only note of colour came from some of Tomas's paintings that were pinned to the wall. One of them had two figures with the words 'Mummy' and 'Daddy' scrawled below. It looked just like any other child's picture of his parents except that the father's figure had turned out to be a quarter of the size of the mother's.

'He's not smaller,' Jarka said quickly when I pointed this out. 'He's just further away – in his memory.'

Not far away enough by the sound of it.

Jarka fetched a bottle of slivovitz from the cupboard and poured a couple of glasses. She offered some to Elena but she didn't want any. There were a lot of things the old woman didn't want that evening – me in her house being top of the list, and she made no attempt to hide her opinion.

'You shouldn't have brought him here,' she'd grumbled when we arrived.

'He knows everything,' Jarka told her.

'Yes?' Her little black eyes were spitting hostility. 'And how long before all of Prague knows about it?'

Jarka had told her not to be so stupid and they'd argued about it for a while but the old woman wasn't listening and was now clucking and hissing around the kitchen like an egg frying in hot oil.

'There,' Jarka said as we walked back up to her car. 'That wasn't so bad was it?' We'd only been there twenty minutes at the most, leaving the same way as we'd come.

'Elena didn't seem too happy about it.'

'Oh pooh, she'll come round to the idea. She doesn't like anything new.'

'Who is she?'

'Elena? She used to be our housekeeper. At home – when I was a child. Some people said she was my father's mistress. But it's not true. He had a mistress in Nice.' She grinned, her teeth bright in the darkness.

'Long way to go for a night out.'

'It gave him an excuse to get out of the country from time to time. Besides, Elena was far too ugly to have been his mistress, even in those days. Tomas thinks she's a witch.'

And Tomas might be right, I observed to myself.

'Come on, let's eat,' she said. 'I'm starving.'

But we didn't eat, at least not straight away. When we reached her flat, Jarka closed the curtains and in the velvet darkness of her bedroom she undressed, slowly and thoughtfully. Then she did the same for me, not speaking but touching and stroking the bare flesh she uncovered with her fingers and her lips and her hair.

Back in London they tell you never to get involved with women. They distract you from your work, compromise you, take your eye off the ball. The little grey men in Whitehall who make up the rules would prefer it if field agents left their emotions in a cardboard box in the lost property office of Victoria station before leaving the country, all bundled up neatly along with their national insurance number and the name and address of their next of kin. But there are times when the rule book has to be torn up and chucked out of the window if you are going to remain a fully paid-up member of the human race with heart and soul intact.

And this was different. The first time we'd made love had been sudden and clumsy, as most first attempts are, the hormones locking horns, the adrenalin screaming through the veins. This was altogether quieter, more gentle, Jarka's breasts and hips a pale phosphorescence in the darkness, her voice soft. I think she was looking for reassurance, the comforting intimacy of love-making, more than anything else that night. When she came, her thighs astride my waist, nipples grazing my chest, it was with a small sound in her throat as though she had found something she'd lost.

For a time afterwards she lay face down, her arms locked over her head, lost to the world. Then with a start she remembered the reason she'd wanted to come back here. Leaping up, all energy and life again, she went through to the kitchen and opened the fridge, its light glowing up on her magnificent breasts and on the curve of her belly with its dark triangle of feminine hair below. If I'd been old Degas – who as far as I know never was in this situation – I'd have been reaching for my sketch book then and there. Fortunately I didn't have to do anything but lie and watch as she collected a few things in her arms, rummaged in the drawer for a corkscrew, and came back, pleased as a schoolgirl who's arranged a midnight feast in the dormitory.

I guess we must have made a lot of crumbs as we ate but I can't say they kept me awake that night.

'Sit up,' she said the next morning. 'I'm going to draw you.'

I rolled over, opening my eyes just wide enough to get a fix on the bedside clock. 'Jesus, it's only seven-thirty.'

'Drawings take time.'

It didn't sound like standard procedure to me. I can't believe those Renaissance patrons had to put up with being drawn first thing in the morning, particularly when they were hung over, unshaven and feeling steam-rollered after a hard night's work with their Renaissance mistresses.

'Don't I get any breakfast first?'

Jarka came over and held out the doughnut she was eating. She was wearing nothing but a long tailed shirt, the slits up either side showing more thigh than is good for one's digestion at this hour.

'Is this all I get for a night of unbridled passion?' I asked as I bit off a piece.

'I'll get you a cup of coffee.'

I asked her whether there was a phone. She brought it across, trailing its extension flex behind, and dumped it on my chest. I put a call through to Vlasek's office. He'd said first thing in the morning and I took him at his word. Somewhat to my surprise he was in and sounding brisk and efficient. I seriously wonder if the fellow ever did anything as human as sleep.

He wanted me over at some address later that morning and gave me instructions how to get there. I think he had formed some suspicion of what I was up to by the end because he said, 'Where are you?'

'In bed,' I told him. 'Where any sane man should be at this hour.'

He said 'Quite', as I knew he would and rang off.

'Who was that?' Jarka asked as she handed me a steaming cup of coffee.

'Vlasek. He used to run the cold war single handed.'

'Do you trust him?'

'I don't have to; he has to trust me.' Maybe that's what kept him awake.

Jarka settled herself at the end of the bed, her legs crossed, a pad of paper on her lap and began to draw. I watched the way in which the tip of her tongue peeped out at the corner of her mouth as she worked, her eyes flicking up at me from beneath the crown of golden hair. It's strangely intimate to be in touching distance of someone so completely absorbed.

'What happens today?' she asked after a while.

'I'm going round to have a look at Kupka's hoard of paintings, check them out with a knowledgeable expression on my face and then get the hell out of there.'

'Is that all?'

'It's all I need to do. After that it's up to Vlasek and his crew.'

'He'll take them, will he?'

'Storm in like the American cavalry I hope, flags waving and bugles blowing.'

Jarka glanced up at me with those cool grey eyes of hers. She was in a schoolmistressy mood that morning.

'How will you know you're looking at the right ones?'

'They've got a mark on the back.' I'd been briefed on this back in London. 'Ceauşescu had all his pictures stamped with a symbol; it's an eagle shaped into a sort of circle – hard to describe but I can recognise it when I see it.'

'It's strange, isn't it?' she observed. 'All the dictators of the last two centuries have identified themselves with eagles.'

'Budgerigars don't have the same image.'

Jarka made a change to her drawing, rubbing out some lines and blowing the remains off the paper. 'Are you sure that Kupka doesn't suspect what you're doing?'

'I'm sure he does. But he needs the money and that means he's got to take risks.'

'What's he like?'

I was going to be asked this same question by a pack of grim-faced analysts when I got back to London. And they'd pore over everything I said, weigh it and evaluate it and come up with policies that could send our lives spinning off into outer space. But the devil of it was that I had no real answer, either for them or for Jarka. Not one that made sense, anyway.

'He's several men at once,' I said. 'He only lets you see what he wants you to see. He's an actor, always playing a part – he says so himself. But he's clever. Everything he does is staged to have the right effect.'

'In what way?' Now that we were talking about the man himself she was really interested.

'Take yesterday's little show. He calls me over to this wretched little church and gave me a long spiel about how he had been trapped in there when it burned down in the Easter Coup, how he managed to escape into the crypt and how he rose from the ashes to lead the people in their crusade against the communists. Then I discover that the place caught fire ten years earlier, that it wasn't blood-crazed commies that started it but bad wiring and that Kupka was never anywhere near the place at the time. The whole thing was a load of rubbish he'd cooked up on the spur of the moment.'

'I don't understand.'

'No, neither did I at first. In fact to begin with I thought he must be off his rocker. Then I realised that it was like one of those parables in the Bible. He wanted me to understand what he's up to, the way he thinks and feels, which isn't easy to do in a hurry, so he didn't even try. He invented a colourful little story instead. It's not true but it has the right effect.'

'Does that worry you?'

'Yes,' I said. 'It worries me like hell. The moment anyone starts wandering off into a fantasy world to get what they want you're in deep trouble. I think Kupka's a great deal more dangerous than anyone realises. The sooner we find this treasure hoard of his the better.'

Jarka was thoughtful for a while. 'Once you've found it, will you be going back to London?'

There was no change in her voice but I caught the change of tack just the same. She was no longer talking about Kupka; that had been put back into second place.

'Yes,' I said. 'I have to for a while.'

'Will you be coming back?'

'Yes.'

As I said it her eyes flashed up from her drawing, studying

my face, trying to gauge in that brief instant whether I was telling the truth.

'Good,' she said. Then she grinned, breaking the mood, and held up the drawing for my inspection. 'What do you think?'

It was me all right. Just the head and neck and the line of the shoulders drawn in long, fluent strokes of the pencil, but it was alive, real.

'That's extraordinary.'

'Do you like it?'

I said, 'It's brilliant.' And I meant it too. I'd seen drawings by her before but until then I don't think I'd realised how talented she was.

'It's good, isn't it?' She grinned smugly.

'I don't put on that expression, do I?'

'Yes, you do – when you're talking.'

'Can I have it?'

'No,' she said. Rolling her long legs off the bed, she scrabbled in the drawer of her dressing table for a pin and stuck the picture up on the wall, standing on tiptoe, the shirt lifting to reveal the full sweep of her thighs. 'I'm going to put it there until you get back.' She glanced round at me, pleased with the deal she'd struck. 'You can have it then.'

The address Vlasek had given me was for a sour-faced building in a street beyond Nameski Republiki. It didn't look the kind of place you'd want to live in unless you had to and, by the look of the boarded-up windows, there weren't many people around who had to.

I pressed the bell and it was answered by a young man in a denim jacket. He had a couple of days' stubble on his face and the steady eyes of those who don't go looking for trouble but know how to handle it should it come along.

'Follow me,' he said when I told him who I was. His eyes swept the square where buses were gunning their engines in the cold air, then he closed the door and led the way up a flight of stairs. On the second floor landing he climbed through a hole that had been knocked through the brickwork into the next building. Down the dimly lit passage, our footsteps hollow on the bare floor, and through another similar hole – whoever this lot were, they were no respecters of other people's property. With a jerk of his thumb he directed me up a spiral staircase into a garret room tucked under the roof.

It was in semi-darkness. On a tripod in the centre of the floor stood a pair of powerful binoculars, pointing down through the grimy window to the street below. Behind it a chair, a single bed to one side, magazines scattered across the floor and in the air that indefinable smell of boredom and cigarette smoke that always seems to settle over surveillance operations.

There were two men up there already. One was sitting on the end of the bed, a plastic cup of coffee in his hand. The other was Vlasek, looking distinctly out of place in his spotless black overcoat and polished brogues.

'Ah, Capek. Good to see you. Take a look at this.' He nodded down towards the street below.

The window was cracked and repaired in places with sticky-tape. A few pieces of glass were missing, an icy draught lancing in through the gaps. Through one of them I could see the row of buildings opposite.

'Black door by the grocery shop,' Vlasek told me. 'That's the one; headquarters of the National Reform Party. They own the whole place. Kupka hasn't shown up yet. I doubt whether he'll put in an appearance until you arrive.'

The two others were watching me with that deadpan curiosity of men who've had the monotonous routine of their work suddenly galvanised into life but don't know why. They weren't likely to know either.

'I need hardly tell you that we don't want any heroics,' Vlasek went on. 'Just find out where the paintings are stored and leave. And don't get into any sort of conversation about them unless you have to. You don't know enough about art to fool anyone that you're a dealer.'

He seemed to share Jarka's low opinion of my abilities. I can't blame them: between them they were right.

'There's no point in wiring you up; they'll almost certainly frisk you when you go in. If they found a microphone it would rather defeat the purpose.' He gave a bleak smile which I understood to mean that if they found one they'd flay me alive and feed the remains to the crows. 'Do you think you'll come away with one of the paintings?'

'Could do.'

'Whatever happens, we need to know immediately whether you've seen the pictures. Better not to make any direct contact – give us a signal. When you come out, have your coat buttoned up if you've seen them, leave it undone if you haven't.'

Vlasek was impressive once he got going, issuing his instructions in blunt sentences as he paced about the confined space of the garret, the eyes of the other two men following his every move as though their jobs depended on it, which they probably did.

'Got that?' Vlasek enquired.

'Closed if I've seen them – open if I haven't.'

'That's it. Good . . . and Capek.' He gave another of his wintry smiles. 'Once you've seen them, that's it. We'll handle the rest. Understood?'

'Yes,' I said. 'I understand.'

'As from now your part in this is finished.'

London might have their own views on this point, but I wasn't going to rock the boat so I said, 'Don't worry. As soon as I've seen those pictures I'll be on a plane and out of the country quicker than a cork out of a bottle.'

As it happened, things turned out very differently.

CHAPTER THIRTEEN

I sensed there was something wrong the moment I turned up.

The man behind the desk at the top of the stairs looked me over with disinterest as he lounged back in his seat. He was thick-necked and corpulent with eyes no bigger than buttonholes and a body that was trying to burst out of his shirt. When I told him that I wanted to see Jaroslav Kupka he didn't move a muscle.

'He's not here,' he said.

'He will be.'

'Not that I've heard.'

I had a sinking feeling in the guts. 'Then I'll wait.'

He gave a shrug that said I could do what I liked and switched his attention off.

I sat down on a metal framed chair by the head of the stairs. To call the headquarters of the National Reform Party functional was to glamorise it. The floor was covered in lino that was beginning to ripple with age, the walls stuck with posters and memos. Through the glass panel in the door off to one side I could see an empty passageway that led away to the back of the building.

After half an hour that felt like four, the telephone on the desk rang. The friendly receptionist picked it up, gave a couple of grunts and put it down again.

'You're to go on in,' he said.

I followed his directions along the passage and down a couple of flights of steps. A boy in overalls was waiting for me. He can't have been more than nineteen with ears that stuck out like jug handles.

'You Capek?'

I told him I was and he looked me over dubiously.

'You armed?'

I shook my head. 'You can check if you like but they've already been over me, when I first came in.' Which was some time ago now. It was just as well that Vlasek wasn't listening in on any hidden microphone; he'd have fallen asleep with boredom.

'Just asking,' the boy said sulkily. 'There's no harm in asking. Okay then, come with me.'

He led the way down into a low stone cellar and then into a second much larger one that lay below. It was dark and gloomy as a secret chapel and I could see at a glance that it was centuries older than the rest of the building.

There are generations of cellars below Prague. They've been stacked up on top of each other every time the level of the city has been raised to stop the place from flooding. It's not uncommon for completely modern buildings to have vaults below them that date back to the Middle Ages.

All the way down I was hoping we were going to reach some separate chamber, sealed and dry and stacked with valuable paintings. But no such luck. This lower cellar was completely empty.

'Now we come to the interesting part,' the boy informed me. Standing with his legs spread wide he lifted a heavy trap door set in the stone floor.

It opened to reveal a dark hole beneath. The smell that came out of it rocked me back on my heels. It was foul and organic and strong enough to make me want to throw up.

Without further explanation the boy climbed down into it.

'Where are we going?' I asked him as his head sank out of sight.

'Out of here.'

'Why don't we just go out the front door?'

He looked up at me as though I were mad. "Cos you

gets your photo taken by the police across the road if you do that.'

Love-fifteen down to Vlasek, I told myself grimly as I followed the boy down into that stinking hole, gingerly feeling my way down iron rungs in the dark. All around I could hear water dripping, the sound hugely magnified in the confined space.

When he reached the bottom, the boy clicked on a torch and I realised – if my nose hadn't told me already – that we had come down into one of the city's sewers, a circular tunnel some ten feet high, the glazed tiles glittering like mother-of-pearl in the beam of light.

'Weird, isn't it?' the boy said as we made our way along the narrow cat-walk, our footsteps echoing and booming around us.

I don't know how far we walked, it's hard to measure distance in that featureless landscape. Everywhere there was the sound of water; it dripped from the roof, slunk down the curved walls, roared in from pipes at the side. Beneath us, at the base of the sewer, was a thin stream of some fetid and slow moving liquid, the contents of which I didn't want to even think about. It glimmered like the Thames in the moonlight. Rats scuttled ahead of us, their shadows vast flickering fingers. I know every alleyway and passage of Prague but this was a kingdom that I didn't even know existed before.

Fortunately the boy seemed to know where he was going and I followed him through this maze of stinking tunnels until we reached a steel door in the wall. He cranked back the bolt and we stepped through into a passageway. It was drier, fresher and, coming from where we had, it smelled like a spring meadow.

At the far end the lights brightened, there was a sudden tug of wind and, to my astonishment, we found ourselves on the platform of the metro. We took the escalator to the surface, the boy silent, more apprehensive, now that we were in a public place. When we came out in the street he nodded towards a car.

'That's the one,' he said and without further ceremony vanished back down into the metro.

We were on the far side of Namesti Republiki, I realised as I went over to the car, a quarter of a mile from where I'd set out, a quarter of a mile from where Vlasek was waiting in that garret room of his. There was no time to contact him. Already the driver had stepped out of the car; he was holding the rear door open for me. The plans we'd made earlier that day were now useless.

I was on my own.

It was a familiar sensation, like greeting an old friend you haven't seen in a while. And not one, I should add, that I had particularly wanted to see either.

As we drove out of Prague I wondered how long it would be before Vlasek realised that things had gone awry. And what would he do about it once he had realised? Not that there was much he could do, come to think of it, and knowing him he wouldn't even try, just tut-tut, light one of those vile cigarettes of his and go back to his office.

It was not a complete disaster, however. Kupka was devious enough to have lied about where he was holding the pictures but presumably, now that he knew he had me alone, there would be nothing to stop him from showing them to me.

For two hours we drove westwards while the sky darkened and the coral pink light of the winter evening split the horizon. I didn't try talking to the driver. He didn't look the talkative type and anyway he was separated from me by a glass screen. The car was equipped with a little bar, decanters and cut-glass tumblers fitted into the panelling, but I doubt whether it was put there for my benefit so I gave it a miss. Besides, they wouldn't have liked it back in London if I had – sun not over the yard arm and all that.

And so I sat and watched the countryside sliding by, vast

and untamed after the cosy farmland of England. Eventually, as it was getting dark, we emerged from a wooded valley and there on a promontory of rock stood one of those Teutonic castles that sprout so freely in these parts, complete with turrets, pointed roofs and all the rest of the paraphernalia that they used to add to buildings in the Middle Ages to remind visitors that this was private property.

I didn't have to ask the driver, the back of whose head I was now on familiar terms with, to guess that this was Kupka's weekend cottage. It was just where he would live, an extension of his self-image, part of the fantasy world he was busily building up around his huge body.

Not that it wasn't impressive: chuck in a few circling crows and a dog or two baying in the distance and it would have passed for the backdrop to any Dracula film.

At the foot of the crag was a lodge – guard-house might be a better description of it, judging from the double gates and the twelve foot electric fence that ran off on either side into the fir trees. As we drew up, a couple of capable-looking characters disembowelled themselves from inside, exchanged a few words with the driver, pressed their faces against the rear window to give me the hard stare and ordered the gates to be rolled open.

The car proceeded on up the hillside, swinging through hairpin bends, until it crunched to a halt in front of the house. Without waiting for further instructions I went inside, the door opening magically as I approached.

The hallway was much in keeping with the outside, wooden panelled and decorated with the stuffed heads of the animals who were unfortunate enough to have got in the gun sights of some previous owner. A man-servant appeared from backstage, black-suited and efficient, and told me that the master of the house was in a meeting.

'If you would care to wait in here he'll see you when he is ready.'

He showed me through into a small drawing-room, a cosy

enough place with bookshelves around every wall, a fire burning in the grate and the flattened skin of a tiger snarling up from the hearth, and closed the door behind me.

I went over to the window and looked down into the valley. Lights twinkled away into the distance, above it the remains of day still glowing in a stone-washed blue sky.

After twenty minutes the door opened. I turned, expecting it to be Kupka or that well-oiled man-servant of his, but it was a woman.

'Ah, there you are,' she said, coming towards me.

She was strikingly beautiful, sleek and dark and graceful as a panther, dressed in riding gear: a tweed jacket that flowed in and out in the same places as she did, a white silk shirt beneath and a yellow silk scarf tied as a cravat at her throat.

'I heard you had arrived.' She smiled and offered me a slim hand in greeting.

When you're a teenager you dream of the time when you might be smiled at by a woman like this; when it comes you feel like a teenager again.

'I'm Éva,' she added. 'Jaroslav's wife.'

Her eyes held mine for an instant, the smile unwavering, as she saw me calculate that she must be twenty years younger than him, a hundred pounds lighter and ten times more desirable; a wildly improbable match on the face of it, but then power and wealth are the only two effective aphrodisiacs going.

'Strange place to go riding,' I said, nodding towards the sheer drop of the rocks below the window.

'Ah, no,' she said. 'The stables are down in the valley. There wasn't a proper road up here until recently. You had to leave your coach down there and walk up on foot, a barbaric arrangement. I had it changed when we came here.' She spoke lightly, correcting me without being so rude as to contradict me. 'You poor man,' she added. 'You haven't given yourself a drink. Let me pour you one.'

She strolled over to the tray and picked up a decanter. Her

hair, which reached almost to the small of her back was black and glossy as her polished riding boots below. For a moment she stood, one hand on her hip, her head turned from me in the way women will when they expect to be admired.

Then she glanced round to check that I was doing so. 'Scotch?'

I nodded. 'Ice, no water.'

As she handed me the glass a sound outside caught her attention and she glanced out through the window.

Whatever it was that Kupka had been attending to was over. Four or five men had come out into the driveway, their bodies splintering the light of the doorway, and were making their departure. A few words called out, a raised arm, then the slamming of car doors and they were gone.

'I must go and change or I'll be late for dinner,' Éva said. She removed herself in the same feline way as she'd arrived, pausing in the doorway to add, 'Mirek will show you to your room.'

'I don't think I'm staying.'

'Of course you are.' Her smile was an invitation in itself. 'It's much too far to go back to Prague tonight.'

I didn't want to upset their social arrangements so I followed the man-servant they called Mirek to a room on the top floor. It was hardly one of the state apartments, more like a servant's cubicle but adequate enough, especially for someone who had never asked to be put in there in the first place.

'If there's anything more that you need you may ask,' Mirek informed me from the doorway.

I glanced out of the small window. It looked down into a courtyard at the rear of the building. I said, 'Nothing that I can think of offhand.'

'Do you have any luggage, sir?'

'Can't say that I do. Why, are you expected to dress for dinner?'

Mirek's face never moved. 'The chef will prepare something for you in the kitchen should you require it.'

As good a put down as you'll get from any English butler. 'When do I get to see your boss?'

'When he is ready to see you sir, I imagine.'

'Sounds reasonable,' I said. If he went on cutting me down to size like this I was going to fall through a crack in the floor. 'Tell me, Mirek, how long have you known I'd be staying here tonight?'

'I was informed you'd be a guest here yesterday, I believe.'

That's what I thought: everyone knew about my social arrangements except me.

'Is that a problem, sir?'

'No problem, Mirek. I just wanted to make sure I wasn't putting you out by turning up unannounced.'

Mirek didn't look put out. My guess is that you could billet a troop of Cossacks in the place and he wouldn't be put out.

'If you ring when you are ready,' he told me, 'I'll show you down the back stairs.'

There was some sort of dinner going on that evening. As I sat in the kitchen, putting away paprika chicken and rosti cakes, I was surrounded by a bustle of activity: loaded dishes trundling up in the dumb-waiter, flunkies coming and going in relays, the Hungarian chef, whose accent could have been cut on a salami slicer, fussing about the place, cursing anyone who came within earshot.

The wine, I noticed, came from somewhere underground – curious for a castle built on rock. As Mirek emerged on one occasion, a couple of bottles in his hands, I asked, 'Is there a cellar down there?'

'There is, sir.'

'Cut straight into solid granite?'

'I believe it was used as a powder store in early times.'

'Quite a feat of engineering.'

'Indeed, sir,' he agreed as he shimmered off with his two bottles of house plonk.

It was well over an hour later, after a silver tray of coffee had slithered away up the dumb-waiter, that Mirek returned to say that the master of the house was ready to see me.

And about time too, I told myself as we went upstairs into the dining-room where two waiters were clearing the remains of dinner from the table.

Telling me to wait, Mirek went through to a room beyond, closing the door after him. I stood and looked around the walls. They were decorated with fans of weaponry, flintlocks, pikes, crossbows. At first sight I assumed them to be old but on closer inspection I noticed that they were reproductions – efficient, well greased and very functional looking reproductions. I was about to take one down when the door opened again and Mirek said, 'You may come in now.'

I went through into a drawing-room, beautifully furnished in soft toned silks. There were five or six men in there, all dressed in black tie, none of whom I recognised except Ivan Teige standing by the fire and Kupka who sat heavy as a sack of grain on a sofa at the far end of the room. Neither of them showed any sign of recognition in return.

As I came in they fell silent, looking me over with that cool, appraising interest that punters give to a new race horse in the paddock. One of them, a gaunt-looking individual, put down his coffee cup and said, 'Why have you come here tonight, Mr Capek?'

'I didn't come here. I was brought here.'

'What is it that you expect to find?' He bared his teeth as he spoke, neither a smile nor a grimace but a sort of involuntary tightening of the facial muscles.

'I've come here, as I think you already know, to see the Ceauşescu paintings.' It sounded a bit formal but that seemed to be the way they wanted it that night.

There was silence. The gaunt fellow bared his teeth again, and said, 'You work for the British government, Mr Capek.'

'That's right.'

'For the last fifteen years you have been in this country on what I can only describe as clandestine activities.'

'That's right.' Christ, we'd been over all this before. I glanced over at Kupka and said, 'I think this was understood from the start.'

Kupka made no attempt to reply but sat, his eyes hooded as though he were half asleep, a glass of whisky moored to one hand. Whatever the point of this party, it was evidently put on for the benefit of the junior officers, not for him.

'And yet now,' the gaunt man continued, 'you are asking us to believe that you are also an expert on paintings.'

'I'm not an expert,' I said as smoothly as I could. 'I'm a dealer.'

'I thought they were the real experts?'

'Not always. In my case I'm more of a go-between.'

'But still—' the blighter wasn't letting go, curse him— 'you must know about paintings.'

'As much as I need to know.'

'I think we'd like to know exactly how much that is, Mr Capek.' It was Teige who said this. He'd been standing listening to us with the repressed frustration of a man who doesn't think the questions are cutting deep enough. He glanced round at the others. 'I think we'd all like to know just how far Mr Capek's knowledge extends.'

There was a murmur of agreement.

'It's easy to claim that you're an expert, with connections in the art world and collectors at your fingertips. What we want is some proof.'

I gave a little shrug. It wasn't particularly hot in there but I could feel the sweat beginning to prickle down my spine.

At that moment the door at the end of the room opened. I looked round, hoping fervently that at the very least it might be Mirek coming in to announce that the house was on fire and we had only seconds to evacuate the place. But it was Éva.

Since I'd last seen her she'd slipped into something tight and shiny, a coral pink dress that clung to her as though its life depended on it. It was slashed up to the hip and shimmered with every movement of her body. Lazily she strolled across the room and coiled herself at the feet of Kupka, the generous sweep of one thigh coming in view. He put his hand on her head and absently stroked the sleek black hair. Éva flashed him a smile and then turned those slanted eyes of hers to me.

Damn her, far from interrupting the show she'd come to enjoy it.

'If I were to show you this,' Teige went on when she was settled, 'what would you make of it?'

Propped against the wall were three pictures – if I hadn't been in such a funk I might have noticed them there before. Teige picked up the nearest and placed it carefully on a chair.

I had no idea what to make of it. Given half a chance I'd have been over there with a magnifying glass looking for a signature, looking for anything that might give me a clue to what it was. But I knew that art experts don't do that; they judge a picture on its style and technique alone. So I stood back and studied it in a leisurely sort of way while my mind went racing back to the hours I'd spent going round the galleries with Jarka. 'First try and tell which century it comes from,' she'd told me.

That was easier said than done. The painting was a landscape: sun-drenched fields, distant hills, an evening sky. It could have belonged to any century. I fumbled through my mental notes like a schoolboy with a crib under his desk. Over to one side were some trees, dark and brownish coloured in the shadows. That rang a bell. I remember Jarka had said that if a picture was dark it could be either Dutch or dirty.

This one certainly wasn't dirty. It had a sort of glossiness to it. And the little wispy clouds were pure white. But it didn't look Dutch either. I don't know why. Too many hills, that was it. It just wasn't flat enough for Holland. Then I noticed the steeple peeping up in the background. Now that had to be English, didn't it?

The others were all waiting expectantly. I felt a trickle of nerves in my stomach. How long had I been staring at it? Too long. I made a little grimace, that of a man who is coming to a difficult decision and said, 'You wouldn't get as much for that as you might expect.'

'Why do you say that?' Teige asked.

'The real market for Victorian pictures is Britain and America but it's been oversaturated recently. And the recession hasn't helped either.' I threw in the last for good measure. I doubt whether Teige knew much about such capitalist diseases as recessions.

Teige made no comment. He glanced over to Éva who said, 'How much would you expect to get for it, Jan?'

'At auction or privately?' I was still throwing any spanner I could lay hands on into the works.

'At auction.'

'Thirty thousand pounds sterling,' I said casually. Was that the sort of price English landscapes fetched? I'd no idea.

Neither did Teige. He was watching Éva, waiting to see how she reacted. I felt a small spark of satisfaction. He didn't know any more about paintings than I did. It was Éva who was the expert – that's why she'd come in, I realised. It wasn't to watch the spectacle; it was to run it.

'Thirty thousand?' She gave a frown. 'Are you sure you're right about that?'

I wasn't sure about anything. It could have been thirty million for all I knew but now that I'd given my opinion I was going to have to stick with it.

'Given the right sale,' I replied. 'With the right collectors you might get five thousand more.' I was holding my hands behind my back to stop them from shaking but I was relieved to hear that my voice was still more or less steady. 'But that would be the limit.'

Éva was silent. She ran one hand up the snakeskin of her dress and smoothed her hair back over her shoulder. I glanced up at Kupka. He sat rock solid, glass in one hand, his face inscrutable. The gaunt man had his teeth bared.

'That's a shame,' Éva said with a shrug. 'I was hoping it would be more like fifty thousand.'

'Five years ago you might have been.'

'How disappointing,' she said. 'But you would know.'

Christ, I hadn't been far off the mark. With the sudden release of tension that flooded through me I felt like laughing out loud.

But the moment was short-lived. Teige wasn't going to be beaten so easily. His expression was stony. He picked up the next picture and put it in front of the other.

This time I went up close. It was the only way of seeing what it was.

'Please.' Teige was liberal with the sarcasm. 'Take a good look.'

It was a chalk drawing of an angel, its arms upraised, wings spread wide. That was useful. As far as I knew most things with wings came from Italy. I straightened up. After the last effort I decided I could rest on my laurels.

'Italian drawings aren't my field. I'd need to have a test made on the paper before I could comment.'

Teige accepted that as a draw. 'And this?'

'Do I get a prize at the end of this, Ivan?' I tried a note of levity but it went down like a lead balloon.

The painting he now wanted me to look at was larger than the others. It was a stormy, desolate scene. Angry clouds above and a pink, unearthly light below. I went over to where it stood on the chair, ran my thumb across the gritty surface, stood back and went on the attack.

'Hardly worth the canvas it's painted on.'

The wrong answer. Teige didn't need to be told by Éva this time. He knew what it was. A smile jumped ready-made to his face; it was predatory, triumphant.

'That,' he said quietly, 'is a Goya.'

'Good heavens,' someone said.

Teige stood waiting. The look in his eyes was malignant. I smiled. He might think he had me by the short and curlies, but what he didn't know was that art experts can never be wrong.

'It's not a Goya,' I replied. 'It's a copy of a Goya.'

This stopped Teige dead in his tracks. He glanced at the painting and then back at me, uncertain. But Éva's eyes had narrowed. She got to her feet, her legs slithering upright in that dress of hers, and came to stand in front of the painting.

'Why do you say that, Jan?'

'The brushwork's too heavy, too unfeeling,' I told her. My mind was grappling with that name. Goya: he was Spanish wasn't he? Jarka had shown me some pictures of bullfights by him. She'd been very impressed by them. What was the name of the big gallery in Madrid? The Puerto? The Pablo? One of the secretaries in the office had been there on her holidays last year. She'd come back raving about the place. No, that was it – I turned to Teige. 'I think you'll find the Prado will confirm it for you.'

He didn't reply. I think he'd lost confidence in speaking. In the end it was Éva who said, 'My goodness, you do know your pictures.'

'You must have realised it was a copy.'

'I always knew there was a possibility. I rather hoped you weren't going to confirm it.'

I've never believed in guardian angels; if I've had one all these years he has been notable for his absence. But all was forgiven. In the last fifteen minutes he'd saved my bacon several times over and for that he deserved a medal and two weeks off harp-duties.

Éva's mind had now moved on to more practical matters. 'Which one of these do you want to take with you?'

'The landscape.'

She asked me why that one in particular and I told her because it was the most valuable, which I'm sure is how any red-blooded art dealer with an eye to earning a fast buck would have spoken.

'You think you can get thirty thousand for it?' She wanted to be sure.

'I'd be surprised if I couldn't.'

'Is that before or after your commission?'

'After.' I was in a generous mood.

'What do you expect to make yourself?'

Here was another mine-field that I didn't want to wander into so I just said, 'I won't starve.'

'No,' she said slowly. 'I don't think you will.'

I took the painting from where it stood on the chair and turned it over. My heart missed a beat. The back of the canvas was blackened and dusty. There were a couple of labels on the frame and nothing else – no stamp, no symbol of an eagle formed into a circle.

Éva said, 'You seem surprised.'

'This isn't one of them – ' I could hardly believe my eyes – 'it's not one of the Ceauşescu paintings.'

'No,' she said. 'It's mine.'

'But I came here to see them.'

She gave me that enchanting smile that could melt a man in his tracks and said, 'No, Jan, that's what you thought you came here to see.'

CHAPTER FOURTEEN

There was nothing I could do. If I'd refused to take their wretched picture it would have looked very strange indeed. Art dealers sell paintings, they don't get too sniffy about where they've come from.

Besides, it was just a test I told myself later that night as I lay on my bed staring up at the ceiling in the darkness. Another of their infernal tests. They wanted proof that I really could find a buyer who would pay the market price and ask no questions afterwards. Teige had said so himself. It was only sensible, I suppose. But why did they have to be so blasted sensible? Why couldn't they just throw caution to the wind and take a chance for once?

The worst of it was that they'd called my bluff. I was going to have to go ahead and sell the blasted thing now. They were going to love that back in the office.

The only good news was that it shouldn't be too difficult. Éva had said she reckoned it was worth fifty grand, so it shouldn't be too hard to get thirty-five. I might even get more and the department could pocket the change. That should cheer them up.

But it was the frustration of it. Until the last moment I'd been so close to finding those paintings. In fact as I turned over that canvas I thought I had done it. As it happened I was still as far from finding them as I'd ever been.

Having said that, there was one other alternative left open to me. They hadn't actually shown me any of Ceauşescu's paintings. But that wasn't to say they weren't here.

*　　*　　*

I waited for an hour, listening to the sounds of the house below. The others had all left or gone to bed long before, but I gave them a bit of time to settle down.

Eventually, around one in the morning, I got up and went downstairs. The hallway was dark and ghostly, the embers of the fire cutting jagged shadows from the rows of antlers. Working my way towards the rear of the house I found a door that led out into the courtyard. I wasn't too worried about burglar alarms. When you've got an electric fence, a pack of dogs and a small private army of security guards to look after the place you don't need a bell on the end of a microchip.

It was a raw night, the wind tugging at my hair as I stepped outside. Above the castellated rooftops, clouds raced against the moon. Keeping to the shadow of the wall I went down a flight of stone steps into the courtyard.

It's not easy to search a house as large as this one, particularly in the dark when you don't know your way around and there's a danger of bumping into some prowling member of the staff at every step.

I worked methodically, starting with the outhouses on the far side of the courtyard. There was nothing much of interest; most of it was garages, three long black limousines rowed up beside a little sports number which I guessed was Éva's. Beyond it, a workshop with some heavy duty equipment and storerooms.

Back in the main building I made my way down to the kitchen where I'd had supper, feeling my way around the work surfaces until I reached the door to the cellar. As I opened it, a breath of cold, dank air reached up from below. Cautiously, I felt my way down the stone steps, testing each one with my foot before taking it, and switched on the lights.

There was enough wine down there to float a battleship, all stored in racks that reached up to the ceiling, the bottles laid out neatly, necks down, labels upwards. Presumably Mirek's pride and joy.

In the room beyond was some shapeless object under a canvas wrap. For a moment I thought I was in luck. I untied one of the securing ropes and lifted the cover. But it was just a generator, a functional-looking piece of machinery that was probably vital up here during the winter.

There was a sound behind me. I ducked down, but a voice caught me.

'Stay right where you are!'

I straightened up.

It was Ivan Teige. He stood at the foot of the stairs, arm out straight, a gun in his hand. With the other he reached across the wall, flicked on more lights.

'What the hell are you doing here?'

I moved out from behind the generator.

'Just looking for a glass of water.'

He came towards me with short, quick steps. The gun didn't even waver in his hand.

'What do you want?'

'I was taking a look around,' I said easily. 'I couldn't sleep. Thought it might be worth having a tour of the house.' The muzzle of the gun was so close now I could see the first twists of the rifling in the barrel. Above it, Teige's eyes blazed in his pale face.

'They're not here, Capek,' he said quietly. 'Do you think we're fools? Do you think we'd just leave priceless paintings lying around the place for you to find?'

'You'd know the answer to that better than me, Ivan.'

He gave a sneer. 'You don't fool me, Capek. You might have talked your way round the others, filled their heads with all your promises and your boasts. But you haven't taken me in. I know what you're after.'

'Do you, Ivan?'

'Of course—'

'You may be wrong.'

'Don't try to bluff, Capek.'

'You think I'm down here looking for a few old paintings?'

It was my turn to sneer at him. 'You must be dreaming, Ivan. Paintings? Do you honestly imagine I'd go to all this trouble to get hold of a few pictures?'

Teige said nothing, but a shadow of doubt had passed over his face.

'You have no idea, have you?' I felt quite sorry for him. 'You've no idea what's hidden down here. No one's bothered to tell you, have they?'

'What are you talking about?'

'It's not paintings I'm looking for. It's this.' I pointed up at the ceiling.

And like an idiot he looked up.

Deflecting the gun with my left hand I hit him, right on the point of the chin that he had so generously presented to me. It was just a jab, there wasn't time for anything more ambitious, but he went down in a satisfactory way, head jerking back, knees buckling so that he landed in a tangled, and I hope rather painful, heap on the stone floor.

The gun was still in his hand. I gave his wrist a kick and it skittered away. Grabbing him by the collar I hauled him up into a sitting position. He was still conscious but only just, his head lolling to one side, a trickle of saliva worming its way out of his mouth; hardly the most attractive sight.

I pushed him back against the canvas covering of the generator, my hand rammed up under his chin, and as I did so a voice lashed across the room.

'Leave him!'

I glanced round.

It was Éva. She stood in the entrance to that cellar, her eyes flashing with anger. She was dressed in a white silk night-gown that reached to the ground, the light shining through from behind so that the silhouette of her body was plain as day. It was quite a sight. Give her a halo and a set of wings and I would have sworn she was an avenging angel standing there.

'What are you doing?' she enquired archly.

I let Teige go and stood up. There weren't many excuses that came to mind, certainly none that would get off the starting blocks, so I just said, 'Trying to knock a bit of sense into your friend here.'

Teige had staggered up to his feet and was leaning back against the generator, clutching his neck in one hand. Why he should hold that I don't know; I'd hit him three inches higher up.

'He was down here,' he spluttered. 'I found him down here . . . looking for the paintings.'

'Is that true?' Éva's small, oval face was turned up to me.

I said, 'I wanted to see them.'

'He means to take them,' Teige croaked.

Éva looked him over, and not with too friendly an eye in my opinion, and said, 'Would you leave us, Ivan? I wish to talk to Mr Capek alone.'

'I must tell Jaroslav.'

'Tomorrow,' she said. 'He's sleeping at present.'

'He means to steal them, Éva.'

'Go to bed,' she said sharply.

For a moment Teige stood there, still clutching his throat, torn with indecision. He wanted to stay, but he was designed to take orders, everything in Teige's make-up compelled him to do as he was told. And so finally, with a bob of his head and a black look in my direction, he left the room.

Éva waited until he was out of ear-shot before turning to me.

'Why did you come down here?'

If I had hoped that she had banished Teige so that we could have a pleasant little chat together I was wrong. Her voice was cold as the Arctic dawn.

I said, 'I wanted to see the paintings.'

'Why's that?'

'To see whether they exist for a start.'

'Oh, they exist,' she said lightly. 'They're not here, of course but they exist all right. Although what good it would do you to see them I can't imagine.'

'I want to get some idea of their value.'

'Like you did for those after dinner?' She smiled that slow, slanting smile of hers and drew away, looking round the cellar with detached interest. It was probably the first time she'd been there.

I said, 'You seemed impressed at the time.'

'I was,' she agreed. 'You were so nonchalant, so knowledgeable. It was a beautiful performance. It's just a shame that you know nothing about pictures.'

'Are you trying to tell me that I was wrong about them?' I made a last-ditch attempt at bluster but Éva wasn't falling for it.

'The Goya is genuine. Not only would the Prado verify it, they've been pestering me to sell it for the last five years. The drawing is by Rubens and is Flemish not Italian, as anyone with the slightest knowledge of art would know. As for the landscape, it's no more English than I am, or, for that matter,' and here she had the cheek to give me a malicious little smile, 'than you are.'

I don't know why I'd thought she was just a decorative addition to the house earlier on. She was as sharp and dangerous as a jewelled dagger.

'Why didn't you say so at the time? Why did you let me go on like that?'

Éva considered the question.

'Because my husband trusts you,' she said. 'He is convinced that you are the right man to handle this rather sordid business. And I'm sure he's right; he has an instinct for these things.'

I didn't like to ask her how he'd react if he found he was wrong; I didn't want to know, and with any luck I wouldn't be around to find out when the time came anyway.

'And now,' Éva said, 'it's time we all went back to bed. We've done enough talking for one night.'

'That picture.' I stopped her as she was leaving. A question had arisen in my mind that urgently needed answering. 'Is it worth as much as you said?'

'I've no idea.'

'You said it was worth fifty thousand.'

'I hope it is, Jan.' She flashed me that malicious little smile of hers again. 'For your sake, that is. Your life won't be worth a shred if it's not.'

I didn't sleep much during what was left of that night. Restless thoughts and schemes kept me awake but eventually, in the early hours of the morning, I dozed off into a troubled sleep in which I dreamt I was back in that hotel on the border. I heard the car draw up, saw the figure beside me go to the window, but as the gunfire burst out and the glass exploded before my eyes, it wasn't some indistinct memory of a scientist who stood there but Éva, her arms spread, the car headlights shining through her nightdress, her body warm and inviting and that mocking smile in her eyes.

The gun fired again, just a single shot this time. I opened my eyes and realised this much wasn't a dream. I'd heard it distinctly.

Getting out of bed I creaked over to the window but there was no one down in the courtyard. I went through to the bathroom, washed and shaved, nearly cutting my throat at the sound of more shots from outside. I checked my face in the mirror. My eyes were slightly pink. I rolled out my tongue. It wasn't.

Hauling on some clothes I went downstairs. Mirek was hovering in the hallway. He told me that Kupka was outside.

'Is that him firing a gun?'

'He likes to shoot some clay pigeons when he first gets up.' He hesitated, wondering whether to confide any further information. 'He says it helps his metabolism.'

'I prefer a cup of coffee myself.'

'I'm sure the kitchens can provide one.' Mirek liked to take everything literally.

I went out through one of the French windows in the dining-room. It was a clear, cold morning, the gravel crisp, the sun across the valley almost blinding.

Kupka was standing on the rocks, kitted out in an old tweed suit that had seen a bit of weather in its time and a felt hat on the back of his head. He glanced round as I came up.

'Ah, Jan.' He sounded faintly surprised, as though he'd forgotten I was still around. I didn't take it as an insult; after the skinful he'd put away the night before it would be a miracle if he could remember which century he was in. 'Sleep well?'

'Like a log.'

'Good.' He dropped a brace of cartridges into the breech, holding them in the cleft of his fingers so that they went in as one. There was no trace of sarcasm in his voice so maybe he hadn't heard anything of my activities in the night. Snapping the gun shut he threw back his head.

'Pull!'

The trap was fifty yards away across the rocks. At the command, the gamekeeper who sat crouched behind it released the trigger. I watched as a pair of clays skimmed out across the valley, scissoring together and parting again, just specks in the sunlight. Kupka pivoted, the gun coming into his shoulder in a fluid action. He took the furthest first, the black disc vanishing to dust, then the next as it came naturally into the arc of his swing. It burst also, a single fragment careering off erratically. A polished performance. He must put in a lot of practice; shooting straight with a shotgun is nothing to do with natural talent or masculine prowess, it's simply a matter of practice.

'I need to be getting back to Prague,' I said.

'Of course you do.' Kupka opened the gun and the two spent cartridges ejected with a soft pop. I could smell the warm scent of the cordite. 'Get someone to drive you in.'

'It's okay, I've got someone who'll do it.'

'Suit yourself. Tell Mirek to warn the gate-house first.' He lifted his head again, the gun rising in anticipation. 'Pull!'

I watched as two more clays burst above the valley. As he broke the gun again he said, 'I hear you were prowling around the house last night looking for the paintings. Is that true?'

'I didn't come here to play games.'

'No,' he said slowly. 'No, I can see that. But you'll have to be patient, Jan. This business can't be hurried.'

'Who told you?' I asked.

'Ivan. And he tells me you weren't too polite to him either.'

I gave a shrug. 'He should have stayed in bed.'

Kupka studied me with his small, bright eyes. 'You've made yourself a dangerous enemy there.'

'That's his problem.'

'No, Jan, you should be careful. You've no idea what's going on; you don't understand. This is much bigger than you realise. We're just the pieces in a game. None of us are in control. You don't realise that; I do, and I'm warning you to be careful.'

At the time I didn't pay too much attention to what he said. I imagined it was just another of his theatrical statements. It was only later – much later – that I appreciated that what he was trying to tell me out there on that sunlit promontory was the plain and literal truth.

CHAPTER FIFTEEN

Back in the house, I put a call through to Michal and told him
to get out here as fast as his clapped-out banger could manage,
giving him the directions that I had extracted from Mirek.

He arrived a couple of hours later, the car wheezing to a
halt before the front door. For a few minutes he sat and stared
up at the house; then he got out and tried staring at it from
that angle.

'Holy Mother, you've got some friends, captain,' he said.
'It's big, isn't it. I mean, it's really big. Like a sanatorium.'

'That's more or less what it is.'

'Did you nick one of the ashtrays?'

'No, only this.' I put the painting in the boot. It had been
taken out of its frame and wrapped in brown paper, a sheet
of plywood on either side of the canvas. Done up in this way
it was about the size and weight of a briefcase.

'What's that then?' Michal wanted to know.

'The family silver.'

Michal got back in the car. That's what makes him such a
useful assistant: he doesn't ask questions. It isn't that he has
been trained not to, just that he lacks any sense of curiosity.

On the way back, through the forests that keep the valleys
of Czechoslovakia in endless twilight, I gave him a message
to pass on to Vlasek. I made him repeat it a couple of times
until I was sure he'd memorised every detail correctly.

'Don't worry, captain, I've got it.'

'And tell him that there's no point in him watching the
National Reform Party headquarters any more. They've
rumbled him; they get in and out through the sewers.'

'Best place for them.'

'They come out at Namesti Republiki metro.'

Michal nodded sagely as though this were only to be expected and said that they were a right pack of bastards.

'Why do you say that?'

'Because I won't be able to say it once they get in power.'

There was something slightly chilling about his certainty. 'You reckon they'll take over?'

'Bound to, captain. The whole country's behind them.'

'But not you?'

Michal spread his hands, lifting them off the wheel as the car did eighty. 'In my time, I've seen fascists and I've seen communists and do you know, captain, they all look the same to me.'

I thought of Kurz with his piggy eyes and I realised he was right. When you come down to it, there's no real difference between a communist policeman and a fascist policeman. Whatever you call them, they all turn out to be a dab hand with the red hot poker, or the electrodes, or the tweezers, or whatever other instrument it is they happen to favour.

When we reached the hotel I told Zora I wouldn't be needing my room any longer. She took the news without any overt show of emotion.

'You never seem to use it anyway.'

I couldn't see it was any of her business but I said, 'I've been out of town.'

'Not that it matters to me. If you men want to waste your time playing cards that's your funeral. Just don't go trying to tell me you're staying in castles in the country. It's more than human endurance can bear.' And with that she disappeared through the bead curtains that separated the hotel from her private lair.

I went upstairs and put a call through to Jarka. She was surprised to hear me and started with a torrent of questions but I cut them short.

'Come round here, quick as you can. Room 64.'

'Oh yes?' She was behaving as though this was a scene from a French farce. But I damped down her enthusiasm when she arrived ten minutes later, grinning like a Cheshire cat, by showing her the painting.

'What do you make of that?'

She took it in her hands, scanning it closely. 'Is this one of them?'

'No, it's not. It's clean as a whistle; one of Kupka's own. What do you think it's worth?'

'Not much. What do you want to get for it?'

'Thirty thousand?'

She went off into a peal of laughter that sent my spirits diving. 'You must be joking, Jan.'

'I've never been more serious in my life.'

'You'll be lucky to get one thousand.'

I could feel the sky closing in on me. 'That bad, eh?'

'It's a skunk, Jan. Practically amateur.'

I mentally cursed Éva with every foul word I knew. Jarka looked at me, suddenly chastened.

'My poor Jan. You didn't say you could get thirty thousand for this, did you?'

'They said it was worth more.'

'Who said that?'

'Kupka's wife.'

Jarka's eyes narrowed. 'Éva?'

'You know her?'

'Of course. Everyone knows her, always parading herself around Prague as though she owns the place.'

It was unlike her to be so vindictive. 'She knows a thing or two about paintings.'

'She's a conniving bitch,' Jarka said. 'You can't trust anything she says.'

'I don't think I will in future.'

'She should have stayed in the Bucharest gutter she came from.'

I'd like to have stayed and learned a little more of Éva Kupka but time was pressing.

'Look, I must get going. I've got to get down to the station.'

'I'll drive you,' Jarka said. The flash of anger that had come over her at the mention of Éva had passed as quickly as it had come.

'No, you'll stay here. Wait for at least ten minutes before leaving.'

She looked at me, puzzled, until it dawned on her what I was saying. 'You mean you're being followed?'

'I'll be surprised if I'm not.'

It was well after midday by the time I reached Hlavni Nadrazi, the main station of Prague. It wasn't crowded as it would be later in the afternoon, but busy just the same, men shuffling through the barriers and women standing to drink cups of bitter coffee. Destinations were fluttering on the departure board, whistles shrilling and trains gliding from the platforms with their antlers pressed to the overhead cables, their drab green paintwork raising the faint sensation that the place was under military occupation.

I bought a paper from the kiosk and sat on one of the metal benches. The painting was beside me, resting on the ground. After ten minutes I got up and left it where it was.

No one noticed; no one called after me. The two men working on the telephones nearby didn't even look up.

Going up to the big open cafeteria that overlooks the station from the first floor I leaned against the balcony. From there I could see the bench where I'd been sitting and the wrapped parcel that was still perched beside it.

A man sat down beside it. He wore a donkey jacket with the collar turned up. He lit a cigarette, cupping the flame in his hand. A couple of puffs and he moved on.

He took the painting with him.

I watched as he made his way through the crowd to the exit

where a car was waiting. It's hard to be sure at a distance in a busy station but it seemed to me that he didn't go unnoticed. There was another figure, moving quicker, shouldering his way after him, his arm raising to catch the attention of a driver. But it could have been chance. Time would tell.

I bought a first-class ticket for the Paris-Praha express. There was still twenty minutes to go before it left but the train was waiting at the platform, doors open, a uniformed attendant fussing over his sleeper reservations. I wasn't going far enough to need bother myself with him, so I climbed aboard, found an empty compartment and sat down, feet up on the seat opposite. No one else tried to come in; one man can make a compartment appear very full if he puts his mind to it.

It was only as the train was leaving that the door slid open.

'Ah, Capek. I'm glad to see you've made yourself comfortable.'

'I assumed you'd travel first-class.'

'Is there another?' Vlasek was surprised to hear it. He sat down opposite, briefly flicking the seat where my feet had been resting with his gloves. 'Just a couple of them,' he said when he was settled to his satisfaction. 'They're following your driver in a rather unpleasantly coloured fawn Citroën.'

'And me?'

Vlasek gave a little smile. 'My dear Jan, I wouldn't be sitting here enjoying the pleasure of your company if there had been anyone following you.'

'I suppose not.' The train was drawing out through the suburbs of Prague, the wheels clattering and complaining on the points.

'Meanwhile, we have nothing more strenuous to do than try to pass the time as best we can.' He was carrying a briefcase, one of those plump leather affairs that lawyers used to carry. From it he took out a bottle of wine and a couple of long stemmed glasses wrapped in a white napkin.

When they'd been filled we touched them together. Vlasek took a sip and made a little noise in his throat to declare himself satisfied.

'Did I gather from your amusingly inarticulate friend that you were taken out to Kupka's home last night?'

'Through the sewers.'

'Really? How unfortunate.' He lit a cigarette. I nodded towards the no-smoking sign but he didn't seem to be bothered by it. I suppose there isn't a conductor in the country who would have dared to enforce it.

'But from the fact that you are now trying to smuggle a small and obviously canvas-shaped object out of the country,' he went on, 'I can only assume you didn't find what we are looking for.'

Vlasek would never be so impolite as to pump me for information but he wanted it just the same. So I gave him a brief résumé of what had happened since I'd last seen him. He listened in silence, touching the cigarette to his lips, letting the smoke curl up before his eyes.

'If the pictures are not in there,' he said, when I was finished, 'where are they?'

'I've no idea.'

'Has it occurred to you that they might not be in this country at all?'

'They keep telling me that they are.'

'Yes,' he said in that silky way of his. 'But that could just be a game, a way of stringing you along.'

'Why should they want to do that?' I couldn't see what Vlasek was getting at. He'd been so long in the business of bluff and double bluff that his mind was always a couple of moves ahead.

He refilled the glasses and sat back, his eyes flicking around the empty compartment as though assuring himself that we were alone. 'Can I ask you something?'

I couldn't see how I was going to stop him so I told him to fire away.

'Why did they send you out here?'

I shrugged. 'Prague's my patch.'

'It seems strange to send a man all the way from London just to ask a few questions. Especially a man like you. A little like cracking a walnut with a sledge-hammer.'

'Perhaps they were expecting some sort of trouble.'

'Perhaps they were,' Vlasek agreed calmly. He took a sip of his wine and gazed out of the window. 'In the old days,' he said after a moment, 'when I was working for the previous management, we used to be given some sort of explanation with our orders, the party line – you know the sort of thing. It didn't always make sense but that's because we were rarely given the full story. Over the years I developed quite an instinct for it. I could always tell when I wasn't being given the whole truth. It was nothing tangible, just a sensation – a sort of uneasiness.' He paused, his eyes coming round to me. 'Of late I've been feeling it again.'

Strangely enough so had I.

We reached the Czech-German border later that afternoon. A waiting car drove us to the checkpoint on the main autoroute.

It had changed quite a bit since I was last there. Gone were the customs officers with the diamond hard stares and the itchy trigger fingers; gone too were the mirrors they used to trundle under the cars to check for illegal passengers, and the cubicles where travellers could be stripped and searched and beaten senseless if there was a suggestion that they had something to hide. Now all you had to fear was the tedium of a thirty minute queue and the threat of a rubber stamp on the nice clean page of your passport.

We waited in a room overlooking the road. There were blinds on the window so that we could see out but no one could see back in. Uniformed officers brought us coffee in plastic mugs and clicked their heels and saluted, as those brought suddenly and unexpectedly into the presence of their superiors tend to do.

After half an hour of this Vlasek said, 'Ah, there he is.'

It was the man I'd last seen carrying the wrapped picture across the station. He was driving a black Mercedes. I watched as he nosed it into the queue of cars and cut the engine.

Vlasek rested one finger on the blind, opening it wider. He gave a little nod of his head, drawing my attention to the fawn coloured Citroën he'd spoken of earlier. It had joined the queue about three cars further back. A neat piece of timing. Any closer and they would have been too obvious, any further back and they'd risk losing the car in front as it drew off.

What happened next was almost artistic. One thing I've noticed about the eastern sector is that they tend to be a shade more artistic than us. There was never much difference in our intentions, or in our deviousness, for that matter, but I've always noticed that the eastern sector is inclined to be a shade more imaginative than we are in their methods. It's as though extra points are scored for style.

And this had style. As the Citroën drew to a halt, the two inside leaning back in their seats in boredom, the car coming up behind ran straight into its rear.

There was a hollow crunch. Small pieces of orange plastic scattered across the road; the panel work of the boot buckled.

The two men in the front seat didn't move. Not surprising really, the last thing they wanted was to start an argument.

The car behind wasn't taking the matter so lightly. The driver and passenger were out in a second and hammering on the Citroën's windows, looking much like irate tourists who've had their day disrupted – curious when you consider that the last time I'd seen them they'd been telephone mechanics in the railway station.

When the drivers of the Citroën didn't open the door, one of them kicked the front wing. That had the passenger out, still very placatory, not looking for trouble. Someone slapped him across the head. The other came out of the driver's seat. Tempers rose; there was shouting, a face was punched and all hell broke loose.

It was over in moments. The door to the guard-house burst open and a bunch of uniformed officers came spewing out to break up the party. Orders were barked, arms twisted, and, despite furious protestations from the two in the Citroën, all four contestants were marched inside. The occupants of the others cars just stood and gaped.

Beside me, Vlasek gave a little grunt. He had watched the performance with the rapt and slightly distant expression of a choreographer on the opening night of a new ballet. There was a knock; the door was opened and the wrapped painting that had been extracted from the boot of the first car was brought in.

Vlasek took it from the officer and handed it across to me.

'Have a good trip. I don't think those two will be troubling you any more.'

CHAPTER SIXTEEN

London was looking battered, grey and familiar, much as my own face does in the mirror on the morning after the night before.

On the way in from Heathrow airport the taxi driver asked me where I'd been; when I said Prague he told me his sister had been there. At the time I earmarked the information for the mental waste-paper basket but, as you can see, it never made it.

As soon as I reached the office I was summoned down to see Sutherland. He's the head of station, a small man with the neat, meticulous habits of those who spent most of their life in the army.

'What's going on, Jan?' He was pacing the room, hands thrust into the pockets of his tweed suit. It was a Saturday and normally he would be down in the country.

I took his question to be rhetorical and made no reply.

'You went over to Prague to collect information. Not only do you refuse to come back, you go to ground and break off all lines of communication. Do you realise we've been trying to contact you for over a week now?'

It hadn't been my intention to be thrown in the Vltava river, or to have a red-hot poker waved in my face for that matter, but there was no point in pointing this out to Sutherland. He imagined operations ran to a tidy and pre-ordained schedule.

'You seem to think you are running some private vendetta of your own out there.'

I said, 'Phones can be tapped.'

'And now you pitch up here with some damned painting you expect the department to sell. This is the Foreign Office, man. We don't sell trinkets from a barrow in the market. What ever got into you?'

'I have a lead.'

'As an art dealer?'

'It was an option that offered itself at the time. I took it.'

Sutherland stared at me as though I'd taken leave of my senses. 'You're a field operative, Jan. Your job is to collect intelligence and pass it on. If you want to play parts you should go to RADA and wear tights and talk in a funny voice.'

'My brief was to find the Ceauşescu paintings. If you allow me back to Prague I can still do that.'

'Back?' He repeated the word thoughtfully as though it embraced a concept entirely new to him. 'You're not going anywhere until we've had a full review of the situation and particularly the part you've played in it.'

'I can find those paintings. I'm very close now.'

'So you keep telling me.' Sutherland studied me with those bright rodent eyes of his. 'But, as I understand it, to return you need thirty thousand pounds in your pocket.'

'Thirty-five.'

'That's a lot of money.'

'You have the picture I brought.'

'Is it worth that much?'

'Certainly.'

Unfortunately it wasn't.

The first thing I'd done when I came into the office was to send Sophie, my secretary, up to Sotheby's with it. They'd turned out to be closed on a Saturday so she'd used her initiative and taken it round to the National Gallery where she'd dug out some boffin who knew his stuff.

'It's German,' she said, dumping the canvas down on my

desk and perching herself on the edge. '19th century; no one famous.'

'What's it worth?'

'Five hundred.'

'Thousand?'

'Quid. He said it would be worth a bit more if it had a decent frame.'

'That's great,' I said. 'I can't very well ring up Éva Kupka and say "can you send along the frame" on the off chance that it's worth twenty-nine and a half thousand pounds.'

'No, you can't.' She grinned at me. The trouble with the well-educated and rather beautiful daughters of Field Marshals is that they think money is just money, something you haul from a bottomless pit with the aid of a cheque book. 'What are you going to do?'

'What are the options?'

'There aren't any,' she said. 'You'll just have to go grovelling to Sutherland.'

'He'll dock the difference out of my pay.'

'He can't.'

'Don't bank on it.'

'I'm not; it's just that you don't earn that much.'

I stared at the painting and mentally consigned all devious women to the fires of hell. If it had only had that little eagle stamped on the back I'd be a hero by now, invited to dine at St James's Street clubs by Whitehall mandarins eager to discuss my promotion. Instead I was standing in the corner with the dunce's hat on my head.

'I could just shoot myself.'

'You haven't got time for that,' Sophie said, sliding off the desk and straightening her skirt. 'You've got to write your report.'

I've always admired writers, not for what they write but for the fact that they can write anything at all. I find it almost impossible. I know what I want to say but as soon as I try putting it down the words get stuck and won't move across the page. But for the rest of that afternoon I scratched away at my report. When it was finished I passed it over to Sophie who took it to pieces and completely rewrote it, firing out questions, adding and enlarging the text, tapping her pencil on her well-flossed teeth as she went about it. Sometimes I think she should be running the department; occasionally I think she does.

By the time she was finished, it wasn't a bad piece of work, if I say so myself, and it created quite a stir. First thing next morning, before I'd had time to get the coffee granules and boiling water together in a cup, Sutherland was on the phone.

'I want you down in the country,' he said.

'Where do you live?'

'Not here,' he said testily. 'Stephen Bathurst's place; Sophie knows the way. She'll pick you up in half an hour.'

I glanced at my watch. It was nine-thirty. I must have slept longer than usual; it was the effort of writing that report.

'And Jan,' he added, 'wear a tie, would you? You're invited to lunch.'

I'd never met Stephen Bathurst – Sir Stephen Bathurst as he is to me – but I knew his name just the same. He was one of those advisers you hear about, rarely appearing in public himself but influencing policy from the think-tanks and select committees that lie buried beneath the surface of every government. A tough operator from what I've heard. He'd made his fortune in the steel industry back in the sixties, a success he put down to a lean work-force and relentless pressure on the trade unions.

But now that aspect of his career was almost irrelevant. Industry had put him into business with the Soviet empire. He'd been wined, dined and generally fêted by every country it contained and was now rated as a leading expert on Central European affairs.

Sophie drove me down to his house in her open-topped Golf. She was kitted out in nothing more formal than jeans and an open-collared shirt but the brooch at her neck, the scarf tied to her handbag and the Gucci shoes she'd kicked off while she drove, matched her with the rolling countryside we were speeding through.

'You're the kiss of death to my social life,' she said, her fingers thrumming on the wheel in time to *The Greatest Hits of Abba*. 'I was meant to be at a Horse Trials this afternoon.'

'Well, you'll just have to watch me on trial instead. You'll find it much more exciting.'

'You're not on trial, Jan.'

'No? You think I've been asked down here for the fresh air?'

Sophie turned her head to me. 'Sutherland's read your report. He's impressed. I don't think he had any idea what you've been doing out there.'

'I'm sure he hadn't.'

'I'm impressed too—'

'That's because you wrote the report.'

'No, you've achieved a lot. No one else could have done what you've done. You shouldn't be so down on yourself. If they'd left it to the embassy we'd never have got anywhere.'

It does the ego good to have this kind of endorsement from a girl with long blonde hair flying in the wind but it didn't help to answer any of the questions that were breeding in my mind.

The wealth Sir Stephen Bathurst had amassed over the years had provided him with an estate in Gloucester. Not, as it turned out, one of those glitzy outfits with swimming pools tailored into Georgian orangeries and stately lawns laid out as landing pads for helicopters, but a gritty Tudor mansion with gnarled stone walls and mullioned windows.

The housekeeper who opened the door told us that Sir

Stephen was in the garden and pointed to where a column of smoke rose above a beech hedge.

He was burning the remains of a greenhouse.

'You must be Capek,' he said as we approached. Reaching out a long, thin arm knotted with muscle he shook my hand. His grip would have cracked a walnut. 'Just the man I need; could you give me a hand?' He indicated a sizable part of what had been the greenhouse, lifting one end in expectation. 'That's it, get your hands right underneath. On the count of three.'

Between us we hefted the thing up on to the fire. A great rush of sparks flew up with the impact. Bathurst stood back, wiping his forehead with the back of one hand. Dressed in old corduroy trousers and a checked shirt rolled to the elbow, he was a tall thin man, lean as string, in his early sixties.

'Damned thing fell down in the storms. I've been wanting to get rid of it for weeks.' Taking a red handkerchief from his pocket he cleaned his hands and then thrust it away again, one end still trailing out behind. Then with no preliminaries he said, 'So Kupka's started a fund-raising exercise, has he?'

I said he'd started one on a big scale. Bathurst nodded and tossed another piece of the condemned greenhouse on the fire.

'Can't say I'm surprised. It was only a matter of time before he began making a nuisance of himself with that National Reform Party of his. He's been harbouring ambitions for some time.' Another piece of wood was consigned to the fire. 'I met the blighter once in Berlin. He had the cheek to tell me Great Britain was a second-rate power; meant it too. He's an empire builder. The question is, what we are going to do about it?'

He spoke in short bursts, as though a great many thoughts were passing through his head and he only bothered to mention a few.

For the next fifteen minutes he cross-examined me, going through the sequence of events I'd laid out in my report, digging and prying into every crevice of the information while

Sophie stood at a discreet distance fanning the smoke away from her eyes.

As grillings go, it wasn't too bad. I just told him what I'd seen and heard and let him draw his own conclusions. All the time he kept lobbing pieces of wood on the fire until, finally, when he had kicked the thing a few times with his foot to make sure it would bed down into a solid core, and satisfied himself that he'd learned as much from me as he could, we went back into the house.

It was low and dark with oak beams and windows cut into thick walls. Hanging in the entrance hall were four mirrors; there were two more in the drawing-room. It was strange, Bathurst didn't strike me as a vain man who would want to see his reflection at every turn but there they were.

Sutherland had arrived and was skimming the newspapers. He greeted Bathurst in the brief way of those who've known each other some time and maybe they had. From what I've learned of the English, I shouldn't be surprised if they hadn't been to school together and would revert to calling each other by quaint, incomprehensible and apparently insulting nicknames the moment they were alone.

'We've been doing a bit of work in the garden,' Bathurst told him. He poured drinks all round, ending with a large whisky for himself. He took it to a chair and sat down, knees apart, head thrust forwards.

'From your report I gather that you think Kupka's wife is implicated in this business.'

'She's Romanian and she's sharp as a razor. Added to that she's the only one amongst them with any real interest in pictures.'

'So I gather,' Bathurst said. 'Never met her myself. The only time I came across Kupka he was married to someone else. Nice girl, wonderful figure. I can't think how the man does it; he's built like a tank, drinks like a fish but he manages to surround himself with beautiful women.'

'Maybe something to do with his bank balance,' I said.

'I'm rich,' Bathurst replied flatly. 'And all I get to comfort me in my old age is Mrs Tucker.' He nodded towards the housekeeper who had come in to say lunch was ready. She tut-tutted coyly at the mention of her name and removed herself with a flourish; anyone would think he'd suggested a pre-prandial quick one in the potting shed.

'I can believe it though,' Bathurst said when she'd gone. 'For some time she was mistress to a Red Army general; she must have made a few contacts – Éva Kupka that is, not Mrs Tucker. She was the wife of a corporal who had the good sense to pass away and leave her culinary skills to me. Shall we go in?'

'How long has she been married to Kupka? I asked.

'A couple of years.' It was Sutherland who made the reply, looking pleased with himself for managing a contribution. 'About the same time as the balloon went up in the eastern bloc.'

'So she could have brought the paintings out with her.'

'A sort of dowry,' Bathurst agreed.

And I'm sure that is how it was. It was not a marriage those two had, more like a business arrangement, a pooling of resources. Which is not to say they didn't show every sign of affection – I could remember vividly the way Éva had sat at his feet, while I was sweating over the value of her damnable pictures, and allowed herself to be stroked by Kupka, for all the world like a cat that's allowed the cream from the milk when it's been good. But still I sensed a formality to it all, a merging of two equal and opposite powers rather than a marriage.

During lunch, which was solid and nourishing and British, roast lamb with mint sauce and a piping hot gravy made with a hint of cranberries and a good slug of port wine, the subject turned to a more general discussion of Czechoslovakia. I'll say this much for Bathurst, he knew his stuff. There wasn't a nook or cranny of the political landscape that had missed him. He spoke fluently, I might say effortlessly, on everything from the baroque architecture of the city to the future of the car industry in the new market economy, while outside the sun broke through the cloud, turning the mirrored room to the rich, golden glow of a meerschaum pipe. Somewhere in the distance, in the trees, something hard and reflective was winking as if a message was being sent to us by heliograph.

It was only later, when we had gone through to a private study of his, and he'd poured us each a glass of malt whisky, that he returned to the business in hand.

'I think we must accept as inevitable now,' he said, the bottle in one hand, the screw top in the other, 'the fact that Kupka intends to seize power in Czechoslovakia. I think we must also accept that he'll probably succeed. It's the right psychological moment for him to move, with the memory of communism still painful and the country beginning to slide into chaos under the new regime. Whether he intends to get there by peaceful means or just grab power in a coup remains to be seen, but the UN has already been briefed on the possibility and I myself have spoken with the PM.'

I'd been aware of all this and had spent some time in the last few days thinking it through, and yet it was only as Bathurst laid out the facts in that little study of his, safe and cosy and miles from the country itself, that I came to full realisation of the storm that was about to break.

'The implications aren't too good,' Bathurst continued. 'With Kupka in power – a man who at the best of times is unstable, at worst deluded, if Capek's report is anything to go by – the political geography of Europe will alter completely. He'll turn the place into a fortress state that will threaten every country that surrounds it. The whole stability of the area will be turned on its head. I don't think it is an exaggeration to say that our grandchildren could be paying for the consequences of what is about to happen.'

There was silence in the room. Outside the light still winked at us from the trees. Bathurst took a pull at his whisky. I remember wondering whether he knew that he shared at least one weakness with Kupka.

'In normal circumstances I'd say that this was a domestic matter that the Czechs must sort out themselves and, apart from lending advice, I'd tell them to get on with it. This man Vlasek,' he prodded his glass in my direction, 'sounds a competent fellow and evidently aware of what's going on in his own backyard. But these are not normal circumstances. Kupka has already anticipated world reaction and has started to take steps to ensure that it won't foul up his plans. In the last year he's been courting every industrial nation in the west, offering vast concessions in mining, agriculture, electronics, to anyone who will back his horse. And it's working. I don't mind telling you there are those in the Cabinet here in Britain who are actively encouraging Kupka's claim.'

'What can be done?' Sutherland asked in that detached, cultivated way of his, as though he were debating the solution to a knotty problem in chess.

'In the short term we must play what cards we have. Fortunately we have a man on the spot and I thank God that we decided to use him.' His steely eyes turned to me directly for the first time since we'd come in here. 'Capek must get back to Prague and destroy those pictures.'

'Destroy them?' I couldn't keep the surprise from my voice.

'It's the only way.'

'Stephen.' It was Sutherland who murmured an objection. 'Won't there be a bit of a stink if we do that?'

'There'll be the most God-almighty row; there'll be angry letters to *The Times* and art lovers topping themselves all over the world, but we'll just have to weather that. While those paintings exist there's a chance that Kupka can use them; Christ, he might even have engineered legal ownership of them by now. No, they must be destroyed, and they must be seen to have been destroyed.'

'That may not be as easy as it sounds,' I said.

Bathurst wasn't listening to any dissent. 'This policeman – Vlasek. Can't you get him to help?'

'He'll help me to find them, but he'll do everything in his power to stop me damaging them.'

'Then you'll just have to do it when he's not looking, Capek,' he said drily.

'I'll need a banker's draft for thirty thousand pounds if I'm going to go back.'

'I'll arrange for you to get it,' Bathurst said. He gave a little smile. 'I'm sure the Treasury will see it's a small price to pay for the stability of Central Europe.'

I left them to work on the rest of the whisky together and went outside. Across the lawn, Sophie was sitting on a swing that hung from the branch of a beech tree, casually kicking herself backwards and forwards with one foot. She looked up as I came over.

'That sounded like boys' talk in there,' she said.

'And we never even got round to the dirty jokes.'

'I thought I'd leave you to it.'

'Very wise.'

She looked at me with those steady blue eyes of hers. 'Are they sending you back, Jan?'

I nodded.

'I thought they would.'

'Why did they put me on the job, Sophie?' I asked the question that had been nagging me ever since I found Pesanek's body in the flat.

'You're the best man for it.'

'They didn't know they needed a field agent. It was meant to be a quick chat, no problems, no hang-ups; they could have sent the vicar from the English church.'

Sophie stopped the swing with one foot, twisting round as it slowed. 'Why are you letting this worry you?'

'It doesn't add up.'

'Maybe they're just giving you a chance, Jan,' she said quietly. 'You needed another chance.'

She was right, of course. When I came back from Prague after two years in jail I was washed up, an old horse put out to grass, but it hurt to hear her say it. I stared away across the lawn.

'Don't fight it, Jan,' she said.

'You think I should be thankful?'

'You're doing what you're best at, Jan.'

'Maybe.' I was watching that light. It was winking again, and this time it was winking from a different position than it had earlier.

It shouldn't do that.

I said, 'Do you have the keys to your car?'

She looked up sharply, catching the change of tone in my voice, but she reacted quickly enough, hoisting them out of her back pocket.

I went back into the study. The two men were talking. I cut into their conversation.

'Is there a rifle in the house?'

Bathurst looked up in surprise but he didn't waste time with questions. 'I've got a couple of .22s,' he said. 'I keep them for shooting rabbits; they any good to you?'

'Can you show me where they are?'

He led the way through the kitchens, where Mrs Tucker was washing up lunch, and down into a utility room at the back of the house. There were coats and boots and fishing rods laid out on racks. In a steel cabinet in the corner were a selection of guns: a pair of 12-bore Purdeys, engraved and glinting darkly, a plainer box-lock and two rifles. I took one out. It was a lever action Martini, a good, solid mechanism, virtually unchanged from the time they were used at Rorke's Drift. I grabbed a handful of shells from a box, pushed one into the breech and dropped the others in my pocket.

They felt very small and ineffective.

'In God's name, man. What are you intending to do with that?' It was Sutherland who asked from the doorway where he stood still holding his glass in one hand.

'Someone out there's eating the lettuces,' I said as I brushed past him.

In the hallway I wrapped the gun in my overcoat and took it out to the car, stashing it barrel downwards in the passenger seat. Sophie had left the swing and was standing in the drive, her hands on hips. She didn't say anything as I drove off.

Turning out of the drive, I headed back in the direction we'd come from earlier that day. It was just a country lane, scarcely wide enough to allow two cars to pass, that wound its way through open countryside with wooded hillsides and sudden vistas over sunlit fields.

I wasn't driving at any speed, almost dawdling.

It was after a mile or so that I saw it. A dark blue Ford Escort. About a hundred yards behind. It was just the occasional glimpse as I took the corners. Nothing out of the normal there. I turned off into a side road and after a while the Ford was there again. I tried one more deviation and when it was still with me I knew for certain.

Gradually I pushed up the speed, swinging the car through the bends in the road. It took them well, a polished piece of machinery. A long straight stretch opened before me. I went up to eighty, changing down into third as I came to the corner, hearing the engine whine with the sudden deceleration. I glanced in the rear view mirror. No sign of the other car yet. I hit the brakes and the car slewed across the road, its tyres screeching. If Sophie had seen me she'd have had a fit.

As the car came to a halt by the verge I pulled the rifle from my overcoat and stood up on the seat, twisting round to face back down the road, the gun resting on the roll-bar of the car. I cranked the breech shut.

And only just in time.

The Escort came round the bend at speed, heeling over like

a ship in a gale. I drew a bead on the front tyre and squeezed off a shot.

There was no response. Could a .22 penetrate a wire-walled tyre? I'd no idea. It was not something I'd tried before.

The driver had spotted me; the car was slowing rapidly. I flicked open the breech, reloaded and fired again.

This time I hit.

I saw the bonnet dip, the rear end waggling as the driver wrestled with the wheel. The tyre was flapping like old washing in the spin drier. Then the car spun round in the road and turned over on its side, grinding to a halt about thirty yards away.

It lay still, its windscreen frosted, steam rising from the radiator. The rear wheel was slowly turning. Apart from that there was no movement. The driver appeared to be stunned. I jumped down into the road. As I did so there was a sign of life from inside. The side door lifted in the air and a man clambered out.

As his feet hit the road he turned towards me for an instant and I recognised him.

It was Ivan Teige.

CHAPTER SEVENTEEN

He saw me coming and ran.

Crossing the road, he leapt down into the ditch, landing on all fours, pulling himself out with his hands, and crawled through the hedge beyond.

On the far side was an open field, a wide expanse of plough. Teige headed off across it, moving slowly, the loose soil spitting up from his feet. Swinging off at an angle he made for the grassy track that ran down one side.

By the time I had reached the overturned car and shouldered through the hedge, scratching my face and hands, catching the barrel of the rifle in the dense branches, Teige was a hundred yards or more ahead of me, running down towards the woods at the far end of the field.

At one point he stumbled and nearly fell. I gained ten yards in the time it took him to recover. The muscles of my legs were straining with the effort, breath hammering in my lungs. But in the primitive ritual of the chase, that all-consuming instinct of the hunter and the hunted, I felt nothing. All I knew was that Teige was here where he shouldn't be. That he had seen what he shouldn't have seen. And for that he must be tracked down and caught.

Coming to the edge of the woods, Teige wavered for a moment. The way into the trees was barred by a thick undergrowth of nettles and brambles. He glanced round to see how far back I was, how much time he had. Then he darted away to one side.

I veered off the path on to the plough, cutting off the corner of the field to intercept him. But Teige had scrambled up onto a piece of farm machinery that lay rusting in the brambles. Throwing himself on it, legs and arms outspread, he struggled across and fell into the woods beyond.

I was still thirty yards behind. All the way across the field I'd been gaining on him, closing the distance inch by inch. I was younger than Teige and fitter. It was only a matter of time before I caught him. But now he had the advantage. Woods would give him cover; woods would give him the chance to get away. The frustration of it burned through my veins like a fire.

Without bothering to find a way through, I burst straight into the undergrowth, feeling the brambles dragging and tearing at my clothes. One barbed strand caught my ankle and I fell face down as I came through the other side.

I scrambled to my feet. The steep hillside was thick with beech trees and silver birches. Beneath them a soft brown carpet of leaves. I could smell the damp soil, see the ranks of silver green tree trunks falling away into the distance.

But there was no sign of Teige.

I held still, blood pounding in my head, lungs heaving. He could be hiding, as a frightened animal will hide, crouching with its head down and eyes stretched wide, staking everything on the hope that its pursuer will pass.

I held my breath, summoning silence from my labouring body.

And I heard him. Off somewhere to the left of where I stood. I could hear the rattling of the chalky soil as he plunged down the hillside, hear the cawing of the startled rooks in the trees above. I followed the sound, ducking beneath the branches that whipped in my face, slipping and sliding down the crumbling earth until I saw him.

He was running erratically, weaving between the tree trunks, frantically grabbing at branches as he passed to steady himself. Suddenly, for no good reason that I could see, he veered off to one side and ran across the angle of the slope.

Then, catching at a tree, he came to a halt.

The soft chalk crumbled beneath his feet. He fell to his knees, still holding the trunk in his arms. His head turned and he looked back. He picked himself up, hands on the ground, and scuttled away to one side. But after a few yards he stopped again.

I couldn't see what was holding him, why he had stopped so abruptly. He was crouched on all fours, staring up at me. His face was white. I could see his mouth open, shoulders heaving as he panted for breath.

As I approached he dropped to his back, one hand reaching into his jacket. When it came out there was a gun in it. He rolled over on to his chest. His arms stretched up, reaching towards me. The hands closed around the butt of the gun and he fired.

The shot went high. I heard it cracking through the branches above my head. I jumped to one side; threw myself into the nearest tree, nearly winding myself with the impact. It was too narrow to shield my body. But before I could move to a better position he fired again.

Leaves spurted up just behind my foot as the bullet cut a white scar in the chalk.

I stood up straight, back resting against the trunk, reducing the exposed area of my body as far as I could. Fumbling in my pocket I took out one of the .22 shells. It didn't look as if it was up to the job I had in mind but it was all I had. I cranked open the breech, saw a flash of gold as the spent case flicked out, and rammed it in.

I turned my head. Over to my right was a larger tree. It had thick moss-covered roots that clung to the soil like the tentacles of an octopus. If I could reach that it would offer some cover, give me the chance to get a shot back at him. But it was further back, higher up the hillside. It was going to be a scramble. Teige would have the chance of a clear shot at me as I went. But I needed to be there. I had to take the risk. If I could get him to fire again and then moved immediately I might get away with it. It's almost impossible to get a second shot off accurately if it's hurried.

I was bracing myself to make the move when Teige spoke.

'It's too late, Capek.' He was speaking slowly, his breath labouring the words. 'There's nothing you can do now.'

I twisted round on the tree trunk and looked down at him. He was up on his knees, leaves clinging to his clothing. The gun was held out at arm's length as though it were a crucifix held up to a vampire.

'I know what you're doing,' he called out. 'I know your game, Capek. It's over. Finished.'

If he wanted to talk that was fine by me. I edged away from the tree, the rifle held low in my hands, muzzle aimed at his chest. There's nothing more futile than the sight of two men pointing guns at each other – unless you happen to be one of those two men. At least then you know the odds are more or less even.

'Stay where you are!' Teige ordered. His hair was awry, his sweating face streaked with mud. There was a cut to his forehead and blood was trickling down his cheek, dividing and separating like a family tree. I took a couple of steps forwards. Fragments of chalk dislodged and went tumbling down the hill towards where Teige was now clambering to his feet.

He didn't like it. His voice rose to a shriek.

'Stay where you are!' He glanced back over his shoulder as he spoke and I saw for the first time what it was that had brought his escape to such an abrupt halt.

He was standing on the edge of a quarry.

Not ten yards beyond him the ground fell away like a cliff. Off to the left I could see the eroded face of the chalk, a lip of soil dropping over the top, the roots of the trees dangling beneath. No wonder he had thrown himself on the ground in such a hurry. A few strides more and he'd have been over the edge.

'Looks like you picked a bad route,' I said, but Teige shook his head and pulled back his lips in a smile.

'There's nothing you can do now.' He was getting his breath back. 'I've seen it all. I know what you are, Capek.' He wiped his forearm over his face, smearing blood and sweat. The gun didn't waver. 'I knew. I always knew what you were doing. Now I have this.'

With his left hand he reached into his pocket, pulled something out and held it out to me. All I could see was that it was small and yellow but it didn't take a great stretch of the imagination to guess that it was a spool of film.

'It's all here, Capek. I saw it all. I've got the evidence.'

What do you do in the circumstances? Reason with him? Play for time? I moved down a little closer.

'There's nothing there that will prove anything,' I told him easily.

'Don't fool yourself. You're finished.' He shook his head as though disgusted by the whole business. 'I knew. Right from the start I knew. You never fooled me, Capek.'

There was a little rush of stones at his feet.

I said, 'You don't know what you're talking about.'

'I smelled you as a phoney from the very beginning. They should have listened.'

'Maybe they should, Ivan.' I wanted to get closer. There's always a chance if you can get in close enough.

'I told them.' His voice was rising. 'I warned them.'

'But they didn't listen to you, Ivan. And they probably won't again.'

There was another small rush of stones but Teige didn't notice them. He was shaking his head. 'Oh, they will now, Capek. They'll listen very carefully when they see what I've got.'

And then it happened.

At first it wasn't much. The branches of the tree beside Teige gave a shiver. Then came a small sound and the ground at his feet appeared to shift.

He glanced down, his knees braced. For an instant the gun was off-target. But before I could move he'd regained his balance. His eyes swung back to me, the barrel steadied.

He gave a smile and stepped to one side.

A crack appeared in the soil above him. His foot slipped. The smile vanished. He dropped to his knees. And suddenly the whole hillside land-slipped around him. Earth and stones went cascading down. Pouring over the edge of the cliff.

Teige had fallen to his face. His arms and legs were spread-eagled on the ground, grasping out, trying to get a hold. But the ground was sliding away beneath him. There was nothing he could do. His eyes were fixed on me. There was a look of disbelief in his eyes as though I'd caused it all to happen. The gun had come out of his hand but the other was still clenched around the little spool of film.

At the lip of the quarry he came to a halt, his feet dangling over the edge into space. With his one free hand he grasped the stem of a small sapling. It was bent double, the roots tearing with the strain. Teige's face was white, mouth wide open in fright. His breath was coming in short, fierce gasps.

Of the rest I remember very little. It is often that way and it may be for the best. The mind thinks and calculates but it leaves no trace in the memory. All you remember are the decisions. And they seem to come from outside like a voice issuing instructions.

I moved down to Teige, skirting the area of bare chalk where the soil had shifted.

He lay still. One hand clung to the root of the sapling. The other grasped the spool of film.

I stood over him.

He looked up at me, searching my face for mercy. But he saw there was none.

I took a step forwards. There was hate and anger in his eyes. His teeth were bared.

I kicked his head and he let go of the tree.

As he fell his body turned over backwards like a diver

performing some complicated stunt. Then he hit the chalk
sides of the cliff face and was suddenly galvanised in action,
his limbs spinning like a broken doll's, before he thumped
into the ground far below.

A shower of stones followed him down. They started a
small avalanche that covered his body the moment it came
to rest.

The spool of film still lay on the cliff edge by the sapling
he'd been holding. I picked it up, pulled out the long ribbon
of smoky grey celluloid, exposing it, wiping out the pictures
he'd taken such pains to take. I tossed it down after him. It
went down slowly, the film fluttering out behind the yellow
case like a streamer going over the side of a liner.

It looked tiny and insignificant. Not worth the effort.

Certainly not worth dying for.

'You mean you killed him!'

'What did you expect me to do?'

'God, man, was that really necessary?'

'He'd seen us. He had pictures.'

'Was there no other way?'

'Yes,' I said. 'I could have brought him back here, locked
him in the broom cupboard and asked him not to tell anyone
what he'd seen.'

Sutherland stared at me in disgust. He was having trouble
in coming to terms with what had happened in the last forty
minutes. All these years he has been reading reports, assessing the results, reprimanding those that haven't performed
satisfactorily and I don't believe that until that moment he
had the slightest idea of what any of it actually means.

'It seems excessive,' he said but Bathurst cut him short.

'Capek's right. It was the only way. This man knew too
much. If he had been allowed to get away it would have
ruined the whole operation.'

'That I don't doubt,' Sutherland said.

'In the circumstances I don't see he had any alternative.'

Sophie came into the room. She closed the door and stood there, pale and erect like a page-boy.

'I've rung the office. They'll send someone.'

'Someone?' Bathurst asked.

'A bag man.'

Bathurst looked for an explanation. Sutherland gave a little grimace as though apologising for this loose language.

'To tidy up,' he said. 'After Capek's . . . performance.'

'Ah, yes.'

There was silence in the room. The evening sun glinted on the silver coffee-pot, on the glasses still waiting to be removed on the tray. Then Sutherland asked me, 'So, what happens now?'

'I must get back to Prague.'

'Now?'

'The sooner the better. Sophie can drive me up to Heathrow.'

'But is that wise?' Bathurst asked. 'Won't this man have reported what he's seen?'

It was the question for which none of us had an answer.

CHAPTER EIGHTEEN

Had Teige managed to get a message back to Kupka? That was the question that turned over and over in my head as I flew in to Prague that night.

Back in the cosy security of Sir Stephen Bathurst's drawing-room it was easy to say that he hadn't had the time; to reassure yourself with the comforting thought that he would have been too busy taking his photos to have bothered trying to make contact with Kupka.

But as the plane came in to land, none of it seemed quite so certain. It would have taken only a moment for him to have made a phone call. He'd had the opportunity. At any time throughout lunch he could have slipped away, found a phone box and spilled the beans.

The thought of it froze the blood in my veins.

But what could he have seen? It was only the meeting with Bathurst that I had to worry about. The rest could be explained. Teige must have picked up my trail somewhere in London. At the airport possibly, or my home. He would have seen me going into the office. But that didn't matter. I was bound to go to the office when I came back. It would have been strange if I hadn't. The only part of my behaviour I couldn't talk my way out of was why I'd gone down to the country, why I had briefed a man known to be a leading expert on European affairs. That was the giveaway; that was what let the cat out of the bag.

But Teige wouldn't have tried to make a call while I was still there, would he? If he'd sneaked away while we were having lunch he might have missed something. I might even have been gone before he got back. No, he wouldn't have done it. He'd never have taken the chance.

It was a reassuring thought, and yet somehow as the plane touched down, the wheels screeching on the tarmac, I didn't feel reassured.

Jarka was waiting for me at the airport. As the automatic doors puffed open I saw her standing there among the doleful committee of taxi drivers and corporate chauffeurs who were waiting. Her shiny helmet of hair flashed as she waved her arms above her head.

'I've been here for hours,' she said as she hugged me round the neck. 'I thought you were coming in the flight before. I've just been standing around waiting. People were beginning to think I was a call-girl.' She pounced on the duty-free bag I was carrying. 'Did you get my scent?'

'The most expensive one in the shop.'

'Of course – and a bottle of champagne. What are we celebrating?' She was wearing faded jeans tucked into brown boots, and her old bomber-jacket. Beneath it her white T-shirt was moulded provocatively to the curve of her breasts.

'I don't know,' I said. 'Nothing in particular. My safe return to the land of my fathers, I suppose.'

'Is your mother foreign?

'No—'

'You should say "land of my parents" then.' She'd opened the little box of perfume and sprayed some on her wrist. 'It's very disrespectful. Here, smell this.' She held her wrist up to my nose. Her eyes were bright with excitement and I can't believe there wasn't a man watching who didn't feel a twinge of envy.

The VW Golf was in the car park out in front of the airport. Jarka ignored the exit and drove straight out of one side of the place, the tyres bumping over the kerb.

'So, how much did you get for that picture of yours?' she asked as we reached the autoroute.

'Thirty-two thousand pounds.'

'But that's more than a million crowns,' she said in amazement.

'It's not as much as I said I'd get.'

'But it wasn't worth anything.'

'The grey men in Whitehall have coughed up. Just to keep the ball rolling. If I don't do something useful with it they'll take it out of my pension.'

'Why didn't they give you the whole lot then?'

'They reckon it looks more realistic if I don't come back with exactly what I said.'

'In that case they should have given you more, not less.' Jarka was indignant.

'They never give more.'

'Have you got the money with you?' She twisted round in the seat, as if she might be able to see wads of used notes glowing out of the suitcase which was lying on the back seat.

'It was transferred into a bank in Liechtenstein. I didn't get to feel the stuff.'

'Mean, aren't they?' We came out of the Letna tunnel and there was Prague spread out before us, St Nicholas glowing like a hot coal, the castle hill green and gold in the floodlights. Jarka suddenly thumped my knee with her fist. 'Oh, I haven't told you, I've got a commission. Someone's asked me to make some drawings of his family. He's a lecturer at the Charles University. He wants me to draw his wife and children. Not bad, eh?' She stopped at an intersection, her head cocked as she watched the lights changing. 'How much do you think I can get for doing a drawing?'

I'd no idea. 'Is he well off?'

'No, I shouldn't think so. Lecturers don't earn much, do they. They wouldn't all wear those scruffy suits if they were well off.'

'Havel wears a scruffy suit and he's not doing badly for himself.'

'He's a playwright, my darling.'

'How about ten thousand crowns each?' I suggested. It was around £250.

Jarka nodded. 'That's about what I thought. It's not fair, is it? You get a million crowns for a worthless bit of canvas and I only get ten thousand for slaving away on a masterpiece. I could have got more by hanging around the airport tonight.'

She parked in the coal market, two wheels up on the kerb and got out.

'Don't you think I could get a bit more than that?' She wrinkled her nose in dissatisfaction. 'I was thinking of asking for fifteen thousand – maybe twenty. It's not easy to make a good drawing.'

'I'm sure,' I said. 'Don't take my word for it. Ask what you think's right. I'm not renowned for my valuation of pictures.'

When we reached her flat I put a call through to Kupka. A voice I didn't recognise answered the phone. It said it would transfer me to a private extension and with that the line went dead.

I waited. Jarka's living-room was in darkness. The only light came from the kitchen where she was busying herself with the champagne bottle and glasses. I thought of Teige and the black thoughts that had vanished in the warmth of Jarka's welcome returned.

Then Kupka came on the line.

'Jan,' he boomed. 'Where are you?'

'Prague. I've just got in.'

'So soon. I wasn't expecting you for a day or so. I thought you'd be living it up in London.'

'There's no reason to delay, is there?' I was nervous and it made me abrupt.

'That depends on what is making you delay, Jan.' He gave that little chuckle of his and I could picture him, sitting vast and solid in a chair, a glass parked in one hand and that malevolent smile of his glittering in his eyes.

I said, 'I need to see you.'

'Of course you do. I'll be in Prague in the next day or two. We'll meet, have a drink, talk things over.'

'No, I'm coming round tonight.'

'Are you, Jan?' A silkiness came into his voice. 'And what's the rush?'

'I can't hang around any longer. We've wasted too much time already. I'm coming round to you tonight.'

There was silence on the line. Then Kupka said, 'My, my. We are being efficient. Very well, I'll send a car. It won't be with you until at least ten. Where are you?'

'I'll be waiting by the Legii bridge.'

I put down the phone. Jarka was standing close, holding two glasses of champagne. She gave me one.

'You're not going already, are you?'

'I have to,' I said. 'I must get this over with.'

She was standing close, her hips brushing against mine. She touched my face with her fingers. They were cool from the chilled glass.

'Are you worried?'

'Scared stiff.' I hadn't told her about Teige. I didn't want her to know. It was nothing heroic. It was just that while no one else knew of the fears that haunted me they weren't mentioned. And that way I could fool myself they didn't exist.

'When do you have to leave?' she asked.

'A car's coming in an hour or so.'

She kissed me, her lips just tasting mine. I could smell the scent I'd bought her, feel her breasts nudging against me.

'A lot can happen in an hour.' She kissed me again and this time she closed her eyes, her mouth opening in invitation.

'There was a big demonstration the other day. The National

Reform Party and the SL and all the rest of those fascist pigs marching around with flags and banners.'

'When was this?'

'The day before yesterday – just after you'd gone. I went up to Wenceslas Square and had a look but I could hardly get near. The whole place was jammed with people.'

'What were they demonstrating about?'

'Nothing really, just showing us that they were there. It was more like a parade than a demonstration.' Jarka sat up, drawing the bedclothes around her hips and crossing her arms over her naked breasts. 'It was eerie. A lot of the men were in uniforms, black and khaki. Some of them had guns. And there were tanks.'

'Tanks? Where did they come from?'

'The newspapers said it was a peaceful rally but there were tanks parked in the street up by the National Museum. I could see them. They were like big iron toads.' She turned and looked at me in the dark. 'I thought we'd seen the last of them; I thought that was the whole point. No one seemed to be worried. No one apart from me seemed to be worried that there were tanks and uniforms in Prague again.'

'Was Kupka there?'

She nodded. 'He made a speech. On the steps of the museum, just above the place where that poor boy burned himself.'

During the Prague spring of '68, the country's only real attempt to overthrow the communists, a student from the philosophy faculty of the Charles University had set fire to himself in protest against the regime. It was an emotive part of the city's history, exactly the kind of thing Kupka would play on. He'd keep it subtle, just place himself near the memorial stone and let the collective imaginations of the audience make the connection for themselves.

'What did he talk about?'

'I don't really remember. I could hardly hear from where I was. But he used a lot of words like "destiny" and "cause".

The newspapers put all of them down; they had pictures of
him on the front page. But they didn't mention the tanks.'

'They're not going to pick a fight with him. Not yet. He's
too powerful.'

'It's frightening, isn't it?'

I rolled out of bed and began to tug on my clothes. 'If
Kupka begins to lose popularity the newspapers will suddenly
rediscover their souls and pitch into him.'

'But he's not going to lose popularity, is he?'

'No, probably not. Not yet anyway.' I sat on the edge of
the bed. Jarka had lain back. Her arms were spread out on
the sheet, the soft pads of her breasts pale in the moonlight.

'Do you have to go?' she asked.

'It's nearly ten.'

'Will you be back tonight?'

'No, probably not.' I'd no idea what was coming. The
future was a vague mist of possibilities. I said, 'I'll ring you.'

It was well after eleven when I arrived at Kupka's fortress
house in the hills, but that didn't bother me. Time was
running out. Even if Teige hadn't already given the game
away it wasn't going to be long before someone began to ask
where he was and why he hadn't returned. And if I was still
around when those questions were asked all hell was going
to break loose.

Lights were burning in many of the ground floor windows.
There were cars parked in the drive outside. Mirek opened
the door with the faint disinterest of a man who is spiritually
removed from the rest of the human race.

I followed him through to the dining-room.

The scene that greeted me as the double doors opened
could have come from another age. The room was in near
darkness. Candelabra lined the long table and the remains
of a log fire glowed in the hearth, the soft light of the two
flickering on cut-glass and silver ware and on the weapons
that lined the walls. Seated around the table were twelve or

more men, dressed formally in black tie. A hush settled over the room as I came in. Their heads turned towards me.

It was like being summoned before the Inquisition.

At the head of the table was Kupka. He made no movement, offered no sign of recognition, but through the candlelight I could feel his eyes on me, searching my face.

'So,' he said. 'You're back.' It was just a statement, devoid of any feeling, devoid of any real meaning.

I faced him down the length of the table. Now that I was here, the cold fear that had gripped me for the last few hours was gone. In its place was a fierce anticipation that burned in my veins like a raw spirit. I've met it before. It's the fire that spurs men into battle, that leads them to perform unaccountable acts of heroism. It's not bravery, just a madness.

'Your trip went without incident, I take it,' Kupka said.

'I sold your picture.'

'So I see.' His eyes burned into me.

'It's what you wanted.'

'Yes, Jan,' he said. 'You've done well; we're pleased with you.' He lifted one hand and made a sweeping gesture, taking in the darkened room, the silent figures around him. 'So, I'm here. I'm waiting. Now what is it that you wish to see me about so urgently?'

'I want to see the Ceauşescu paintings.'

He smiled. 'That's out of the question.'

'Then there's nothing more I can do for you.'

'You're asking too much.'

'No,' I said. 'It's you who are asking too much. I got that picture of yours out of the country, as I said I could. I found a buyer, as I said I could, and I've transferred the money into your account. I've done my part of the bargain. Now you must do yours.'

Kupka's head had sunk in his shoulders. 'You didn't get as much for the picture as you said.'

'You're lucky I managed to sell it at all. I'd promised my

clients that they were going to get some important pictures, pictures that haven't been seen for over fifty years, not a piece of junk that they could pick up at a local antique shop. It was a miracle they didn't throw it back in my face.'

'You're not seeing the paintings.'

'Then there's nothing more I can do for you. Unless I can take back something good in a hurry they're going to lose patience, and I can't say I blame them. Christ, so far they've got no real proof that you have these things at all.'

'You have my word.'

'And what's that worth?'

'That's enough!' Kupka said. His small eyes blazed in his head. 'Who are you to be making demands? Who are you to be issuing orders? You are an agent, a middleman. You will do as you're told.'

'In which case you won't make a penny. You say you want to sell these paintings but you make it impossible for anyone to buy them.'

'One,' he said. 'I'll give you one painting.'

'I have to see them all.'

Kupka held up a finger. 'One.'

'I can't do this blindfolded,' I told him. 'I need to be able to tell them what's there, what sort of quantity we're talking about.'

Kupka was about to say something more when Éva's voice cut across him.

'No, Jaroslav, he's right.'

Every face was turned to her.

She had come through the door at the far end of the room, dressed in a short black dress, its severe outline decorated with a single brooch that glittered in the villainous way of large diamonds. She strolled up to the table.

'If Jan is going to sell these pictures he must be allowed to see them,' she said. 'It's only fair.'

I expected Kupka to tell her not to interfere. But he didn't. He just looked at her with a thoughtful expression.

'Jan's proved himself a useful friend,' Éva said. She turned those slanted cat's eyes of hers to me. 'We must trust his judgement.'

Kupka shifted in his chair.

'Very well, my dear,' he said. 'If that's what you want we'll show them to him.' He lifted his glass, took a shot of whisky.

'You don't have to do it yourself,' I said. 'Your friend Teige could do it.'

Kupka put down his glass, slowly and deliberately, and stared at me across the candles.

'No,' he said softly. 'I'll do it myself.'

He knew. I swear that as he sat there, turning the glass in his thick fingers, his eyes hard as stones, he knew what had happened to Teige. But for some reason he wasn't letting on.

All he said was, 'Now can we be allowed to go to bed?'

I was shown up to the room overlooking the courtyard that I'd slept in before. I hadn't brought any luggage with me; I hadn't known I'd be staying. But someone had laid out a few essentials: soap, towel, a razor and toothbrush.

I washed and undressed and got into bed. The door hadn't been locked but I had the distinct feeling that I was a prisoner in this little chamber. Before leaving, Mirek had run his eyes around the room as though mentally assessing the escape routes.

But he needn't have bothered. I'd got what I'd come for already. I didn't need to go prowling around the house.

I'd had a long day but I didn't feel like sleeping. After my confrontation with Kupka the adrenalin was singing through my veins. I lay in the dark staring up at the ceiling.

After an hour or so, just as I was beginning to doze off, there was a sound in the passage outside.

I was suddenly wide awake.

The handle turned. But before I could move, the door

opened softly and Éva came into the room. She made a little gesture with her hand, forbidding any sort of remark. Closing the door silently behind her she crossed the room to stand at the end of my bed. The moonlight gleamed on her white silk dressing-gown. Against it I could see the silhouette of her sleek black hair.

'Seems to be a habit of yours,' I said. 'Walking around the house in your nightie.'

She ignored the comment and stood gazing down at me.

'How did you get that money?' she enquired.

'Hot chocolate—'

'What?'

'A cup of hot chocolate. You'll find it does wonders for your sleep.'

She frowned and gave a shake of her head. 'I'm not talking about that,' she said sharply. 'I want to know how you got so much money for that picture.'

I shifted up into a sitting position. The bedclothes fell away from my bare chest, but I don't think it was the first male torso she'd seen.

'I got it as an advance,' I told her. 'It was a sort of sign of goodwill on their part. I told them that the goose wasn't going to lay the golden egg until it was given a little sweetener.'

'That was convenient.'

'If I don't come back with something distinctly more tasty they'll have it back off me with interest.' It was closer to the truth than she knew.

'They can't have been too impressed when you told them you wanted thirty-five thousand pounds for it.'

'I didn't tell them I wanted that much. I told them you did.'

Éva nodded and her dark eyes flittered around the room. 'It wasn't very clever what you did just now.'

'I wanted to see the pictures.'

'You made Jaroslav angry. He doesn't like to be black-mailed, particularly in front of the others.'

'If I hadn't twisted his arm I could have been waiting for the cows to come home before I got anywhere.'

'You take too many risks,' she said. 'It's very foolish.'

She sounded annoyed and sulky as though I was a servant of hers who'd misbehaved. I shifted the direction of the conversation. 'How did you get hold of these paintings?'

Éva stood still as a statue.

'What makes you think it was me?'

'You're Romanian and you're the only one around here who seems to know anything about pictures.'

She thought for a moment. Then she sat on the end of the bed, sliding one of her magnificent white-clad thighs onto the eiderdown. I could feel it pressing against my leg.

'They were a sort of inheritance,' she said.

'You must have some useful relatives.'

'It wasn't like that.' In the darkness I could feel her eyes studying me. 'When the revolution started they were taken out of the palace and hidden for safety. The task was given to a senior officer in the army. He was executed a few days later. After that no one knew where they were. It had been kept a secret, you see.'

'But you knew, did you?'

Éva looked at me in silence. Then she said, 'He was a friend of mine.'

I refrained from making a comment. A woman can always get more out of a man than a trained interrogator. Provided she's good enough in bed, that is.

I said, 'So you thought you'd take them.'

She gave a toss of her head, the long black snake of her hair glistened. 'Why not? They didn't belong to anybody else.'

'Finders keepers.'

'You can be very glib,' she said crossly. 'I don't like that in you.'

'They're valuable are they? I mean really valuable?'

'As if you'd know.'

I wasn't going to be put down that easily. 'I hear there's a Raphael madonna.'

Her head turned quickly. 'What makes you think that?'

I couldn't very well tell her that an expert in London had spent some time assessing what may be in the collection. His report on the subject had been passed on to Whitehall where it was passed around until eventually it ended up on my desk. So I said, 'Just a rumour.'

'You'll have to wait and see what's there for yourself.' She slid herself off the bed, the white silk robe gleaming as she straightened up. She glanced across at the door and then back at me. 'You realise that what you are doing is very unwise. Once you've seen those pictures you know more than you should and that's dangerous.'

'That had occurred to me.'

'I'm glad,' she said softly. 'It's important you understand what you are doing. Jaroslav can be very . . . brutal when he has to be.'

CHAPTER NINETEEN

For most of the next day I waited.

Kupka had gone into Prague at crack of dawn without leaving any instructions for me, or even indicating when he might be returning. The shadowy figures who had provided the decorative border to the dinner table the night before had also evaporated. So I was left to roam about the house by myself.

Not that I was by myself, as I discovered the first time I tried going outside. A couple of heavies had been laid on to keep me company. They kept their distance, never getting close enough to talk to, never talking to each other for that matter, just standing silently watching me wherever I went. Why they were thought necessary I can't imagine. An electric fence that can keep out intruders can easily keep in one man who doesn't want to escape.

Éva put in an appearance later that morning. She was dressed ready for riding in a black jacket and starched white stock, her hair tucked into a hair-net. I asked her when I was going to see the paintings but she just shrugged.

'When Jaroslav comes back, I imagine.'

'When's that?'

She didn't like to be questioned. 'You're very impatient. It doesn't do any good to be so impatient.' And with that she removed herself, driving off down into the valley in her Mercedes.

Around one Mirek announced that the chef had prepared lunch for me. So I sat in the kitchen and ate a plate of sandwiches while my two shadows stood outside in the passage and allowed themselves the indulgence of a brief conversation. I don't know why they didn't talk more. Maybe they didn't like each other. I can't say I blamed them. I didn't like them much myself.

It wasn't until later that afternoon, just as it was beginning to get dark, that a blue van turned up, winding its way up the valley to park outside the front door. The driver got out and had a word with the two heavies. One of them put his fingers in his mouth and gave me a whistle.

I went across to them.

'And there I was thinking we were never going to meet,' I said affably.

He told me to shut up and get in.

There were no windows in the rear of the van. Come to that, there were no seats either, just a few straw bales rowed up on either side. I sat down on one of them. The two heavies took up position opposite, knees apart, hands clasped in the cleft of their thighs.

'Where are we off to then?' I asked.

They didn't answer, just stared at me with their pale Slav faces. It was the first time I'd been able to take a look at them at close range. They were a solid, powerful looking pair with that strange sense of stillness that comes to all potentially violent men. Pinned to the lapel of their leather jackets were the red badges of the SL, the circle with a lightning flash through the centre. I wondered whether these two had been part of that uniformed army that Jarka had seen parading around Wenceslas Square.

The door was slammed shut and we moved off. I could feel the van rolling from side to side as it made its way down into the valley. It stopped for the gates to be opened and then swung to the right as it came out into the road.

After that I couldn't say where we went.

You hear of kidnap victims who manage to calculate the route they are driven along; clever-dicks who catch the sound of a waterfall, get a bearing on a church bell, memorise each turn in the road so that they can reconstruct every mile of the journey when they come back later on. But I didn't hear anything that could help me.

All the time the two heavies sat and stared at my face as though trying to read my mind. They needn't have bothered. For all I knew we were on the moon.

But it wasn't hard to realise that we had driven into Prague. I could hear the jangling of the tram bells and the roar of their steel wheels, feel the thrumming of our own tyres over cobbles. But where we were in the city was impossible to tell. For half an hour the van kept swinging around, lurching to a halt and moving off again. I wouldn't have been surprised if the driver wasn't taking us around in circles just to keep me disorientated.

Finally it swung sharply to the left, bumped over a ramp and came to a halt. The driver slid open his door and banged on the side of the van. One of the two heavies reached down behind the straw bale and took out a canvas sack.

They put it over my head.

And suddenly I was in darkness, that total and impenetrable darkness where all sense of space and balance are lost. Unceremoniously they pulled the sack down to my waist and tightened the neck.

I could hardly breathe.

One of them gave an answering bang on the door and I heard it open. Strong hands grasped my shoulders, pulling me out of the van. I stumbled as my feet reached the ground but they held me upright, propelling me forwards.

'Steps,' one of them said after a few yards.

He didn't say whether they went up or down. But I discovered a moment later when the ground disappeared beneath my feet. Again I lost my footing and would have gone plunging down head first if they hadn't held me.

Cautiously I made my way down gritty stone steps. I was beginning to sweat inside that sack. The air was growing stale.

My head was filled with the thick, overpowering stench of the canvas. It was like some resin. I've never been claustrophobic but as I stumbled down in the darkness I began to understand what it must be like.

I didn't count, but we must have gone down thirty steps before the ground levelled out. I was pushed forwards a few yards and then brought to a halt.

I stood there, swaying slightly. In the blackness of the sack I could plainly hear water dripping, sense the men who stood around me.

Then Kupka's voice said, 'Ah, so you've made it, Jan.'

I turned around, trying to identify where he was.

He gave a little chuckle. 'My, my, you are a picture. What a sight. You should see yourself.'

'I'd like to see something,' I said.

'Yes, of course. Can't keep you trussed up like this all night, can we?'

He must have given some sign because I felt the ropes around my waist loosen and the sack came off over my head.

The sudden brightness of the lights blinded me but the air was cold and fresh as a mountain stream and I drank it in gratefully.

'So,' Kupka said after a moment. 'Here you are, Jan.'

I blinked over to where he was standing ten yards away in the arch of a stone doorway. He wore a long black overcoat and a Homburg hat on his head. In one hand he held a rolled umbrella. It looked very small against his huge bulk.

'Really,' he said, looking me over in mild disapproval. 'The things you do to earn a crust.'

'It's more than a crust I'm after.'

'Your hair's a mess,' he said.

I couldn't see that he could complain about my appearance but I combed my fingers over my head. Now that my eyes were growing accustomed to the light I could see that we were in a low, vaulted cellar. My two guardians were standing on either side of me, silent and respectful now that they were in the presence of their master.

'Come along then,' Kupka said.

I followed him through the arched doorway into a long passage. Naked bulbs dangled from the ceiling. Beyond it another cellar, the darkened entrance of a passage opening on the far side. It's like this in Prague. The whole subterranean world was linked together during the war, cellars knocked through into the next, so that it could be used as an air-raid shelter.

Kupka walked ahead of us through this labyrinth, his hands in his pockets, the umbrella dangling from his forearm. Eventually, at the end of a passageway, we came to a wooden balcony. It overlooked a single large room.

It must have been fifty feet underground but it was carved and columned, the ceiling spanned with graceful fan vaulting, like a banqueting hall.

I stood on the balcony beside Kupka and looked down at the floor. It was divided into rows by plywood panels, all about ten foot high. And on them hung paintings.

Hundreds of them.

'There,' Kupka said. He ran his hand around in an arc that took in the whole display laid out beneath us. 'Is that what you've been looking for?'

'Yes,' I said. 'I think it is.' I could feel the excitement beginning to wake in my stomach, puttering up into my veins like one of those old outboard motors starting up. They were here. I'd found them. Until that moment I hadn't dared believe I'd do it; I hadn't really known whether they existed at all. But now they were here, in my grasp.

I followed Kupka down the steps.

Three more men were waiting at the bottom. They were armed with bulky automatics at their waists. The two guardian angels who'd brought me had removed themselves, gone back to the entrance. It wouldn't do to have unexpected guests arrive while we were in conference.

Now that we were here, Kupka had lost his earlier caution and was keen to show me round the display. I think he wanted me to see them, he wanted me to appreciate this legacy that had fallen into his hands.

Together we walked down the avenue of paintings, while he pointed out battle scenes, huge portraits and little sketchy landscapes that caught his eye. Occasionally he would turn one, showing me the eagle motif stamped on the canvas.

'I think of them as orphans,' he said. 'Small, helpless creatures evacuated during the war for their own safety only to find themselves lost at the end of it, to be passed from one institution to another with no one to care for them.'

It was a fanciful idea and maybe he believed it. It's extraordinary the notions that people will come up with to convince themselves they have a right to what is not theirs.

'Now it's up to you,' he went on in that warm, hospitable voice of his. 'To find them real homes where they will be loved and cherished.'

'In return for vast sums of money.'

'Of course,' he agreed. 'But for you as well as me. What do you make of this one?'

We were standing in front of a large picture full of fawns and satyrs and plump girls whose clothes wouldn't stay on. But I hardly gave the thing a glance. I was trying to work out where we were, what part of Prague we had burrowed beneath. But there was nothing I could see to give me a clue.

'These are good paintings,' Kupka said seriously as we moved on. 'Highly important pictures.'

The pillars that supported the ceiling were ornate, with carved animals and twists of foliage around the top. They had to be old. But that wasn't saying much: all the cellars in Prague are old. I felt a clutch of panic. I was never going to be able to find this place again. Any minute now my time would be up. I'd be put into that stinking sack and taken away and I'd never be able to work my way back.

'What are you going to do with all the money you're going to make from these?' Kupka asked.

'Invest it,' I said with the kind of nonchalant shrug I thought a shrewd art dealer would use. 'Buy more pictures; plough it back into the system.'

'Will you come back to live in Prague?

'I could do. It hadn't occurred to me, but I could do.' I ran my eyes around the cold, ill-lit interior. There must be some clue to where I was: a date, a coat of arms. But there was nothing that caught my attention, just damp walls and bare flagstones. Over in one corner was a small door, metal framed and studded with nails, but that was no help. There must be a thousand of those in Prague.

I'd been silent too long. I glanced back at Kupka. 'Why do you ask?'

'No reason. But I'd be interested to know if you came back here. I could use a man like you.'

'I'm just a civil servant.'

'You say that but you are resourceful. You get what you want. I can always use a man who gets what he wants.'

'I'm not committed to any political party,' I told him mechanically. The paintings were here, hanging all around me on the panels. Maybe I should finish it now. Forget about trying to get back later, seize the opportunity and destroy them while I had the chance. They'd burn wouldn't they? All this wood and canvas, it would go up like a bonfire.

Kupka gave a little chuckle. He was standing in front of me, his hands planted in his pockets, his head cocked to one side as he studied me.

'I don't believe you,' he said. 'You say you have no interest in these things but you're determined to sell these pretty things here.'

'That's for the money. I told you from the start, I'm only interested in the money.'

'And I think you're one of us,' Kupka said softly. 'I've been watching you, Jan. I think you want to see this country on its feet again, capable of looking after itself.'

Two of the three men were over by the steps. They were leaning against the wall, off-guard, disinterested. The other was standing a few yards back behind Kupka. If I were to get his pistol I might be able to hold the others. I could put it to Kupka's head. They'd never dare fire with a gun stuck up their master's ear, would they? But how would I ever get a fire started?

When I made no reply, Kupka flattered himself with the notion that I was thinking over what he'd said. He gave a grunt and said, 'I'm right, aren't I?'

I could feel the adrenalin beginning to pound in my blood. I was going to have to do it; I was going to have to give it a go. I'd no idea how to get the fire started; I'd no idea how I was going to get out of the place afterwards, but I was going to have to try.

There was no alternative.

Kupka was talking now; talking about the future, about how it was going to be, but I wasn't listening. I was measuring the distance between myself and the armed guard standing behind him. Five paces, maybe six. He was powerfully built but heavy-bellied. And he wasn't concentrating. He'd be slow. And I had surprise on my side.

'What do you say?' Kupka asked. 'It's not like you to be so dull-witted, Jan.'

'I need time to think.'

'Think? You don't want to think, Jan; you want to react, follow your instincts.'

There was a sound in the passageway above. I looked round at the rows of paintings. I could feel the blood racing in my veins. That madness, that sudden desire to defy every judgement of common sense and instinct, was coming over me.

It had to be now.

Kupka was staring at me. His eyes were suddenly angry. 'What are you waiting for?'

I opened my mouth to reply but didn't speak. From the passage above I could hear footsteps, coming towards us, slow and erratic. I looked down at the two men standing at the foot of the stairs.

They had heard the sound too. They were looking up. It was too late. The moment was passing. I tensed to move. Kupka sensed it. I think at that moment he realised what was happening.

He stepped back a pace.

'Jesus Christ,' he whispered.

At that moment a figure limped out of the passageway on to the balcony above our head.

And I recognised him.

I recognised the skull-like head; I recognised the pale eyes and the thinning hair; I recognised the look of hatred in his face as he pointed one arm down at me and screamed, 'Stop him!'

It was Ivan Teige.

CHAPTER TWENTY

He looked like a figure from hell. His neck was braced, a bandage wrapped round his forehead. One arm was clamped to a crutch, his right leg in plaster. In the blackest grip of a nightmare you could never see a more terrible sight than Ivan Teige as he stood on that balcony, his eyes red-rimmed, mouth stretched wide as he shouted down at me.

What he was saying I didn't hear. My mind was numb. I stared back at him stupidly. He couldn't be there. I knew he couldn't be there. I'd seen him slither over the edge of that cliff.

Teige was dead.

The others were beginning to move. Like a slowed-down film, I saw the two men at the foot of the steps come towards me. Frame by frame they broke into a run. The heavy-bellied one closest to me was crouching. His gun was in his hand. The barrel was raised. I could feel them closing in on me. Only Kupka remained still but he seemed to be growing in size, swelling up in fury like a barrage balloon rising from the ground.

My limbs reacted before my mind had comprehended what was happening. I began to run, falling backwards, turning as I went. Without worrying where I was heading, I fled down the avenue of paintings. Huge canvases loomed overhead. They were dark and flat, stretching away down an endless corridor.

Then there was someone at the far end. He appeared suddenly. I cannoned into him before he could loose off the gun in his hand. He threw his arms around me. I brought my knee up into his groin, heard the breath burst out of his lungs and he fell aside.

But I had lost momentum. Someone caught me by the shoulder, spun me round. I gripped him by the arm, aimed a kick at his shins. Then came a blow from behind.

The lights burst before my eyes. Slowly the room toppled over on to me and I fell into the dark hole beneath.

I have only the vaguest image of what happened next. I remember lying on my back with someone's foot on my face. He was stamping on me, slowly and repeatedly. I rolled from side to side but the foot kept pounding on my face.

I opened my eyes but there was nothing there.

Voices were speaking in the distance. I felt a blow in my ribs. I could sense space behind my back and none in front. Gradually I realised I was lying on my face. It wasn't a foot pressed against me but the ground.

My head was heavy. I turned it to one side. I was still rocking from side to side.

That part was real.

I was in the back of that van. I could see a couple of legs close to me. I tried moving but someone gave me another kick. That was real also. Dimly I heard a voice say he'd do it again if I didn't lie still.

I did as I was told.

I could feel pain now. It was lapping up my spine into my neck, like waves breaking against a beach, growing stronger all the while until it burst into my head. I gave a groan. There was blood on the metal floor. I moved my tongue to speak but there was more in my mouth.

I must have passed out again because the next thing I recall was the doors of the van being wrenched open. I was dragged out of the back. There were bright lights blinding my eyes, gravel beneath my feet. Above me loomed a black silhouette. It had turrets and gables.

I was back at Kupka's house.

*   *   *

They took me inside. Through a side entrance, into the
kitchens. Low lights, gleaming aluminium, the terracotta
flagstones passing jerkily beneath me.

The door at the far end was opened and I was hauled down
into the wine cellars. The two men holding me were in front.
I could hear something clattering down the stairs behind but
I guess that was my feet.

Lights came on. The racks of wine bottles glinted darkly.

They dropped me down on the stone floor. My coat was
unbuttoned and torn off my shoulders, the shirt after it. I
heard the material rip as they pulled the sleeves clear of
my hands.

One of them straddled my head and lashed a rope around
my wrists. As he worked I could see the little red badge on
his lapel jiggling about.

I was going right off that cursed symbol.

The other was on a chair. There was a metal ring in the
ceiling, set in the boss of the vault ribs. Stretching up, he
poked the tip of the rope through and jumped down again,
drawing it with him as he came.

Immediately I felt the tension on my wrists. It pulled my
arms up in the air. Then the two of them put their weight on
the rope and I was swung up off the ground into a standing
position. They tugged again and my body stretched upwards,
arms wrenching in the sockets of my shoulders.

They tied off the rope and I was left dangling there, neither
quite standing nor hanging. The two men stood before me,
silent, impassive. Why did the bastards never need to speak?
Could they communicate by telepathy? One of them gave my
chest a push and I swung round in a slow circle, my feet
dragging sluggishly along the ground.

Satisfied with their work they drew away. One sat down
on the chair, the other leaned against the wall. They watched
me in silence. I don't know what they expected to happen.

I wasn't going anywhere.

*   *   *

For over an hour I hung there with the eyes of the two men on me. My back was aching, shoulders screaming with pain. But I tried not to think of it. Pain develops if you allow yourself to dwell on it. I counted the wine racks, multiplied the number by five, then by seventeen, forcing myself to concentrate on the calculations. From time to time I rolled my head around, trying to loosen the knotted muscles, grunting with the effort.

The two men watched. They weren't curious or amused; they weren't even interested. I thought of what I might do to them if I could get my wrists free. It made me laugh and that's a dangerous sign. I started on another mathematical calculation.

Then came the sound of footsteps on the stairs. I craned my head around to see.

It was Ivan Teige.

He limped over to me, the long black overcoat flapping. His sunken eyes were bright and feverish. They flickered across my body to the rope above, checking the job had been done to his specifications. Then he parted his lips over his teeth in a smile.

'So, Capek,' he said softly. 'It looks like it's over for you.'

I opened my mouth to tell him what I thought of him but no sound came out.

'You were so close, weren't you?' he said, caressing the words with pleasure as he spoke. 'You must have been so pleased with yourself. What a shame that I had to turn up just as you'd found what you were looking for. You can never have guessed that was going to happen, can you? You can never have dreamt that I would come back to foul up your plans.'

He was speaking quietly, as if this were some private confidence that he didn't want the others to hear.

'You thought I was finished; you thought I was done for. But you were wrong. That was a miscalculation on your part. You should have checked, you should have made sure before you went. It was a mistake and now you'll pay for it.'

He turned and hobbled over to the two men, the crutch tapping on the stone floor. They spoke together. The one on the seat came over to me. He stood there for a moment, sizing me up, his head cocked to one side. Then, taking a leather-bound cosh from his pocket, he swung back his arm and hit me in the ribs.

It knocked the wind from my lungs so that I couldn't even cry out as the pain seared up through my chest. I swung around on the rope and he hit me in the kidneys and then again in the ribs, further up at the base of the shoulder. I couldn't breathe. My lungs were screaming for air but as each blow smacked into my helpless flesh the muscles constricted around my throat so that I just hung there, choking and panting, the sweat pouring down my body.

This wasn't any sort of random beating, it was a professional operation delivered by a man who knew how to inflict pain. And all the while Teige stood watching, nodding in satisfaction. After a dozen or more swings of the cosh, he barked out an order, commanding my tormentor to stop his work.

I saw that another man had come into the cellar. He was carrying a canvas bag and a length of bamboo cane. Teige went across to him, his crutch a sharp staccato rhythm on the floor, and took them from him. He had the chair placed a few feet in front of me, commanding it to be moved a few inches to the side and a shade closer, before sitting down and taking the canvas bag on his lap. Unclipping the crutch from his arm he rested it against the side of the chair and opened the flap of the bag.

I watched in a cold fascination as he took out a heavy battery and set it on the floor before him. Attached to the terminals was a length of flex, on the other end a small black box. Teige took it from the bag and cradled it in his hands.

'How much do you know about electricity, Capek?' he enquired conversationally. 'Did you learn about it at school? Did you pick up the basics while they were training you to spy for your country?' His eyes flickered up to me.

'Not your country, of course. Just the one you've sold yourself to.'

His fingers were busy on the black box, screwing a second flex to the brass terminals.

'The principle is not difficult to understand. Electricity is like a river. You can think of the amps as the width of the river and the voltage as the speed of the water flowing through it.' Taking the loose end of the flex he separated the two exposed wires that protruded from the end, stripping away the insulating cover with a knife. 'It's quite simple really. If you make the river narrower, less water gets through so it has to flow faster; if you make it wider more is allowed to get by, but it travels that much slower. You get my point? Either way the quantity is the same.'

Taking the bamboo cane, Teige held the flex to one end and bound it in place with insulating tape.

'This battery I have here is only twelve volts. There's nothing dangerous about that. It'll hardly give you a shock. But by passing it through this adaptor I can accelerate the voltage a hundred times. And that makes it quite a different proposition. It becomes suddenly very dangerous, very dangerous indeed.'

Carefully he parted the two wires at the tip of the cane so that it resembled a two-pronged fork. His pale eyes came up to me. They were bright with expectation.

'But fortunately, because the voltage is increased, the ampage is severely reduced. That means it will give you a shock but it won't actually kill you.' He stood up, the electric prong in his hand. 'Not,' he added almost to himself, 'for a long time, that is.'

Now that the moment he'd been waiting for had come he was unhurried, almost lazy. He was tantalising himself, prolonging the delicious sensation of anticipation.

There was a sound from the staircase and he glanced round.

It was Éva. Dressed in black, with long legs and bare arms.

Silently she came into the cellar and leaned against one of the wine racks in the darkness.

She'd come to watch. The bitch had come to watch me die.

Teige gave her a respectful little bow. It was all manners and courtesy now, a ritual that was going to be acted out like some medieval play.

Then he took a step towards me, placing his plastered foot on the ground, shuffling the other in behind, slowly limping his way up close. There was a sheen of sweat on his upper lip.

I pressed my head between my straining shoulders. Suddenly I wanted to talk, to shout abuse at the bloodless vampire.

'Where did you learn these tricks then, Ivan? I thought you were a journalist. I didn't know journalists were taught how to torture people.'

'Don't talk, Capek. It's too late to be clever now.' Teige held the forked wires up to my face. The exposed filaments were ragged and bushy.

'Where did you learn to do it then?'

'Silence!'

'What was it? The StB—?' My voice cut short as the prongs touched the base of my neck. There was a sharp crack. Pain shot up my body like a firework and every nerve-end screamed in unison. I felt my body jerking with the current, the rope biting into my wrists.

Then I slumped down, my head lolling to one side.

'That's it, isn't it?' I said weakly. The compulsion to talk was driving the words out of my throat. 'You were one of them, weren't you Ivan? You were one of those bastards who tortured and maimed people for fun. You were a communist pig along with all the others—'

Again the words vanished in a scream as the prongs dug into my flesh and my body jerked and kicked as the pain went spearing through me.

'You're all the same!' I spat the words out of my mouth. Sweat was pouring down into my eyes. Across the darkened room I could see Éva leaning against the wine rack. Her lips were parted, her thighs pressed together. One knee had raised itself as she watched, exposing the top of her stocking.

Then the prong went into one armpit. The pain was an explosion. Every muscle and fibre of my body was cramped in agony. I shouted some more, the words almost meaningless now, just a spark of life that I could feel and hold on to.

'You're all the same – fascist, communist – you're all the bloody same.' And the prongs were in my stomach and my back was arching until I thought it would break.

Gradually, as the shocks burnt through me, I felt my strength begin to go. Defiance was ebbing away. I shouted and babbled out words but they had little meaning. Resistance was weakening; the will to survive was slipping away. Like it or not, I was giving in. And strangely I felt my mind beginning to detach itself from the experience.

I was no longer thinking.

Like a wreath of smoke my thoughts lifted out of my head and rose up to the ceiling. I could see myself hanging there on the end of the rope, jerking and dancing to each touch of that pronged fork, the blood streaming down my arms from the knots cutting into my wrists. I could see Teige, the hatred iridescent in his white face, and beyond him Éva watching in silent enjoyment. From a distance I could hear the screams of pain that poured from my throat and the blubbering for breath that came in the pauses between.

Then slowly and serenely my thoughts floated on up into darkness and I passed out.

I'd lost all sense of time.

I don't know whether it was hours or minutes before consciousness began to return. At first it was just a notion, a sense of being. Then gradually I became aware of the straining of my arms. The bruising of my body came awake, throbbing slowly and sickeningly.

I opened my eyes but could distinguish nothing. My head

was on its side. I pulled it upright and the cellar swam into focus. Memory returned, scene by scene.

I craned my head around but the place was deserted. The light was still on but Teige and his cronies had gone. They'd probably called it off when I passed out. It's no fun torturing someone who can no longer feel pain.

Above my head I heard the rope creaking in the silence.

For an hour or more I hung there, drifting on the edge of consciousness before a sound caught my attention.

The door at the head of the staircase had opened. There were soft footsteps.

It would be Teige returning to finish off his work. He'd be waiting for me to come round. I turned my head towards him.

But it was not Teige that I saw emerging out of the shadows but Éva. She was still in her black dress but her shoes were off. Silently she crossed the floor on stockinged feet.

'Give you a thrill, does it?' The words were a croak in my throat.

'Keep your voice down,' she hissed. 'If it hadn't been for me you'd be dead by now.'

There was a knife in her hand. For a moment I thought she was going to use it on me but reaching up on tiptoes she put it to the rope around my wrist. With small grunts of exertion she tried to cut it through but she wasn't tall enough to get any pressure on the blade. Hurrying across the floor she picked up the chair and set it at my feet, clambering up on to the seat.

Her firm stomach was pressed against my face, her hips rocking from side to side as she sawed at the rope. I could smell her scent, feel the softness of her dress. Then the rope parted and I fell to the ground, a groan breaking from my lips as the muscles were jerked from the position they'd been locked in all these hours. Éva was unsympathetic.

'Be quiet!'

I rolled over, feeling my stiffened arms cracking as the blood flowed through them again.

'Get up,' she ordered impatiently.

I was trying but it wasn't easy. Massaging my shoulders I made it up to a kneeling position. Éva stood above me, her legs apart, hands on her hips. Her voice was urgent.

'For God's sake get up! They'll be back in a few minutes.'

I stumbled up on to my feet. Strength was returning, flooding through my veins like a warm glow.

Without waiting to see if I was following, Éva darted across the floor and up the stairs, a flash of darkness in the shadows. As soon as we were in the kitchen she closed the cellar door and locked it.

'Why are you doing this?' I asked her but she gave an angry toss of her head.

'Don't ask questions. Just go.'

'I must know—'

'Just go!'

We came out into the darkened passage. Éva pushed me in the direction of the rear door and without another word she was gone, disappearing silently into the house.

I was confused by this sudden turn of events but I wasn't going to stand around puzzling over it right now. If fate hands you an unexpected bonus you grab it and ask questions afterwards.

Keeping to the wall I made my way down the passage, not moving too fast. Nothing gives the game away quicker than the sound of running feet. Antlered heads lined the way, a mirror glinted in the moonlight.

Half-way down the passage was a door leading outside. It was the one I'd been through before. I put my hand on the knob, opened it a crack and looked out.

Through the narrow aperture I could see the courtyard, the silhouette of the outhouses beyond. Clouds were racing overhead. At the head of the steps stood a guard. He was leaning against the parapet, his arms locked around his chest in the cold night air.

I tested the door. It was heavy and solid. And it opened outwards.

I rapped on it a couple of times and started waggling the heavy knob from side to side.

Then I stepped back a pace.

I heard the guard turn around at the sound. He came over to investigate, his footsteps crunching on the stone. As his shadow passed the crack of light I lifted one foot and kicked the heavy door out at him.

There was a muffled thump as it made contact. He gave a curse and fell back against the parapet. I stepped outside. The door had caught him a beauty. In the moonlight I could see he was clutching his face, his nose pouring blood. But he was still upright. The door had practically staved in his skull but he wasn't out cold. Catching sight of me he staggered to regain his balance.

But he was too late.

Grasping him by the lapels of his jacket I swung him round, driving his head into the wall. I felt the impact run through his body. And with that he retired from the immediate proceedings, falling to the ground with a clatter.

I ran over to the head of the steps and then, on second thoughts, went back to where he lay. Taking him by the shoulders I pulled his jacket off and put it on. It was brown leather and warm as an electric blanket. Pinned on the lapel was that little red badge.

I'd just joined the club.

Tucked in his belt was an automatic pistol. I took that too. Just a precaution. I've noticed that if you are polite but firm people will do what you want. If you have a gun in your hand at the time you don't have to bother with the politeness bit.

Hurrying down the steps I crossed the courtyard. It was lit only by a single bracket lamp above the doorway to the outhouses so I can't have been more than a shadow as I slipped by.

There was only one way out and that was through the big entrance gate which led out on to the driveway.

And that was a different proposition altogether.

The front of the house was illuminated by powerful floodlights. It was like some stage set out there, every detail clear as day.

I stood in the comforting darkness of the archway, my back to the wall, and looked out across the expanse of gravel. A couple of cars were parked out there, along with the blue van I'd been locked into.

They were only twenty yards away but it could have been a mile.

The unnatural white lights burned up from the ground beyond, cold and merciless. Nothing could pass them unnoticed. I thought of those border fences I'd known in the old days: the barbed wire, the trip ropes, the orders barked out over the megaphones, the machine gun posts standing like skinny black silhouettes in the glare of the lights. And I felt sick.

I couldn't go through with it.

I looked back at the darkened courtyard, the mountain of the house above. It was only a matter of time before Teige found I had gone from the cellar, only a matter of time before that guard came too and raised the alarm. I took the pistol from my pocket, checked that the chamber was loaded. I tucked it into my belt and turning up the collar of the leather jacket I stepped out into the bright light.

I wanted to run. Every instinct in my body pleaded for the chance to run, to sprint across that space into the sheltering darkness beyond. But I made myself walk, my legs unsteady, hands trembling in my pockets, eyes fixed on the far side of the driveway.

The gravel crunched beneath my feet. It was loud enough to wake the dead. I could feel my shoulders tingling. At every step I was expecting to hear sudden cries behind me, alarms going off in the night, the sudden crack of a rifle.

But there was nothing.

I reached the cars. Instinctively I glanced in the window of one but there were no keys dangling invitingly from the ignition. They wouldn't have done me any good if they had been there. I was never going to drive out past that gate-house down in the valley.

The lights were before me now. I could see them planted in the ground just a few feet away. I couldn't hold myself any longer and bounded forwards, diving into the wonderful cover of the pitch blackness beyond. And then I was running as fast as I could go, my legs hammering over the rocky ground in relief.

The hillside fell away sharply and I plunged down a few feet, tumbling over. As I came to a halt I rolled over on my side and lay for a moment panting hard. The great house was above me, bright and menacing against the night sky. But I knew I was invisible from it now.

I looked around. Earlier that morning I'd spent some time examining the crag of rock on which the house stood. I hadn't realised at the time how useful that knowledge was going to be.

I knew that directly below me was a cliff-face, not impossible to get down in daylight but extremely dangerous at night. And I didn't fancy ending up in a heap at the base of it as Teige had done. I might not be as lucky as he had been.

Further round was a ravine. I remember thinking that it would have been the only means of approach for an invading force. Methodically I worked my way around the crest of the hill, losing height whenever I had the chance.

All the time the brilliantly lit edifice of the house loomed above me and I felt the lurch of panic in my belly again. I wasn't getting away from it. It was twenty minutes or more since I crossed the driveway and I was still no further away from the place. I forced myself to look down, to concentrate on the rocky terrain beneath my hands and feet.

Then I found it, a deep crevasse in the rock, strewn with

boulders. Lying on my back I slithered downwards, letting gravity take me, steadying the fall with my feet and my elbows. In places I was able to stand and run forwards, clambering and jumping between the rocks. Somewhere below me there was water. I could hear it chattering and splashing in the cleft of the rocks. A stone dislodged beneath me and I fell, rolling over on my face until I came to a halt against a boulder in a shower of little stones. A knife edge of pain drove in between my ribs and I realised for the first time that at least two of them were broken, the legacy of that leather cosh.

I was picking myself up, the acrid smell of earth and torn moss in my nostrils when a commotion broke out from the house above. There were raised voices, shouted orders. I heard a car door slam shut, its tyres tearing at the gravel as it moved away and I knew that whatever headstart I had given myself was over.

Someone had found I was missing; someone had raised the alarm.

From where I was I couldn't be seen, but I crouched low against the hillside, feeling that fierce charge of energy, part fear and part excitement, that every hunted animal knows.

Keeping low I moved on, dodging between the trees, feeling the sting of branches whipping against my face. Half a mile off to my right, and only a little below me now, the lights in the gate-house had come on. Three or four men had spilled from the doorway. I could see them pulling on their jackets, kicking the sleep from their minds. One was shouting instructions and above his voice I heard the sound I dread most: the baying of dogs.

I ran for my life.

The ground was levelling out now and I was able to move more quickly, bounding over the grassy patches, scrambling across rocks and fallen trees. I could see a clearing in front of me. It was the road. It had to be the road. I felt a surge of excitement. I ran out into the open and stopped dead in my tracks. It wasn't the road.

It was the electric fence.

I'd forgotten about it. In my determination to get down the rock face I'd completely forgotten about the electric fence that ran around the base of the crag.

It stood in that clearing, glinting wickedly in the moonlight; ten foot tall and completely impassable.

I felt like falling down and weeping on the ground. Until that moment I'd thought I had done it; I'd thought I was free. Instead I was caught like a rat in a trap. I looked through the wire mesh at the open ground beyond. It seemed so close, so easy to reach but I knew that if I came within a few inches of that fence it would burn me until I was a blackened cinder.

In the distance I heard the dogs.

It filled me with a cold, primeval fear. Without thinking where I was going or what I intended to do I began to run along the line of the fence – just getting away, putting a few extra yards between myself and those creatures.

I was easily visible out there, I realised. I headed back into the shelter of the trees, scrambling up a rise in the hill. There was a pile of logs in front of me. They were the trunks of fir trees, stripped of their branches, gleaming ghostly in the dark. They must have been felled to clear the ground for the fence.

A spark of hope flashed into my mind. A chance; there was just a chance. I clambered up on the pile and tried to shift one of the logs. It was too heavy. I lay down and kicked at it with my heel. It moved, rocking from side to side. I gave it another kick, catching the rhythm, waiting until it was on the crest of its rise and kicked again. Two more and it dislodged and went clattering down the pile.

I watched, holding my breath, as it rolled down towards the fence.

But it didn't have the momentum. Bucking a couple of times over the rocks it came to a halt a few feet from the base.

I swore under my breath. It wasn't much but it had been something, an idea, a possibility. Now the gleam of light it had offered was extinguished and I was faced again with the bleak prospect of running until I was caught. Worse than that, I had wasted valuable time.

I scrambled down to the ground and paused to listen. The dogs were there, distant but audible. Then the log lying out there caught my attention.

It was taller than the fence. And it was heavy.

I ran down to it and took hold of the narrower end, dragging it away from the fence. Lifting it up I hefted it on to my shoulder, dropping to my knees with the effort. Pushing it up again, arms straightening, I struggled up to my feet and began to raise it into a standing position.

The baying of the dogs was closer now. It gave me a desperate strength. Grunting with the effort, the cords of my neck standing out like guy ropes I lifted that tree trunk, walking my hands down its length, forcing its head up into the night sky. At one point it unbalanced and I had to fight it, legs braced, lungs straining for air. But gradually I regained control of it and began to move it upwards until I had it on its end, its base ten yards from the fence.

There was a yelping sound in the trees to my right. A hundred yards away, maybe more. It was the dogs; they had picked up my scent. They'd be coming now, homing in on their prey.

Cradling the tree in my hands, directing it as it began to move, I let it topple forwards. Half-way down I added my own weight, thrusting down on the base with all my strength.

It came slicing down out of the sky, picking up speed as it went, and plunging headlong into the fence. There was a crash. The air was suddenly alive with brilliant blue sparks that crackled up into the sky. Above it I heard the shrieks and twangs of wires breaking under unbearable tension.

The fence sagged under the pressure but it wasn't crushed as I'd hoped it would be. The tree bounced lazily on the wire and came to a halt, lying at an angle across the mesh with its head about my own height off the ground. From the sullen crackles and the sparks that fingered their way along the wires I realised that the current was still alive.

But the tree had done its job. It lay there like a gang-plank. All I had to do was climb up it. I stood back, assessing the task and at that moment I caught a movement out of the side of my eye.

I glanced round.

A dog had materialised out of the trees. It was an Alsatian, a sleek powerful creature, its coat almost white in the moonlight. It ran like a wolf, teeth bared, eyes sulphur yellow.

The moment for decision, for reasoned logical thought was past. I jumped up on that tree-trunk, arms out on either side for balance, and ran forwards. For the first few yards there was no problem. Then one foot slipped to the side. I managed to keep upright and kept going. The tree-trunk rolled slightly. I was close; just a couple of yards from the top. But my balance was gone and I fell, toppling away to the side. At the last moment I dived forwards, hurling myself at the rim of the fence.

I'm certain one of the wires hit my hand as I cleared the top, but if it did it must have been broken because there was no flash, no sudden paralysing shock. I flew through the air and hit the ground on my shoulder, bowling over like a falling stone.

I came up on to my knees, ribs screaming in protest, and looked back at the fence. The dog could see me there. Its sight, its scent, every instinct of its body was locked on its target. Disregarding the wire mesh between, it bounded straight at me, teeth bared. As it leapt there was a flash and sharp crack, like a conjuror performing a trick. The dog gave a kick in mid-air and fell dead on the ground.

Picking myself up I ran down into the sheltering trees beyond. Only a few yards into them I came to the road. I crossed it and began to climb the hillside beyond.

There was no sense of strain or effort as I worked my way up. I felt almost light headed. Below me I could hear the guards' voices. They'd found the broken fence and the dead dog; they knew where I'd gone but I very much doubted if any of them were going to try following me over that tree trunk.

Cars came out of the driveway, sweeping off down the valley in either direction, but they were never going to find me now. I was free and the knowledge of my freedom filled me with that fierce, wild exhilaration that only those who've escaped death can experience.

CHAPTER TWENTY-ONE

After half an hour of climbing through the trees I began to notice small details: the bark of a tree, the lichen on rocks. I looked up and realised that dawn was coming, a pale salmon-pink light splitting the horizon. It took me by surprise. For some reason I had assumed it was still the middle of the night.

I sat down at the base of a rock and looked down the valley. Kupka's house was some two miles away, standing clear of its surroundings, grey and austere in the cold morning air. There must be some butts being kicked in there, I thought, some heads being banged together. All the time I was climbing I had seen cars pouring in and out of the entrance gate. They'd be scouring the local villages, posting look-outs in railway stations and bus stops, trying to work out what direction I'd be heading.

But they weren't going to find me down there.

The sun crept up above the hillside. The air was warming slightly. I felt a drowsiness coming over me. I found a hollow at the foot of the rocks, dragged some fallen branches and grass over it and crawling underneath I fell into a deep sleep.

I couldn't tell what time it was when I awoke. The sky was brighter, the sun, hidden beneath thin scudding cloud, much higher. But without a compass to tell me where north lay I couldn't judge the hour.

The exhilaration that had carried me up the hillside had worn away. I felt stiff and cold and pitifully hungry.

Climbing on over the crest of the hill I followed a track

downwards until I came out in some fields. There was a lane beyond that weaved its way down through orchards and scrubby woods until it intersected with a larger road.

Here there was a garage.

I studied it from a distance. It was just a single shed with a forecourt in front boasting a couple of pumps. A single light was burning in the kiosk behind and smoke was trickling from the tin stack above. Parked round the back was a lorry.

As I approached I tried to improve my appearance as far as I could, combing down my hair with my fingers, zipping up the leather jacket so that it wasn't so obvious that I had no shirt on beneath. The gun I took out of my belt and buried in my right pocket.

There was only one mechanic in the place, a stubby character in blue overalls. He was sitting behind the till in the kiosk reading a newspaper. He flicked down one corner when I came in.

'Do you have a phone?' I asked.

'What do you want it for?' He was taking in the mud-stained and crumpled clothing, the unshaven face.

'There's been an accident. Up the road. I need to make a call.'

He gave a grunt and nodded towards the phone on the wall.

'I don't have any change,' I said. On second thoughts I felt in the upper pocket of the jacket. It held a thin mock-leather wallet. I thumbed through it, found a hundred crown note. 'Small change that is.'

He took the note and handed me a coin in its place.

'I'll give you the change when you're finished,' he grunted.

A trusting sort. I prodded the coin into the box and dialled. Jarka came on the line almost immediately. I could sense her panic before she even spoke.

'Oh God, Jan where are you?'

'In a petrol station in the middle of nowhere.'

'There've been people here,' she said in a rush. 'They've been through my flat.'

'Are you sure?'

'They pushed in the lock.'

'Were you there?'

'No. I was out. They turned the place upside down. Oh God, Jan, what's going on?'

'They're looking for me.'

'They followed me. They're here now, outside.'

'You must get out of there,' I said. 'I'll meet you somewhere.'

'I can't.' She was close to tears. 'I went up to see Tomas this morning. I didn't realise. They followed me. They know where he is.'

The mechanic was watching me over the flap of his paper.

'They might do something,' she said. 'I'm frightened they might do something to him.'

'Go and get him,' I said. 'Pick him up and take him down to the Old Town Square. I'll meet you there in an hour. Maybe a bit longer.'

'Yes,' she said. 'All right.' Now that she had something positive to occupy her she was calmer.

'And keep in with other people. Don't get caught by yourself. You're all right while you're in a crowd.'

'What's happened, Jan?'

'I'll tell you when I see you.'

'Are you all right?'

'Top of the world. Now get going.'

I put the phone down. I'd been intending to get Michal out here but that would take time. I turned to the mechanic. He lowered the newspaper on to his lap in anticipation.

'Can you give me a lift up the road?' I asked.

Without hurrying he folded the paper and laid it on the counter. He didn't look too friendly.

'Why's that?' he asked.

'There's been an accident. I told you. I need to get back there. I'll pay you for your time.'

He weighed the words as though testing their value and dismissed them.

'There's been no accident,' he said. 'You weren't talking about no accident on the phone there.'

'Look,' I said. 'I just need a lift, okay?'

'And I think you should stay here nice and calm while I call the police.' Reaching under the counter he drew out a wrench and got to his feet.

I said, 'I don't think that's a good idea.'

'You just stay where you are.' He was holding the wrench out to one side as he came round the counter as though tempting me to give him the chance to use it. 'You're the one, aren't you? You're the one they were talking about on the radio just now.'

'I don't know what you're talking about. I just want a lift up the road.'

'And I say you're not going anywhere.'

That's the way of it. You start off being polite and you wind up using a gun. I pulled it from my pocket and levelled it at his head.

He stared down the barrel in surprise, the wrench held low in his hand.

'Drop it!' I said.

The wrench clattered to the ground.

'Give me the keys.'

'Who are you?'

'I'm not half as bad as you think.' I don't know why I should want to justify myself to him. It might have been because he looked a decent enough type, or it might have been that I myself wanted to believe that what I was doing was right.

'You're the one they were talking about, aren't you?' There was a sort of awe in his voice.

'Give me the keys.'

He was staring at the gun as though it had a mind of its own and might go off without encouragement.

'You won't get away with it,' he said.

'Give me the keys.' I put my thumb on the hammer and drew it back. The sharp click had its effect. The mechanic nodded towards the door.

'Over there. On the peg.'

I glanced around. A bunch of keys were hanging from a nail behind the door. I edged over and unhooked them.

And that was the moment he decided to be a hero.

I don't know whether he'd been watching too many films but as I tucked the keys into my pocket the idiot decided to have a go. Dropping his head he lunged at me, his arms spread wide like a charging bear. And that's a stupid thing to do.

I brought my knee up into his stomach and he doubled up. Stepping back, I brought the gun down on the back of his head and he rolled forwards, hitting the wall with a crash, and subsided on to the floor.

'What the hell did you want to do that for, you stupid son-of-a-bitch?' I shouted in exasperation. But I doubt whether he even heard me. His eyes were unfocused, mouth sagging open.

I went over to the phone box and jerked out the flex. Then I went outside and climbed up into the cab of the lorry. It was a rudimentary piece of kit, the gear lever loose, the clutch spring too weak to do anything more than lift the pedal a few inches off the floor. I twisted the key in the ignition and the engine turned over without starting. I tried again but there was no response. On the third attempt the battery began to flag. Just my luck. I went to the bother of nicking a lorry and the damned thing didn't work. I counted up to ten and tried again. This time there was a flutter of life. The engine gave a cough, smoke belched from the exhaust, and it began to turn over.

I nursed the revs until it was running smoothly and pulled

out into the road. I'd no idea where I was. I drove for a couple of miles until I came to a T-junction. There was a sign to a town I'd never heard of. For some reason I decided I didn't want to go there. So I headed off in the other direction, goading the machine to the upper range of its speed which was around forty miles an hour.

There was no sign of life. The road seemed to stretch on forever without getting anywhere. After living in an overcrowded place like England you forget how much open space there is in this country. But eventually I reached a small village and from there I was able to work my way across country to the autoroute into Prague.

With smoke belching from the exhaust, the cab shuddering like a defective food-mixer, I made my way up the slow lane of the autoroute. The Russians used to boast that if war broke out they could reach the Channel in three days. With machines like this in their service they'd have been lucky to have done it in a month.

As I rumbled along I thought of that wine cellar, of Teige, of my escape down the cliff face but most of all I thought of Éva cutting the ropes around my wrist. What, in God's name, had induced her to do that? It certainly wasn't any sort of feminine compassion. She'd have been quite happy to see me die. There had to be a reason for her to have set me free, but however I twisted the problem around in my mind I couldn't see what the hell it could be.

By the time I reached the outskirts of Prague my backside was raw from the juddering of the seat and my hands and feet were numb from the draught that was whistling in through every orifice of the cab.

I ditched the lorry in a back street and took the metro. It was no use driving any more. By now the mechanic must have passed on the theft to the police and while you can get away with a short spin up the autoroute there's every chance of being spotted in heavy traffic.

It was after four by the time I reached the Old Town Square. Jarka was sitting at the base of the Hus monument, Tomas on her lap. They looked a dejected pair. Her arms were wrapped protectively around his shoulders, her eyes sweeping the square like twin searchlights.

Catching sight of me she leapt to her feet and taking the child by the hand she came running across the cobbles. She was wearing a fur hat and a long grey military overcoat, buttoned up to the neck.

'I thought you were never coming,' she said breathlessly. The cold had brought the colour out in her face.

'I had trouble getting a lift.'

'We've been going in and out of shops just to try to stay close to people.'

'Good for you.'

She laughed nervously. 'It seemed silly.'

Tomas was looking up at me. His face, beneath its mop of golden hair, was bright with the excitement of this adventure.

'You're Mummy's friend, aren't you?'

'That's right,' I said. 'And with friends like me who needs enemies?'

'I remember you.'

'Did anyone follow you here?' I asked Jarka.

She nodded. 'Yes, I think so. It's hard to tell but I think those two men over there are. They've been here all the time.'

I only needed a brief glance in their direction to know she was right. They were over by the white façade of St Nicholas. One of them was leaning against the wall, his knee cocked up beneath him, the other smoking a cigarette as they watched the world go by with a lazy indifference.

Jarka was gazing at them with wide grey eyes.

'What do we do now?' she asked.

'We go for a walk.'

To the passing crowds we must have looked like any other

family out for a stroll. Jarka tall and handsome in her fur hat, Tomas trotting along beside her, hopping from one foot to another as he tried to avoid stepping on the cracks between the paving stones. I was the only incongruous part of the picture, rough and unshaven, my trousers torn at the knee from scrambling down that rock-face.

'What's happened?' Jarka asked urgently as we passed the Estates Theatre.

'I made a mess of things,' I told her. 'Teige turned up. I thought I'd got rid of him back in England but he showed up just as I was looking at the paintings. He blew the whistle on me.'

'You saw the paintings?' Jarka was talking under her breath.

'They're here in Prague. Locked up in some cellar. God knows where it is. I was blindfolded on the way down.'

We came out in Wenceslas Square. Stalls were selling glass and wooden dolls and high-peaked Russian military hats. I glanced back over my shoulder. The two men were with us, about twenty yards back, shouldering their way through the crowds.

In a small voice Jarka asked, 'What do you mean, you thought you'd "got rid" of him?'

'He followed me over to England.'

'You mean you hurt him?'

'I did my best.'

She was silent, biting her lip in the cold air. Across the street I saw a ticket office, a small queue of people pushing their way inside.

We went over and joined them.

'This is a theatre,' Jarka said, looking up at the billboard as I bought tickets with the last remaining note I had in the wallet.

'That's right.'

The performance had already started when we reached

the darkened auditorium. A girl indicated free seats with a torch.

'What are we doing here?' Jarka hissed as we sat down.

'Watching a play.'

It was a Black Theatre, the stage in darkness, the actors dressed in black so that the only things showing were the luminous skeleton figures painted on their tunics. It had scared the willies out of me as a child. I glanced down at Tomas but he seemed quite unworried. They must be breeding a tougher generation these days.

Casually I looked around the audience. The place was less than half full that afternoon, small groups of spectators dotted around the rows of seats, all keeping as far from the others as possible.

'Are those real skeletons?' Tomas asked in a loud whisper.

Jarka told him they were only pretend. She was looking pale and worried. I turned towards the back of the hall. And there were the two figures from the square.

They had taken up position against the back wall, just beneath the exit sign. The girl with the torch was encouraging them to sit down but after the briefest of conversations she realised it was wise to let them stay where they were.

'I saw a skeleton in a church,' Tomas said. 'Elena said it had come out of a saint.'

Jarka had seen the two men herself now. She looked across at me, the expression on her face an unspoken question.

'How did they get it out of him?' Tomas wanted to know.

I told him it took a lot of practice. There were no other exits to the place. I stood up, taking Tomas by the hand.

'But didn't it hurt?' he asked as we moved out into the aisle.

Someone told us to hush.

We walked down towards the stage. The skeleton actors were dancing and jigging in time to the piped music. As we came close I could hear the thudding of their feet on the boards. It made them seem suddenly more human.

'Where are we going?' Jarka's voice was urgent in my ear.

'Get on the stage.'

I jumped on to it as I spoke, pulling Tomas up behind me. As I did so I glanced back to the rear of the hall.

Until that moment I don't think the two men had noticed what was going on in the dark. But they saw it now and they reacted quickly enough, jerking out of their lethargy, running forwards.

Jarka had jumped up on the stage beside me. I grabbed her by the arm, pushed her towards the back curtain.

One of the skeleton actors put himself in our way.

'Get off, you fools,' he hissed.

I pushed him aside but he caught me by the sleeve. The two men were coming down the aisle, thrusting their way past some newcomers looking for their seats.

But they'd left it too late.

Wrenching my arm free I put my hand on the actor's face and pushed it away. He didn't weigh much more than the skeleton he was imitating and he went down in a heap, colliding with one of the others who was coming to help.

There was shouting now, the audience beginning to rise to its feet. Jarka had already vanished backstage, dragging Tomas with her. I followed, catching them up in the wings.

There was practically no light back there. A low lamp glowed on a desk. A couple of technicians stared at us stupidly as we passed. One of them shouted something but his voice was lost in the clatter of our footsteps.

A flight of steps led down to a passageway. Tomas stumbled as we hurried along it. I picked him up and carried him like a teddy-bear under one arm, hauling Jarka along with the other. But she needed no encouragement and ran like an athlete, her greatcoat billowing out around her flying feet.

There was a door at the end of the passage with a bar-lock. It burst open as we hit it and we were outside, breathing in the cold evening air. I glanced back up the passage as I shut the door. There was no sign of the two pursuing men.

We'd come out in an alleyway, one of those depressing spaces between buildings that thinks it needn't be decorated as no one important will ever see it. There were dustbins and old cardboard boxes. It led back out into the Na Prinkope, a few yards from where we'd gone into the theatre.

Merging into the crowds we made our way down into Narodni Street, catching a tram to the Nove Mesto. It was practically empty. Jarka sank down on the red plastic seat, Tomas beside her. She didn't say anything about what had happened in the theatre but after a moment her eyes flicked up to mine and I saw they were thoughtful.

'Those weren't real skeletons,' Tomas told me. 'They were just people dressed up. I saw.'

It was cold in the tram. Jarka blew warm breath into her gloved hands and held them to her cheeks. Then she did the same for Tomas. Sitting there together they looked so alike it was uncanny.

'Where are we going?' she asked.

'To see a friend of mine.'

I took them to a street near the Karlova, a quiet, remote part of the city where the buildings were crumbling and settling but still majestic, like a row of old dowager duchesses at a debutante's ball.

At the head of a flight of steps guarded by two stone dogs I rang a doorbell. Jarka stood beside me, Tomas on her hip.

'Who is this?' she asked.

'You'll like her.' I wasn't as certain as I sounded.

The door was opened by a thin, anaemic young man. He looked at us uncertainly.

'Yes?' His eyes were two pools of warm chocolate.

'We've come to see Irena. I'm Jan Capek.'

He nodded quickly. 'Ah yes, you rang earlier. Please come in. She's expecting you.'

With quick, apologetic gestures he led the way upstairs, ushering us into a drawing-room. It was small and cosy and crammed with the memories of a long life: silver framed photos on the mantelpiece and on the piano, pictures packed tight along the wall, pieces of china and jade cluttering every other surface, all flickering in the light of the fire that was burning in the grate.

I hadn't been in that warm, dark room for five years but as I came in the sight was so familiar it could have been yesterday.

Sitting at a table by the fire was an old woman. She was dressed in a flowing black robe, a green eye-shade around her forehead. With long, elegant fingers she was turning the cards that were spread out before her.

'Jan.' She didn't look up from her game as she spoke. 'I heard you were in town. How kind of you to condescend to see us.'

She pointed to a chair. I brought it over to the table. She inclined her head towards me.

'You may kiss me.'

I leaned over and brushed my lips across the parchment-thin cheek. She made a wicked little sound in her throat that might once have been a laugh.

'Was that you on the radio this morning?'

'Doing what?'

'Escaped convict on the run. Dangerous and not to be approached. Was that you?'

'Probably,' I said. It explained the garage mechanic's garbled conversation.

'I thought so. When you rang this afternoon I thought, I'll bet that was Jan they were on about.' She looked up at me with eyes that had been washed of all colour. 'So what can I do for you?'

'I need somewhere for the night.'

'And how about these two refugees you've brought with you?' She nodded over to where Jarka stood in the doorway, her hands on the child's shoulders.

'Them too.'

Irena wasn't to be hurried. She turned a card on the table, moved it to another pile. Then she looked up at me again.

'Are you in trouble, Jan?'

'Let's say there are a few people around Prague I'd rather not bump into socially for a while.'

'The police,' she said. 'Why don't you go to the police? Why do you have to come troubling an old woman with your problems?'

'The police wouldn't be ideal.'

'No?' Irena turned her attention to Jarka. She studied her as she stood there in the shadows. Then she lifted her arm and beckoned her over with one bony finger.

'Come here, girl.'

Jarka stepped forwards. As her face came into the soft pool of light cast by the table lamp Irena made a little ticking sound in her throat.

'You are welcome to stay here,' she said to me. 'You are always welcome. But this girl doesn't stay in my house.'

'It'll only be for twenty-four hours.'

'You know who she is?'

'Yes,' I said carefully. 'I know who she is.'

'And you think to bring her here?' Her eyes were riveted on to Jarka who stood with her arms folded around Tomas, her head hanging. In her fur hat and overcoat, the firelight winking on the big brass buttons, she looked like a Czarist sentry being reprimanded for some petty misdemeanour.

I said, 'We need your help.'

'And I have no help to offer the daughter of Zetlivsky.' How she knew who Jarka was I've no idea. But then there are a great many things the old woman knew that denied any rational explanation.

'It's not her that needs help,' I said. 'It's me. She's just got caught up in it.'

'I'm not having her in the house, Jan.'

Jarka hadn't moved but I could see she was holding her lower lip in her teeth to stop it trembling.

'She can't help who she is,' I said.

Irena turned over one of the cards in her hand and studied it. She placed it carefully in position on the table.

'No?' The question seem to cause her some amusement.

'We can't go to the police.'

'I can see that.'

'Besides,' I said, 'you owe me a favour.'

Irena lifted the thin pencilled eyebrows painted on her forehead. 'I owe you a favour? I thought it was you who owed me.'

'I will do after this.'

The old woman considered, not a flicker of expression animating the cold, aristocratic features of her face. Then she turned to Jarka and said, 'Let me see your hand, girl.'

Obligingly, Jarka took off her glove and spread out her palm. The old woman drew it forwards into the light of the desk lamp and pored over it, running her fingertips across the lines.

'What do you see?' Jarka asked softly.

Irena shrugged. Folding the fingers closed again she pushed the hand away. 'Nothing.'

'We must make arrangements,' she said, getting to her feet and drawing the black lace robe around her shoulders. 'If we are to have guests we must prepare some rooms. I'll get Josef.'

She went out into the passage, impatiently calling his name. He appeared from the kitchen, quick and attentive as a spaniel. Jarka watched them talking together.

'I can't stay here,' she whispered. 'She hates me.'

'No, she doesn't. It's just her way.' I'd known it was going to be tricky bringing a stranger into this house; I hadn't expected it to be that bad.

'She'll tell the police about me.'

'That's one thing she won't do. She's a scary old bat but she's one hundred per cent trustworthy. I used to hide here when things got hot in the old days. There's a little room in the attic. I used to hole up there until the coast was clear.'

'You have strange friends.'

'She'll make a bit of a fuss but you'll be safe here.'

'Can she really read hands?'

'If anyone can, she can. She's a medium. Quite a famous one. You'd be amazed who's come to see her over the years.'

Irena swept back into the room as we were speaking, her robe rustling around her like the wings of a bat.

'Josef's making up some beds,' she announced.

Jarka said she'd come and help but the old woman brushed the suggestion aside. Now that she had made her decision she had lost her earlier hostility.

'No, leave it to him. He likes doing these things. He's meant to be here to study but he's more use in the kitchen than anywhere else.' She gave another of her dry cackling laughs. 'I've put you in the double room upstairs,' she said to Jarka. 'You can share it with the child. Jan, you'll have to go on a mattress next door.'

'You're very kind,' Jarka said carefully.

'And if those arrangements don't suit you, you'll have to work it out for yourselves.'

Jarka's eyes met mine for an instant. 'No,' she said quickly. 'That's fine. Is there somewhere I could give Tomas a bath? I'd like him to go to bed as soon as possible.'

'I'll show you,' Irena said. 'And take your things off, dear. You look as though you're standing on guard.'

Jarka pulled off her hat, giving her shiny blonde hair a toss as it came free, and picking up Tomas she followed Irena out of the room.

I went across to the window and drew back the curtains. But the street below was deserted. Irena came back into the room. She took a bottle of brandy and a couple of short glasses from the Japanese lacquered cabinet behind the door and set them on the card table.

'So,' she said, sitting down. 'And who is it you're running from, Jan?'

I twisted the cork from the bottle and filled the two glasses. I passed one to her and said, 'Jaroslav Kupka.'

'You always did pick your enemies.' We touched glasses. The old woman's eyes smiled. 'It's good to see you, Jan.'

'And you.'

I drank some of the brandy, felt it burn down into my stomach and realised suddenly how hungry I was. I hadn't eaten a thing since lunchtime the day before.

'Do you know him?' I asked.

'Who, Kupka?' Irena screwed up her nose as though trying to remember. 'No. I've seen him around, but I've never spoken to him.'

'He hasn't been to see you professionally?'

She gave a snort and flapped the idea away with her hand. 'Not that one, Jan. He's a dark planet. They travel alone.'

She raised her eyes to the doorway. Josef stood there, waiting for a break in the conversation before asking what was to be done about dinner.

'Are you hungry?' Irena asked me. 'You must be. I'll go and see what there is. It won't be a feast. I never seem to need to eat these days.'

She got to her feet, shooing the young man back into the kitchen with her hand. I stopped her before she left.

'What did you see?'

'Where?' Her eyes hooded slightly, knowing what I meant.

'In her hand. What did you see in it?'

'Nothing. I told you.'

'There was something. I could tell.'

The old woman glanced over to the door but Josef was gone. 'Why do you ask? You always tell me you don't believe in all that.'

'I just want to know what you saw.'

'Blackness.'

'There must be more than that.'

'Hands aren't books.' The old woman's eyes were pale as washed stones as she spoke. 'You can't read stories in them. But when I touched her hand I felt darkness. It's all around her.'

'You didn't say.'

She smiled sadly. 'Don't dwell on it, Jan. It's just an old woman's fancy.'

CHAPTER TWENTY-TWO

There was nothing edible in the house. Jarka and I pooled together what money we had between us and gave it to Josef, sending him off into the night to buy what he could. While we waited for him to return Irena produced a couple of bottles of French claret.

'You've got a beautiful house,' Jarka said admiringly. Beneath her overcoat she wore jeans and a black polo neck sweater with a fine gold chain around her neck.

I pulled the corks from the bottles and set them by the fire to warm.

'The commies wanted to take it,' I told her. 'But the Chief of Police was a client of Irena's. She told him she'd put the evil eye on his family if they touched the place.'

Irena gave a little snort. 'That's nonsense. It was just inefficiency. Whenever I filled out those forms they loved so much I put down that it was a boarding house and they took my word for it.'

Jarka had been looking around the drawing-room when her attention was caught by a writing desk. She went across to it and crouching down she ran her fingers across the inlaid woodwork.

'This is by Pavel,' she said, glancing round over her shoulder.

'Pavel Pesanek,' Irena agreed. 'He did good work.'

'That's extraordinary.'

'You know him?'

'I used to work for him,' she said, straightening up. 'This is different to the ones he was making when I was with him.'

'It must have been twenty years ago I bought that. He was just starting out on his own.'

'It's lovely,' Jarka said, stroking the polished woodwork with her fingers.

'How could you tell it's by him?' I asked.

'It's signed. He always signed his work. Come and look.'

She drew me down beside her and pointed to a piece of inlaid wood near the base. It was in the shape of a tortoise, beautifully worked.

'He always signed himself with that,' Jarka said. 'It was the sign above the door of the house where he was born.'

I looked at that tortoise closely. I'd seen that same motif before but for the life of me I couldn't think where.

Josef came back with eggs and bread and some thick slices of bacon. We ate at the scrubbed table in the kitchen, Tomas sitting on Jarka's lap in his pyjamas, his hair brushed.

I'd managed to borrow a shirt and razor from Josef earlier. As I was shaving Jarka had come into the bathroom. She'd sat on the edge of the bath and studied the bruises on my upper body in silence. Then slipping outside she'd spoken with Irena, returning a few minutes later with some antiseptic cream.

'Sit down,' she'd ordered.

I perched on the bath beside her and let her work the cream into the raw skin of my wrists and chest. Her fingers were cold and the cream stung like a wasp.

When she was finished she knelt down, wrapping her arms around my waist, her head buried in my neck. After a moment she lifted her face to me.

'Do you have to try to kill yourself all the time?'

'I was trying not to.'

'You're the most resourceful man I've ever known. There are so many better things you could be doing with your life.'

'That's what I think until I try making a list.'

She looked at me steadily. 'I don't think I can cope with someone so hell-bent on killing himself.'

'Were you thinking of trying?'

'Yes, Jan,' she said slowly. 'Of course I'm thinking of it.'

A sound outside made her turn her head. It was Tomas calling. She got to her feet, running one hand through her hair.

'And that's the other thing,' she said, tossing her head and suddenly laughing. 'I don't think I can cope with a man who rubs antiseptic cream in my hair every time I touch him.'

When dinner was over Jarka put Tomas to bed. In the bag she had been carrying over her shoulder she had brought a few of the child's possessions: pyjamas, green felt slippers, a teddy bear. But there was no book so she made up a story for him, weaving together a whole lot of little incidents, half imaginary and half real, into a long adventure of which the child was the hero.

She had quite an imagination. All along the boy sat listening intently, occasionally checking a detail for clarification, his eyes fixed on his mother.

When it was finished and she'd switched off the light I said, 'I must be going.'

Jarka nodded. I'd already explained to her what I had to do. She touched my cheek with her fingers.

'Take care,' she said, keeping her voice down in the way people do when they are trying not to wake a child who is clearly not asleep.

I went up to the attic and opened the skylight window. Kicking my feet over the sill I climbed out on to the roof and made my way along the parapet at the back of the house.

It was a journey I knew so well. Every slope of the roofs, every chimney and wall was familiar and as I scrambled over them the accumulated emotions of the past came back to haunt me. Distantly I relived the cold clutch of fear, the dryness of the throat, the strain and tension that

I had known in the monotonous days I'd spent hiding in this house.

The only difference that night was the view. As I worked my way across the rooftops, Prague was spread out beneath me like a glittering galaxy, the castle and churches glowing like golden suns in the darkness. It had never been like that in the past. Lights were frivolous and expensive and hadn't been allowed. The city was as dark as it would have been in the Middle Ages.

A metal ladder took me down into a narrow alley which led through into the street a block below Irena's house. From there I walked over to a *pivnice* in the Old Town.

It was downstairs, in a low cellar from which the sound of voices and the reek of beer and sweat and cigarette smoke couldn't escape. As I pushed aside the heavy curtain door they hit me simultaneously.

I looked around. Waitresses hurried by with loaded trays. A game of cards was under way, someone had a dog tied to the leg of a table. Sitting in an alcove on the far side of the room, and looking about as out of place as a diamond in a coal hole, was Vlasek.

'No,' he said.

'It has to be.'

'I forbid it.'

'There is no other practical solution.'

Vlasek took a sip of his wine and placed his glass down on the circular green beer-mat. He glanced around the noisy room.

'If you destroy those paintings it will be an act of vandalism for which neither you, nor those who have instructed you, will ever be forgiven.'

I said, 'I can't help that.'

'Working with you over the last few days has been a pleasure.' Vlasek spoke in his soft, well-enunciated voice which betrayed no trace of emotion. 'I don't deny it. In many ways it has given me some hope for the new order which we find thrust upon ourselves. But if you destroy those paintings I shall have no alternative but to arrest you.'

'As you did before?'

'This is no idle threat, Jan.'

'And will you set me up this time?'

Vlasek paused. His cold grey eyes studied me. 'I don't follow you.'

'That microbiologist who suddenly decided to sell himself to the West, who was suddenly so eager to get out of the country with his pockets full of secret papers. It was a bit obvious, wasn't it?'

'You went for it, Jan.'

'I didn't have much option at the time.'

There was silence across the table. Vlasek's eyes had hooded. 'I didn't realise you knew.'

'You get a lot of time to think about things in jail.'

He nodded thoughtfully. 'Yes,' he agreed. 'I suppose it was a little . . . obvious, as you say.'

An accordion started playing next door. The sound came rolling over the babble of voices between us, a thin, trembling melody. Vlasek listened for a moment, then he turned to me.

'Why are you doing this?' he asked. 'Why do you want to destroy these pictures?'

'It's for the best.'

'Is that so?' he said. 'I can't help wondering whether there's not more to it than that. Things have not been easy for you in the last two years, have they? You've been taken off active duty, made to sit at a desk in London. As far as I know, this is the first time you've been back in Prague since you were released. Naturally you want to do well, to show that you haven't lost your touch.'

'That's not the reason.'

'No?' The question was so light it hovered between us.

I shook my head. 'I'm doing it because it has to be done.

You know it as well as I do – or you would if you weren't so damned educated. It's what they are that's confusing you. If they were anything else but paintings you wouldn't have a second's hesitation. You'd burn them and say it was a job well done. But because they're art treasures you come over all squeamish and think they must be saved.'

'That may be true.' Vlasek gave a nod as though acknowledging a fine academic point. 'But then art treasures have a life of their own, Jan. They don't belong to you or me. They are a legacy, something we inherit to pass on to future generations. Without them we are little better than animals.'

We were entering into a level of conversation that I wasn't designed to handle.

I said, 'I'll make a deal with you.'

'Really?' I don't think anyone had tried bartering with Vlasek before. 'What sort of deal?'

'Come with me when I do it. If you see anything in that collection of paintings that you think is too valuable to be burnt, take it with you.'

'What exactly are you saying?'

'I've seen them,' I said. 'I walked up and down those pictures like a sergeant major inspecting them on parade, and I don't think they're worth much.'

Vlasek smiled faintly and made a little movement of his hand, as if to acknowledge that he was entering the realms of bad manners, and said, 'But then you don't know anything about paintings, do you Jan?'

'No. But I walked around the National Gallery and I saw all those pictures in there, and I saw these ones in the cellar. And they don't look the same; they didn't somehow *feel* the same.'

'That's interesting—'

'Is it a deal?'

Vlasek leaned back. 'It's a fascinating proposition, Jan, but you're forgetting one thing.'

'Which is?'

'You don't know where these paintings are. And until you do, the whole subject of what you do to them is pure speculation.'

The house was in darkness when I climbed back in through the attic window. I tiptoed down the stairs carrying the suitcase that Vlasek had passed on to me. I'd got Michal to take it over to his office earlier that evening.

Undressing in the little box room where Josef had fixed up a mattress, I crawled under the blankets. As I did so the door opened and Jarka slipped into the room. She was wearing only her black polo-necked sweater, her bare legs flashing in the dark as she crossed the room to kneel down beside me.

'How did it go?' she whispered.

'Much as I thought.'

'Was he angry?'

'He's not pleased. But at the same time he thinks I'll never find them again so he's not too disturbed either.'

Crossing her arms, she stripped off the sweater, her breasts bouncing lazily as they came free, and crept under the covers beside me. Her feet were cold. She gave a shiver and wrapped her arms around my chest for warmth.

'There must be some way of finding them.'

'There must,' I agreed. 'I just don't happen to know what it is.'

'What can you remember?'

'They're in a big damp cellar somewhere in Prague.'

'There must be more than that,' she said. 'Think back. What's the first thing you can remember about the place?'

'We drove around in circles for a bit then turned in to the left. There was a bump and we stopped. I reckon it was a courtyard.'

'How do you know it was Prague?'

'I could hear it.'

'There are a lot of places it could have been.'

'No,' I said. 'It was only an hour's drive and there were trams and church bells.'

'Could you tell which bells?'

'You must be joking.'

Jarka accepted that was a long shot. 'So you were taken down some steps. What did you see?'

'The inside of a sack.'

'When it came off—'

'We went through a lot of passages until we came to this big cellar stuffed with pictures.'

Jarka lifted herself into a kneeling position, the blankets around her shoulders, and looked down at me.

'Describe it.'

I said, 'You're a very restless person to sleep with.'

'I know. Tell me exactly what it looked like.'

'I'm not good at these games.'

'Try,' she urged.

'It was big and rather grand. We came in one side, about half-way up the wall. There were some steps down, wooden. I reckon they were modern.'

'Why do you say it was grand?'

'It had all these vaults.' I made an imitation of them with my fingers. 'And there were columns down the centre.'

'Romanesque?'

'Don't keep coming up with these words. It was old, like those castles in the Hollywood B-movies where they have sword fights up the stairs.'

'What was the floor like?'

'Stone.'

'No tiles or patterns?'

'Just stone. There were patterns on the columns. The tops of them were carved into the shapes of fishes and deer and that kind of thing. And there was a little door at one end.'

'Is that all you can remember?'

'The walls were wet.'

Jarka said 'Hmmm' and lay back on the mattress.

'What do you make of it?' I asked.

'I think it's a damp cellar somewhere in Prague.'

'Well done, Dr Watson. You've cracked it.'

She was gone when I woke up the next morning. I got up off the mattress with a groan. My whole body felt stiff and rusty. Flicking open the suitcase, I tugged on a pair of trousers and went down to the bathroom to shave. I didn't recognise the person reflected in the mirror; he was nothing like the dashing hero of my imagination. I put on a clean shirt and pulling my guernsey over my head I went through to the kitchen.

Tomas was sitting at the table, putting away a plate of scrambled eggs that had been cooked by Josef.

'Morning,' I said.

Josef bobbed his head and smiled at me with those big brown eyes of his and asked if he could get me anything.

'I could use a cup of coffee if you know where to find one.'

He busied himself with the percolator. I sat down at the table and ran my hand over my face, just checking it was still there. The air was warm with the smell of breakfast.

'Do you know where Jarka's got to?' I asked him.

'She's doing things,' Tomas informed me.

She appeared at that moment, a wad of paper in her hand.

'Good afternoon, Jan.'

I waggled my head to show that I always knew the old jokes were the worst. Jarka sat down opposite, spreading the paper out on the table and smoothing it flat with her hand.

'You've got new clothes,' she said.

'Vlasek brought my suitcase. He's a born butler.'

'Lucky you.' She plucked the neck of her sweater. 'I'm going to have to wear this for the rest of my life.'

Josef put a cup of coffee in front of me.

'I want you to describe the tops of those columns you were talking about,' Jarka said, plucking a pencil out from behind her ear. She was looking fresh and healthy, her skin glowing. I don't know how she could look so good at this time of day. I felt like one of those squashed apples you find under trees in the winter.

'What, now?' I said.

'Yes. First thing in the morning is the best time for the concentration. The metabolism is starting up and the mind is clear.' She glanced up at me smugly. 'At least it is with most people. You tell me what you saw and I'll draw it.'

'What good will that do?'

'There's a historian I know at the university. He's been making records of all the old parts of Prague. If we showed him what they look like he might be able to tell where they come from.'

'He might.'

'It's worth trying.'

I took a sip of coffee and tried to picture the columns. 'They were bowl-shaped,' I said. 'But sort of square.'

Jarka looked up, the pencil poised over the paper. 'What do you mean?'

'If you look at them from the side they were shaped like mixing bowls. But from the top they were more square.'

She nodded and made some lines on the paper.

'Like that?'

'Taller.'

She made some adjustments to the drawing.

'That's it,' I said.

She flashed a smile. 'You see it works. Now what was the design like?'

'One of them had a couple of fish twisted together.'

'Normal fish, or those dolphin things with lips?'

'Normal, like herrings. And their heads were facing downwards.'

Jarka scribbled away for a few minutes, turning the paper round when she was done for my approval. 'How's that?'

Surprisingly, it wasn't far off what I'd seen.

'Then there were leaves all around them,' I told her. 'Those stylised ones you see on church pews.'

She worked away at the drawing, adding shading when it was complete to make it look solid. After that we moved on to the two deer and a third column that I could only vaguely remember seeing.

After an hour we were done and Jarka inspected her handiwork critically, adding small improvements here and there before going next door to call her historian friend.

'He's working at home this morning,' she said when she returned.

'Where's that?'

'Up north, beyond Holsovice Park. We'll have to take the bus.'

'What's wrong with your car?'

'Is that a good idea?'

'Did you use it to pick up Tomas?'

She shook her head. 'I went on the tram.'

'Then no one will know where you left it.'

Jarka's friend lived in a second-floor flat of what had once been a private house. He was a tall, untidy man with sandy hair and a jumper that looked as though it had been knitted by a beginner.

Jarka knew him well enough to kiss him warmly on both cheeks and ask after his sister. She introduced him as Erik.

'He knows everything about Prague,' she told me.

Erik clucked in protest as he ushered us through into the front-room. The furniture was covered in a teetering pile of books and papers. Generations of cups of cold coffee stood sentry between. Erik suggested we sit down but it was out of the question.

'These were below ground level?' he said, perching himself on the edge of his desk and looking through the drawings.

'Deep down,' Jarka told him.

'What's up above?'

'Jan can't remember,' she said quickly. 'He was there a long time ago.'

'But these drawing are accurate, are they?'

'Not far off,' I said.

Erik thumbed through them, wrinkling his nose as he searched his memory.

'It's hard to say really,' he muttered after a while. 'It could be anywhere. By the look of them I'd say they were fifteenth century. But you can't be certain.'

'How many parts of Prague go back that early?' Jarka was coaxing him along. I'd bet she knew the answer but she wanted to encourage him to think for himself.

'Most of the old town,' he said. 'And parts of the new. That was laid out in the late fifteenth century. And of course the castle hill goes way back beyond that. But it's unlikely to be up there.'

I said, 'The walls were damp.'

'Probably below the level of the river. Most of the cellars in the old town are. It only takes a crack in the wall to flood them.' He tapped the drawings. 'It's these fish. They're interesting.'

'In what way?' Jarka asked.

'Usually when you see a fish motif in a building it's a symbol of Christianity. It was a sort of pun. The Greek word for fish is IXOYE. The letters form the initials of the words Jesus/Christ/Of God/The Son/Saviour.'

There was a slight bravado to the way he dashed off this piece of academic trivia. Jarka thought so too; her eyes flicked up to mine for a moment and she smiled.

'But they are normally a flat outline in a building. These are different. You're sure they are in Prague?'

'Certain.'

Erik ruffled his hair with his hand. Then getting to his feet he scanned the shelves of files above his head. He pulled one down. It was fat and green and started haemorrhaging photos the moment it opened.

They were black and white pictures of buildings, close-ups of doorways and window frames and gnarled old stairways. One that had dropped to the ground showed an evil-looking gargoyle with bulging eyes and pointed tongue.

'Take a look at this,' Erik said, pulling a photo out of the pile.

It was of an arched courtyard, very dilapidated, with ivy round the columns and grass disturbing the level of the flagstones.

'What do you make of that?' He pointed to the carved capitals. 'Was the one you saw anything like that?'

I studied the columns closely, Jarka peering over my shoulder.

'Here,' Erik said. 'Have a look through this.'

He gave me a magnifying glass. Through it the picture sprang up at double the size. I trained it on the capital of one column. It was carved into the shape of two inter-twined fish.

'That's them,' I said. 'Almost identical.'

Erik nodded to himself.

'Where is this?'

'Mittzenburg Castle. It's over on the Czech-German bor-der.'

'How long does it take to get there?' Jarka asked.

'A couple of hours' drive,' Erik said. 'Probably more.'

'It couldn't be the one Jan saw.'

'No, it couldn't,' Erik said. 'You said the one you're looking for is in Prague, right?'

'Oh yes, of course.' Jarka flushed slightly at her mistake.

'I was just making the point that there is something remarkably similar out there in the countryside.' Erik was looking slightly puzzled.

'Who owned this Mittzenburg castle?' I asked.

'The Oberhart family. They were a big noise in the Middle Ages.'

'Did they have a house in Prague?'

Erik caught my drift. He thought for a moment, then nodded to himself.

'Yes, by God. They did.'

He flopped the photos down on the overloaded desk and going over to a bookshelf he pulled out a leather-bound book. He leafed through the pages until he came to a crudely illustrated map of Prague.

'It was knocked down after the Thirty Years War,' he explained, smoothing down the page. 'But before that they had a palace on the southern side of the old town.' His fingers were moving across the old map. 'It was hard up against the city wall about here. It's gone though. There's nothing left of it.'

'What's there now?' Jarka asked.

'Oh, nothing much, a few shops and office blocks. The only part that survived is now that little church—'

'Called St Peter-in-the-wall.' I filled in the name without even looking at the map.

I knew it already.

Kupka had practically told me.

CHAPTER TWENTY-THREE

I rang Vlasek from a phone box down the road and told him what I'd discovered. He didn't waste much time. When I called him again forty minutes later from Irena's house he gave me an address off Narodni Street and told me to get round there as fast as I could.

He was waiting for me in a deserted apartment on the fifth floor, the collar of his black overcoat turned up, a cigarette in his fingers. There were a couple of other men in there when I turned up but he banished them into the passage.

'That didn't take long,' he observed.

'I took the tram.'

He smiled briefly, knowing that I knew perfectly well what he was referring to. 'I mean it didn't take you long to find this cellar of yours.'

'Ah, yes, well I had a bit of luck there.'

We went through to the kitchen at the back. The single sash window looked down over St Peter-in-the-wall. It looked very small down there, its roof speckled with new tiles, scaffolding clinging to its medieval walls, dwarfed by the drab apartment buildings that surrounded it.

'How many workmen did you see when you were in there?' Vlasek enquired.

'Maybe twenty.'

'That's what we thought.' He stubbed out his cigarette in the sink and flicked the butt through the opened crack of the window.

I said, 'You've had someone in there today?'

'We delivered a consignment of cement half an hour ago.

The driver had to go inside to get the invoice signed. He estimated the work-force at around fifteen but there could have been more elsewhere.'

'I can't think of a better way of keeping an eye on a secret hoard of paintings than to have twenty beefy builders working overhead.'

'We'll have to wait until they knock off work before we do anything.'

'They're bound to leave some sort of security.'

'The concierge in the office across the way reckons they have a couple of guards on duty at night.'

'Can you distract their attention for a while?'

'I expect so. But, Jan . . .' Vlasek turned from the window to look me straight in the eye. 'After that it's between you and me. No one else goes in there tonight. No one else even knows what's down there.'

I nodded towards the two characters out in the passage. 'What do they think this is all about?'

'Drugs.'

'But the newspapers keep telling us that there's no drug trade in Prague.'

Vlasek allowed the ghost of a smile to flit past his face. 'That's why it's being handled so discreetly.'

I moved closer to the window and looked down into the street below. There were a few cars bumped up on the kerb, a row of dustbins queued up by a back door.

'Have you managed to find the entrance I was taken in through?'

Vlasek shook his head. 'There are several courtyards around here that fit the description. It could be any of them. We'll have to go in through the church, find our way down.'

'You're sure there *is* a way down?'

Vlasek smiled faintly. 'I'd be very surprised if there wasn't.'

*   *   *

'I want to come with you.'

'No.'

'I must!'

'It's better that you stay here.'

'I don't want to,' Jarka said crossly. 'I'll go mad if I have to stay here all evening.'

'What about Tomas?'

'He's quite happy watching telly with Josef.' She was looking at me defiantly. 'Please let me come, Jan. I won't get in the way, I just want to be out of the house for a while.'

I relented.

'I suppose there's nothing to stop you sitting in a café down the road.'

'No,' she agreed, 'there's not.'

It was a breathlessly still evening as we drove up towards the Old Town. The castle was reflected in the mirror-smooth river, lights winking out from the lilac dusk. There's no city that's seen more bloodshed, tears and violence over the years than Prague but it holds it secret behind this serene façade.

'Are you cross with me about something?' Jarka asked.

'No—'

'You've been very distant all day.'

'I'm sorry.'

'Where were you this afternoon?'

'I had things to do,' I said vaguely.

She glanced round at me and then back at the road. 'I shouldn't ask,' she said softly. 'I'm sorry.'

She parked near the National Theatre and we walked round into the bright lights of Narodni Street. It was comforting to be amongst people out for the evening, people on their way to restaurants and clubs and cinemas. Jarka walked along beside me, her hands buried in the pockets of her overcoat, her attention fixed on the pavement.

'This is close enough,' I said as we turned off into the darker streets of the Old Town. There was a *vinárna* further up, small, crowded and cheerful. 'Wait there until I get back.'

'How long will you be?'

'An hour maybe.'

Jarka's face was turned to mine. She looked pale and worried. There was a question in her mind, she parted her lips to speak it but then she gave a little shake of her head and whispered, 'Be quick.'

It took me a few minutes to find Vlasek. He was sitting at the driver's wheel of a Skoda about fifty yards back from the church.

'Lost the company car then?' I asked as I slipped in beside him.

He was wearing the same black overcoat as before, above it a cap that cast a shadow over his lean face. There was a cigarette in his hand but for once it wasn't in its amber holder. He nodded towards the door of the church.

'Seventeen of them have come out since knocking off work.'

'Any idea how many are left?'

'A couple turned up about fifteen minutes ago. I reckon they're the night shift.'

'Two's not too bad. Even your lot can handle two, can't they?'

'Yes,' he said drily. 'I expect so.'

I peered up the street at the church. It was just a dark outline against the street lights beyond.

The minutes ticked by.

Vlasek lit another cigarette and drew on it for a while. Then he said, 'Tell me something. How did you know?'

'How did I know what?'

'That you were set up.'

Coming at this moment, as we sat waiting in the car, the cold grip of anticipation on us, the question seemed strangely out of place. I glanced round at him in the dark.

'Does it matter now?'

'I'm curious to know.'

I thought back to the hours I'd spent thinking it over for myself. 'That scientist I was with,' I said eventually. 'He knew it was going to happen. When that car drew up outside the hotel room he went to the window and started waving his arms.'

'You think he was signalling?'

'At first I did. Then I realised that he can't have been. They would already have known where we were.'

'Why do you think he did it then?' Vlasek seemed genuinely interested.

'He was trying to stop them from opening fire while he was still in the room.'

'Do you think so?' He looked up the street to where three drunks had appeared, silhouetted against the light.

'What he hadn't realised was that I wasn't the target. It was him. He was the one they had come to execute.'

'What makes you say that?'

'I was always useful to you alive. He wasn't.'

'That's a cynical attitude.'

The three drunks were weaving their way down the street, shouting incoherently.

'Who was he then?' I asked.

Vlasek frowned and made a movement of his cigarette as though this was beside the point.

'A dissident.'

'Was he really a scientist?'

'I believe so. Not of any importance, but sufficiently knowledgeable to pass himself off as being knowledgeable to those who aren't.'

'What did you offer him then? A free pass to the West if he played the game?'

'Something like that.'

'You didn't tell him that he was never going to be allowed to get away with it.'

'No,' Vlasek agreed. 'But then he should have worked that out for himself.'

The drunks had come to a halt now up by the church.

One of them, who was in such a state he was practically being carried, slipped to the ground in a heap. Relieved of the burden, his mate lurched across the street and hacked at a door with his foot.

A window opened and a woman's angry voice told them to keep their voices down. It was greeted by a storm of abuse from all three below. One of them threw a stone. The door-kicker gave her door another couple of kicks, then, lurching across the street he kicked the door of St Peter-in-the-wall for good measure.

His friends tried to drag him away. A fight broke out. They were shouting wildly. One broke free and threw another stone up at the church window.

There was a crash of breaking glass.

At this the church door opened and a security guard appeared in the entrance. He was a big, capable-looking fellow with a truncheon in his hand. But before he could use it, the nearest drunk hit him in the side of the head. It was a quick, efficient blow, remarkable for one who only moments earlier could hardly stand.

The guard dropped like a suit of clothes with no one inside it. As he hit the ground he was carried inside by the three now very sober-looking drunks and the door closed.

A van drew up. The driver got out and opened the back doors. The two security guards were carried out of the church, feet first and both unconscious, and loaded inside.

'You're right,' Vlasek said as the van removed itself. 'Our lot were able to handle it.'

We climbed out of the car and walked over to the church. Our footsteps echoed in the cobbled street. I glanced up at the windows but there was no one watching. That's the way of it. People in Prague have learned what to see and what not to see.

'Here.' Vlasek handed me the canvas bag he'd been carrying. It was heavy for its size. I checked the contents briefly and swung it over my shoulder.

As we reached the studded door he said, 'Naturally I don't have to remind you of the agreement we made?'

'I haven't forgotten.'

'You destroy nothing without my permission.'

'That wasn't exactly what I said.'

'No,' he agreed. 'But then you don't make the rules.'

The inside of the church was dark and silent as only large empty spaces can be.

A couple of working lamps, set low on the wall, glimmered light across the stone floor. Beneath them stood the table where the two security guards had been passing the time until minutes earlier. They seemed to have made themselves comfortable. Scattered across the surface was a pack of cards, a can of beer and the untidy contents of a newspaper. Only the overturned chair gave any indication of the sudden end that had come to their reign.

'Do you have any idea how to get down to the crypt?' Vlasek asked.

'None.'

'There must be a staircase somewhere.'

He glanced through a metal grill into a side chapel. The carved figure of the Virgin was still in place. She smiled back at us placidly. Beyond it was a door. It led through to a vestry.

Vlasek took a pen-torch from his pocket and played it round the walls. The place was stacked with timber and building tools, a few hard hats on the pegs where the white cassocks of choirboys should be hanging. Apart from that there was nothing.

He flicked off the torch and moved back into the central aisle of the church.

'Didn't he say anything?'

'Just that it was somewhere below. He said he'd hidden down there until the coast was clear.'

Vlasek was walking aimlessly around the church, his hands

folded behind his back, checking the walls and columns for a possible cavity. I shot him a question.

'Don't your men think it's odd that we have come in here alone?'

'They don't think.'

'That's handy.'

Vlasek stopped his meandering and looked at me through the twilight. 'It's different here. People don't always expect to understand what they are doing. They accept that they are the pieces of a jigsaw. Only someone up above is able to see the picture.'

As he spoke I found the image of Kupka returning. I could see him standing there in the church, hear his voice.

'There was something,' I said. 'He told me that he found his way down to the crypt because he *knew* a bit about these buildings.'

'Really?'

'I don't know whether that means anything.'

Vlasek looked around the church thoughtfully. 'Crypts are usually under the altar. The clergy always liked to be buried directly below it. They thought it put them that much closer to God. But I've looked up that end and I can't see anything. Unless . . .'

He paused for a moment then walked over to the altar. It was at the other end of the aisle, covered in a builder's wrap. On it were piled some large cans of paint and an empty milk carton.

Vlasek flicked back the covering. It revealed nothing more than a plain stone facing. He tried round the back and as he did so he gave a little purr of satisfaction.

'Ah, now this might be what we're looking for.'

He'd found a flight of stone steps. They led down beneath the altar like the companion hatch of a ship.

I followed him down into a room so low that we could neither of us stand upright. The air was musty. Vlasek played the torch around the walls and thin shadows leapt and danced away from the pillars.

'A crypt,' he said. 'Unfortunately nothing more.'

The place was full of graves. They were laid out across the floor in neat, orderly rows like the beds in a hospital. Vlasek rested the beam on the nearest. It had the carved effigy of a priest resting on top, his hands folded over his chest, his bearded face serene in the knowledge that a dreary lifetime of prayers and hymns had put him on the direct route into heaven.

'Over here,' Vlasek murmured.

His torch had found a low archway off to one side. Beneath it gaped another flight of steps. They ended in a door, black and studded with nails.

At first I thought the thing was locked. It didn't budge when I turned the handle. But it was just stiff with age. Putting my shoulder to the woodwork I eased it back on ancient hinges.

Beyond was an impenetrable wall of darkness. But I knew the moment I stepped inside that this was the cavernous hall I'd been in before. I could sense the scale of the place, feel the cold clutch of its damp air on my face.

Vlasek ran the torch around the floor and in the thin blade of light the avenues of paintings flickered up into view. He gave a little grunt of approval.

'The stairs,' I whispered. 'They're over there.'

Following the wand of torchlight we made our way over to the wooden steps, Vlasek stopping occasionally to touch the beam on the glassy surfaces of paintings.

At the foot of the steps was a light switch. Vlasek reached out for it but I stopped him.

'Wait until I'm up the top.'

I climbed up to the head of the stairs and glanced down the passage. There was no sign of light at the far end. I put my back to the wall and nodded down to Vlasek.

'Okay.'

As the lights flickered awake the hall opened around us, the rows of paintings lining the floor, the vaults of the ceiling meshing above our heads like the branches of a forest. I'd seen it before; I knew what to expect but the scale of the place was still awesome.

I stood waiting, ears straining for the sound of approaching footsteps. But there was nothing apart from the dripping of the water down the walls. Kupka evidently reckoned a couple of guards in the church was enough.

'Give me that torch.'

Vlasek lobbed it up to me. Following the beam I made my way along the passage, retracing the steps I'd made the first time I was brought here, until I reached the steps leading up to ground level. At the head of them was another formidable-looking door. It was locked and there was no sign of a key.

'We're going to have to go back the way we came,' I told Vlasek when I returned.

He was studying the paintings and made no reply.

I left him to it and went over to the opposite wall. It was built from heavy stone blocks two feet square. They were smooth and moist, the mortar between them crumbling to the touch.

Dumping the canvas bag on the ground I took out a hammer and cold chisel. I drove the point into the cleft between two blocks and began to gouge out a hole, twisting the chisel between each blow of the hammer, pulling it back to release the gritty remains of the mortar before driving it in further.

In the confined space the ringing of steel on steel was deafening, each stroke echoing around the hall, but I worked relentlessly until I'd dug a hole in the wall some nine inches deep.

I took the chisel out and examined the mortar clinging to the tip. It was wet and pasty.

'Is this going to work?' Vlasek asked. He'd given up his study of the paintings and come across to watch.

'Like magic.'

From the bag I took a small brown paper parcel and unwrapped it on the floor. In it was a battery and a clockwork timer wrapped in flex, beneath it a small piece of Semtex. It was not the standard, rusty red variety they use for blasting in quarries but the infinitely more powerful Semtex H, the kind terrorists like to use. It was soft and yellow in my hand like a little marzipan sweet.

Vlasek had produced it for me, not before he'd told me frostily that such materials were not available to the police and he'd have to put in a request to the military. I don't know who he thought he was fooling.

I tried out the clockwork timer, checking to see it ran smoothly. One fault there and we'd both be requisitioning harps and halos before we left. Satisfied it was in working order, I buried the two brass electrodes in the plastic explosive and screwed the wire at the end of one to the battery. Gently, I rolled the soft doughy substance in the palms of my hand until it was the size and shape of my finger. I glanced up at Vlasek.

'Are you letting me go ahead with this?'

'Yes.'

'No Raphaels that need to be saved?'

'No,' he said.

I fed the explosive into the wall, pushing it all the way to the end with the wires. As I did so a trickle of water came out of the hole and ran down the wall.

'This used to be part of the city walls,' I said, ramming some of the mortar in after the explosive. 'On the other side was the moat.'

'So you keep telling me.'

'As soon as this goes up we're going to have a flood on our hands, so be ready to run for it.'

'How do you know this?'

'I was talking to a surveyor this afternoon.'

Taking a piece of pale coloured putty from the bag I

broke it into four parts, handing a couple of them over to Vlasek.

'Bung those in your ears.'

He took them gingerly. 'This isn't more of that explosive, is it?'

'You'll be the first to hear of it if it is.'

I cranked the clockwork timer round to its maximum extension of five minutes, screwed the final wire to the battery terminal and said, 'Okay, let's get the hell out of here.'

We had plenty of time but we didn't waste any of it. As soon as that timer began to tick we were up the stairs quicker than a vicar leaving an orgy. The passage was in the direct line of the blast. We ran to the end, ducking round into the safety of the cellar beyond.

'Hold your nose,' I told Vlasek but I needn't have bothered. He was already doing it.

The explosion when it came a few minutes later was scarcely audible in that constricted space. It was an impact, a sudden sickening concussion like being dragged deep under water.

The force had blown a six-foot hole in the wall. As we came back into the hallway I could see it gaping open like a great brown wound in the stonework. Dust and smoke had risen in a sulphurous cloud which was rolling across the vaulted ceiling towards us. The nearest paintings had been scattered, the shock wave cutting a swathe through their ranks like grape shot into an infantry division.

We paused on the balcony, eyes streaming, lungs choking on the acrid smoke, and stared at that hole. The explosion had carried clean through the medieval stonework. I could see the bared soil beyond. But there was no flood, no sudden rush as the river water poured in.

I couldn't believe my eyes.

We stood on the balcony, momentarily paralysed. Vlasek took the two plugs from his ears and dropped them on the ground. I heard them patter across the wooden boards.

Then there was a movement.

It was over to the left, twenty feet from the hole. It was very slight, just a fractional shift in the stonework. At first I thought I was mistaken. But Vlasek had seen it too.

The wall had bulged inwards, the heavy blocks easing themselves, the smooth surface of the wall disfiguring. But that was all. It was just a momentary reaction that stopped as quickly as it had started.

We stood there in silence, breathing hard.

Then some little cascades of mortar trickled to the ground. The stonework bulged again. Right across its length this time. And to our astonishment the whole wall began to cave inwards.

I'd somehow assumed that as soon as the stonework was breached, water would come spraying in. But it was mud that brought that wall down, a great lava flow of the stuff, black and stinking. It bulldozed its way into the hall, making practically no sound as it came through the side of that cellar, carrying the remains of the medieval wall with it, oozing forwards, crushing the rows of paintings in its path, crumpling the canvases as though they were playing cards.

We stood there, stupidly, watching that mud-flow advance towards us. Then we both reacted together.

'Get out of here!' I shouted to Vlasek. And as if on cue the lights went out.

Together we clattered down that flight of wooden steps and fumbled our way towards the little door in the wall. In the pitch dark I could hear the splintering of crushed wood, smell that tidal wave of mud as it came towards us and it filled me with a wild, irrational panic.

What if we didn't make it? What if it reached that far wall before us? I could picture the cold embrace of the mud as it rolled over us, pinning us down, squeezing the breath from our lungs.

Something hit me on the shoulder and fell across my path. I tripped across it, hitting the ground. It was a painting. I could feel the drum-like canvas as I scrambled up to my feet. Throwing it aside I ran forwards and met the stonework of a wall.

I'd lost all sense of direction.

Then I heard Vlasek's voice.

'Here!'

His hand came out, contacted with my sleeve, pulled me to one side. I felt the solid frame of the door. And then we were running up the steps into the little crypt above.

There we paused, backs against the pillars, breath whooping into our lungs in great, painful gasps.

'You see,' I shouted between each bout. 'It worked.'

'Worked?' Vlasek's voice was a screech. 'You call that working, you crazy son-of-a-bitch. That didn't work, it was just a stupid, dangerous piece of luck. You deserved to be killed – we both deserved to be killed.'

And for no reason we began to laugh, long and helplessly. It was the relief, the sudden release from danger. By the time we finished we were both shaking like frightened rabbits caught in the glare of a car's headlights.

At the head of the stairs above was the glimmer of the lamps. Soberly now, we climbed up into the church. God, it was silent. We can't have been down in the cellar for more than twenty minutes but as we stood in the aisle it seemed like a year.

I looked at Vlasek. He was still breathing hard, dirt and plaster dust whitening his shoulders, his cap askew on his head.

'God, you look a mess,' I said.

'Believe me, compared to you I'm elegance personified.'

'You didn't take anything then?'

'I did, as a matter of fact.' Vlasek reached in his pocket and took out a scrap of material. 'I thought I'd keep this.'

It was a piece of canvas. He must have cut it from one of

the paintings. But I couldn't see why he'd bothered. It didn't show anything identifiable.

'Other side,' he said.

I turned the canvas over and there on the back was the little eagle symbol of the Ceauşescu collection.

'Just in case anyone doesn't believe what we've done.'

I left him and walked back to the *vinárna* where I'd told Jarka to wait. She was standing further down the street, her arms clasped around her chest for warmth. As I came close she heard my footsteps and turning around she hurried towards me. Her eyes scanned my face, looking for a clue to what had happened.

'Have you done it?' she asked.

I nodded.

She paused, waiting for me to add something. When I didn't she grinned and said, 'I got so bored waiting in there. I thought I'd walk about for a bit.'

We walked down to the street where her car was parked.

'How did you do it then?' she asked. She was watching me as she walked, looking for some response.

'Knocked in the wall. The place is flooded with mud.'

'Oh,' she said. Then she added, 'It's finished then.'

'Yes, it's finished.'

'I'm glad.' She was imploring me to confide in her, to tell her what I had felt and seen.

'I couldn't have done it without you.'

She shook her head with a little laugh. 'That's not true, Jan. It was you who found them.'

'If you hadn't been there in Pesanek's workshop that day I wouldn't have been able to even start. '

'I wasn't very nice to you, was I?'

'Then you came to me with the address for the stone-mason's yard. And you insisted on coming with me after that, always ready to be helpful, always ready to show the way.'

Jarka paused, her face pale in the streetlamps.

'What are you saying?'

'I couldn't help noticing that whenever I had a difficulty you always managed to find a way round it.'

'I wanted to help you, Jan.' Her voice was unsteady.

'You did. You led me to that cellar; you made sure I found it.'

She was staring at me, her eyes wide and liquid.

'Why did you do it, Jarka?' I asked.

She looked at me for a moment longer, then her eyes dropped to the pavement.

'I had to,' she whispered. 'They knew about me.'

'*Vysehrad*?'

She nodded. 'Them,' she said. 'And Kupka. They said they'd report me to the police if I didn't help them.'

'And you agreed. Just like that.'

'I had to!' Her head came up, her eyes suddenly imploring. 'You must be able to see that. I had to do as they said. There was nothing else I could do. They knew who I was.'

'It wasn't your husband you were hiding Tomas from, was it? It was Kupka.'

'You don't understand, Jan!' She sat down on the wall behind her and began to cry, her hands clenched in her lap, head bowed.

'What did they tell you to do?'

'Just to find you, give you that address, that's all.'

She was sobbing freely now, her shoulders jerking as she fought for breath. It would have been so easy to have sat beside her, to have comforted her in my arms. But that would have sent out the wrong signals.

'You're quite an actress,' I said.

Her head jerked up, tear-stained eyes round with shock. 'You don't think I was acting? Not all the time?' She searched my face in desperation. 'You can't believe that, Jan!'

'I don't know what to believe.'

'It was just at the beginning, Jan. Not all the time. Not

later. I didn't know what it was going to be like. I was just
told to give you a message. That was all.'

'But then Kupka wanted more.'

She looked away, focusing on the past. 'He rang me, told
me I had to stay with you. I didn't mind by then, Jan. I wanted
to help you. We were together, you know that.'

'Why didn't you say something?'

She began to cry again, shaking her head. 'I couldn't, Jan.
He would have found out.'

'If you'd told me.'

'It wouldn't have worked, Jan! You don't know what he's
like. He knows everything; he can find out anything he wants.
I couldn't tell you. I just thought that if I helped you it would
all be over and then . . .'

'And then?'

'And then we could be . . . together,' she said in a small
voice. Her eyes came up to me, calmer now. 'I didn't know
it was going to be the way it was, Jan. I thought I could just
pass on what they wanted and it would all be over. I didn't
know how it was going to be with us.'

I believed her. She'd fooled me once but this time she was
telling the truth. There was no reason for her to lie.

She held my gaze for a moment and then looked down at
her gloved fingers twisting together on her lap.

'Why did Kupka want you to do it?' I asked.

'I don't know.'

'He did everything to lead me to those pictures. First he sent
you. Then he called me round to that damned church of his
and practically told me they were down there. Why?'

'I don't know,' she said.

'There must be a reason.'

'I don't know!' She was suddenly angry. 'I didn't know
anything, Jan. They didn't tell me. Until I talked to you that
first day I hadn't even heard of those paintings.'

'From the very beginning he wanted me to find them and
destroy them.'

'I don't know anything about it, Jan.'

It was getting late. I glanced up the street to where Vlasek would be waiting by the church. Jarka read my mind.

'You're not going, are you?'

'I must talk to Vlasek. There's things to be done still.'

'Are you coming back afterwards?' Her voice faltered.

'Maybe.'

'I thought . . .' Her voice trailed off. She didn't know what she thought.

I said, 'I'll see you later.'

I walked away from her. Up the street with its tiled arches and its wrought-iron lamps. At one point I looked back. She seemed to sense it for she paused too and looked back at me.

I turned away.

It wasn't her fault, I told myself. She'd done what she had to do. It was Kupka who was to blame. He'd manipulated her as he manipulated everyone around himself. And now that he'd finished with her . . .

Kurz.

Suddenly, in my mind's eye, I saw Sergeant Kurz. He too had served his purpose. I saw him on the marble slab, those two small holes punched through his chest. He had died because he had known more than was good for him, because he could be of no more use.

I swung round.

Jarka had reached her car. Her hand was on the door.

Blackness – Irena had seen blackness around her. I called out her name. I'm sure I called out her name; I told her to stop.

But she didn't hear.

She opened the door of her car and there was a bright light. For a moment I could see her silhouetted against it. But it was all right. It was just the inside bulb coming on.

So bright in the darkness.

Then the sound hit me, throwing me back against the wall.

The car was suddenly a ball of orange flame, lifting up in the road, turning over as though in slow motion and falling on its side.

I ran back towards it. I don't know why. There was nothing I could do to help.

And what I saw will haunt me for the rest of my life.

CHAPTER TWENTY-FOUR

I flew into London on the following evening and went straight round to the office. Sophie was sitting at her desk waiting, *The Times* crossword puzzle propped on one knee.

'Hallo, Jan.' She dropped the paper and got to her feet, straightening her skirt. I didn't need her to tell me that I was looking terrible. I could read the thought in her eyes.

I said, 'Is Sutherland here?'

'No, he left at about six – before you rang.'

Damn the man. He was always around, interfering with my work when I didn't need him. When I did he was gone.

'Can I get you anything?' Sophie was motherly.

I shook my head and dumped myself down in my seat. It didn't sound pleased to see me. I put a call through to Sutherland's home. He sounded surprised.

'I thought you weren't coming back until tomorrow.'

It seemed pointless to inform him he was wrong about that. I said, 'I need to talk to Sir Stephen Bathurst.'

'What, tonight?'

'I'm going down there now. There's something I must tell him. I want you there as well.'

'Can't this wait until the morning?'

'No. I have to be back in Prague tomorrow.'

'Very well. If you feel it's that urgent.'

'And get on to your chums in Special Branch. Have them send round a team. I don't want any eavesdroppers as we had last time.'

I put down the phone. Sophie was perched on the edge of the desk. There was a thoughtful expression on her face but she knew enough not to ask unnecessary questions.

I said, 'Can I borrow your car?'

'I'll drive you.'

The roads were clear after the rush-hour traffic and we made it down to Bathurst's sprawling mansion in under two hours. It was looking like a Christmas card, the gabled roofs jagged against a starry sky, the mullioned windows glowing in the dark. The only thing to spoil the effect was the row of cars parked in front and the two plain-clothed officers stamping their feet in the driveway.

'Do you want me to come in?' Sophie asked.

'You'd better, you'll freeze to death out here.'

'I don't mind waiting.'

'Better to come in.'

Sutherland was waiting for us in the hallway. He was looking neat, dapper and out of humour.

'This is a little embarrassing,' he said. 'Sir Stephen's got guests to dinner.'

'I think he's going to be interested to hear what I have for him.'

'He'll be out in a moment.'

'No need to trouble himself, ' I said, and opening the doors I went into the dining-room.

There were only a handful of guests around that candlelit table but they were a fair reflection of Bathurst's status. At a glance I recognised a Cabinet minister and the chairman of a City bank.

My appearance silenced the conversation in the room.

'I'm sorry,' Sir Stephen Bathurst said from the end of the table. 'I thought I'd made it clear I would be coming out in a few minutes.'

A flicker of annoyance had crossed his face when I came in but he recovered quickly enough and now faced me with an expression of ruffled tolerance. He was wearing a dark green smoking jacket, the silver grey hair and aquiline features above lending him an air of aristocratic elegance that takes centuries of breeding to achieve. 'But now that you are here,' he added, 'what is it I can do for you?'

'I've destroyed the paintings as you wanted.'

It was an absurdly indiscreet remark to make in public and I heard Sutherland beside me say, 'Good God, man.'

But Bathurst was unmoved. His eyes flitted round the faces at the table and he said, 'So I gather. As a matter of fact we were discussing that very subject when you chose to burst in on us. It seems it was a remarkable achievement on your part, Capek.'

'It wasn't any sort of achievement.'

'No? Well, we'll know more of that when we've had time to read your report.'

Which was his way of saying the subject was closed until then.

'I was allowed to destroy those paintings,' I said. 'I was practically encouraged to do it.'

'That sounds a little fanciful,' Bathurst began, but I cut him short.

'I was led to them. Oh, they made it rough along the way – I doubt there were many who realised they were meant to be helping, not hindering me – but all the way I was led, shown where to look, fed clues to help me along the way.'

Candlelight flickered on the mirrors round the wall. The faces round the table stared at me with glassy eyes.

'Are you sure you're not imagining this?' Bathurst asked gently.

'I thought so at first. But I was wrong. I was led all the way. Hell, at one point Kupka's wife unlocked the door and showed me out of the house. There was nothing imaginary about that. Kupka wanted me to destroy those paintings.'

Bathurst studied me thoughtfully.

'But why should he want you to do that?'

'Because they weren't worth anything.'

'Come, come, man. With the best will in the world I simply can't accept that. The pictures that Ceauşescu appropriated for himself were good. I think that was established from the start.'

'The ones I destroyed weren't.'

'But you're not an expert, Capek.' He smiled apologetically. 'You said so yourself.'

'I'm not. That's why I took Colonel Vlasek with me. He can recognise a masterpiece when he sees one. I told him he could take anything that he rated as too precious to be destroyed. There was nothing.'

They were paying full attention now, turned in their seats to face me, the hostility that had greeted my arrival gone. Even Sutherland had moved round to listen. He was looking at me with those quick, dark eyes of his.

'Why?' he said. 'Why should he want you to destroy them if they were worthless?'

'To protect the valuable ones.'

'You say there are valuable ones?' It was Bathurst who asked.

'Of course, but they were removed weeks ago. What I was shown, what I was allowed to destroy publicly and finally, were the rest, the irrelevant ones, the rubbish. That way the others could be sold without arousing suspicion.'

You could have heard a pin drop in that elegant room.

'Picture it,' I said. 'Two, three years from now if a major painting by Titian, or by Rubens or by any of those other artists that collectors go wild about, is to come on the market it can be sold without a murmur. No one will wonder whether it came from the Ceauşescu collection. It can't have. The Ceaucescu collection was obliterated, everyone knows that. It was one of the scandals of the modern world; an unspeakable act of vandalism carried out by a philistine who knew no better.'

After a moment Sutherland said, 'My God, Jan, can you prove this?'

'I think so.'

Bathurst had been staring into the darkness, but now he said, 'Where are these other paintings, then?'

'They've been sent overseas to Kupka's supporters. You said yourself that there were people in high places who supported his cause. They now hold the paintings. I imagine they've advanced money to him in the meantime. A temporary arrangement. When the witch-hunt has died down, they'll put them on the market and regain their cash – with a little profit in it for themselves no doubt, not to mention the harvest they'll expect to reap when Kupka comes to power.'

'Do you have any idea where they are?' Bathurst asked.

I hesitated. This was the part I wasn't sure of. The rest I knew. I had the facts, it had simply been a matter of putting them together. But now I was going into the realms of speculation.

'Kupka had his hooks into a Czech girl living in Prague. She was the daughter of a high-ranking member of the Communist Politburo and had no permit to be in the country. This gave him the chance to blackmail her. I don't know if you've heard, there's a nasty little outfit called *Vysehrad* that makes a speciality of unearthing that kind of dirt.'

'It was in your report,' Bathurst said flatly.

'She worked for Pavel Pesanek. He'd been a member of the party in his time so he had some sympathy for her, I daresay, and gave her a job. That made him an accomplice and Kupka was able to force him to act as the front man for his operation. He made Pesanek sell the paintings. When one was exposed, Kupka had him killed.'

'You think this Pesanek had the paintings shipped out of Prague before he died?'

'He was a cabinetmaker. He exported furniture all over the word. My guess is that he had the cream of the Ceauşescu collection built into some of his handiwork and sent it all abroad.'

'You don't know where?' Bathurst asked.

'He kept the export orders in his workshop. I had a look through them yesterday but I reckon he would have removed the vital ones. Records are dangerous things.'

'So you've no idea where they've gone?'

'Pesanek was an artist and like all artists he put his signature on his work. It's a little tortoise design set into the wood. Quite distinctive. I was shown one the other day. At the time I realised I'd seen it before but I couldn't think where. It only came to me later.'

'And where was it?' Bathurst asked.

'Here.'

There are moments when all reality seems to slip away and you move and speak without conscious thought. This was one of them. Reaching across the table I picked up the cut-glass port decanter and threw it at the nearest of the mirrors on the wall.

'Good God!' Sutherland spluttered.

Two of the guests had jumped to their feet. A chair fell over with a crash. Everyone around the table was staring at me in horror. Only gradually did they follow my gaze and look round at the broken mirror on the wall.

And then they saw it.

Through the broken shards of glass still clinging to the frame had appeared a face. It was the sweet smiling face of a mother. She had a veil across her head and carried a child in her arms. There was a glow to the picture, a sort of radiance to the colours.

'I'm no expert,' I said to Bathurst. 'But from what I've learned, I'd say that's a Raphael.'

CHAPTER TWENTY-FIVE

Jarka's funeral was held on the following afternoon. There was no one there apart from myself and Vlasek. We stood side by side in silence during the brief ceremony, a small guard of honour, outnumbered by the priest and his two assistants. Tomas wasn't there to see his mother buried. The old woman, Elena, who was now in sole charge of the child, thought the experience would only upset him further. Whether that was so I can't tell but couldn't help wondering whether, in some obscure way, there wasn't a measure of spite in her decision.

It was a beautiful spring afternoon, the first of the year, but nothing was going to lift my spirits that day. It was not just the funeral and the vague awareness, even at that stage, that I was burying some part of myself in that grave that weighed so heavily on my mind. There was something more, a sense of futility that had been with me ever since I left Stephen Bathurst's house.

'He's going to get away with it,' I said to Vlasek as we left the cemetery. 'For what he's done he deserves to rot in hell, but he's going to get away with it.'

'I fear that may be so.'

'Do you know what he said? When I smashed that mirror he just sat there with a little smile on his face and told me that there was nothing illegal in what he's doing. And he's right. There's not a court in the world that will link him with the damage he's caused over here. Or Kupka for that matter. They'll just pick up the pieces and go on as though nothing had happened.'

'You're a true Slav,' Vlasek said. 'Such a pessimist; always on the look-out for the dark side of the cloud. You've tracked down what, eighteen major paintings; you've punched a hole so wide in Kupka's organisation that the whole world can see into it. That's something to be proud of.'

'Maybe . . .'

We came out of the cemetery gates. Vlasek's car lay sleek and black along the kerb, its rear door opened.

'Come back with me,' he said. 'We'll open a bottle.'

'Later. There's something I must do first.'

'Ah yes . . . I was forgetting.'

The priest hurried past us, nodding his thanks, hurrying on to wherever priests go on spring afternoons. I watched him walking away, thin ankles showing beneath his black robes.

'Do you know what really gets up my nose?' I said to Vlasek. 'It's knowing that Bathurst chose me specially for this job.'

'Is that so bad?'

'They could have used any one of their bright new men but they chose me, one of the old lags from the cold war, a jail bird down on his luck. That's what really gets me. He used me because he knew I didn't have a scrap of knowledge about paintings; because he knew I'd do as I was told and, worst of all, he used me because he knew they could disown me if things went wrong.'

'And what he forgot,' Vlasek said as he got into his car, 'was that he was using the best.' He smiled, one of the rare times I've seen Vlasek smile with a twinkle in his eye. 'At least,' he added, 'I like to believe that. Sometimes when I look back over the last thirty years and wonder why we didn't ever achieve what we set out to achieve, I console myself with the knowledge that we were put up against the best in the business. Please don't disillusion me now.'

I walked up the castle hill to the house beneath the Strahov monastery, approaching through the garden as I had in the past. There was no reason to do so any longer but it was the only way I knew. Absurdly, I hadn't any idea which house it would be from the street side; I didn't even know its number.

The old woman answered the door. I was expecting her to greet me with a look of mistrust, even hatred – she blamed me personally for what had happened to Jarka – but if anything she seemed bewildered when she saw me standing there.

I went upstairs, a little uncertain, not sure how to explain my purpose now that I had arrived. But as I came into the kitchen I realised with a jolt that it didn't matter. I wasn't going to have the chance to talk to the old woman in private.

For sitting there at the table was Jaroslav Kupka.

He'd been drinking. I could tell the moment I saw him. He was slumped in the chair and he was breathing through his mouth. He made no movement when he saw me but his eyes glittered with an evil humour.

'You must be very pleased with yourself, Jan,' he said thickly. 'You must think you've been very clever.'

I made no reply and this seemed to irritate him. He frowned and spoke with greater force.

'It makes no difference, you realise that? What you did was irrelevant. It changes nothing.'

I said, 'I know.'

'It won't even register as a footnote in history.' He stared at me sullenly as though wondering whether it was worth wasting his breath on me. Then he said, 'Anyway, what are you doing here?'

'I've come to take the child.'

'Take the child?' He repeated the words in amazement. 'And where would you be thinking of taking him exactly?'

'Back to England.'

'So that he could be brought up like you, Jan? So that he will grow up a mongrel, neither one thing nor the other? Not part of the country where he was born and

not accepted by the one he lives in, is that what you want
for him?'

'What alternative is there?'

'The child will come with me,' Kupka said.

'With you?' I could scarcely keep the disgust from my voice.
For Kupka to take Jarka's child was obscene.

'And why not?

'What can you possibly offer him?'

'Wealth, security.' Kupka's voice was soft. 'The chance to
live in the country he belongs to.'

'And what will you tell him when he asks what became of
his mother?' I asked.

'I shall tell him the truth, Jan, which, if you don't mind me
saying, is something you could never do.'

'It's out of the question. The child will come with me.' I
spoke roughly, overriding what he had to say, but Kupka just
smiled.

'You're too late, Jan. It's all arranged. The child has
already left.'

'Then he must be returned. It would be better if Jarka's
husband was traced, wherever he might be, and he was passed
over to him. At least then he'd be with his father.'

Kupka stared at me for a moment, his eyes unblinking.

'I am his father,' he said.

The shock must have registered on my face because Kupka
smiled again. It was a mocking, arrogant smile. He took a pull
at his flask that was clasped in one hand and with a sort of
weariness he said, 'Oh Jan, do you mean you've come all this
way and still understand nothing?'